PRAISE FOR JOHN M. KELLER

"One of the most original and most brilliant of the new crop of
young American fiction writers."
—*Roll Magazine*

"I knew I was in the presence of not just a conscious stylist with
a mind well stocked with image, likeness, mashal, but also a
storyteller capable, as the best are, of overcoming 'plot,' and
turning it into event—a journey not for characters alone but for
the reader. I continue to read his stories, each one surprising, and
wait for the novels the bio note promises."
—Robert Kelly

ADVANCE PRAISE FOR *KNOW YOUR BAKER*

"Keller has Juárez in his bones. This intricate novel is people
talking—the good priest, the bad cop, the woman about to be
murdered...Ciudad Juárez beats the lies of nations into the dust,
and Keller has written the city's poverty and gore in bold colors
and cold gales of anger. Feel the rumble of the slow train
a'coming? That train is death and filled with dead girls and dead
men and dead dreams. Hop on board for *Know Your Baker*."
—Charles Bowden, author of
Some of the Dead Are Still Breathing

"Alternating parallel narratives, *Know Your Baker* is a witty and
imaginative first novel, enhanced by an intrinsic elegance."
—Jonathan Baumbach, author of
Dreams of Molly

Know
Your
Baker

ALSO BY JOHN M. KELLER

A Bald Man With No Hair

John M. Keller

Know Your Baker

DR. CICERO BOOKS

Copyright © 2013 John M. Keller
All rights reserved.
Reservados todos os direitos de tradução e adaptação.
Tous droits de traduction, de reproduction et d'adaptation réservés
pour tous les pays.

This book is a work of fiction. Names, characters, places and
coincidences are a product of the author's mind or are used fictitiously.
Any resemblance to actual events, locales, persons or animals, living or
dead, is entirely transcendental.

www.knowyourbaker.com
www.drcicerobooks.com

Cover adapted from artwork by Manuel Zardaín
Dr. Cicero Books
New York Rio de Janeiro Paris
First Edition
Manufactured in the United States of América

ISBN: 0615717063
ISBN-13: 978-0615717067

for the dying city, and its dead: for the girls and women and their families; for whoever goes to hell with delusions of fixing things; for chuck and the photographers and journalists and the strawberry girl; and for padre haroldo, s.j., that brazilian bicycle priest

PART ONE

ya se fue

I have a terrible memory, but some things I can remember perfectly. Entire epochs and details of my history have escaped my memory (the children's literature I read as a young adult, a vacation to Chihuahua City with my family when I was 17, a number of festive, memorable birthdays…), but I can recall colors, objects and dialogue with rare precision during other moments, such as the time I stared confoundedly at the word "memoir" on a vocabulary examination for five minutes before guessing and moving along, or serendipitously discovering the grand opening of a local branch of a national taco dynasty. When I looked back upon the beginning of the longer lunch days, I remembered what Art said almost verbatim, how the third fight between the Martínez twins panned out (Nico, the minutes-elder Martínez, dropped his brother in two impressive rounds) and the nauseated look on Julio Poitras' face as he flew down the corridor between the gym and old buildings, poised to hurl. My memory did suffer some contortion and convolution over the passing years. During the first and only time Art ever asked me if I knew my baker, I see myself wearing a sweater (in some odd accident of memory), but I wouldn't have worn a sweater until years later—after I'd moved to New York. Otherwise, I remembered that day with such rare clarity, it was as if some sort of memory chip had been miraculously inserted into my head, saving the data. And this was the moment I recalled as I sank into the couch, just after I hung up with Art's mother, just after she told me that Art had vanished, had been gone for more than a week now and had left in his place a painting.

It had been during the beginning of the longer lunch days, when lunch would from then on last thirty minutes rather than fifteen. We hadn't been surprised by the over-the-intercom announcement a week prior. Simply, Julio Poitras had thrown up during fifth-period gym, and two days later his sylphlike mother entered the principal's office in an all-black wardrobe and exited a minute later, a subtle grin on her face. We were not amused when the extension of lunch (which was referred to as the lunch "hour" by the faculty) pushed the last bell from two-forty to two fifty-five, thereby causing after-school programs to commence fifteen minutes en retard, their subsequent finales to be fifteen minutes later, and the time between the end of school and the end of the day drawn closer together like illness and death.

Having grown accustomed to eating in fewer than fifteen minutes, this additional fifteen now seemed frivolous, like a zipper on a shirt collar with buttons. Since the announcement, no one could seem to talk of anything else ["Now I can't watch…" *such-and-such TV show*, "But my dad starts work at three, and he used to drop me off before…" "¡No mames, Julio Poitras!"] Scattered about the cluttered outdoor tables, my classmates talked zealously about the extended day until a

4

third fight at the park between the school's toughest blades, the Martínez twins, overrode its importance.

Art was oblivious to the chatter about this new issue. Even then, as a freshman in high school, his conversations were like a crazy old Colombian man tied to a tree. "I'm going to revolutionize the world," he said. "Va a cambiar conmigo, güey." I nodded, agreeing. Of course he would. I sipped my soda.

"You're not paying attention to me," he said, and I knew that I hadn't been. I was thinking about how thirty minutes was too long, how I'd finished my sandwich in less than four, and my coke was gone too. "You'll see one day," he continued. "I'll paint the mountain completely white and use it as a palimpsest for my creations. You know what I'll write?" I shook my head, and my eyes scanned the outdoor cafeteria tables for some napkins.

"I'll write, 'know your baker.' Do you know why?"

I nodded, intimating that I did, but he went on: "Because we don't know our bakers anymore. And *you* can't even possibly know your baker. You live on the Westside."

It was true—I *did* live on the Westside, and it had been my most shameful demerit ever since my dad's business had expanded from a single warehouse selling brake pads to several and our family moved across the mountain to live among the rich folks. All of my friends and classmates lived on the Eastside, and on the Westside there was nothing to do. It didn't make sense to me that the rich people lived on that side of town, away from where everything was happening.

But knowing my baker…what did Art mean?

"Who is your baker?" I asked.

"His name is Jim."

"What's so special about him?"

"It's not so much him *himself*. It's the fact that I know him, that I know my baker. Don't you understand?"

Even then, I had a feeling that Art knew something I didn't. That, as he suggested, my ability to understand this, and other important things, was obstructed by the yuccas and cacti and the three-thousand-foot mountain that divided me from him, from his side of town. I imagined Art and his baker—an older man, probably about forty, with a long white baker's hat and a precisely shaved face—sitting together, conversing. In this imaginary scene, Art has his arm around his baker. He is laughing and patting the man's back at the same time.

"No, I *do* understand," I said. Some time passed. All we had was time—still twenty minutes of it. "Art, did you call that girl?" I asked.

"I can't call girls at a time like this. All the girls are dying," he said. It was evident that everything affected, or appeared to affect, Art on a personal level, and oftentimes while talking to him I felt like I had been the instigator of the world's malevolence, as if I had a hand in the intractable Juárez murders to which he was referring.

"I didn't know we were talking about the murders again," I said, my guilt seeping out from my pores like the smell of death emanating from a body washed up on the riverbed.

"You can't be human and not talk about the murders…" His face lit up with an expression that quickly faded—perhaps he knew he had taken it too far, had associated yet another, only vaguely related topic, to the border's greatest pestilence. "No, I haven't called her yet. She's got to feel it first, and I know it will take her at least a few days to realize what hit her."

I was accustomed to hearing Art talk this way—he was the type to give himself nicknames, wear a skull-cap during summer, do his calculus homework in graffiti, come late to school and offer "a sudden moment of revelation" as his excuse…yes, to paint the mountain a snowy white and use it as a canvas.

It wouldn't have surprised me then—seventeen years ago, amid the highly theatrical dispute over the elongated lunch period—to know that Art's story, his bio, his existence would later be of international importance, throw the highest of morals into question and the world of art into a whorl. Although we would lose touch for several years at a time, I had long counted Art as one of my greatest lifelong friends. There is something impenetrable about the ties formed in youth—before great successes and failures, before university and one's departure from home, before life's great romances, back in the days when years traveled much slower through time. So even though we hadn't spoken in the past two-and-a-half years, a phone call or a letter—even an email—would have caused our friendship to pick up right where it left off. I was fully comfortable with the characters in my life coming and going the same way characters in Dickens novels come and go. They enter with great ceremony, then disappear as if for good but always return, and when they do, the relationships grow denser. In fact, in some ways, I was perfectly happy with the idea of explicitly cultivating friendships as such, forming deep relationships, then allowing a fallow period to transpire before rediscovering them and watching them bloom anew.

Regardless of this temporary fallow period in which my friendship with Art then dwelt, it was impossible to ignore his rising renown in the world of art and his celebrity-at-large. At first there were occasional moments when his name came up—the volume of my TV would rise suddenly and his name would spit through the plasma in reference to some art opening, exhibition or gala. A few years before, while interviewing one of Hollywood's stylish new luminaries for a profile piece, I'd asked her what she planned to do while in New York. She said, "Go to the Housing Works Bookstore in SOHO, see what's shaking Off-Broadway and then take in the new Art Serrano exhibition." It had come to pass, without my realizing it at first, that my dear old friend Art had become the name-brand painter of the new century, the man who defined the era and time in which he painted. I hadn't understood this fully until Joaquín Guzmán, a friend of mine whose interest in the art world was strictly pornographic, said to me, excitedly, when he learned of our friendship: "He's the Michael Jordan of the art world!" This was long before Art had disappeared.

Art was known especially for his range, for an œuvre that defied categorization by medium and genre. His earlier paintings were remarkable duplications in scale and color of the objects of our world. Quickly, he developed an affinity for lithographs, and in El Paso he turned these into murals, often depicting themes used to represent the border between the United States and Mexico, then very carefully blending these styles before next graduating to his famous paintings that exaggerated the human form and, according to one eminent art critic, "changed forever the way both artist and spectator view the world." Later, Art used his paintings to communicate messages and ideologies—especially those pointing out the ills of globalization; these, stylistically, were vast departures from his earlier, true-to-scale paintings. Perhaps his signature, however, was his audacious use of color to provoke in the viewer the sensation of seeing the world for the first time.

Although I rarely saw photographs of Art, when I did encounter one, it always struck me as interesting that his face had changed so little in the seventeen years since that day in the cafeteria. His father's family was full-blooded Aztec; his mother was English (an anomalous cross-breeding experience in El Paso) and, though Art's siblings were tall and more Anglo-looking, he peaked at just a bit over five-four and was an uncanny relic of one of the world's greatest civilizations.

I had changed immeasurably since high school. Although then I had been a scrawny kid, the quintessential nerd with glasses, and feet and ears larger-proportioned than the rest of my body, I was now a fuller-figured man, my black hair was whitening on the side of my head, and I wore contact lenses (glasses only for reading). At thirty-five, I had finally settled comfortably into my career as a journalist, having spent the past several years as a contributing editor for several national magazines and published a book of essays entitled "The B-35," which sold poorly, as it was named after a bus.

Aside from the press that caught my eye, I often thought of Art, especially Art as he was in those days—destined for success, the brother of three stunning sisters, the son of a Mexican entrepreneur and an English university professor who taught at the University of Texas-El Paso. And while his artistic success was what the world had so propitiously latched onto and, though his interviews and articles were focused on his art, the conversations we would have in our sporadic times together almost never touched on our professions, art or writing, even though I can't recall exactly what we did talk about.

And, nearly a year before, while working on an article in Seville, Spain, I saw a college-age kid wearing a T-shirt with the words *Conozca a su Panadero* written upon it in a sort of graffiti font. I knew immediately the slogan had been Art's creation, but I never saw the shirt again. Although I had intended at the time to contact Art, I was writing a profile about an ancient war vessel that had been uncovered under an old sevillano port, and the story had consumed me, thinking in my first language fatigued me and, after I left Spain, I forgot about the T-shirt entirely, the way the world had forgotten about Seville.

This particular afternoon of the call from Art's mother I had just finished writing another fairly horrible story on a musician/celebrity, a twenty-one-year-old with a mawkish voice who said, "Even though I'm an adult, I'll still show my belly-button [in music videos] because I don't want to dress like a mom." On my couch with my feet hanging off the sides so that the blood rushed to my head, I almost fell answering the phone, and managed only a strained, truncated "Hello."

"Hello…" she said, and in an English accent that has never failed to delight me, she immediately told me what happened, thankfully excluding the *How are you?/Great/And yourself/Not so well, I mean…/What?/Well…* Art had moved back to El Paso a year before to devote himself completely to recapturing images of Mexico, the border, his youth, and had taken up an apartment on South El Paso Street downtown, just blocks from the border. One night after his mom had called him several times and received no answer, she drove to the apartment, knocked for several minutes and eventually entered using a key Art had given her no more than a week before in case of emergency. There she found the room in order ("a rare sight"—Art had always been messy) and discovered two envelopes and a handwritten note placed squarely on the small bed. A new painting hung on the wall. The note said, "I have decided to take my own life, which belongs to me. You will not find my body—don't look for it. Why? The answer is obvious. And yet, if the answer were as obvious to everyone else as it is to me, then perhaps I would still be here. I send my love to my friends, and my family, in un-dying quantities." The envelopes were addressed to *me*, which is why she called, or "phoned," as she put it. (It made me feel like a sort of accomplice, as if I might know something, despite not having spoken to Art in so much time.) Then the painting—all she would say was that I needed to see it in person. There were already several different interpretations of the work, though that of Professor Keating, who had flown in from Grenoble, France, where Art had been a Montparnasse fellow for two years, had become the most widespread. But I would learn about all of that as soon as I arrived.

"As soon as I arrive?"

"Yes, you must come," she said. It was then that her smooth, authoritative voice cracked, and she cried violently, a wretched wailing sound that forced me to keep the phone a few extra inches away from my head. Then I heard Art's dad's soothing voice in the background, calming her.

I was slow to make distinctions between fact and fantasy when it came to events of great significance. I didn't feel happy about a magazine award I'd received until a few weeks after I accepted the award. I didn't weep until three months after my mother died. By the time I mourned the loss of an ex-girlfriend with whom I'd broken up, she was already living with her next boyfriend. I was the part of the snow that melted last.

But hearing Hector Serrano's soft, reticent voice consoling his wife added an extra dimension to the drama and made it real. In this moment, I truly registered the gravity of the situation, that a plot usually reserved for a movie or book had entered my life, my world.

The loss of friendships had been a recent motif in my life—one friend had died in a boating accident, another married and had to schedule his encounters on a calendar (What's your confirmation number?), a third hit it big on Broadway, declared himself out-of-closet (which was an interesting thing to reveal as epiphany several years after opening a gay-and-lesbian bar in Chelsea) and became increasingly unavailable to his closest friends. Now Art. Even though I hadn't talked to him in years, he was my final link to that place called adolescence, that place of firsts in all their forms: El Paso, the border, the city and site of the perpetual in-between.

"I'm sorry," I said, trying to get her to stop crying. "I'll be there." I was surprised to hear myself give in so easily, though as soon as I said it I understood that I needed to go. I knew for some odd reason that it was important I be there, if not because of the mysteries, then just to have an excuse to go back to see if the places of the past still existed.

"Thank you," she said, sniffling, stifling the heavy ululations that seemed almost histrionic in the same way that a Southerner's Southern accent often sounds overwrought.

I held off calling the airlines until later that afternoon. Instead I lay back on the couch and reminisced about high school—of Julio Poitras' mother sashaying through the school, the absurdity of discipline and pedantic high school bureaucracy, the way that in each of life's stages we always feel as if we are just one step behind arrival. I began to debate with myself the pros and cons of an abbreviated lunch period.

(*We'd get home earlier, but Julio and others might regurgitate their food. But—Julio and others would get used to it. We'd get home earlier...*) I conjured the small figure of Art eating lunch, his head somewhere in the clouds. I remembered the girl he had met the night before on the bridge between the countries...Was it true that Art Serrano was now dead?

Within a few hours of the phone call, you couldn't go anywhere without hearing Art's name. News crews, beginning with the local bureaus of wire services and then the national magazines, newspapers and television networks, descended on El Paso in a frenzy. Ella Serrano and family declined interviews. On the major news channels, Keating, the American professor who had recruited Art to Grenoble, managed only to boost the mystique by claiming Art's swan song work had been the "perfect artist's suicide note in visual form," though he would not elaborate on why (and no one was allowed access). The media's importunity increased, piggybacking on talk of even further greatness—*immortalizing* greatness—and soon the event had festered into a media blitzkrieg.

I received my first phone call a few hours after Art's mother had phoned—from a young reporter on staff at a publication I worked for. He quoted another El Pasoan, a neighbor of theirs who had watched Art grow up and responded in post-suicide-quote cliché: "But he *wouldn't* commit suicide. They were the happiest of families."

"Yeah, but he wouldn't just *disappear* either," I said. "I don't think the potential for killing himself *or* disappearing were part of his character, so if you rule one out for that reason, you have to also rule out the other. And because it has to be one or the other, both become a possibility," I said, not necessarily endorsing the suicide theory, but also not espousing the idea that people's intentions are worn externally (consider the longevity of some with tattoos of skulls).

"So, you think it *was* a suicide?" he said.

"I don't know. I haven't even…" I swallowed, "…seen the painting." I listened to myself contribute to the hype. "Look," I said. "It'd be better if you didn't ask me anything just yet. I've just potentially lost a very close friend, and I don't want to comment until I have something to say."

"All right," the guy said. "I respect that. Just promise me you'll keep us up to speed on this one. Do you have a pen? My number is…"

I didn't think Art had committed suicide. As soon as Ella Serrano called and told me what happened, I immediately decided he'd run away, had vanished to another country, another part of the globe, to the Europe in which he had spent the better part of his life—or farther beyond: to Thailand? Sri Lanka? India? The mystery to me had been more in the *why* or the *where* rather than the *what*. He hadn't even revolutionized the world yet. How could he possibly kill himself now?

Why is it that our first thoughts on a subject, the first reactions that grip our senses, become the basis by which we judge all other consistency on a particular subject forever? Even if we change our minds completely, there will always be that starting point. This is why we understand the layout of some cities and not others. This is why we forgive some people over and over again but can't forgive others once. We stake our lives on these—these first moments of intuition. An encounter with a girl in a bar, the urgency of the moment, the words that sound like what you've been trying to say all your life…you fall in love and everything springs from one night, one confident pick-up line, one collision of time and space. I didn't think Art had committed suicide and, even when the evidence later suggested otherwise, I still believed he was alive.

I stood on the stoop of my brownstone talking with my roommate, Camille. The traffic light a few blocks over painted her face a shade of red. The wind blew. The onset of winter dressed us in layers of thick apparel. I watched her smoke a

13

cigarette. Camille had moved in two months before, in November, after breaking up with a guy she worked with in an advertising firm in midtown. She ended up quitting, changing jobs and moving deeper into Brooklyn—here, to Prospect Heights. When she could not endure whiling away the hours indoors but still did not want to join the world, she came to this stoop or walked into Prospect Park and hid under the gingko trees.

"When was the last time you were there?" She asked, the green now inhabiting her face.

"It's probably been more than ten years. After graduating from high school, I never went back. My parents had moved on to Boston, and I moved out with them a few weeks before school ended. We kept a few things in the house. I returned there after a long weekend and slept in the empty house with my sisters as we finished the school year. We threw a small party there when I graduated, and then I never saw the city again. There were so many human goodbyes that I never really thought to say goodbye to the city, to do something like, say, unearth a cactus and bring it along."

"You had *cacti*?" she asked, emphasizing her grasp of the plural.

"Yeah, but not the ones you're thinking of, the ones that on first glance resemble a bunch of little green men standing in a field holding their arms like this…" I placed one of my arms in the position of a bicyclist signaling a left turn and the other in the reverse position. "…They're actually the kind of cacti that stay close to the ground, that grow limbs the shape of the palm of your hand."

"Oh," she said.

"And you grew up in Denver, right?"

"Yeah, most of the time," she said. "That's not to say that I was detached or anything. We moved around a lot. Military family. But we always seemed to find our way back there. There's a lot to do in Denver." She added, "Even if you're dead."

"I've never seen that movie," I said.

"What movie?" She flicked her cigarette theatrically. "So, you've got your bags packed?"

"Yeah."

"What time do you go?"

"Noon to Chicago. Two-thirty from Chicago to Albuquerque. Four-thirty to El Paso. I get there at six."

"That's not so bad," she said, ashing into the flowerbed.

"Well, yeah, but it's back in time the whole way."

"Mountain time, baby."

She finished the cigarette, then went for the mail, handing me my stack and then opening her solitary slice of mail, her first paycheck. "Look, they calculated my year to date," she said. "If they knew me better, they'd know it's going to take longer than that."

I casually opened the bills and listened to her talk about the first two weeks at her new job ("My boss said 'Get back to work,' with this snide look on his face. I couldn't tell if he was joking or…"). I sifted through my mail looking for a letter. Instead, there were only bills, each telling small stories about my life—the water I consumed, the light I used, how many people I talked to, how *often* I talked to them…if I talked to them from home or not. I thought of Art and his new life, dead or alive, where no longer would the statistics of his life come to him through the mail.

"…My boyfriend Joe, my *ex*-boyfriend Joe," she clarified, "would have probably gotten up and walked on the boardroom table if anyone said something like that," she concluded. "I promised myself I wouldn't talk about him."

"I did that, too," I said. "With my last girlfriend a few years ago. I think not talking about them is like spending all day on a boat and then afterwards trying to tell your body you're back on land."

"You're right. I need to talk about him. Just not now."

An extended silence brought the end of our conversation. Thunder erupted from the sky, but the best it could do in its ferocity was float small pillows of snow to the ground. We moved back into the apartment, and I spent the night lying in bed thinking about Art, the past, this boat I drifted on called New York, and how the next day I would be leaving this thundering, freezing island to return to a place that existed only in burned pigments of memory.

The Great American Southwest—lip of the lower Rockies, fountainhead of Tejano music and the Western, nerve center of the hardscrabble American desert, fixture of supernatural visits and landfill of military laboratories, fissure of newsworthiness, gateway to Mexico, dusty cradle of lost ethnic groups under four different flags in 180 years—sprawled from my window in desolation, a language of green specks of color spattered on a worn brown surface.

The Albuquerque airport had been dull. During their layovers, people slouched in their chairs in what seemed like galactic boredom but was really more likely complacency. They spoke to each other laconically, the way the breeze whispers in a mountain valley, and used small gestures to communicate. Occasionally, homecomings of relatives stirred them, but they were much more subdued than the frazzled people of New York and Chicago, who moved with the bustle of lives that could not go any faster.

I alternated between reading one of the El Paso papers and a novel about a British man who kept accidentally murdering people in Germany but, when I couldn't concentrate, I eavesdropped on a pair of teenage boys, who I could easily discern were from El Paso by the way they spoke.

…But you said you're going with your mom to the mall tomorrow, no?

Yeah, you wanna meet there at like five, bro?

No tengo dinero.

Don't worry, I'll spot you five.

Cool, then. Let's meet at Cielo Vista. This chick I know works there. You should see her, güey. My friend says he scammed with her last week after the football game. He said he had his tongue down her mouth for an hour and a half.

Who?

This tall white guy…

"Austin High School is considering implementing the use of mandatory uniforms this next fall in an attempt to curb violence in and outside of the school. Despite the implementation of metal detectors, locker and car checks, two Austin students were killed in a gang fight just outside the school this past Wednesday," the newspaper reported.

I'm going to get her a birthday gift.

What are you going to get?

I don't know.

How old is your mom going to be?

49.

Buy her a candle or some flowers. Get her a Thalia or Marc Anthony CD, so she'll feel young.

Damn, fool, I'll figure it out.

I recognized an earlier version of myself in their conversation, but in the fifteen years that followed, my parlance had taken on that of one born and bred in Manhattan. French words popularized in magazines (repartee, blasé, passé) took the place of the occasional words that sprinkled my sentences from my mother tongue. The undetectable flat accent of the midlands curbed out all the nos and bros. Spanish became more of a novelty, a credit on a laminated résumé, a dictionary of words to express a culture apart from my adopted one.

The plane was touching down soon. I had forgotten that the airport was parked between the city and the desert and, like landing on a small island, you always think you're going to crash into the expanse of ocean or desert before a runway and civilization could save you. The plane weaved into the troposphere, the wheels emerged from underneath the wings, and the plane landed without event.

They knew me immediately. "Omar!" the old man cried out. Ella Serrano grabbed me and kissed me on the cheek. Their faces wore stretched, forced smiles, and I knew that their minds were elsewhere. We left El Paso International Airport, "International" because it flew to Mexico (by the same logic, the car I drove in high school could have been christened an international vehicle), and headed for their van. The air was cold and dry; the early evening forced forth one last burst of sunlight to try and make up for the clouds in the sky.

We exchanged the dialogue of people whose lives had been wrought by tragedy, and so the words were more forthcoming. For a period of a few hours, I replaced Art as their son. They masked their pain in the roles of hospitality, reconnecting to me through the handful of anecdotes I supplied to represent a period of years that spanned three presidencies. I didn't expect them to know much of anything about me after high school, but it appeared Art had kept up with me the same way I did him. They knew the details of my life—how my mom had passed away a few years before ("We're so sorry," she said), the story I did on the Spanish vessel ("Aren't you glad you're Mexican and don't speak with the accent of the Spaniard?" he asked), my oldest sister's wedding ("The picture in the invitation…she's beautiful," she said). I stayed in Art's old bedroom, where Art had occasionally slept after lunch in the late afternoon. Paintings and drawings bedecked the walls of his room and flowed into the hallways and into the living room. It reminded me of the Picasso museum in Barcelona, where his works are organized chronologically, his evolution as an artist affixed to time. Art's biography twisted up the staircase.

Hector Serrano rolled tortillas on the kitchen counter. The smell of the onions and peppers stirred up a current of dormant taste buds in my mouth. The Chilean wine relaxed me. We began talking about Arturo, as his parents called him, without even pausing for the awkward digression that uncomfortably leads people into the grave subjects at hand. The story of their son, of Art, stayed at the forefront of conversation and never left our lips until we said goodnight.

They were convinced he was dead. They'd never gone more than two days without talking to him, even when he was living abroad, even in the obscure and inaccessible places—the periphery of Oaxaca, Mexico, the remote Irish mountain region called Mao. During the past few months, they had noticed a wearying depression, a fatigue that had dimmed his usual mirth. He spent weeks at a time away from them, lost in his work and never getting anywhere. He used to show them the finished work, one to two and sometimes three a week but, in the past several months he hadn't produced anything, except for the one painting.

The other reason they said they knew he was dead was because of his unimpeachable honesty. If indeed the painting was an artist's suicide note, if indeed he had written "I have decided to take my own life, which belongs to me. You will not find my body—don't look for it...," then he was dead, they were sure—he would never have inflicted upon them so much undue suffering. But, the question remained: if he were dead, where *was* his body? How does one remove himself from the world without any evidence of the fact?

I tried to persuade them that not all hope was lost, but after a while I realized I was only trying to convince myself. The sun faded behind the Franklin Mountains on the Eastside first. On the Westside, it would slip behind the horizon ten minutes later. I gave up trying to plead my case. I was here to give one more perspective on the painting and then to read the letters addressed to me, and inform them as to what information was contained therein. In a few days, they would open up the apartment to the general public, showing Art's final works, and finally make their statements to the media. They would handle the other postmortem details neatly, wrapping the issue of death up in a trim layer that would culminate in statistics (suicide rates, real estate numbers, the span of his life as indicated on his tombstone) and a funeral of bleak consolatory attire and Forget-me-not pats on the back. The earth would spin on its tilt quickly, and the energy of his soul would slowly, but eventually, completely dissolve, leaving behind nothing but the capsule of the pill, an idea without a body, a name, an image—and some really expensive paintings.

The sunrise brought with it the morning light, which stretched over the city like a new idea. I sat on the front porch and listened to front doors slam shut and garage doors open and wives shout after their husbands to remember to call if they're going to be late. They left with plastic bags holding egg-and-sausage burritos and lunches that unpack like takeout.

Snow lightly patched the ground, and so I wore my jacket and what my bellicose Polish landlord had disdainfully referred to as "this hat of winter"—a skull cap. I hadn't commented on *her* choice hat of winter, which looked as if it were made by a tailor anxious to get rid of superfluous wool. Hector Serrano brought me coffee, and I agreed to go with him to Horizon City to pick up a part for his truck. Soon we were paddling through the slow current of drivers on Interstate 10, where the traffic moving five or ten miles per hour below the speed limit was the rhythm of life. His truck maintained an invariable speed and stayed in its lane, and by five-thirty, El Paso and its metropolitan sprawl behind us began to huddle together and exist as a seemingly singular concept.

Hector's thick black head of hair was slicked back in the style of his era. He drove with one hand on the wheel and chatted with me about the state of the city—the downtown revitalization, the subpar mayor (Were there any the city had loved?), the metal detectors and school uniforms. Then he said, suddenly, "I think Art is alive."

"What?" I said, shocked by the abruptness and the certainty of his statement.

"There were times he didn't call when he was abroad, when I just told Ella he had for her own peace of mind. But it's not just that. I just don't think he *would* kill himself. I know you haven't seen him for some time, but wasn't Art always a few steps ahead of the game, didn't he have some sort of sense behind all the dreams? Or am I just being a father, not able to think his son would do something like that?" He kept driving with one hand, wiping away a tear, or what might have just as easily been a speck of dirt from the spot below his eye.

"I agree," I said. "I also think he's alive…But I don't understand. Last night you were *sure* he was dead."

"If my wife thought for a moment that Arturo were still alive, she'd do exactly what he said not to and start looking for him. She'd suffer far more thinking he was still alive than dead. I don't think hope will do any of us any good."

I didn't say anything. By saying nothing, I imagined he thought I was tacitly agreeing with him about what was best for his wife, about that understood sentiment among many men that women were the weaker gender, fraught with emotion and incapable of handling crises, when in fact, through life I had learned that it was often the opposite, that women were the more resilient, that they met life's most exigent circumstances with steel souls and never crumbled until it was over, that *they* were the survivors when the rest of us were gone. Before long, we arrived in Horizon, turned off on a bumpy dirt road and slid into a spot on the front lawn of what looked nothing like an auto repair shop. Hector conversed with a man seemingly beyond age, who wore the end of the nineteenth century with a digital wristwatch. After I was introduced, the man asked if he could talk to Hector for a few minutes alone, so I walked to the edge of the road where it met the fence, kicking gravel with my toes, looking out at the vast fields of cacti and wondering if Camille would be as impressed by the genuine article. As I turned back toward where Hector was standing with the man, I saw the man reach forward and hug Hector Serrano and then the two visibly letting go of one another. The man then walked into the shop and picked up a bag containing a head gasket for his truck, insisting with his hands that Hector Serrano not finish producing the paper he held in his wallet.

She was showering. He was sleeping. The day before, Camille had asked me to call her and let her know that I had arrived safely, so I picked up the phone and dialed my apartment.

"Hello?"

"Camille?" I said.

"Yeah, who did you expect...a burglar? A burglar probably wouldn't answer the phone. Besides, my voice is too sexy. Were I one for larceny, at the very worst...the *worst*," she emphasized, "I'd be thieving large amounts of cash from well-endowed old men." For nine-fifteen in the morning, she was wired.

"So, how've you been?"

"Pretty good. I've started talking about Joe to a tape recorder," she said as if she hadn't seen me the day before. "This way I don't bore the hell out of any of my closest friends, pay exorbitant psychoanalysis fees, and I can still cradle these neurotic feelings I can't seem to stop having. So...what are you doing?"

"On my way to see the painting, as soon as Art's mom wakes up. Otherwise, the atmosphere's been less plaintive than I expected. It's strange to be back here in this city. I feel like I've time-traveled rather than flown across the country. It's a different kind of déjà vu, the more literal kind, where you know there are certain places in which you existed before, and you're seeing them again."

The phone beeped; someone else was calling our Brooklyn landline.

"Wanna get that?" I asked.

"Right. Just a second."

About thirty seconds later she returned. "It's for you," she said, pausing, as if she expected me to emerge from my room to take the phone from her.

"Are you still on the phone with them?"

"Yeah."

"I guess you should probably tell whoever it is I'm not home."

"Did I tell you who it was?" she asked.

"No," I said, amused.

"Oh, I think it's a telemarketer," she said. "I'll tell them you're not home." She hesitated. "Just in case they ask, when do you think it would be best for them to try you again?"

"You'd better give them the number here," I said, laughing. "Ask if it's an emergency."

"All right. I'll be right back," she said. After a few seconds, she returned: "They've hung up!" she exclaimed.

"Hmmm," I said. "Well, I just wanted to let you know I've arrived safely. If anything comes up, such as more urgent calls from telemarketers, the number here is, do you have a pencil?

"A pen."

I gave her the number.

"By the way, I almost forgot, you *did* get a call from a magazine, some important magazine, though I forgot which one. The guy's name is Jack Walsh. He didn't elaborate. He just said he wanted to talk to you about Art, and I assume he means your friend rather than the subject."

"Thanks for clearing things up."

"Well, I've got to go to work," she said. "I'll talk to you later. Call me tomorrow if you want. I want to know about the painting."

When we hung up, I noticed that the door to the Serrano's bedroom was open, so I went back to Art's room to grab my notebook and, when I returned to the kitchen, found Ella Serrano waiting for me.

"Ready?" she asked, seemingly prepared for any answer.

23

This time we went toward the downtown, a mess of vacant twenty-story skyscrapers, mostly art-deco, a hub for the interstate trains and local and international buses, several parks and a commercial zone with wall-to-wall shops chock-a-block with customers. The commercial area ends at the bridge, linking the downtowns of the two massive cities and creating the largest international border community in the world. El Paso had probably looked about the same fifty years before—only the dress of the people who traversed the streets and their means of transportation would have given it the otherworldly vibe of the past.

We turned right onto South El Paso onto Overland, parked on the street, then entered the apartment building that looked as if it could just as easily have been an apartment building in New York.

"Last door on the right," she said, as we walked to the end of the hall. She found her keys in her purse, slid the key into the door and turned.

The apartment was massive and contained several bedrooms and a studio with high-ceilings and a few doors—one that led to a bathroom, another to a closet. A collection of blank canvases several meters long leaned against a glass table in the corner. A floor lamp without a shade that looked like a microphone stood in the middle of the floor, next to the bed.

The back wall was replete with art of varied skill and complexity. One stood out immediately. It was larger than the others and was of an empty art gallery with the various canons of the pop art epoch—Warhol's soups, Lichtenstein's comics, Jasper Johns' American flags, Keith Haring's busy silhouettes, then works that I didn't recognize—a woman toweling herself in a bathtub, the image of Frida Kahlo wearing a lime-colored shirt against a pink background, several Mexican boxers in a ring—all spaced equally along the three or four visible walls within the mock gallery.

"He did that one about six months ago," Ella Serrano said.

"So, it's not *the* painting?" I said.

"Turn around," she said.

I turned around to face a wall that was empty except for a mirror, and then was jolted by what I saw inside it. I walked a few feet in the direction of the mirror. I found the spot in the room from which Art must have intended the mirror be viewed. I stood on this imaginary "X" mark on the floor and stared into the mirror. Everything in the room was reproduced exactly as it was, except for me. The mirror did not reflect back my image. Instead I saw the reflection of the edge of the room, a bookcase next to it holding a candle, a vase, several stacked books and, above it, the artwork—the pop art gallery, a painting of Piccadilly Circus unpopulated, a portrait of an Aztec woman turning a bowl. I moved closer to the mirror, impressed by its bizarre anamorphosis. Closer up you could see, smell, feel the paint; you could tell it was a painting, but it was realistic enough to make you doubt reality for that smallest interval of time—a second—which was all that was really needed. I looked over at Ella Serrano, who looked back at me expressionlessly. Art Serrano had managed to exclude himself from a mirror, disappearing from something from which no one can hide. The words of Professor Keating—"perfect artist's suicide note in visual form"—gave my disorientation and astonishment a soundtrack, the words repeating themselves in my head, circling in my brain, in and out, as when the body heads down the inevitable path toward sleep. I couldn't take my eyes off the mirror. Could it be that Art wanted to look at the world one last time and see it as it would exist without him? Did this mean that he really was dead?

My eyes stayed fixed on the mirror. I didn't exist either.

vero

The train headed north. She leaned against the window and fell asleep. Through the window the landscape morphed into the desert of Chihuahua; the silhouettes of mountains in the distance rolled up from beyond the flatlands as the train rounded the earth. Her cousin Pablo was peddling mazapanes and *Lucas* up and down the rows—and to much success. Uncle Armando and Aunt Laura slept under a sarape in seats next to her. She awoke to silence and darkness. As if in a sleepwalk, her eyes blinked and she rose. She walked toward the bathroom, advancing two cars at first, whereupon she came upon a large window through which she could see the city they were descending upon, a mass of greenish lights that spread forever into a future that was as incalculable and dim as its lights.

Verónica left quickly, dropping the wad of bills into her purse, not even looking back at Benito, who rested peacefully, a beastly look of pleasure tamed by sleep. She knew he would awake soon; enraged by her absence, he would throw a fit and eventually begin to sulk, but by the time he found her again, he would be ready to continue their fevered relationship, ready to saddle up for lust but finding himself bestriding love all over again. Verónica prayed hard, cold prayers of devotion and repentance. The cathedral in its enormity enveloped her, calmed her, frightened her, and she came every morning to list her sins.

Padre Osvaldo, gray-eyed and monkish—a slightly pained look on his face and forehead—took her confession, giving her short penances despite the consistency with which she broke the same commandments. The younger priest, Padre Humberto, didn't understand Osvaldo's clemency. Humberto openly referred to her as a puta and adamantly held to the notion that the larger the sin, the greater the penance. "That we even allow her to confess every day is beyond me, since all she confesses are the same sins committed with different people," Humberto said.

"Find me a woman—a girl—more pious," Osvaldo retorted. "But I'm worried about her. She's too young to have lived all of this." Padre Osvaldo turned to look at the image of Guadalupe, her hands clasped, her head bowed. "May Our Lady protect her…" *And you, Humberto, for your tremendous compassion*, he nearly added.

Verónica wanted to sit at the bus stop, on the ground like a teenager, but she held her body up and waited for the bus to Satélites to come. The early-morning traffic in a city that woke early to beat the heat, but only ended up being beaten by it, bustled past her in droves, little noting the bags under her eyes like rainclouds or the remnants of makeup that caused her to blink tears. Finally, the bus came, and she was whisked away to the colonias far from the center, in a seat she shared with a man holding a colostomy bag, still content, however, that she wasn't aboard one of the nieves, those trucks that transported women to the maquiladoras, the factories that turned Juárez into the epicenter of the modern-day gold rush, a place with so very little gold.

When she arrived at their vacant apartment, the one she shared with Esmeralda and another girl, she went immediately to her bed, and that's when she found the note from Esme: "Vero—Your aunt Laura called last night right after you left for work. She told me she would call again this morning. That's all." Verónica could suddenly feel the blood in her veins and hear her heartbeat intensify, as if in the rhythm of its beat were encoded messages, and the messages had changed. Had it really been her tía? Verónica tried to imagine the conversation, that authoritative voice that commanded attention—that would cause even a seasoned PRI candidate to stop shaking hands. Then the gentle voice of Esme, her mentor, who could spell perfectly in Spanish and even knew some English. What had they talked about? What could Aunt Laura possibly have wanted?

Just over a year before, Verónica had been with her mother, in Coatzacoalcos, Veracruz, living on the middle floor of a three-story house. Her father, a German infantryman who'd remained in Mexico after his assignment, had died of tuberculosis when she was ten. She hadn't wanted to become an orphan. There is no such thing as a Mexican orphan, her mother told her. Her mother's eyes were hard and her skin was like clay, and the crease of her smile had been indelibly embedded into her countenance. Those nights, as her mother's disease trickled through her veins, Verónica stayed up to nurse her, listened like a tape recorder to her stories and prayed every night until morning to keep her mother alive. Every night, her eyes burned with the need for sleep. She fought but always relented. She knew her mother had been fighting and giving up over and over.

Within a week of her mother's death, Verónica was already with Aunt Laura and Uncle Armando, on a one-way ticket to Juárez. Two weeks later, she was waiting by the phone for a call from the maquila factory, a place where printer ribbons were made, where she could make between thirty-five and fifty dollars a week if she worked quickly enough and stayed on extra hours.

And she got the job, and she worked hard, walked through the colonias to the place where the women waited for the nieves every morning—and she never complained and always smiled, even though living like this was tearing at her will to live, was making her feel like the printer ribbons she worked with, which were strong but sometimes snapped. She met Esmeralda, an eighteen-year-old girl destined to act, poised to follow in the footsteps of Salma Hayek, Vero's fellow ciudadana from Coatzacoalcos, but secretly hoping for a rich boy to impregnate her. At first, Verónica found a way to do both jobs, to sneak away after work with one man for an hour or so, but soon she found it made much more sense to sleep with men for ten to twenty dollars a night. And, though selling herself seemed infinitely worse than working in the maquilas, it was a decision made, rather than one condemned to, and Verónica found herself much happier—that is, until the colonia began to talk.

Every evening before going to work, she would go to the cathedral—Nuestra Señora de Guadalupe—and confess to Padre Osvaldo and the other priest. She would go out of her way to the cathedral because it reminded her of the one in Coatzacoalcos, which was infinitely smaller but cut the same silhouette in the sky at night. And the priest with the discerning gray eyes would make her feel safe and comfortable, almost the way a good father makes a daughter feel, and she could leave the church in the evening with confidence, ready to rule the world of the night, the world in the alleyways and side-streets by Avenida Juárez, a world where she was free and where men like Benito came to her to

29

flee their wives and girlfriends only to find love where it did not belong.

Soon, however, the chismosos caught sight of her and did what they did best, and word spread like an airborne virus over las colonias in and out of windows and eventually into the ears of Laura Delgado, who said to her sobrina, "¿You want your streets? You can have them."

And here she was, orphaned.

She fell asleep dreaming of her aunt. Like Vero's mother, Laura's face was as hard as clay but, instead of a permanent smile, no true expression dug its lines into her countenance, as if she had lived a life of equal misery and joy. Laura was saying something that Vero struggled to hear, which only added to her aunt's frustration. When Vero had given up completely, she realized that Laura was not herself, that she was really her boss at the maquila factory, a boss who had never supervised her before but, for some reason, today, was doing so. Vero put the red plastic tape over the delicate, rust-colored part of the ink cartridge and was immediately handed another. She steadied her hand and put the small strip in the perfect position and then passed it onward.

But then the supervisor came rushing over to her and showed her that she had been putting all the red strips of tape upside down, on the wrong part of the cartridge. The ink was exposed—worse, damaged eternally. The phone rang. The supervisor's lips did not move, but Verónica heard her say that it was the boss. And you know what the boss is going to say. You know what he'll do. Suddenly, Vero awoke to the sound of her phone ringing. She ran to get it, but was too late.

The pain returned to her belly, and to somewhere else, somewhere near her throat, somewhere she could not point to—the place that she had always designated as the location of her soul. She was already feeling the enthralling sensation of Laura's dominion again. She lay back down on her bed and wondered at the word "dream." How could a word like this have such a positive connotation while also symbolizing everything that was beyond her reach? Why were her dreams when she slept no better than the ones while she was awake? Why did her dreams always have to turn into nightmares?

Again she fell asleep, daydreaming about dreams. This time she dreamt not of images, but of herself, thinking. She was lying on her bed thinking, when she realized that she didn't have to work today or any day and that Esmeralda and she were going to the discotecas, somewhere like Amazonas, and that's why Esme was dressed in a sequin dress that twinkled, that matched her glittery makeup. Verónica was excited for the moment, the preparation, the destination, the having a place to go, but then she realized she had nothing to wear, nothing but her clothes from the factory. And then Esmeralda intervened, leaving the room and returning with a dress, not something that sparkled but something equally as elegant—sexy.

Those were the nightmares and fantasies that found pathways inside her head. They were filled with equal happiness and sadness—the kind of phantasma that would leave someone looking like Laura.

Esmeralda stood over Vero as she slept. She wanted to wake her. A businessman had come from the other side and tipped her fifty dollars. He told her that he could see her becoming a famous star—a Sharon Stone, a Demi Moore. She could barely concentrate on what she was doing with her head so far in the clouds, but the man seemed to be enjoying himself, and she could tell he would be back. No one ever tips that much unless they're returning, she thought.

But Vero slept, disappeared like she wasn't coming back. She wasn't the type of girl who slept tossing and turning and, when she was younger, this had always scared her mother, how she slept through everything—radio noise (tests of emergency broadcast systems, commercials ten times louder than the programs they interrupt), extreme weather (hurricanes and other tropical storms, Veracruz nortes), alarm clocks with varied sounds and ludicrous volumes. Her parents would shake her, pour cold water on her face and scream at her in their different languages. But the only thing that she would wake from was sleep.

Esmeralda could go days without sleep, and often she did. The last time she had slept was the night before last and, if necessary, she was willing to go two nights in a row. For the first time in a while she had money and as she sat on Vero's bed, she imagined all the possibilities—what she could buy—shoes, black pants, name-brand makeup that didn't run, a cheap camera, a tape with that song—"La Calle de las Sirenas," a meal at a restaurant, a fashion magazine, dark jeans, a manicure…She could have her fortune read and find out once and for all if she was going to be a star. Or she could take the week off and sleep and listen to the sounds of the neighborhood during all of the day's stages.

Esmeralda had dreams, too, but sometimes she really did want it to be easier, just to fall in love with some kid with money. She was pretty enough, but she felt as if her beauty was fading—she could already see lines underneath her eyes and blue veins forming above her eyelids. Her thighs were thicker, and she noticed an inconsistency in the curvature of her nose she had never noticed before. What could be worse than getting old? She should find someone now while she still attracted men. It was all unfair, this game of life, spending your days preparing to welcome your dreams and then watching everything be turned over to chance. Esmeralda turned to Vero sleeping. A loud siren passed through the apartment windows and distracted Esme from her thoughts, but Vero's expression remained deadpan. Esme rested her head on Vero's chest and listened for her resting heartbeat.

When half an hour later she awoke to find Esmeralda at her bedside, staring at her absently, Verónica shrieked. "¡No mames! ¿Qué te pasa, Esme? ¿And what time is it? ¿What time are we going to Amazonas?"

Esmeralda had wondered what would happen when Vero awoke to find her sitting there, but she still hadn't taken the thought far enough to rouse herself to action. "I'm sorry. I had something to tell you."

"¿About my aunt? ¿Did she call again?"

"No. No. About something else. About last night."

"¿But what happened last night?"

"¿Last night—wait, what is this about Amazonas?"

"¿Oh…we are not going there, are we?" Verónica said, and her face showed the disappointment of a dream not transferring into reality.

Esmeralda got up and found her purse, then moved closer to Verónica on the bed and pulled out the fifty-dollar note. "But we are," she said.

"¿Esme, where did you get that?"

"That's what I was going to tell you. This rich, chilito gringo gave me fifty extra dollars last night."

"¿And La Madre knows?"

"¿How could she?"

"¿So, fifty dollars all to yourself?"

"And you. Let's go to Amazonas tonight."

Verónica thought she would die before that could happen. She couldn't imagine circumstances any better than being able to go to Amazonas on a Saturday and being like a fresa and wearing jeans rather than a short skirt. She liked it better when men tried to charm her rather than to offer her money, and even if someone did, she would not take it. On second thought, why would they even offer her money? To offer a sixteen-year-old girl money would be insolent, a deliberate disregard for the way women should be treated. Suddenly, for no reason at all, or perhaps because they were linked together in disturbing the order of her universe, she thought of her aunt and the phone call, and she once again wondered what it had been about.

"¿Esme, what did my aunt say?"

"I don't know, only that she would call you again."

"It must be important. She doesn't have a phone. ¿Did she sound distressed?"

"No. She sounded nice."

"¿Nice? ¿Are you joking? She's basically a witch."

"She sounded nice."

Verónica ached to know what it was her aunt had been calling about, but she needed to get ready and so her mind drifted to thoughts of the night and Esme's prospects. Esme had been like an extension of her mother, and Verónica wanted to do something nice for her, but she couldn't yet think of what.

She selected a white top, jeans and a crucifix necklace, hung them up, and then went about showering, lingering longer than usual to massage her face, arms, legs. She wet a washcloth in warm water from the sink and let it soak into her face, then did the same with cold water, alternating the two to allow her pores to open and close; she had learned this from the atmosphere—the clashing of four seasons and varying types of precipitation that created healthier, refreshed worlds. After Esme had showered, they started applying their makeup—mascara, glittery eye shadow, a light foundation, lipstick.

Esmeralda offered her tissue paper. "For your chichis, mamita."

They left in a rush, remembering the fifty dollars only after climbing down eight staircases, then going back and grabbing it, along with other, suddenly-necessary things: gum, a spray of perfume, another brush through their hair, some added mousse...before catching the white city bus (direction: Pronaf) riding through the areas with high-rise apartment buildings, then small residential areas, and finally the constricted streets of the municipio, crowded with honking cars and taxi bugs without customers, before turning onto the street with the theme superstructures—Chihuahua Charlie's, Ajuua! and Amazonas.

After spending fifteen minutes in line, they went through the metal detectors and Esme paid the admission fee for both of them, in dollars. It was as if they had come from the other side, had spent their early evening getting ready in their separate bathrooms with mirrors behind them and to the side—mirrors that always told them they would never grow old, that when they were successful celebrities and actresses, they would be even more beautiful. Verónica took Esme by the hand, and they walked down a long corridor aside the large room, where people were dancing to the latest hits from Proyecto Uno, Shakira, Illegales, Ricky Martin, Kabah, Fey, Maná, and King Africa, though most of the people in the club would have probably danced to the sound of a drill tearing away at a concrete slab.

Evidence of forest—pines, hemlocks, the limbs of great trees—dangled onto the dance floors, above heaping, sweating teenagers doused in cologne, perfume and the scent of rum or tequila. Three güeritas in the corner took shots from the rambunctious tequila-shot transporter, his wares as tentacled as bagpipes. Older, breastier girls danced on large platforms above the main floor. A taller, younger guy spilled his drink on an older, shorter guy, and words were exchanged, sharp fists dug into chests; the bouncer threw them both out. Vero and Esme were asked to dance by two guys claiming to be "chilangos from Mexico City"—their hair gelled meticulously, their teeth straight as plates before the first earthquake. "¿Aren't chilangos *always* from Mexico City?" Esme asked. "Good point," one said. They danced to Popocatépetl as if the song had become real and magma had spewed forth from the great volcano and their feet couldn't touch the ground.

Outside, the lines grew longer; the tolerance toward fake IDs carried by fifteen-year-olds grew lower. Six brothers, four of whom were twins, pleaded with the bouncer to let the youngest one in. Two El Paso girls showed their chests to bypass the thirty-minute line. Two others tried after them and were sent to the end, where guys allowed them to cut ahead for flashes of bras and other underthings. The parking lot in front of the restaurant-turned-discotheque reached capacity. The streets filled. Traffic nearby stalemated. Shouts from the line to arriving parties kept those just-arrived from cutting in line with their friends.

Inside, Esmeralda was looking for Vero. She had gone to the bathroom and maybe lost her way to where they had been dancing. Esme's heart pounded like a tambora, the drum beating by itself in a constant, imperturbable rhythm. The place was cramped. The two guys split up and began to look for her at opposite edges of the club. Twenty minutes passed. The guys found each other again. Thirty. They found Esme. Where was she? Esme imagined the scolding she would give Vero when she found her. She could see the girl, only a year younger, apologizing, and she knew already that she would mean it. Every fifteen minutes Esme found herself back in the bathroom, retracing the steps she would retrace until the end of her life, looking at the floor tiles and the bathroom stalls, analyzing these things as if they might someday yield clues. And the next day, when Esmeralda, with Vero's aunt and cousin and the investigating officer, returned to the club in daylight in the time when the darkness of the earth is to become yet again a mystery until the night rises again, Esme would stare at those tiles and examine them and wonder how Vero had disappeared, as if she had somehow squeezed in between them and stayed a part of Amazonas forever.

Maybe Verónica never made it to the bathroom. Maybe on the way she was intercepted by a mammoth guy of about thirty who hit on her, his tongue flailing from inside his mouth, his mouth calling her names such as puta or mamá; he asked her to kiss him. He smelled of a thousand years' worth of liquor, as if he had been drinking since the Aztecs first chopped through a mexcalmetl plant to discover the first traces of tequila. Maybe she fled from him and left the club through the back door, the V.I.P. door, getting stamped so that she could come back in. Then she sat down on the curb and cried the same ten centuries' worth of tears, all the oppression and sadness and sacrifice to gods and women dying if they left their home after six. Maybe then there was a sympathetic man who sat next to her, and she felt close to him, immediately, the way we do when we are led somewhere by force of escaping something else. And he consoled her and said the nicest things anyone had ever said to her—that her face reminded him of a commercial and her smile was like magic. He had told her the sad story of his daughter, who'd died a few years before, who was just about the same age as Verónica when she was diagnosed with cancer. Vero's mother died of cancer, too, she told him. And she knew what it was to lose something. He had a necklace that his daughter had worn, and he thought it would make her feel better, as it would make him feel better, if it were hers. She couldn't possibly take something so important to him, but he told her to follow him to his car anyway, around the corner past the lights of the News, back to the avenue, where the cars screeched down the streets with abandon. Maybe, then, the man told her it was a few blocks further, and only then was she remotely skeptical, only then did she mention Esme, and by then they were farther away—too far—where the lights of the superstructures fell away like the last shadows before nightfall. Maybe to prolong the anticipation and start to see and smell the worry, he walked her farther than he needed to in order to be safe. Maybe this was his game. Maybe it was there, on some empty lot that he raped her. Or maybe he got her into the car, and she continued to appease him because that was all the hope she had left, and maybe he didn't touch her until he drove her all the way to where her body was dumped—to the Lote Bravo, all the way over there, in the desolate, rotten part of the desert, where he killed her.

the manners games

Mannerlesshattan, that's what he called it. It was a common conversation among Mexican expatriates and other internationals, the educated elite, people from the South, even people from the boroughs. It was agreed—in Manhattan, the manners of the previous centuries had vanished, and in its place was brash, cosmopolitan sneer.

"And I'm not talking about just opening the door for someone else. That's what most people think of when they think of manners—opening doors. There's more to it than that." These words came courtesy of my friend Joaquín Guzmán, a Columbia University humane studies fellow from Monterrey. Joaquín was a thirty-two-year-old man with a short-attention span, a proclivity toward violence in the form of nipple-pinching and, when saying something he considered of the utmost importance, he would often look at me sideways, which was odd because this was the least aligned my ear and his mouth could be.

"I don't see many men walking on the side of the sidewalk closest to traffic the way my dad did with my mom," I offered.

"…They'll do more than shut the door in your face," he continued. "I asked a subway conductor once what time the day-passes run out and he just shook his head. He didn't even look at me, huevón."

"Sometimes trying to get people to listen to you is as difficult as trying to get them to not listen to you…" I began, but he cut me off.

"Mannerlesshattan," he said, clearly pleased by the invention. "That's what this place is. In fact, this whole country can go to the devil."

Talking about manners with Joaquín stirred up pleasant memories of the past, of high school, and specifically of the Manners Games, which had commenced somewhere around the time of Martínez v. Martínez II and a few weeks before the longer lunch days. That's when my classmates could be found doing such things as buying bouquets of flowers for first dates, tipping imaginary hats and, in a mass exodus after school, rushing across town in the hopes of arriving in time to open doors once class let out at the all-girls school (this, of course, had been complicated by the beginning of the longer lunch days).

My friends and I could now be found answering the phone with "May I ask who is calling, please?" or "¿De parte de quién?" We ate with our forks in our left hands, sneezed on our wrists if we didn't have tissues and began calling our parents "Señor" and "Señora" or "Sir" and "Ma'am." Some friends of mine developed particular techniques about how to deal with consecutive doors (walk through the first one, then open the second, holding both), revolving doors (get the spinning started, then step back) and doors controlled by electricity (make as if you are going first, then, at the last

39

moment, step aside and exaggeratedly wave the person through). The Manners Games impelled many of us to consult our grandfathers and, if they were still alive, our great-grandfathers, in order to discover the more antiquated and forgotten incidences of manners or those on the brink of desuetude. This caused a lot of confusion, especially because some manners ran in conflict with others, and a committee to establish which manners to defer to in the case of a draw had not been established. Things began to get even more complicated when large groups of students could be found outside classrooms, no one wanting to be the first to enter.

Art was unimpressed by the Manners Games, calling them exaggerated attempts to impress rather than to show people respect, which was, he said, the purpose of manners. (It was he who drew our attention to the versatility of the Spanish word "educación," which encompassed both "education" *and* "manners"). Art had been dabbling in impressionism at the time and was still years away from finding icons among the brilliant artists that inhabited the border and Mexico, but he was content not to involve himself in yet another passing trend. And like all good and bad fads alike, the Manners Games disappeared almost overnight, especially as many students were then getting their driver's licenses and driving automobiles tended to inspire rebellion rather than the revisiting of social decorum.

It was manners—probably something closest to Art's notion of manners, I believe, that kept the Serranos from reading the letters addressed to me. Of course, they knew that by doing this, it was possible that they would never know what Art had written to me. They knew what had become of me, but they didn't know whom I had become. In El Paso, everything stayed the same—sometimes new street signs or park benches were put in to "beautify" a city steeped in the visions of the past—but New York and every place not-El Paso had the power to change a person.

With Art's mother standing by, I walked from one end of his studio to the other several times, almost pacing, seemingly looking for information that might have been, if you had seen me, stored somewhere within the hardwood floors. Eventually, I stood still in the center of the room, once again in front of the painting.

"Would you like to see the letters?" she finally asked.

I nodded. She took them from her purse. On the return address, I recognized a handwritten font that tilted into italics and formed into the letters of his name. The mailing address bore my name, but there was no address. As she had informed me earlier, they had been in a safety deposit box since the day after she had discovered them. The investigating officers had never seen them, Professor Keating had never heard of them, and the Serranos, if I knew them at all, had honored the name on the outside of the envelopes that denoted their responsibility and ownership to be mine alone. The letters were sealed. Ella Serrano immediately turned to leave, telling me she'd give me a few minutes alone with them and, though I assured her that this was unnecessary, she found her way out anyway.

I opened the letter and began reading.

Compa,

Listen: I was on a train in Belgium when two men came through the train and started yelling at a dark-skinned man. They shook him up like la migra, searched through all his stuff and took him away. The only thing the police missed was a book. So I took it from under the seat, read a few lines, then I heard your voice telling the story of a kid who spent his life dreaming of running the subway. Even though the kid was someone else, he sounded like you as a kid. He had glasses and big-ass shoes. I didn't need to look at the cover to see that you wrote it. Only you could write a whole damn book about public transportation.

When are you going to write a book about la frontera? You know it's your duty to keep things alive when everything else is dying. For you I have painted El Paso and Juárez—a true-to-life landscape, except the colonias are in downtown El Paso, underneath the skyscrapers.

I'm coming to New York in October, and I'm leaving you my email address so that you can send me your information. I don't even know where to send this, carnal. The publisher?

Keep pushing things to their limits. Make sure to smell nice. Drink juice. Fry mangos. Read the newspaper. And don't forget to shave every day before school.

C/S,
Arturo Serrano
Ciudad de México

The second and heavier of the envelopes was typewritten. Neither my name nor return address appeared on the envelope, but it had been attached to the other by a paper clip. Without further ado, I carefully tore apart the back flap of the envelope and pulled out the papers, reading from the cover page:

The Last Will and Testament of Arturo Serrano

Perhaps anyone who deals on a regular basis with deaths—and particularly suicides—would have expected to find a will somewhere among Art's meticulously-organized, surviving materials, but I certainly hadn't anticipated finding this among the two envelopes I had been so mysteriously bequeathed. Again, I wondered why I had been the selected recipient. Art had friends, college classmates, professors, people with whom he'd shared studios over the years, roommates, sisters and cousins, yet he had chosen *me* to receive this envelope, this will, this final renunciation of all things his, all things material.

As wills go, and I had seen several in my years of journalism, his was remarkably professional, included a statement on family members, costs of administration allowances, and he'd had it notarized at the courthouse just a few weeks prior. His older sister, Carla, would be executor. His assets—he didn't have any debt—would be deposited immediately into his parents' account. His apartment would be sold after three years; money had been set aside to pay the utilities (nothing was to be moved in the room—clearly, I imagined—so that the painting would continue to reflect everything, except for the viewer, back). His paintings that had not been sold would also be turned over to the estate. After the larger financial matters had been settled, and there were only few, an interesting array of books, paintings, household appliances, even salad tongs or lamps—anything more important than a toothbrush—had been allocated to a list of people numbering twenty-seven. At number sixteen, I was to receive the painting "El Paso del Norte—oil on canvas"—likely the one mentioned in the letter—and the book *Drink Cultura* by José Antonio Burciaga. Instinctively, I scanned the list for the other book titles, determining that those characterized by the obscurity of the author or the text had been relegated to people such as myself, while the family members and friends who didn't read much were bestowed modern classics (to use an oxymoron from the industry) such as Gabriel García Márquez's *Love in the Time of Cholera* or Willa Cather's *Death Comes for the Archbishop*. I couldn't be certain what statements were being made in the way of explicitly bequeathing moka pots, end tables, the occasional ceramic dish but, based on the books alone, I was sure that quite a bit of consideration had gone into the list. The more I analyzed, the more certain connections (what in humor is called the "inside joke") items and people had to one another. For example, his cousin Mateo was to be given a jersey for the Mexican national fútbol team, even though Mateo despised sports. Quique Delgado, who was probably the least likely to appreciate it among our high school friends, inherited one of Art's most enigmatic paintings, the acrylic on canvas "La Senectud y La Decadencia."

Not all of the items listed in Art's will were in this studio, as Art still kept a large portion of his things in storage in London. I looked around the room to locate several of the items and, upon doing so, discovered something even more beguiling. Nothing in the will was in the mirror's reflection, and some things bequeathed had been left menacingly near, as if to flaunt how deliciously close to the line they could flirt. The painting of the mirror had been left to his parents along with the money, so did that mean they would also stand to inherit all the real objects the mirror reflected? Or to put it another way, did the things reflected by the mirror belong to the mirror and, consequently, the owner of the mirror? (Did this also mean that the new owner of the painting of the mirror had also inherited the missing Art?) When it came to Art and his creations, you could never be sure. He loved these types of games and enjoyed making people speculate and guess about things that were of little or no significance. In high school, he refused to show anyone his grades. We would all come together after class and compare scores. But Art would just say, "I might have got a ninety-eight. Maybe I failed by a few points." This was the sort of thing that irked me infinitely and played right into my compulsion, my desire to always know, something that I'm sure sent me spiraling into a career in journalism, a profession built on knowing things—and not only that—to know them before anyone else did, when it was new, which in its noun form became plural: *news*.

I had nearly forgotten about Art's mom so, when she knocked on the door, I jumped from the spot on the bed where I had been reading the will, giddy with the discovery of its crosshatched ironies.

I called to her to come in and, to spare her the exasperation of a moment's wait, immediately passed her the two documents. "One is a will; the other is a personal letter addressed to me, of no great telling detail, just that he was going to be in New York sometime in October." She looked them over, briefly, and then turned and looked directly at me.

"You might think this settles things," she said.

"What do you mean?" I asked, unprepared for her sudden change in tone.

"Even if Arturo were to be found dead from a car accident, and his body were found on the scene in two pieces, I'd have trouble believing he was dead."

"But he hasn't really deceived anyone before. As you mentioned, he calls home even if there aren't any phones within a hundred miles."

"No...I know that. But this whole thing stinks incredibly of Arturo and his designs. All this extensive preparation for death. He's an artist. Like God. You don't create something and then run away, do you? You stay and watch."

Her conviction forced me to play the other side. I was also partially honoring the agreement I had made in conversation with Hector Serrano not to give way to the possibility that Art was alive. "A lot of people believe God did just that—created the world and then disappeared."

She looked the other way, finding her own glance perplexed upon not being returned by the mirror.

"Don't say anything to Hector. Hope would ruin that man. It will do him a great deal of good to grieve and then be over it."

I didn't tell her how her husband felt. It seemed to fit that they both needed this level of nobility, this feeling that they were taking care of the other. I made a promise to myself,

45

fighting the advances of disclosure that hurled forward from the unknown, that I would not spoil a misunderstanding that connected them on a level deeper and greater than matrimony.

I gave the room one last look, and then Ella Serrano and I left, turning off the lights and rolling down the blinds, leaving the room dark and empty. We found her car parked on the street and drove past what had once been the Palace nightclub, then the Museum of Art and finally the theater, which was in the process of restoration to its heyday, back when crowds commingled in El Paso for movie openings, in the era of the pachucos, when El Paso was a film mecca for the Western and Juárez was a majestic stepaway for the glamorous. Every once in a while El Paso found its way into the national news—a high-profile boxing match, a Bruce Willis movie, or as one of the cities that placed consistently among the top three safest in the nation.

Situated finally on the eastbound freeway and free from the hassle of the downtown streets, which, as in many major cities, require that you turn off your stereo to understand which are one-ways and which might actually not be lanes but instead places for parallel parking, the car slowed when she was speaking and sped when I was talking, at a range of about forty miles per hour. We lunged forward to eighty miles per hour and faster as I asked her when she thought they would hold the funeral, to which she replied that she wasn't sure, but that they would wait for all of their children to arrive—and then she changed the subject, mentioning that on her walk north toward the border she had come across Father Rahm St., the street named for a Jesuit priest who was famous in El Paso mid-century. She said she hadn't thought about him in ages, but she said that Art, taken by the things he had learned about the priest in a book he had read in college, had gone to where the priest had relocated, a city called Campinas, near São Paulo, Brazil, where he had worked for a year or so teaching art to street kids in one of the priest's professionalization programs. "It's so funny that I had forgotten it," she said, adjusting the rearview mirror, as cars sped by us on both sides. "I imagine when you have a son such as Art, who has circumnavigated the globe as many times as some presidents, details like that sort of slip away." She then went on to talk about how in the years following Art had stayed in touch with the priest and talked of moving to Brazil to work with him to bring about social change, so impacted was he by the priest's ministry. As Ella Serrano was prone to loquacity, but not to non sequitur, the conversation did not diverge from its course as she continued to talk about Father Rahm, a man who had been to me little more than the namesake of a street en route to ditching class and afternoon carousing in Mexico. "This priest did more in a year to affect Art's worldview than anyone who came after him. I understand that he even befriended prostitutes and baptized the children of unwed mothers. You know, I never understood all the preoccupation with the rules and regulations, the drawn-out process of annulment, the literal adherence to the Bible. If you've read Leviticus, for example, there are certain egregious sins listed that are so outdated they were probably outdated then, when the book was written…But Father Rahm—he had a very modern slant on things, and he didn't get caught up with little rules that don't have any meaning, did he? Art said Father Rahm would often fast for several days at a time—he even developed a type of Christian yoga, where he'd stand on his head in the mornings, coordinating his prayers with the various chakras. I'm agnostic myself, but if religion were closer to Father Rahm's ministry, I'd find it far more difficult to repudiate, or resist."

The character of Father Rahm appealed mostly to my journalistic ear, the one that listened acutely for instances of contradiction and uniqueness that could be converted into stories of fifteen-hundred to three thousand words. As I would later learn while researching El Paso history in order to pitch his story to several magazines, Father Rahm was the one who had put an end to the notorious gangs of El Paso during the 50s; he founded a Night Court, where gang members themselves convicted and punished their peers through head-shaving or even in organized, public fights. His liberal style of religion seemed even more of a selling point, since many people, myself included, had long battled with and eventually dismissed the world of religion from our lives for reasons similar to those Ella Serrano had described. I began to think I might remember Art saying something about the priest. I did vaguely remember Art had been to Brazil; however, in retrospect it didn't seem he was there for as long as a year. But time is a surreptitious measuring cup—how interesting that we continue to measure it in minutes and hours and years instead of by the weight and gravity of the moments! The evening I spent singing at a karaoke club in Morningside Heights during my graduate school year, for example, calculates at a far greater weight than that of an evening two years ago that I only vaguely remember when I met my friend Joaquín Guzmán, who, as I know him now, is *completely* memorable and probably at the time looked at me sideways as he said something important, as he always does. Ella Serrano continued to talk about Art's visit to Brazil, and I pictured slight objects and shadows of people interacting under palm trees, and her story seemed to end as we parked, as if the distance of the trip indicated the length of the story—rather than the story indicating the length of the trip, as it does in fiction—for Ella Serrano was a university professor and an artist of time management. As she parked the car in the slightly circular driveway curved by the cul-de-sac in which the Serranos' house lay, she turned off the ignition, and I rushed across the front of her car, came to the driver's side and opened the door for her, as if for me the Manners Games had never ended.

tres leches

After making some phone calls to New York, I explained to the Serranos that I needed to leave later that afternoon, given that I was required back in Manhattan to do a story on a subway conductor who had apparently saved several hundred people pushed up against a wall in a subway station without a rear exit (the York St. station on the F-train) by leading them through the unlit, smoky tunnels to the next station. The Serranos didn't seem to mind that I was leaving after so short a time with them. "Business is business," he said. "You're here now, and that's what's important," she said. Having returned the call from Jack Walsh, the magazine editor, I also needed to write a short piece on Art that was to appear in his magazine's "Epitaph" section. I again touched base with Camille, who told me that I had received several phone calls from magazines and newspapers and that she had deferred their questions until I arrived back in the city.

The Saturday afternoon had been warmed by an impressive sunlight worthy of summer, so much that I wondered whether the earth was on course in its revolution. Now that I'd seen the painting, I needed some time for reflection. I knew that Ella Serrano would want to go over the will with her husband, so I decided to do something uncharacteristically El Pasoan and completely New Yorker that left the both of them perplexed (especially after offering every option of transportation short their neighbor's pets)—I took a walk.

Condemned to spend the crucial part of my formative years on the Westside of El Paso, I was only vaguely aware of the vibrant existence of El Paso's Lower Valley. Here, Spanish predominated. Mexican products and restaurants and modi operandi reigned. I left the quiet residential area the Serranos lived in and found my way to Alameda. Somewhere farther east this road intersected Avenue of the Americas, which, as soon as you crossed the bridge, became Avenida de las Américas. This was one of the two free passageways to Juárez, and only once during our weekend and summer night crossovers—when the free bridge downtown was shut down because of a bomb threat —were we forced to use this bridge.

After walking no more than five blocks after turning onto Alameda, I ran into a small panadería in a rundown white building, architecturally linked to the house next door but still a freestanding structure. On the Westside, such a business would be impossible to find unless it existed as some sort of boutique and was done up like an upscale bistro.

As soon as I entered, it occurred to me that I was looking for Art's baker, this powerful figure from Art's youth, a man of extraordinary proportions and, of course, a long white baker's hat. But I was disappointed; no one matched this description. Instead, there were a man and a woman dressed in the indistinguishable white uniforms of meat cutters or doctors.

"¿Le puedo ayudar?" the woman asked.

"Yes…but give me a moment. I don't know yet," I answered in English.

Living in New York, I had been indoctrinated to think that the world's great bakers could only be French, or Italian perhaps, as if using large ovens for baking bread would baffle culinary experts elsewhere, and I was embarrassed to discover how myriad and extensive the bread, in addition to cakes, cookies and candies, in a small bakery in the Lower Valley could be. I surveyed the bolillos, pandulces, conchas with indentures like the lines of a hand, pan de huevo, empanadas, churros, galletas in the shape of pigs and then, turning my attention to another encasement, I saw—and immediately ordered—a pastel called tres leches, the greatest cake in the world; soaked in three different types of milk and served cold, it was something I had completely forgotten about in my years away from El Paso. The bakers here weren't selling the cake in slices and, as I thought it might be nice to bring something back to the Serranos, I ordered the entire cake and resigned myself to waiting to taste it until later.

My sudden recognition of the existence of tres leches caused me to shudder for having forgotten it; worse was the knowledge that other, equally significant things had been lost in the gutters of time. I looked through the lens of the glass through which all these things could be viewed, and to me the glass seemed representative of all the valuable and precious things that were locked away deep within the recesses of the brain, that only memory could awaken.

"¿Algo más?" the woman asked. A look of concern crossed her face, a triangular bridging of the eyebrows.

"Yes," I said, and then for a moment hesitated about whether to ask her. "Do you know if a man named Jim has ever worked here or at any of the bakeries nearby?"

"Jim?" she asked, still not indicating either possibility.

"Yes. I think so."

"Well," she said, "My husband is Jaime, and some people call him Jimmy." As she said this, the man, who had been in the back room, entered the room through a door made of plastic strips cut like fringes he parted on each side. He was a handsome man of about five-foot-six with a bald, perfectly formed pate. "You're looking for Jimmy?"

Jimmy—had that been it?

"Maybe. You're Jimmy?"

"Jimmy Number One," he said. "My son is Jimmy Number Two."

"I'm actually just back in the neighborhood from New York and I'm looking for a friend of mine who used to live nearby. His name is Art Serrano—the artist. The reason I ask is that he used to go to one of the bakeries around here and always used to talk about his baker."

"Art. Of course I know Art. He's been coming here since the beginning of time."

"Have you seen him recently?" I asked, shocked at how immediate my discovery of an association had been.

"Let's see. Yes. I saw him about a month ago. Right after the Raiders/Cowboys game a few Sundays ago."

It surprised me—Art had never really been into football, if that's what he was implying.

"He's disappeared. Did you know that?" I asked.

"Disappeared. Really?" he said, with inklings of remorse and excitement melded into one, as if I were referring to the incidences within a recent telenovela, or, of course, real life.

"Yes."

"I just saw his wife the other day, and she didn't say anything."

"His wife?"

"What is her name—Angela?"

"No…I think we're talking about different Arts."

"Art only comes here when the Cowboys win because otherwise he's broke."

52

"Do you know any other Arts?"

"I don't think so. Amor, are there any other Arts?" he said, turning to his wife.

"Maybe, but I don't remember," she said, then left the room.

"Where did Art go?" he asked, seemingly concerned.

"I don't know," I said. "But it's a different Art. Arturo Serrano. The well-known painter."

"Where do you think he went?"

"I don't know," I repeated.

"Sometimes Art does win a lot of money, but he lost a lot on the Super Bowl last year, and he loses money here and there. That's because he has a weak spot for underdogs. It's a great way to live, but a stupid way to gamble…How did a young man like yourself meet Art?"

I decided to just go with it. "I went to school with him. I'm actually a lot older than I look." I wasn't getting anywhere with Jimmy, so I tried a different technique of getting information from him. "Have you ever heard of the phrase 'know your baker'?"

His eyes widened with recognition. After a brief pause, he said, "No."

"Let me put it this way—do you know of any reason why anyone would want to know their baker?"

"I see," he said, looking me over. "People always come in here, thinking that because they know me, I'll give them free bread. I can't. This is my livelihood."

"Oh, no," I protested. "That's not what I'm getting at. I don't want free bread."

He scrutinized my face like a drunk or someone on stage exaggerating their facial gestures so that people in the back of the audience can still discern an expression. In the meantime, as he continued to look at me, his wife returned with several boxes, cakes for quinceañeras of several layers, each showcasing a girl by herself on the top layer holding flowers, like wedding cakes for weddings at which the groom stands up the bride.

He continued, "The first time I met Art...do you know what he ordered?" He leaned forward onto the counter.

"No."

"Tres leches, just like yourself."

"Is that so?" I wasn't sure I believed anything he said.

"Yes. Tres leches. When you're eating it, you can feel the different types of milk filling your mouth, like three different currents forming into one river in your mouth," he said, pointing at his throat. "I remember the first time I had tres leches..." He peered off into the distance in frozen reverie, transfixed by the memory. After a moment, I asked him, "And when was that?"

"What? Oh, yes, when was that? I was about ten years old, old enough to be in love, and there was a fight between my brother and my uncle over a girl. My brother was three years older than my uncle. My grandmother had fourteen kids, you know, and the last three of them were younger than my oldest brother. The girl's name was Julia, and she was only eighteen and a real *chula*, not a *chola*, like the girls around here who wear their pants around their knees and black makeup on their faces, but a really classy girl, with green eyes. I'd never seen a Mexicana with green eyes before, but we're all Spanish, no? [I nodded.] And that's what my brother told me—that her grandparents were from Spain. So my brother had seen her over at Bronco Meat Market, down further on Alameda, where she was working, and he made a pass at her. I remember the way he came home that day, smelling of heavy cologne that he always wore, but instead of angry and slapping me, he had a big smile on his face. He said, 'Jimmy, I've found the woman I'm going to marry—la chica más guapa del mundo, y con ojos verdes. With green eyes,' he repeated. I was ten years old at the time, old enough to be in love, and to hear that mesmerized me. I kept thinking about it and thinking about it. I took out a notebook of paper and tried to draw what she looked like in my head, but I couldn't do it, because, like your friend, I wasn't an artist."

A man with a thick beard of impressive cultivation entered the store, carefully choosing a half dozen rosquillas, crunchy, snail-shaped, doughnut-holed, sugarcoated bread. He lingered for a moment, asking Jimmy about business and then about "Jimmy Number Two," to which Jimmy replied, "He spent three hours on the bridge last night coming back from Juárez. ¿Can you believe these kids these days? It's that they leave the house at eleven o'clock to go to Juárez for three hours and then end up coming back at six in the morning." The man nodded. "My son just turned fifteen, as you know, and he's just started talking about crossing over. We told him he can't, but then remember when we were young?...It's only a matter of time."

"It was much safer those days," Jimmy said, and they shook hands. "Oh, well. Cuídate, bro."

As soon as the man left, Jimmy returned to the other side of where I was standing and laid his arms on the counter in the same position they had been moments before. "¿Algo más?" he asked.

"What about the rest of your story?"

"The story? Ay, ándale pues—so where were we?...My brother had been taking Julia out for a few months, and about this time my uncle came to the house and no sooner is he in the door is he talking about the new love in *his* life, the prettiest girl he'd ever seen. Really classy, and she went to school at Burges. The more my uncle talked about this girl, the more he wanted to see her, so he called her and asked her if she wanted to come over. I couldn't wait to meet her. I was ten years old, and I remember waiting for this girl to come to my house while I listened to him tell me about how important it was to him to find someone as beautiful as this girl. My grandmother was cooking, my mother and my aunts were in the kitchen, too, and after about an hour there was a knock at the door, and it was the girl. She was taller than I expected, maybe even an inch taller than my uncle, and she had straight dark-brown hair that went far past her shoulders. She was wearing a dress and loop earrings, and even to this day I can picture exactly what she looked like standing in front of the door waiting for my uncle to invite her in. My uncle took a few moments to react. He was nervous because she had not met the family, and he was nervous because she was so gorgeous. And, as soon as she entered, the light caught her eyes, and do you know what color they were?"

I shook my head.

"Green. And I knew immediately. Not even because of all the descriptions of what she was like or how green her eyes were, but because the expression on my uncle's face when he described her was exactly the same as my brother's. I might have taken my uncle to the side and told him because I knew my brother would be coming home soon from his job—I forget completely where he was working—but I didn't. I was too taken by the look on her face, her eyes…*I* was in love, too. Pues, soon enough, my brother *did* come home. He walked into the living room and saw Julia sitting there next to my uncle and said, '¿Qué haces aquí, querida?' With those words, my uncle stood up, full of rage. 'What are you talking about? This is Julia. This is the love of my life.' The next thing you know they are out in the front lawn bloodying each other as if they were the world's worst enemies. Everyone in the house rushed out, including Julia, and my mother and my aunts were staring at her, the cause of all this trouble. And then my grandmother came from inside the house. She was a very big lady. And she got in between both of them and stopped them fighting. And by this time Julia had already escaped. My brother and my uncle didn't talk for a full year but, when they spoke again, they realized how stupid they'd been—and by then they had all but forgotten the girl." He stopped, the dramatic pause of a storyteller in complete control of his art, and he went to get a cup of coffee and refilled it before returning. "And do you know what happened to Julia?" he asked.

"No," I said.

"She owns a bakery." He smiled at me mysteriously, complicitly, and then went on with the story. "Ten years later, I went to a restaurant downtown, and she was working as a waitress. She looked a little bit older, but I recognized her immediately, especially by her green eyes. By that time, there had been many girls in my life, but I would never forget the one I loved first. I was there with some of my friends, sitting in a booth, and she came up to our table and took our order. I kept trying to make eyes at her, but she looked at me strange. When we were leaving the restaurant, I told my friends to wait for me, and I went back up to her, asked her for some matches and wrote down my name and number. I never thought she would call me, but two weeks later she did. She told me she knew who I was and if I wanted, I could pick her up at eight…"

I waited for his wife to reemerge, asking more follow-up questions and, when she did find her way back to the front room, I looked at her green eyes in confirmation of his tale, not because I doubted its veracity, but because it seemed that certain stories required physical evidence in order to be brought to completion, like the story told by an ex-marine, who, at the end of his epic tale of endless torture, pulls up his arm sleeve to show you the horrendous burn mark.

As a wave of customers entered the store, lining up in front of the counter, I decided to make my way toward the exit with the cake, but Jimmy called me back, reaching into the glass and grabbing three or four rosquillas, putting them into a bag and handing them to me.

"On the house," he said.

"Thank you," I said, feeling guilty for squandering some of his livelihood.

"Cuídate, bro," he said, as he turned back to the other customers.

More than an hour had passed since I'd left the Serranos—wanting to return to refrigerate the cake, I turned back toward their home, holding the cake steady and feeling the part of a nervous first-time ring bearer as I navigated Alameda, chilled by winds that hinted of an icy response to the earlier gesture of a summery afternoon and, as soon as I arrived back at the Serranos' home, I felt a sharp pang of loss as I wondered with such strong sense of disappointment what on earth that story had to do with tres leches.

los colores

Let me roll paint on your walls and then tell you a story full of the colors of life. Or better yet, come with me to las colonias, where the colors already exist. Do not look across the river at the gleaming skyscrapers on the other side for disparities between the first and third worlds. Those almostskyscrapers are mostly empty, abandoned a long time ago. Stand with me up high, at the northernmost reach of the Sierra Madres; we are barely sweating, but we can feel what 38°C means, and the heat is bright-colored. The humidity circles other places like vultures, but make no excuses—the boiling point in Juárez is the same as everywhere else. The sun slides down the horizon, splashing tinges of red, orange, yellow and blue upon the canvas of the sky, the clouds empurpled blotches adrift among them. In the early summer, just minutes after eight, the velvet curtain hem closes tightly around the dome of the globe, and

Juárez glistens one last splendid time. Finally, when almost all natural light is squelched out of the city, the Río Grande becomes the river in between feuding green and yellow lights, and the border tells you where the river is instead of the other way around. Those of us women who are most scared—and we are all scared—have closed and locked our doors, and we stay inside until the sun rises again. Now, let us climb down from our perch and take a walk down Avenida 16 de Septiembre. Tonight, red, yellow and green bulbs illuminate the downtown cathedral's neo-classical visage. We turn on Avenida Juárez and eventually arrive at the Strip, which is teeming with teenagers from both sides of the border, their minds awash in the potential of a Saturday night. In their faces gyrate the colors of neon signs and marquees. I know these have only been colors, but in colors are everything, and the details of my story can be remembered through them. When I am finished painting all over your walls, you may return them to their natural colors—their whites and off-whites, beige and plaster. You can pretend that I never told you such a story about colors, and I won't mind. I won't be insulted. I told you the story. It is yours now to do with it what you will.

Black is not the color of night; the night has no color. Ask those who are blind what the color of nothing is, and they will not answer black. The light-skinned girl couldn't see anything, which looked like nothing, as she was dead, and maybe he, who was holding her head, waited to see anything, any glimmer of an object that would cause him to move along, to some place more empty, more devoid. The night was warm; the temperature dropped three degrees within the first thirty minutes of darkness. But there wasn't any movement, so he turned the key to the ignition slightly to allow light to fill the car and opened the door to let it spill out onto the dirt. The door binged, binged, binged metronomically. Maybe he waited a few more moments before getting out, closing the door, and returning to the soundlessness and nothingness of the desert, a noticeable contrast to the sounds of crying and yelling that were so shrill and terrible, that made his occupation in the night so different from anything else.

What had there been about this girl? Were they the same qualities men look for in women they'd like to make their wives? Were they the same qualities men look for in women they see only as whores? Maybe she was just his type—they all were, weren't they? She'd come in to the bar later, after all the other girls; or maybe there were girls who came in later, but it seemed as if she was the last one to enter because she was the last girl he noticed. She'd taken the time to change out of her work uniform, which is why she carried a small bag, which was brown. She was light-skinned, more light-skinned than the others but very obviously Mexican. There's something in the eyes or maybe the lips and you can tell. She had dyed her hair blond, so her dark, natural color was showing only at the roots. He could almost picture the rite—the several girls who watched, the expert who knew how to distribute the dye. At first he just watched her from afar, watched her with his drink, his spiced rum, as he chatted with another man at the bar—a man who wore dark jeans and a brush popper shirt, heavily starched, who was talking about how this was the bar he always drifted to when the sun went down, which was nearly every night, he said. Maybe he waited for her to see him laugh from the bar, to understand that he was safe. Then, he moved across the bar, through the haze of smoke and consent.

"¿Want to dance?" He might have asked.

"No one's dancing," she maybe said. It was true. The bar was a dive. The jukebox was circulating the latest Recodo anthem, but no one was dancing, not tonight, not yet, at this hour when people were still arriving. No lines at the bathrooms yet.

"¿Ok, then how about a beer?" Maybe this man looked really slick in his long-sleeved white dress shirt, the kind of shirt that looked like part of a suit even if the coat was nowhere to be found. "¿What's your name?" he asked her.

61

"María de Los Ángeles," she told him honestly.

What did they talk about for the next forty-five minutes and on the days they met here again? What *didn't* they talk about? The man had the shell of a forty-something, but his heart was that of a man much younger. His clothing was soft. When he spoke, he seemed impassioned, and his references to time were always in the future tense, as if life was something he still had to look forward to rather than only back at. He was the type of man who was loved by everyone who knew him. Time would create distance between him and the people with whom he had once been close, but rarely would anyone who knew him in the present say a disparaging word against him.

Maybe he thought back to that moment, the moment she gave herself to him by accepting a drink. Or maybe he was dutifully concentrating on his task—the removal of her shoes, the delicate setting of them next to her body, the biting into her left breast—yes, this he did after they were dead, well, most of the time, even though he knew this made his actions look much more nefarious. He made no attempt to hide her body. Maybe this entire process took five minutes, as all the rest of the work had been completed earlier in his apartment. Maybe it took an hour. Maybe it took five minutes, but he waited for an hour before leaving. Maybe he liked to smoke a cigarette and toss back a swig of whisky and admire the fruit of his labor, his defiance as he loitered and flirted with the prospect of getting caught.

He knew what would happen next. There would be a time when the girl was expected to be away—the time she was supposed to be at work, for example. Then, the hour she was to arrive home would pass, and her mother would breathe in a small dose of pain and grow increasingly attentive to the clock, but this was what it was to be a mother, so she wouldn't inform anyone yet of her premonitions. Excuses would be made. They were the same kind of excuses made by people when they told themselves they weren't alcoholics or that they were still in love or that they would be young tomorrow, too. When the right amount of time had passed—eight hours to worry and to watch the door and to check the neighborhood and to call around y para enloquecerse más—they would call la policía who would tell them that this sort of thing, señora, happens all the time and they would ask her if her daughter had a boyfriend because she's probably with him and even if she doesn't have a boyfriend she's probably with a guy because sometimes parents don't know their children like they think they do and so on. Maybe he knew every detail of how the day would unfold for the parents of the missing daughters. It was this that he loved, almost as much as how easy it was to get away with this time after time and then watch la policía blame the whole thing on how the girls dressed and whom they hung out with and what kind of Catholic girls they were not, even if they were.

And then, maybe he left the desert and returned to his apartment and turned on the television, sat back and watched the news or a sitcom, maybe MTV, where girls still wore navel rings even though they were climbing into their roles as adults. Did he think about chopping up these girls, too? Or was it a different kind of thrill to murder peasant girls? Were they all the same to him—girls…women? Was it more about the person or the murder? Were these girls special or were they just available?

Maybe the man knew the answer to these questions, understood the psychology of people who didn't need to kill just as some people who do not kill understand the psychology of those who do. Maybe he wasn't like this at all, but maybe he was. The only thing anyone knew for sure—the body of a young girl had just been discovered in the desert, and the girl hadn't killed herself.

Padre Osvaldo, the monkish priest and chief celebrant of mass at the downtown cathedral in Juárez, came-to after his three-day silent meditation only to be greeted with a comment about the notoriously stale, torrid summer weather in Chihuahua. "¿It's rather hot, Father, isn't it?" A septuagenarian priest had asked, daubing his face with a towel. "Indeed it is," Osvaldo said, noticeably irked by the comment, which seemed to make the whole experience of not talking over the past three days unnecessary—like a fútbol player who sits out three months because of an injury only to sprain his ankle the day he returns. He tried not to let the comment annoy him to the point that it would get under his skin, releasing a pin-prick of pain every several hours seemingly without cause; the three-day retreat, the theme of which was "powerlessness," should have had more of an effect on him, he thought. Nonetheless, he hated when he felt powerless, and he hated more than anything redundant comments about the weather—yes, the weather was *always* hot this time of year, and there was no reason to point it out.

From the chapel and his morning prayers, he walked through the convoluted chaos of San Miguel's hallways to the parochial logic of the refectory lines, where priests who wanted no more than cups of pozole still had to stand in the lines for meat. "Por Dios…" he said, under his breath, and found his way to the end of the line, passing through a mess of tables and grabbing a copy of the morning's *Diario*. As soon as he reached for his glasses from his shirt pocket, Padre Humberto, the other priest from the cathedral in Juárez, slipped behind him, patting him on the back. "Padre, good to see you," he said, cheerfully. "¿I pray your vow of silence was as successful as my own?" Humberto had a hint of the celestial about him—something very uncharacteristic in him, so much so that the older priest shrank from what would have typically been his untoward, brushing-off, going-on-with-reading-the-newspaper attitude and turned toward him.

"It was," he said, looking into Humberto's face for more indications of this celestial glow, which had, as he might have expected, already expired.

"Your aura is red today," Humberto said. "All the other priests have white or purple after their three days of rest."

Padre Osvaldo placed his glasses on the end of his nose and unfolded the paper to full-length.

"Padre, you don't have to be so mad," Humberto said. "I was just joking." He then grunted adenoidally—something between a snort and a snore, which was actually his way of laughing.

As the line moved forward, Osvaldo tucked the paper under his arm and gave in to Humberto's attention. "¿So, Humberto, did you make the most of *your* meditations?"

"Yes, of course," he said. "But I've been thinking, Padre…¿Would you be willing to do confession exclusively? I don't think I can anymore."

Apparently, Humberto had been musing upon sections of Leviticus that dealt with touching and absorbing unclean things, and he could feel the grime imploding him, he said, like milk gone bad inside his stomach. At first, Padre Osvaldo despaired of Humberto and all the other priests who were happier in the seminary, lost in debates over mysticism and the tenets of morality, withdrawn from the real world over which these things held sway. But Humberto was right to refuse confession if he felt that way. Besides, Osvaldo hated the business side of religion and was willing to hand it all over to Humberto, who was actually quite a good accountant. There were priests like Humberto who made it easier to be priests like Osvaldo.

"No problem. I can take all of the confessions," he said, actually somewhat relieved that something positive had come from this three-day retreat. Soon, their turns came, and the priests followed the rectilinear path aside medieval-looking tins that kept warm their repast. Some of the younger priests from Mexico City and one novice who was spending his time at La Basilica de Nuestra Señora de Guadalupe called Humberto over, and Padre Osvaldo excused himself to a quiet table far from the instar omnium of the other priests, who had filled the first three tables but left the other nine empty. He dipped his spoon into the pozole and then reached again inside his pocket for his glasses, this time supporting them on the end of his nose. As he did this, a priest set his tray down next to him.

"Hello, Father," he said, in the stentorian voice of a man who never abridges his homilies. "¿You're a Jesuit, aren't you?"

"I am."

He then told the well-known joke that all Jesuits know but never tire of hearing about the priests from three different orders who asked God which of all the orders was best, to which God responded in an email—this was the recent addendum—that he loved all the orders the same, then signing his name "God, S.J." The priest laughed. "¿May I sit down?"

"Please," Padre Osvaldo said, pulling out the chair next to him from the table.

"¿These retreats are never long enough, are they?" he said. The priest moved right on to talking about the weather, disparities in the three regional time zones and finally back to the length of the retreats. Each claim was punctuated by a long pause that seemed rife with finality, and each time Padre Osvaldo riffled the edges of the newspaper, hoping hints would be taken. Instead, it was forty-five minutes before Padre Osvaldo could take a look at the paper. When he did, he learned it had been an unspectacular day in Mexico—the Sociedad Interamericana de Prensa had called for the further investigation of several missing journalists, preliminary gubernatorial election poll results were announced, legislators beseeched Mexico City to look for alternate sources of energy, and four people had died in a car accident on the highway between Chihuahua and Torreón...The piece of news that most thrilled him was deep within, caught in the bleed of crosswords, classifieds and cartoons. It was a story about the apprehension of an Egyptian man for the murder of a teenager in Juárez. The woman had been ripped from life as easily and as unexpectedly as a clothing tear.

Padre Osvaldo stood from the table, left the paper open to this page, took his tray to a garbage can where scraps were collected for a group of stray mongrels the local priest was feeding and went to his room to begin packing.

Back when she still slept with men by profession and was asked her name by clientele, she would always tell them her name was María Magdalena, and the men who knew her and sought her out would always ask for her by that name. The other girls and women would laugh at her to her face and behind her back, but now that she had stopped sleeping with men, the nickname had lost its irony. The girl's roommate, Verónica, the one who was killed, used to hate when the girl called herself that, but nicknames last forever, so there was nothing to be done. She'd ended her career as a woman of the street on a high note—a fifty-dollar bill from a gringo who had since exhaustively scoured the streets looking for the girl who called herself María Magdalena.

The girl, now sitting at a desk in a small second-floor office overlooking the backside of several city buildings, searched for the first letter of the alphabet on her keyboard. On the day she had run into police headquarters on Avenida González and started yelling loudly and ferociously about la policía's apparent reluctance to investigate the murder of her best friend, a woman working for one of the women's rights groups in Juárez had been protesting similarly and immediately found a way to have her hired. She felt natural sitting here at a keyboard, removed from the street below, now devoid of working women, as it was only the early evening.

The girl had an uncanny ability to read and write in Spanish despite having dropped out of school at twelve, after nearly a year of supporting her father and his alcoholism, something she had initially mistaken for a terminal illness because she had seen similar mood swings acted out by a character in a movie—and that person had been dying of cancer of the colon. Her father never lashed out violently against her but managed to destroy nearly everything else in his path: her mother's glass dishes (her mother had died of pneumonia when she was six), the kitchen table, a television, a vase filled with flowers, and so on—and these were merely the physical casualties of his carelessness and rage. As soon as a woman named Rosa, who matched her father drink-for-drink and often even surpassed him, moved in with them, and empty brandy and beer and wine bottles surrounded them like a vigil for the dead, the girl took the paltry sum she made from cleaning an office building several blocks from where they lived—a place where she spent the evenings cleaning and, on her breaks, watching classic Mexican movies and shows like *El Chavo del Ocho* on an old, black-and-white television in one of the offices—and stepped out of her front door into Juárez, the city where she was born, and away from her father forever.

Now, several years later, after six or seven months of weekly tutoring by a volunteer from the university, she had begun drafting letters to human rights organizations and politicians, the media and the private investigators who had been hired collectively by the several organizations that dealt with las desaparecidas; although she wasn't paid much more than a maquila worker, the opportunities were infinite. She'd been enrolled in a course that taught her how to use a computer; after several months, she found it boring and graduated to graphic design, and recently she had been designing brochures and leaflets and a web page for the organization. She was indefatigable. She was driven by pure rage and passion and the determination of someone young, and she devoted herself completely to the work without threat of failure or fear of success. She selected the color icon on the toolbar and ten thousand pixels of blue were at her disposal.

And though she lacked the formal schooling and academic background of a university student, her opinions could not be argued against. The girl had been living and breathing the streets for so long that her intuition was inherently fine-tuned to the problems the center dealt with on a daily basis, and the fact that she was alive and doing what she was doing was a victory for everyone.

Even so, she didn't realize how quickly she was progressing; she only acknowledged the things she did not know. She knew she was weak spiritually and emotionally, and if she thought about her dead roommate for so much as a second, it was difficult to go on for the rest of the day. She found Verónica in everything—eyes, a nose, a quizzical expression, a girl in a crowd who looked identical to her from the back—those slightly hunched shoulders under long, thick hair. How to find a way to remember and forget at the same time. This was the challenge posed by the dead.

She was looking for a particular shade of blue she had seen on a billboard; she pulled up her web browser and typed the name of the product advertised into the search engine, located an image of the billboard, saved it to her hard drive and pulled the graphic up alongside the palette of colors, selected it with the eyedropper and transferred the color to the box she was designing. Then she changed the opacity of the box and slapped another box of the same color on top. *That* was the look she was going for.

She looked out the window, where the streetlamps, round and dim, caused everything to look opaque, and she wanted to use her newfound abilities to cover the faces of the people with brighter, lustrous faces or something like clown facepaint or Azteca masks. She turned back to the computer and the two blue boxes and then decided that if she couldn't superimpose the graphics on the world, then she would find a way to recreate the street on her screen.

In a chair seemingly higher than that of anyone else in the room sat the mustachioed Egyptian chemist, crinkle-eyed, energetic, undeniably brilliant and with an alleged history of sexual promiscuity and violence against women. He sat up straight, did not cower at the claims laid upon him by the police officer, who circumspectly outlined the irrefutable degree of his guilt. If patterns of history repeating itself are to be believed, the Egyptian was more than just the prime suspect—he was a blight, a nuisance, liquid freezing in a glass jar waiting to explode.

The Egyptian was a playboy. He frequented dance clubs and bars packed tightly with girls who worked in the maquilas—girls who all fit the same description—pretty teenage morenitas from the interior of Mexico who were more trusting and oblivious, girls who liked free drinks when they would have otherwise cost them half a day's wage. Despite the fact that he was in his late forties, the girls found him charming; he left an impression like a dent on a car smoothed out and polished new.

On hand in the courtroom were members of the various human rights organizations; the family of the girl whom the Egyptian was accused of murdering; a dozen or so members of la policía; the Juárez photographers, who had documented the story from the beginning; and a monkish priest with a red aura. The ceremony was anything but ceremonious and cut short by the delay of evidence, which would soon, according to officials, arrive. After several formalities—the drama of dicta achromatized into the monotone of just another case number, the Egyptian was escorted back behind the scenes only minutes after having been unveiled.

When the crowd members dispersed, a young woman working for one of the women's rights organization followed after the priest. As soon as she was within earshot of him, she called out to him, and he stopped and turned around. "Padre, I need to make a confession. I...," she said, searching for the right words to continue her sentence.

"Of course," the priest interjected. "We can do it outside," he said, pointing to the double doors in front of them. Together they walked to a plaza complete with benches, the sort of thoroughfare in which pigeons agglomerate, and here in the clamor of heavy street and vehicular traffic, in the deafening noise of the century, did they find silence.

They sat down on one of the benches; she closed her eyes. "Forgive me Father, for I have sinned. It's been eight years since my last confession, and I am only twenty years old. I have slept with more men than whole villages of people. I have stolen, cheated, prayed to become pregnant and wished upon falling stars for fame. I have been doing evil things all my life." He pulled a handkerchief from his pocket and wiped her tears from underneath her eyes.

"You are forgiven, always," he said. "¿Do you have a rosary?" he asked.

She shook her head. He pulled a rosary from his pocket and gave it to her. "Say one rosary tonight before you sleep. Say another one tomorrow morning. You are cleansed of all your sins. You need never go to confession for those things again—¿Understand?" He pierced her line of vision with a heartfelt stare. "I'm not much more than a man, but I'm here for you," he said.

The sun blasted down upon them and darkened their skins. The plaza filled with people passing through, and the buses nearby slid by on routes that knew the precise curve of curbs striving to keep street separate from earth. Palm trees shot up from between brown toes of dirt, and light shadows of blue fading into gray passed onto buildings as clouds in changing shapes enshrouded the sun.

Higher up, above the clouds, everything turned white before fading into nothingness.

two months

The world can change in a day, and it can grow a thick beard in two months. Two months is composed of just under nine weeks, just long enough to take a weekly culinary class in a trendy neighborhood where you can learn to rid your diet of unnecessary carbohydrates, prepare a great French dinner party repas such as lapin au vin épicé avec tarte à la rhubarbe, and meet and marry a woman/man with similar/different interests on the common ground that neither of you knew how to cook (but look at you now!). At some universities and community colleges, nine hours of college credit can be earned, which is just one-third of a graduate degree in some disciplines. Jack Kerouac could have written *On the Road* three times over (it often takes me as long, I feel, to write a paragraph). Off-off-Broadway shows (which sounds like they might be *on* Broadway, but aren't) open and close in less time, despite their acclaim and attendance. During the same amount of time, Art Serrano became the most talked about artist—celebrity indeed—in the United States, and his paintings were already beginning to sell for their posthumous fortunes.

As soon as Ella and Hector Serrano decided to open up Art's studio to the media—indeed, the world—his painting of a mirror came to be viewed as a landmark, a wonder, something of a mecca for art students and a reason for cross-country roadtrippers to spend the evening between Austin and Phoenix lodged in El Paso. There were multiple ways to interpret it, and each seemed to say something about the individual interpreting it, whether speaking to the notion of the exclusion, or occlusion, of the self or the circus-mirror magic that was purely the effect. The headlines and titles of magazine articles never failed to miss the irony of his name: "Is It Art or Not?" "What happened to Art in America?" "What it means to be Artless," and "Where Art Thou?"). Professor Keating's interpretation still reigned as the definitive theory of the painting's meaning. Opinions that speculated Art was still alive tended to be regarded as crazy talk. According to one newsgroup skeptic, Elvis, Tupac and Art were hanging out together in Acapulco, sipping moccachinos at the famous Quebrada. There had been Art sightings in countries so exotic you'd think they were unpronounceable by their own inhabitants.

Another inexplicably odd thing happened: a pair of jeans and a black shirt covered in red paint stains—stains in startling reds initially taken for blood—had been found on the Franklin Mountains near the "C" that had many years before been painted on the mountain in white with the first letter of the name of our high school, next to the bones of a dead mountain goat. These were Art's clothes, the DNA tests confirmed. Police officers scoured the mountain for further clues, but the mountain was like an entire biome of camouflage: a deathly landscape of thorny plants and desiccated earth, and anything that lay across it for more than a few hours was consumed by its dark, dry lapping tongue. The story was reported by numerous news organizations, but neither they nor the police could make any sense out of it, a feat that only added another layer of mystique to the details surrounding the death of Art.

The story also had a very cinematic impact, a certain effect on the imagination, in a way that was as thought-provoking to children as it was to adults, to art-lovers and those who would rather sit outside of museums than wander inside them, to the people who decried mainstream mystery novels as rubbish and to those who read them. Whether you referred to the mirror/painting as a mysterious statement about existentialism or the next stereogram, there was something terribly alarming about a mirror that reflected back anything but the person standing on the imaginary X-mark (which was eventually replaced by an actual X-mark) beholden to the magic of self-exclusion.

A five-dollar fee allowed entrance to the apartment, and proceeds went to a scholarship at the University of Texas-El Paso in Art's name. Magazines, newspapers, art journals, television magazine programs and talk shows all called upon me for interviews that lasted too long and kept me from doing any work. I had been one of the first people to see the painting, I was Art's longtime buddy and the recipient of two-thirds of his postmortem correspondence, and because of my accessibility within the New York metropolitan area, I was contacted so much within the first twenty-four hours of the painting's going public that I began to seriously despair of my career in journalism.

Yes, the world can change in an instant, and several times over in the time it takes for the earth to move one-sixth of its way around the sun. And, though the earth slinks back into the exact same parking spot one year later from when it began its cycle, the planet that returns is a different beast, smoking another brand of cigarettes, facing new universal catastrophes and haunted by different ghosts.

74

KNOW YOUR BAKER

My roommate Camille, a woman who talked about her ex-boyfriend to a tape recorder, tended to walk into other people's unlocked apartment pretending she lived there and accidentally moved large pieces of furniture when she was drunk, immediately noticed that my accent had changed since the weekend I was away in El Paso.

"Your accent used to have the placelessness of an Anthony Hopkins, and now you sound like the next Latin crossover artist," she said, as we sat at our dining room table, she kicking her shoes off, pulling her knees up to her chest and leaning back in her chair so that her head rested against the white wall, several wavy, dark-brown hairs hanging in her face. Camille was still wearing her clothing from work—a dark violet sweater with the sleeves pushed just past her wrists and black boot-cut pants with dark-rimmed glasses.

"I can't help it. This is my natural accent, no?" I sipped on some reheated wonton soup from a place called Jacky Chan's.

"There it is again. You keep adding things to the end of your sentences. 'We should get some Chinese food, yeah?' 'This is my natural accent, no?' You sound Canadian or Irish, not Mexican."

Whether she fully understood the extent of it or not, Camille was astoundingly perceptive about language and often picked up on things that no one else would, which I'm sure worked to her advantage in the advertising world. On a trip through Europe with her ex-boyfriend Joe, she had made a list of things she found interesting about language in the countries she traveled through. According to Camille, the French language was full of words for things good or enjoyable that, if read as English, sounded dreadful, such as pain, poisson, plage, râpé, and crudités—bread, fish, beach, grated cheese and raw vegetables. When she was in Italy, she immediately found the irony in a film poster for the comedy *Not Another Teen Movie*, which had been translated into Italian as *Non è Un'altra Stupida Commedia Americana* (*Not Another Stupid American

75

Comedy)—and she didn't speak a word of Italian. She was always parlaying everyday idioms and vocabulary into social commentary, diarizing on euphemisms and acronyms and commonly misused words (according to Camille, three of the most commonly misused words in the English language—allusion, stilted and literally). She not only knew that I was speaking differently, but she could also point out in which exact ways.

"You just said 'right now,' when you meant 'just a moment ago,'" she proclaimed triumphantly.

"Hey, calm down. I just got back. You're the first person I've spoken to in the past twelve hours. Give me a few minutes, let me step off the plane and go get cambio."

"Cambio?"

"Convert my lingo back. Turn my right 'nows' into just a moment 'agos,' for example."

In the days to come she would point out, usually when I was talking about Art and the border, how "look" had become "watch," "whoa" turned into "eeee," and "dad" became "my dad," even if I was talking on the phone to one of my sisters. A few years before, when (unsuccessfully) trying to find a retired journalist who would teach me shorthand so that I could forever abandon the headache of transcribing from a tape recorder, one of my friends suggested I try cursive handwriting, something I had stopped doing in my early teens. When I first attempted it, I remembered only about fifteen lowercase letters, but, after several weeks of trying to write everything in cursive, the entire alphabet—the full gamut of the compositor's type case, even that bizarre uppercase G—returned to me, the same way this El Paso way of talking was returning to me now.

"You're crazy. I don't understand a single thing you're saying," she said, exaggerating, leaning back in her chair in unprecedented precariousness. "I need a foreign language to speak when I'm drunk. I've always admired people who can do that," she added. With the chair resting momentarily against the wall, she drew her hair up into a ponytail in one hand and struck a pencil through it in three sweeping gestures, immediately transforming the angles of her face through this simple movement. "But, anyway, tell me about the painting," she said and, as my story moved along, she slowly readjusted her seat to the floor and gave me her full attention.

"So," at the end of my story, she asked, "would you have ever thought Art was suicidal?"

"I don't think so," I said, removing myself from the table, going to the refrigerator and pouring myself some juice. "But the problems of our world did seem to weigh heavier on him than anyone else I've ever met. At the same time, I think he had trouble finding a way to reconcile his desire to save the world with his talent for painting. But suicidal? I never would have thought he could do something like that, you know?"

"I know. That's so strange."

"And, even though it's all been spelled out for me, both of the Serranos—his parents—secretly admitted to me, separately, that they think he's still alive. Neither can say specifically why they think that, but they both do. And I think he's still alive, too. I can't explain why either," I said, again sitting down across from her and offering some grape juice from my cup instead of the pitcher. The pitcher was now in the refrigerator.

"I don't know," Camille said. "But isn't this textbook denial? If you haven't seen a dead man's corpse, then it makes you even more likely to deny he's dead. Your friend Art could still be alive of course, but maybe you should at least be prepared to face the fact that he isn't."

She continued: "But if he isn't dead—that's to say if he's still alive, and *not* dead—he's probably going to have to play dead for a while."

"The world would be pretty angry if they thought he might have faked his death," I said. "It's the best way to sell records, or art or whatever, no? I need to write a few more books before I can even consider faking my death."

"You've written a book?" We talked for another few minutes about my essay collection, which had been a flop, the book equivalent of a movie that goes straight to video and then eventually to previously-viewed discount films at a discount pharmacy superstore. She asked where she could buy a copy and I found an extra one in a box deep within my closet. It occurred to me that Camille was probably the person I had found it easiest to talk to in the past several years, though I couldn't explain precisely why; with previous roommates, I'd had only superficial, transient relationships. As my assignments often carried me away from New York, I spent very little time in the apartment and, even when I was in town, I preferred the proximity to other people, whilst at the same time secluding myself by headphones inside screaming, bouncing coffeeshops.

We said good-night, each of us walking the long hallway in opposite directions, as she had work the next day and I needed to begin dreaming about a subway fire I couldn't escape from. As my eyelids closed, I thought about how maybe Camille was right, how perhaps I was at the beginning of a programmed psychological process that began with denial. I wondered what it would take me to get to the next step and, if I never got there, would I completely deny myself the process of grieving over my vanished friend? What importance did these experiences have? Would I be less emotionally connected with the world if I failed to properly recognize the loss of Art? If he were still alive and his death were some sort of prestidigitation, would my grieving his faked death cause me to detest him or never be able to grieve his actual death when it did, eventually, come? These questions drew no immediate answer. I surrendered to their mounting illogic and, soon thereafter, fell asleep.

During the two months, I did several assignments for magazines and newspapers that related to Art's disappearance; for one magazine I wrote a description of the painting, led into from a narrative about what it was like to view the painting without having known anything about it beforehand (and mistakenly thinking *the* painting was the other one with all the pop art canons); for a literary journal, I wrote a piece about the will and my interpretations of why certain items had been consigned to certain people; for a magazine where I was a contributing editor, I wrote a fifteen-hundred-word narrative on growing up with Art, including descriptions of his excluding himself from the Manners Games and his unwillingness to disclose his grades, wanting to paint the mountain white and other things that set Art apart from the masses (for this piece, I unearthed other details, such as Art's early vegetarianism, his affinity for dark chocolate, patronage of florists and cinemas, his contempt for people who spent hours wallowing in relationship angst, the never-fail shine on his shoes and a love for the sound of a tuba and banda music).

None of the projects required me to do any research, which meant that I could write freely from the top of my head, talk to no one, and assume the general role of an expert, and so the details tended more toward periphrastic narrative rather than the facts culled together through inverted pyramid inquisition. My research instead focused on evidence from the past. I found an unlabeled photo album in a box unopened since the past century. How many photos we had managed to take at the bars and antros in Juárez! There, in one, seven or eight people from school—two or three you wouldn't have thought of outside of beaker-and-calculator land, especially at fifteen and sixteen: Quique Vásquez, red-eyed and rum-faced, standing under Julio Poitras, the class valedictorian, who is dancing on a chair with his arm around Patrick Finnegan, a red-headed gringo who had, the caption read (scribbled by Art in graffito-script), "upgraded to *güero*" (*white boy*, in Spanish...) but was now "pedo" (drunk), his mouth open in contrast to Felipe Quiñones, who is wearing a look of constipation and stupefaction and has tufts of hair everywhere on his face where they aren't supposed to be (we called it the inverse goatee), a perfect contrast to Art, clean-shaven and smiling widely and showing both rows of his teeth, his hand palming the back of my head like a basketball.

The stories that came out of each of the nights! Stories about asking girls to dance and stories about fights that cleared boxing rings in the middle of the floor and the story about that time when our quarterback was seen puking and battling with diarrhea in a toilet without a stall and stories about paying la policía after being caught peeing outside, and afterhour taco, fender bender, mafioso and bridge stories.

Another dusty relic I turned to in order to rouse the past from its relentless slumber was our senior year yearbook, a piece of journalism for which I had been entirely responsible, which is why there were large inconsistencies in font sizes and white-space distribution due to my spotty sense of design (despite such natural abilities, my classmates referred to me as El Periodista and my journalism adviser wrote an exceptionally eloquent recommendation that rigged me up for j-school). The senior section filled twenty-five pages—four senior composite photos and biographies fit on each eight-and-a-half-by-eleven piece of thick, uncoated paper stock. Art, like all other students, wore a tie, which was visible underneath his light-blue National Honor Society sash. If memory were ample substitute for the past (It isn't...), I would say that the only time Art ever smiled was in photographs and, when he did, he always showed his teeth, as he did in this photo. What may be more telling are the things he scribbled as answers to the questionnaire that I remember concocting in the never-used stairwell in the old building, where I often hid to avoid calculus class and mundane Mr. Mundo Rivera, whose soporific-style of pedagogy resulted on occasion in his falling asleep in the middle of his own lecture.

Art claimed his favorite class was pre-calculus. His favorite sport to play was soccer; to watch, American football. His student quote was "No lips," which was the line used by students who didn't buy cokes at lunch and wanted sips from other people's sodas, promising that there would be no lip-to-aluminum contact. But what astonished me, when looking back upon this whimsical record of insipid odds and ends, was the final entry on his list, the favorite quote from a book. His was from Ernst Jünger's *Eumeswil*, and it read "…Freedom is based on the anarch's awareness that he can kill himself. He carries this awareness around; it accompanies him like a shadow that he can conjure up."

It's a quote I did not remember reading and, immersed in the frenzy of our senior year, I don't know that I would have taken the time to do more than gloss over the meaning of the words in a search for solecisms. In fact, in the bio next to Art's, "everything" had been spelled "everythink," so it's quite possible that—especially given my work ethic in high school—I hadn't even proofed that page. Nevertheless, the quote was not a detail I included in any of the stories I wrote; rather, I told only Camille. Instead, I included bits and pieces about Art's personality, such as his blend of seriousness and humor. Art's was more of a literal—sometimes epigrammatic or pun-filled—humor, and the things he thought were funny were often things that amused only the two of us. (When someone asked me for my soda with the age-old bargaining plea, "C'mon, no lips," Art, who was often sitting with me, would make them tuck their lips under so that no lip was showing, which he loved because it was very difficult for them to drink like that.)

If senses of humor are like blood types, then I was a universal recipient; I found almost everything funny, so I enjoyed his particular blend of lightheartedness. At the same time, he could shift from something humorous to something completely morbid in less than a second. His was a feeling that everything there was to talk about was fair game regardless of whom you were speaking to, and shifts from humor to sadness, death to a good time out, cancer and baseball, were all legit.

Nonetheless, reencountering the quote from the yearbook had a chilling effect on me, and it reminded me of how much of our actions are so heavily portended in the details of the past, even if it has all but been forgotten. The past does not necessarily have to be remembered. It will show up with keys to your front door, let itself in, sit down, flip through a magazine and wait for you.

The official unveiling of Art's painting occurred exactly one week after his disappearance. It was to be shown several days before, but at the last moment, the Serranos postponed the ceremony so that their daughter Carla could fly in from Mexico City, where she lived with her four kids and a husband who had been in and out of psychiatric hospitals for the past three years but who still elicited her unabashed love and support. Such maneuvering was of little consequence to the Serranos; they simply moved the day of the painting's unveiling forward, which caused the media in El Paso to have to stay two extra days in town, thereby causing them to deepen their coverage, as editors and publishers were reluctant to send their reporters back by plane to wherever they'd come from and, given that news in the United States had reached a dry spell (no elections, scandals, economic disasters, presidential faux pas, sports playoffs, disease scares, movie award shows, holidays, acts of terrorism or terrorist threats), the postponement was a perfect amount of time. Reporters were sent to the three-quarter-century-old brick buildings of our high school, to the various art supply stores in Cinco Puntos and downtown, to neighbors' houses in the Lower Valley and to any place Art frequented (but no bakeries, as far as I knew), in addition to visiting the various monuments and historical sites of El Paso and Juárez. This meant that instead of writing just one story about the unveiling of the painting, they would write several preludes to the actual event and, if they were to write only one story, the story could be more in-depth and enriched with details. In the meantime, the media-at-large continued to search for a number of women who were rumored to have been Art's "lovers" but, for whatever reason, not a one was found and, when Ella Serrano was asked to comment, she said, "*Lovers*...My Art had *lovers*?" in mock disbelief, exaggerating the ridiculousness of the word and leaving it at that.

During the nearly two decades I had lived in El Paso, the city had done very little in the way of attracting tourists. The annual Sun Bowl brought in devotees of certain college football teams and, for a short spell, people very obviously from other parts of the United States converged upon El Paso, our one and only brush with tourism. In the many reports about Art's El Paso, some reporters took it upon themselves to give pen-portraits of the urban landscape, describing, for example, how they found their way downtown from the Camino Real hotel into what one would refer to as "an out-of-the-way cantina," even though no one in El Paso actually called them cantinas. These out-of-town reporters described driving down I-10, a highway that for stretches runs right alongside the borderline, and wrote about the riches of the First World in contrast with the shanties on the other side of the river, only several hundred feet away—"the kind coughs could blow away," one wrote. Or "houses made of little more than the detritus of life," another coughed. These reporters trolleyed across the bridge, stopping at the mercado público and haggling with local merchants for sarapes and pottery and other artisanal items. They were shocked by the size of El Paso/Juárez, "gurgling over the sandbars of the desert beyond" or "spreading outward rather than imploding from the burst of the immigrant population." Unlike local media, however, they recognized the proximity to Mexico and considered the two countries as linked by the border rather than divided by it. And so they represented El Paso by stereotypes but were still able to say something poignant about its size and cohesion with Mexico.

By the time Carla Serrano, Art's taller, Anglo-white older sister arrived at the airport in Juárez, the media had weathered their margarita headaches and their crash course on Art and El Paso. South El Paso Street in front of Art's studio had been closed down, the cops treating it with the ceremony of an Ysleta Street Carnival, which caused vendors to reposition themselves downtown and general crowds to huddle together in air cold enough to make it look like everyone was a smoker as the press awaited their opportunity to see the painting. Another happenstance that contributed toward the overall effect of the hype, which was not unlike the Martínez v. Martínez fights that drew the multitudes to the park by our high school, was the stoic look on Carla's face as she emerged by herself from the building. She walked with the poise of a dignitaire, looking directly into the eyes of the cameras before disappearing into the crowd.

And soon the media were unleashed into the apartment, one after the next, beginning with the New York news nobility whose press passes were like rolled-up hundred-dollar bills at customs, trickling down to what the press liaisons had determined were the lowest levels of rank—regional newspapers and local television stations from nearby cities like Albuquerque and Ruidoso. The national news station that broke the story first used a certain camera lens that allowed the at-home viewer the perspective of someone who had come upon the mirror almost in the same way that I had. Within hours of the gallery's opening, every major news program in the country had broadcast footage of the painting and the border.

And so it was that my friend Art went from being one of the shining stars of the art world (but relatively unknown outside of places like New York and Paris) to capturing the imagination and astonishment of the world. As one comedian on late-night television said, several days later: "Now I wake up in the morning and, before I look in the mirror, I'm scared shitless I won't see myself. Of course, then I do see myself, and I'm equally petrified, so what's the difference?"

One of the more interesting interviews I was called to do during the two months was with Sam Donaldson, graduate of El Paso's Texas Western College (which later became the University of Texas-El Paso) and *20/20* anchor, tenured news reporter of four decades whose infamy began, some say, in the late seventies during his sharp and unwavering coverage of the Carter administration. Donaldson's assistant called and said Donaldson wanted to interview me personally regarding "Arturo," she said, using the name by which I had only heard Art's parents refer to him. I had recently seen an episode of *20/20* in which Donaldson had interviewed Don Haskins, Texas Western's coach several years after Donaldson graduated, popularly known in college-basketball land as The Bear and whose casting of five black players on the starting team against all-white Kentucky won the team the NCAA championship in 1966. During our introduction, I complimented him on this segment, then launched into a story about how Coach Haskins and my father had been friends and fishing buddies during the 1990s, though I hadn't thought much about it until I heard myself telling the story about how the great coach had received hate mail for years from people all over the country, including black people. Donaldson guffawed graciously at this irony, then, waiting for several seconds to pass, asked me if I was ready, as an assistant plugged a microphone to the lapel of my coat. Across from him in front of a white, pull-down screen, I answered his questions as well as I could. Yes, Art had always been an artist. No, he'd never had any idols he spoke much about (not to me, anyway)—no Monets, El Grecos or Dalís, nor Ches or Panchos or César Chávezes. Yes, your extraordinary most-likely-to-succeed sort of student, probably one of the top graduates from our high school. The regurgitated bit about how he would not discuss his grades.

Girlfriends? Not really. Though he might not have told me if he had one. Ditch school? No, I don't think he would ever...Wait. One time he *did*. Only once. He had to organize it himself, come up with the idea on his own, otherwise it wouldn't have been a possibility. Under normal circumstances, Art probably never would have considered skipping. It wasn't something he felt was *to be done* before graduating, no sentimental reasons or fraternity with the guys who skipped school on annual ditch days. But the class we had after lunch was crap, the teacher distraída—one time she put the same assignment on the board three days in a row. Besides, Art had awoken that morning with the need for chile. *Real* chile the kind that burned a hole in your mouth. Yes, thank you, Mr. Donaldson, the border *was* within walking distance of our high school. Yes, the crossing time *did* take about seven minutes on the pedestrian path. I guess I never thought about exactly how long it took. We went to one of Art's favorite places just off the Strip, but it was closed. We went farther into the unknown, uncharted Juárez with Art as our guide—there were four of us—and finally found a place called El Gran Prestigio, as improbable a name for a restaurant as for any business. Art insisted we all order cocas because he said they tasted better if they were made in Mexico.

Mira acá, Westsider, he said, turning to me and pointing at the bottle. *Caña de azúcar, not that sweetener stuff they put in your Westside colas. Real sugar cane. Everything's still real in Mexico, but we got NAFTA now, the first in a series of things that's going to destroy everything, mandar todo a la chingada—cause the maquilas to grow, the rich to get richer and the poor to get, well...they can't get much poorer...* After several minutes, the chile arrived. Tears welled up in Art's eyes from his thoughts, and ours teared up from the chile. *Can you believe all of these factories?* He said, as the tears rolled down his face. *How long before Mexico, too, begins to sell mutated chile that makes you laugh instead of cry?*

What was there about that moment that caused me to recall it for Sam Donaldson in such extended detail? Even though this part of the interview was cut completely, the veteran journalist seemed to allow the digression. I later wondered what it had been—the fact that the greatest details always escape when interviewees ramble through some part of the ruins of the undiscovered past or because he, too, understood that the secrets of the earth could be found in *full* stories—ditching school abroad, drinking real coca. Or was it, instead, Juárez? Was Juárez creeping back into his consciousness? Did he, during his graduate school days, slink into the underbelly, the netherworld or, conversely—as Art referred to it—the place where things were still somehow more *real*?

After the interview was finished and, as his assistants stripped away cables from around him and camerapersons rode their machines to their starting positions, Donaldson turned to me and said, nonchalantly, "Either you spend every day of your life remembering this story so that it still retains the quality of story…or this is the first time you've thought back to that moment, and so it all comes out in one piece like a confession." I thought about the war vessel in Spain, perfectly preserved in the water after all those years.

"The funny thing about Haskins," he said, as if responding to my comment from before, "is that the larger implications of what he was doing never registered with him. He knew that the way to win the championship was by playing his starting five, regardless of their color…He wanted to win."

The Serranos were not as private as you might have expected them to be when it came to the media and coverage of Art's disappearance, and the funeral at St. Patrick's Cathedral was attended by so large a number that several hundred guests, including a number of his high school teachers and close friends of the family, had to stand outside the church. As I had been in El Paso only two weeks before, I told the Serranos I couldn't return in the middle of the week, but I sent my condolences and expressed my regret for not attending.

But, really, the truth was that I could not bear funerals. The last one I had been to was for a friend of mine who'd died at the age of thirty-nine in a horrible boating accident while fishing in a lake in a small town in Vermont. Months later, when reality caught up to me, the thought of his body—his demolished, engine-extricated viscera haphazardly tossed inside the closed casket (even if such weren't the case), my perfunctory comments to his parents, the misplaced apology they replied to with some variation of it not being my fault, and terse, elegiac sentences exchanged among people who didn't know each other disturbed me. Watching ten-second reels of Art's funeral on television shielded me from the uncomfortable feelings that would eventually have arisen from my having been there.

What else was there to note? People were stunned that Art's sisters and mother were so light-skinned. Catalina, the sister closest to Art in age, eulogized. Professor Keating, in from Grenoble, France, remained the spokesperson for the brilliance of Art's painting, saying, "Everything Arturo Serrano painted up until his painting of a mirror had been preambulary to this—his chef d'œuvre, his obra maestra. This piece was the culmination of his talent and, most unfortunately, the culmination of his person." Hector and Ella Serrano sat in the first row on the left-hand side, a row Art and I had shared our freshman year during the candle-lighting ritual when the seniors lit the candles of the freshman. Of course, I hadn't known Art then, and it wasn't until editing the yearbook and coming upon photos from that year that I realized several of my closest friends had, coincidentally, also inhabited that front row. The Serranos cried uncontrollably, as did many of those seated in the pews of the cathedral, but none were more hysterical than Art's youngest sister, twenty-three-year-old Beatriz, on leave from her post in Moscow, where, because of her irresistible charisma and repartee, she was covering politics for CNN's Spanish channel. Beatriz doubled over in such an intense fit of weeping that one completely removed from the event might have thought she was laughing hysterically.

International media in Europe, which I consumed vicariously through Joaquín Guzmán, the regiomontano, international promoter of educación and recipient of an array of illegal cable channels that provided him with access to television programs in countries as overseas as Great Britain, Spain and Israel, favored highlighting Art's body of work, then analyzing his political objectives and artistic activism. According to Joaquín, an Irish news program interviewed Ulick Martin, Dublin's famous fight promoter, who had been responsible for Art's breakthrough exhibitions in London nearly a decade before. Joaquín, who was a sworn caucasiophobe, couldn't help but exclude the Irish from this aversion. He said there was "something about" this Ulick Martin that sufficiently caught his attention in order to stay tuned-in long enough to realize the story was about Art. This something I would later attribute to his thick curly moustache and matching sideburns and the insuppressible laughter that seemed to exit the corners of his mouth regardless of whether what he was saying was intended to be humorous or not. Joaquín, a veritable news junkie and collector of funny names, said Ulick Martin had been so impressed with Art that he bankrolled a special viewing of one of Art's more ideological collections whose exemplar were two paintings, one called "Neoismo," which features the faces of Karl Marx, John Stuart Mill and Benito Mussolini scribbling in their notebooks as an unidentified black speaker with braids moves her hands excitedly, the other revealing a man shrugging his shoulders and standing in front of three nearly identical storefronts, behind which can be seen the tops of row after row of similar colors and schemes, distinguishable only by the slight variation of their names—McDoonald's, McDonild's, McDowell's. In an article I found while searching for coverage of Art's disappearance abroad, a Spanish newspaper reporter interviewed Marta Herrera, a librarian at the Universitat de Barcelona, who said Art had organized several anti-globalization and anti-war manifestaciones in Barcelona, Sitges and other parts of Cataluña, and she was bemused by the recent news because she had not known he had gone back to painting. Had he really, at some point, stopped?

In Paris' *Le Monde*, a photograph of the hunched-over Beatriz, who was somewhat well-known abroad, was used as a lead-in to an article about Art, whose news peg was the funeral. In Berlin's *Die Zeit*, which I saw splayed open on a bench outside the New York Public Library, soaked by rain and left to dry, there was a picture of Art shaking hands with the famous German artist Kristof von Behren at a small conference in München. Journalists had complete and untrammeled access to the funeral, the gallery and the Serrano family, including all relatives who lived in El Paso and the few who lived elsewhere. Having been accustomed to the privacy that was often asked for by families, especially during my three-month stint as an obituary writer at a New York daily in the summer between my sophomore and junior years of college, I had learned that information about people alleged to have committed suicide was often difficult to obtain, but the Serranos were fully cooperative and uncharacteristically vocal, as if they had been phoning the information in themselves. What was it that made them different from these others, those who wanted to grieve in peace away from the shower of cameras and maul of microphones? I didn't consciously seek to determine why they attended to the media so gratuitously, but my mind was wont to wander to places I did not ask it to go, and after hours of arbitration, it eventually settled on *orgullo*—pride. The children of Hector and Ella Serrano were poised for excellence from birth; from thirty-seven-year-old Carla, who had an M.D. from the University of Texas, to twenty-three-year-old Beatriz, they had raised the bar higher and higher with every sweeping success, and Art, as sole heir of the family name, whose life had been filled with achievements no suicide could tarnish or sully, was their child, and the one of whom they were most proud. If ever there was a funeral in El Paso so widely publicized, it would be his. If ever the city had a great son, it would be he. By nightfall, the media had already disassembled and gone their separate ways; in Art's home (I would later learn from Beatriz), family and friends gathered for Hector's famous chile rellenos; for a moment, everyone could be certain the tears in their eyes were, at least in part, a direct result of chile.

From time to time, when remembering Art, I tried to think of what he looked like and only the pictures from newspapers and magazines or the newsreels on late-night television that animated him appeared on the white projecting wall of my mind, where the characters of dreams interact and build their intricate plots, where strong lights burn holes if you close your eyes after directly looking into them, where the memories of the floor plan of my parents' Westside residence in El Paso hovers, constantly available for me to reenter and roam those halls endlessly forever. It suddenly seemed impossible to me to render someone completely through words, yet it was something I'd been trying to do from the very first news article I had written. Even if I found a way to describe Art, a sketch artist would draw something that looked like him but was not him. In the end, those who had closely monitored the news about Art's disappearance were aware mainly of his quirks, his major accomplishments, his atavistic Aztec appearance, his relationship with his neighbors, his academic record, his silence in class discussions. These things together represented a sort of pseudo Art, one who never succeeded to misplace a brush stroke, a man inseparable from his work, whose darkest moment was his last. But who was Art under the covers, behind the closed bathroom door? Who was he one bite into a peanut butter and jelly sandwich?

These chronicles are full of shards and potsherds and broken coca bottles. Whatever memory has lost can be reinvented through objects. As I dug through the boxes containing the letters and postcards and receipts and other documents the color white looking for more information about Art, I eventually found a letter that he had written to me upon my acceptance to a yearlong graduate program in journalism in New York when I was twenty-two and, even though it is unmistakably Art's style of writing, I cannot hear his voice narrating the words.

Omar,

The turkey wrap is eaten. The ducks are walking on a pond of ice. Our paisanos have gone home from a game of baseball in the great park. What is left after this undergraduate education but memories of the past and the sterile drone of the future?

The party will be much smaller. The glasses will be halfway up. You have related to this world and the people within it only so much, then, now, with a postgraduate degree, you'll relate to even fewer, and these relationships will sometimes be small and incomprehensible.

We stick together. Because we will always have a common dialogue. The past and an ability to relate to it from today is our glue, our fusión—the cheese in the turkey wrap, the molecules frozen together, baseball on a balmy early evening.

We speak in abstracts. We enjoy the language of the people who walk, who learned of Metamorphosis and Jesus Christ through the mouth of the red-haired white man. We inhabit our illusions, run to shut the door, make them real and hella hardcore.

This is welcome. Persona grata. This is your houseplant. Watch it grow.

C/S,

Art Serrano
Campinas, SP, Brasil

In the faces of the crowd, I scanned for Art, looked for him in quebradas and street corners and behind magazines instead of inside them. I continued to write and search my memory for anything that might shed light on his death—or disappearance—attempting to recover each detail on first recollection: *entire*, intact, because, if remembered more than once, they might fall apart, never to be put back together again. And after nearly two months of mystique, the country at last turned toward the next great megastory—a famous singer had come down with AIDS after nearly a decade of struggling secretly with the HIV virus. I was spending time above the clouds, cognizant that it could not rain, sleet or snow this high up, and that even though it was probably doing one of the three or all at once in Manhattan at that very moment, I would soon be landing in São Paulo, where winter was a distant memory and everything that had happened over the past two months was something that had happened in another hemisphere, where the rivers flowed backwards and time restarted its sonorous cycle every twelve hours. My head rolled back and forth on the headrest, and I wished for a pillow, a good in-flight movie, or at least a little bit of sympathy.

the gallery

You can grow a thick beard in two months, but not all beards grow at the same speed. Mine seemed to grow faster overnight, like nostalgia or cigarette butts on my brownstone's stoop. When I wake up in the mornings, an older man with sharp, salt-and-pepper stubble on his chin is my stand-in at the mirror during the tooth-brushing interval that precedes all other daily events. Now, aboard the panamerican flight to Brazil, the dense follicles seemed as if they would soon grow into spikes if not sliced off at their roots. In first class, razors were distributed, but I didn't often shave with turbulence at home, so I forewent the process and decided to wait until I arrived at Serra Negra, a small town somewhere nowhere, where I was to meet Father Harold Rahm, the 94-year-old Jesuit priest about whom I was writing for *The Monthly*.

There is something about a twelve-hour flight that invokes entire periods of your life, chunks here and there, glimmers of fruit stands and silly faces and unsatisfying ends of phone calls with girlfriends long since gone and, now, at altitudes so high no one on the ground could possibly detect us up here ahead of our sound, everything was complex and evocative. I once had a friend from Veracruz who had been convinced by a small-town doctor, instead of getting a tummy tuck (which he had been inquiring about), to walk from Xalapa to Morelia, more than six-hundred kilometers, and attempt to trace his history through every event in his life, beginning from his first memory. The doctor said that if he did so, he would change his mind by the time he returned (in addition to saving thousands of pesos). My friend ended up losing twenty pounds and, by the time he returned, the fat from his midriff had already evaporated, but the triumph of the trip was that when the weight returned, he never once again was aware of anything but the tunnels to his soul that had once been eroded by time and circumstance. And he spent the rest of his life remembering.

I couldn't believe so much had happened over the past two months and, as I sat contemplating it from my window seat with two miniature bottles of whisky (which seemed to lacquer these occurrences in the glaze of distant memories), it occurred to me that the two months that had just passed were the first time in about five years that I had not been working on any of my own stories, that I hadn't been writing essays, interviewing sources, seeking out connections or trying to solve problems on the page, and I was suddenly happy to be resuming my career as a journalist, rather than the role of informant I had played these past months. From my crib onward, I had learned countless things about the nature of interviewing, so much that my natural mode of conversation had adjusted itself to journalism. Like a photographer whose camera must always be two seconds away from snapping, my ear was primed for hearing certain details, and I knew how to fast-forward a conversation to focus on certain details that would lead to other questions, always tiptoeing closer, hoping to provoke what lay in the corner of an interviewee's brain to slip out of its slot without his or her becoming aware that it had. A journalist after a career of investigating eventually becomes an expert on a great number of things and, now in my mid-thirties, I found that I was able to make sense of a wide variety of details and allusions that would have otherwise been far beyond my sphere of knowledge. I felt totally blissful at the thought of returning to the self that had never been in front of the cameras but had spent his career always somewhere behind them and, as the plane landed an astounding fifteen minutes early, to the overexcited captain's delight—which he would apologize for when we couldn't dock for another thirty minutes—I felt rejuvenated in places surgery could not touch.

At 19:55, Guarulhos International Airport in São Paulo trilled. The Brazilians at the airport were as noisy as any loud Texan or New Yorker—they spoke a nasal language of ãos and ões, of flat sounds of dohs and dahs and tahs, Spanish stuck into a time capsule and unearthed centuries later by whatever civilization was still toting its humanity around. Two twenty-something guys standing in the back—one a tall, arborescent man—with unkempt hair slithering its way down his back, another, smug in sunglasses, whose erect posture guaranteed him every inch of his sixty would be inventoried were there to be a spontaneous counting and, in contrast to the other's lethargy, made him seem the more important of the two—held a sign with my name handwritten upon it, large brash letters confidently beginning one-third its way through the page and shrinking in size as it reached the edge and realized my name extended several characters beyond what they'd anticipated.

"Boa tarde," I said, this being nearly the extent of what I had memorized from the Portuguese phrasebook I'd bought at a bookstore in Cobble Hill in Brooklyn.

"Hello," the sunglass-wearing man said in English. "Goody morning. You are Omar, I imagine."

"Sí, mucho gusto," I said, taking his hand.

"Prazer. Prazer. Pero, we don't speak Spanish. It is better if the people converse in English."

"The people?" I asked.

"We," he said.

The one with the sunglasses was called Jorge and his hefty sidekick was known as Jorgito, little Jorge. They both looked at me, Jorge said something to Jorgito, and they both laughed—which I found endearing—and then Jorge gestured to Jorgito to take my suitcase, which he was intent on carrying, even when I pointed to the wheels and rolled them with my fingers to demonstrate their function.

Whether we spent any more time in the airport or not I don't remember. Like a bad film edit or a scratched disc, my memory omitted the frame from the lifting of my suitcase to the arrival in the airport parking lot, which was dispiriting, because I often wondered what my first impression of the airport had been, not because anything happened to it or anything happened to me inside it that day, but because I liked airports—the shock of being in a foreign country (or even a place like Utah) comes through full force in an airport through the most subtle differences in the bathroom amenities (in most countries in the world there is a trash can next to the toilet for toilet paper, for example) and the sudden imposition of another language to mark departures and baggage claim signs. But this time the combination of jetlag, disorientation, and the language, which because of the "st" sound, seemed vaguely familiar, somewhat like that of the Russian immigrants I had heard speaking when boarding the Q-train coming from Brighton Beach or the nasal sound I associated with French, together worked to create an easily forgettable atmosphere akin to early childhood—as strange figures loom over us in our cradles, laughing at our most innate expressions, talking to each other in their human language, taking us with them wherever they go so that we never have to remember a single cardinal direction.

The next thing I remember is spending several moments in the parking lot as Jorge waved a remote control in the air, pressing the button repeatedly; both he and Jorgito waved to one another every so often, and each followed the other's hunches for a little while, before they would give up and try another direction. The word "perua" was repeated so often that my lexicographical skills were willing to assert it was an article, basic verb, or profanity. When we did eventually locate what I later realized was called the perua, or van, we were all dripping with sweat, exhausted and embarrassed at how long it had taken.

The air conditioner blasted, the music was a hard rock station turned down to a faint hum and, as we moved from the area surrounding the airport to the highway, Jorge commented on the scenery that passed alongside us, which looked like it could easily be anywhere in the United States—derelict highway gas stations, discount department stores, industrial sites, and other things that had the tropical value of a landfill. I asked Jorge why there was not more evidence of the sprawl of São Paulo, a screaming city said to be between three and four times the size of New York, and he told me that the airport was built in one of the "margins" of the city and, because we were moving away from the center, we would not bear witness to the metropolis' heart. Jorgito stayed silent in the back seat of the perua, and I asked Jorge if he was always this quiet.

"Oh, that's because he speaks Portuguese."

As we got closer to Serra Negra, we began talking about the words that translated perfectly from Spanish to Portuguese and, though there were many, they were not often as obvious as you might think because they were pronounced so differently, such as the name of Brazil's most famous city, Rio de Janeiro—in Spanish, one would pronounce this slightly rolling the "R" and making the "J" into an h-sound. In

Portuguese, the "R" becomes an h-sound and the "J" is pronounced as in English.

Outside, the environment changed completely as we pushed farther away from São Paulo, the plains bundling themselves up into mounds, then hills, and eventually into small mountains. Darkness closed in on us from all directions, and as the nocturnal feature attraction began to reel faintly overhead, the sky became awash in stars and speckled by particles of the dust of the galaxy, the occasional cloud and the moon. "Do you see the white ring around the moon?" Jorge asked. "That means that it is going to rain," he said. Eventually, we made a left turn across traffic onto a small road engirded completely by trees and, moments later, turned right into a clearing that led to the Biazi Grand Hotel, a giant building that hovered above the small tourist town.

"We are arriving," Jorge said.

According to what I could make out of the plan, I would rent a room in the hotel with the help of the Jorges, unpack—then, as Jorge said in English, "wash my face very well," and meet them at eight o'clock back downstairs, where the priest would greet me. I did exactly as was told, even gave my face a good scrubbing after my shave, and, finding myself with an extra twenty minutes to spare from these exercises, decided to pop open my briefcase and review the notes I had assembled for the purpose of the interview.

His story, the story of Father Harold Rahm—known in El Paso as the Bicycle Priest, author of the first American book on Nuestra Señora de Guadalupe and founder of Our Lady's Youth Center, who, with a black leather jacket wrapped over his cassock and roman collar, had famously set himself right in the middle of a fight between the city's two toughest gangs by Sagrada Corazón in Segundo Barrio, and over the next several years completely rid the city of its violent palomillos (gangs) at the end of the glorious pachuco era, in those days when caló spiced the conversational airwaves, Hector

Serrano's slicked-back hairstyle was all the rage and downtown still boomed—was also a story of disappearance. For when he left, the dust swept through the city and then was swept away, and a new era began, and this new era gave way to other eras that dismissed those that had come before as legends and stories, and it was never certain what really happened because very few things were ever documented. These things were, in his case: La Fe Clinic, which had once been called Father Rahm Clinic; *Office in the Alley*, a book co-authored by the priest and published by the University of Texas and once a required text in the study of gangs and gang mentality (doubtless the one Art had read); several mentions in texts that chronicle the history of El Paso; and the street that bore his name, blocks from the international border—the priest's old stomping ground and the epicenter of a city that, like rain that spills onto a rocky mountaintop and goes every direction but back upward, spread outward, and the downtown skyscrapers from decades before were the only evidence that this rule had ever been broken.

The phone calls I made from my Brooklyn apartment told another story of Father Rahm's legacy. The first person I called, the sacerdote at Sagrada Corazón, was well aware of the Bicycle Priest and quite willing to provide me with stories about the famed fight, in addition to allowing me to talk to a volunteer called María, who thanked me for the first several minutes of the phone call for reaching back through time and grasping a symbol of the laurels of the Catholic Church from its last great era. She had been volunteering in the church for what seemed a century and told me about Father Rahm's spontaneous masses on the streets, collection of youth, beggars and other followers who found other lives through *Our Lady*. She gave me the phone number of a priest in Juárez, a Padre Osvaldo, the priest at the enormous neoclassical cathedral downtown who, because of his admiration of Father Rahm, had gone into the seminary after working with him as a volunteer in El Paso. Speaking to me in English as soon as he learned I was calling from Brooklyn, Padre Osvaldo told me about Father Rahm's radio and television programs in El Paso, his quiz shows, his popularity with the palomillos, his charm with the upper classes, his bicycle, his athleticism and the time he tried to learn Spanish curse words but a gang member talked him out of it, claiming it was inappropriate for a priest to use the words of the street. "I wish only that I could have summoned the same powers from the heavens that Padre Rahm did," he said. "We always said that Padre Rahm had a direct line to God; that was years before saying that was a cliché. Now they say that for *any* priest." He told me other stories, rumors from other priests that he was giving communion to unbaptized parishioners or marrying couples who hadn't been officially divorced from previous marriages, things that sometimes got himself into trouble but that, because of all his good deeds and honors and awards and his huge following, never kept him from doing what he wanted to. "He was always in hot water, but he could talk himself out of anything. I guess you could say that he was amphibious," Padre Osvaldo said.

The conversation earlier in the car with Jorge—as Jorgito snored leisurely in the back after several earnest attempts at comprehension, leaning forward unbuckled from the middle seat—turned to a different version of the priest, one who was now in his last fifth of a century on earth, more than forty years removed from his heroics on the streets of downtown El Paso. The reverence with which Jorge spoke of "Padre Haroldo," his international drug conferences, his national television programs, his friendship with leaders in Brasília, Washington, and Rome, betokened a priest who was much more than I had bargained for when pitching the story in New York. I felt incredibly fortunate that Art's mother had recalled Father Rahm, and that this, in turn, had providenced her to mention some of the priest's features that had impelled me to pitch the story in magazineland. Now, as I combed the hair out of my face, I wondered if Art had ever been here in Serra

101

Negra, away from the priest's community of street kids and recuperating drug addicts and alcoholics, where the wind seemed to blow in colors and the moon told stories.

On second inspection, with time to wait, which is why one should always arrive early, the main hall of the hotel was a monstrosity (in the classical sense), and it seemed vacant, because sometimes something has to be large to appear empty. The hotel looked more like a museum of a hotel than an actual place in which one was to sleep and set down his or her bags and use a do-not-disturb sign. The foyer and ground-level hallways and connected rooms seemed only a few cleaning and cooking and decorating crews away from the grand balls of another era. As soon as I walked into a large room with a piano and looked through the windows out upon the garden and its latticework, I heard my name called by a voice I recognized as Jorge's, and I immediately turned around to see, as if carefully choreographed, a cherub-faced white man in a red shirt framed perfectly in between the enormous Jorgito and minuscule Jorge, both of whom were wearing white.

"Hello!" he said, in a voice that was at once Texan. "Welcome to Brazil." I approached him and shook his hand and was surprised by his alacritous movement, his blush-red Irish face. He began to ask me about my trip, how I had found the room and how I was liking Brazil, a question that was repeated so often by almost everyone I met from that point onward that it now seems surprising that Jorge had not asked me the moment I emerged from customs and baggage reclaim. We walked down a long corridor and into a vast dining room that was empty except for a buffet of pasta, fruit and rice and beans that was spread out over several white tables—a bastion of abundance. I followed Father Rahm and the Jorges in ladling large portions of rigatoni in a marinara sauce onto my plate, then adding some cantaloupes and papayas and bread.

"So, what can we do for you?" Father Rahm asked, as soon as we were seated.

I gave him a basic idea of what I wanted to do—to write a detailed profile, following him around everywhere he went, asking him questions from time to time and, then, toward the end, interviewing him for several hours. I would use a tape recorder and take photographs with a digital camera. A photographer from São Paulo would come toward the end of my trip and take more photographs.

"Whatever you want," he said, when I finished. "There are no secrets. Just time."

From him I learned the history of the Jesuit fathers—the Society of Jesus—who had always been a controversial bunch in Brazil. The Jesuits came with some of the first Portuguese ships, which sailed over to the New World to transport back the Pau Brasil trees from which a valuable red tint was extracted and used to dye fabrics. They quickly lost themselves in the culture of the native tribes, such as the Tupi and Guarani, and lived with them in places like the Amazon forest or along the coast of Brazil. More came with the ships that were to bring back the gold from the heralded Minas Gerais. They converted the first Brazilians into Catholics, but they also adopted their customs, ran naked in the forests with them, ate their grub. So much had they learned of their way of life and customs that when the next batch of ships from the Old World came over bringing men who would try to harness the next most valuable resource—the tribe members themselves—the Jesuits took arms and fought against the Portuguese. In 1759, the Jesuits were banned from Brazil by the Marquis of Pombal for their failure to cooperate with the Portuguese rulers. In 1964, years after the Jesuits had re-established themselves in the continent, Pope John XXIII asked several priests from the northern and southern Jesuit provinces of the United States to go to Brazil and other South American countries to create apostolates that would help combat the problems of the poor. The first of these American Jesuits to Brazil was Father Harold J. Rahm.

In Father Rahm's speech was an almost perfect preservation of the 1950s and 60s mode of speech. Although he had returned to the America of the North several times and continued to read English—the major newsweeklies' Latin American editions every week, emails from abroad and books he was lent by American priests and visitors—it was as if his dictionary had not been updated. He used words and phrases such as "shows" when I would have said "movies," "such" to begin a sentence, "dang" in place of "damn," and "the Negro people" when referring to people of African descent—likely a transliteration of the Portuguese "negro." At one point in our conversation, we turned to a very detailed discussion on computers, on which he asked me to later give him a tutorial, and most of the terminology he used in English was either guessed at or translated from Portuguese. For example, he called the printer the "typewriter," and deleting a file "taking it out." As I learned later when I tutored him for an hour or so, every time he talked about signing onto the Internet, he said "going into business," and he thought "ctrl" was an abbreviation for "central" rather than "control."

Forty-five minutes or so of English was enough for both Jorges, and I felt terrible they couldn't understand, always wishing to lapse into Spanish, which Father Rahm also spoke, to clue them in better on what was being said but, as Jorge had said before, they were more likely to understand English, the foreign language they studied in their schools. Eventually the two men excused themselves graciously—"Com licença"—leaving us alone in the colossal dining room. At that point, after mentioning to Father Rahm that I was from El Paso, he proceeded to tell me about several of the things he had done there, all of which seemed exemplary of his fashion, which in many ways represented what seemed to be the quintessential Jesuit way, of taking things into your own hands, basing everything on what the situation required rather than what the rules were. During his twelve years there, he said rosaries on street corners with beggars, prostitutes and drunks; he established an activities center for gang members, which among its myriad amenities housed a boxing ring; he used part of his personal allowance to go to the shows even though his superiors said that Jesuits shouldn't do that sort of thing; he visited gang members in jail and testified for them in court; and during the famous fight, which occurred on the street that would later be named Father Rahm Avenue (but not for this reason), he stood between the leaders of two gangs, picked one of them up and threw him over his shoulder (he said he still didn't know how this happened...). I asked him why he always seemed to confront problems with such bold and unconventional responses, reacting in ways atypical to priests (or anyone else for that matter), and he said it had always seemed to him that the best solutions came from the blending of different styles, genres, theses. In Brazil, the Catholic religion would not have been as effective in the northeastern region of the country had the religions of Africa not been acknowledged. There was nothing wrong with syncretism, he said. Anything that entrenched one's system of beliefs and gave one a greater quotient of goodness could not be faulted if its means were not harmful.

"I see things this way," he said. "I would much prefer to work with a good Protestant than a bad Catholic. If you come and help make good Protestants of any bad Catholics in Brazil, I will cooperate with you."

"And have you been back to El Paso since those days—since the 60s?" I asked.

"A couple of times, but much later, and by then most of the kids had grown up, and of course, those were the days when people kept track of one another through letters rather than phone calls."

From the slower, less-animated way in which he was pronouncing words, I could tell that he was getting tired, so I told him that we had finished the interview for the day. "This

105

is unrelated, but...the artist Art Serrano...I graduated the same year from the same high school as he did. You knew him, right?"

"Yes! Of course I know Art—he's a saint," he said, a vivacity springing forth once again. "He volunteered here, well before he became the Pelé of the art world, and he's always been in touch."

He went on to explain that Art had come to Brazil just weeks after having graduated from college and had originally contacted Father Rahm by letter, indicating that he was willing to volunteer in his therapeutic community but not mentioning how he got his contact information. To Father Rahm, years must have been like slightly longer months—it seems more accurate to measure a moment in a person's life as proportional to their entire time spent on earth rather than by the length of that moment—so the year that Art stayed with him must have seemed considerably shorter a period of time than it was to Art. Because Art was already fluent in Spanish, he was speaking nearly fluent Portuguese by the end of the second month and, much in the same manner in which Father Rahm asked me what he could do for me, he had asked Art something similar, to which Art replied that he didn't know. Father Rahm pointed out that it was great having someone there from the United States because it really expanded the worlds of the drug addicts and alcoholics who spent six months immured in his community that aimed to detoxify them and set them along new, better paths. He said just being in the presence of someone from so far away and having contact with him was antidotal. Art was a slow starter but, as soon as he learned about Father Rahm's other community, the one in the hills where the street kids lived, he requested that he be able to go along with him the next time the priest visited that community. As soon as they reached the campus, away from all the rest of civilization, Art asked the priest if he could stay there and assist with the street kids as a teacher. Art didn't express emotion externally very often, Father Rahm said, but there was something in his face, in his calm, that made it obvious that this was where he belonged. So Father Rahm, assured by Art that he would get on well without him, left him with some of the other volunteers and the street kids, trusting his well-being to his "resilient staff and, well, God." Either way, he said, he was going to have to leave Art at some point, as at the time he was on a five-nation tour regarding drugs, from Rome to Prague to Cape Town to New York back to Prague and then Moscow and, when he returned to the hills after his two months abroad spent hobnobbing for money, spreading word about the concept of therapeutic communities and occasionally visiting with other priests and praying, he found that in addition to having the full attention and faith of all the children, children as young as nine who had been addicted to crack and begged on the streets for money to finance their habit, the kids were beginning to walk, talk and carry on in complete imitation of Art and his Mexican cool, for, if you remember, the priest said, extending his knowledge of Art to include me, he had that way of always blending smarts and street-smarts at the same time. By the end of the year, artisanship—everything from painting to making pottery—had taken over the curriculum on the hills and was used to inform all the subjects the kids were taught. For several years after Art left, the program was continued but, like all good things that die when a leader leaves, it too eventually floundered.

"So they do not practice artisanship anymore in your communities," I asked.

"They do, but not with the same zeal. In the years since, we have not been able to duplicate the success with our street kids that Art had with them during that one year. I will have to show you the gallery."

"Of Art's work?"

"No, of his students' work. You should see what an influence he was."

"Did you hear about his disappearance?"

"Yes. It is true, then," he said, as if my mention of it was a confirmation far beyond the details offered by the international press. "It's very strange, but it does not surprise me...Art did sometimes show up unexpectedly, so it makes since that he would disappear in the same way."

"So you've seen him several times?"

"I've seen him many times. And he emails me often. The last time I saw him was a year or two ago. It was a very strange encounter because it lasted such a short amount of time. He was in a great hurry. He showed up unannounced at the community, hauling ten or so paintings from Rio, where he had been for the last month. I was very excited to see Art, who had brought all of the paintings for me, with certificates of authenticity, so that I could auction them and use the money. But he said he was just passing through from Rio to São Paulo and was already on his way back to Munich, where he said he was living."

"In Munich?" I hadn't been aware that Art had ever had an address in Germany.

Father Rahm went on, seemingly remembering as he spoke, "A curious thing about that visit is that a priest who had arrived at the rodoviaria with Art told me he spent the entire six-hour journey eyeing Art because of his resemblance to João Fabiano, a man who had engineered a large protest in Rio, at police headquarters, against the murders of street kids who had been killed by police officers in death squads. And when Art arrived on our campus at the same time as Padre Adalberto, Adalberto still thought Art was this leader. Eventually, I convinced him that Art's face looked familiar because he was a famous artist. João Fabiano was Brazilian and had a very thick beard anyway."

"And what did Art say he was doing in Rio?"

"Apparently he staged an opening of some of his art and, when the showing was over, he brought some of the pieces to us."

"And you haven't heard from him since?"

"I have. He emailed me about a week before he disappeared."

"Did he say anything strange?"

"No, but he said he was going to be in Brazil soon."

"Do you have that email?"

"No, I already took it out."

That's where we ended for the night. I wanted to continue asking Father Rahm questions, but I was worried about keeping him up too late, even though it seemed he would have been willing to field questions even from his sleep. I walked the priest back to his pousada which, along with a small, derelict chapel, had been given to him by the former owner of the hotel. The sky swarmed in lights. A white ring encircled the moon, foreshadowing rain, and the Jesuit priest, whose mirth had not subsided with his languor, turned to me and said, "Boa noite, Omar!"—Good night.

There were three beds in the room and, naturally, I had to choose one of them on which to sleep. One was queen-sized, but its bedspread had upon it a most horrid design of flowers, a bouquet I doubt any florist would have been willing to arrange without money up-front. The second offered the best choice of the bedspreads, white and simple, but when I lay down, it was not long enough to fit my entire frame and, even though I normally slept in a curled, fetal position, I liked knowing the bed was long enough should I happen to fall asleep in a fetal position, stretch out at some point in the night and then return to the fetal position before awakening. The third bed, like most of the things I settled for in life, was somewhere in the middle.

My bed chosen, I peeled back the sheets and sat down in my underwear with my tape recorder and pressed rewind. I always used tape recorders when I was interviewing, even after I had relearned cursive handwriting, for multiple purposes. For one, at the very beginning of the tape I always recorded the consent of the interviewee to be interviewed. Then, when

I wasn't sure what I had written or the interviewee was talking too quickly, I could always refer again to the taped recording. But the best reason for using a tape recorder is to bring to life the voice of the speaker. I found that when I listened to it a second time, I could focus not only on the words of the interviewee but also the sound of the voice, the timbre, the choice and selection of words. Although some of my colleagues in journalism could memorize what their subjects said verbatim and didn't need tape recorders, I had to listen to the voice again a second time for it to enter the transcript of my memory. Why I needed this second time and was able to memorize things perfectly only then I do not know. Perhaps my memory had a censoring device that said, "If something is said once, forget about it, but if it is said twice, it must be important."

As I began to listen once again to Father Rahm detail the advancement of the Jesuits in Brazil, however, I pressed the fast-forward button and, unwilling to stop it before I knew I had passed through a modicum of material that would be invaluable to me when I later wrote the article, I eventually found my way to the part of the interview where I had noticed the priest was tired and I had asked about Art. How shocking it was to me when I discovered what I was doing. We think it is always our body that must respond to the resolutions of the brain, when, just as often, it is the brain that must pay heed to the discoveries of the body. Like the astronaut who has to look down from space to truly realize that the world is a spinning, blue-green ball, it took fast-forwarding to the parts about Art for me to understand that I had not come to Brazil for the purpose of interviewing the priest, but in order to find clues as to the whereabouts of my friend. How obvious things can seem to us when we are looking at our actions, hearing the intent of our voice, from the point of view of a third party. And when we discover them, we always wonder whether we are truly unconscious of them or if our brain is deceiving us to operate under a different agenda. It had never explicitly occurred to me to look for Art—in fact, I had viewed my trip to Brazil as an escape from the ubiquitous coverage of Art in the media—but now I was convinced that this was why I was here.

I turned the tape recorder off, covered my face with the flowerless bedspread and fell asleep listening to the soothing voice of the Padre, wondering what mass was like in a church with a priest who knew what life was about, in a place where the rules didn't seem to count in the same ways, in a country where religion was still alive.

The next day began on the rolling, winding road away from Serra Negra, Jorge giving historical lessons on the small towns along the way, interspersed with Portuguese language lessons and treatises on life, as Father Rahm slept baby-like in the passenger's seat next to mute Jorgito, and I thought about Camille and the language list she had assembled while in Europe, wondering if certain words here would make the cut, as we sledded down the hilly mountains into flatter lands, alongside towns famous for porcelain or flowers, oranges and knitted shirts and a red glint of a man on the side of the road selling caldo de cana, pure sugar cane in liquid form, and I realized how much sense it made for entire towns to find themselves in the pursuit of one communal goal. When the priest awoke, Jorge desisted from speaking, hallowing in silence, maintaining the appearance of disinterest in the interest of respect. As soon as we docked in Campinas, a miniature São Paulo of chock-a-block high-rise buildings and improbable cram, at the priest's community of recovering drug addicts and alcoholics we met Ednilton, a man who, when we reencountered him in the priest's room after he wrested the priest's bags away from the Jorges, seemed to be applying the intensity and pointillism of an emergency room doctor to the unpacking of the priest's wardrobe. Within moments, two boys entered the room and kissed the priest on the cheek; he pronounced *parabéns*—congratulations—upon

111

them and then scrambled to his feet and rushed to his armoire
to give each of them expensive shirts from his closet. From
there, I was sent on a tour of the facilities, a splendid
panorama of large tropical trees, huts with sapé-grass roofs,
and a fully-equipped bakery and auditorium, while the priest,
according to Jorge, rested for a while at the house of his
friend and accountant, as was his custom. When Father Rahm
returned, I followed him to the city, where he delivered a
lecture about drugs, then to a wedding at a ranch house a few
miles outside of the city where, despite forgetting the name of
the groom, he was the indubitable center of attention. As I
dived into some hors d'œuvres, a journalist from a magazine
called *Olha* cornered me and with his head motionless but his
mouth moving rapidly, like the genre of television cartoons
where what is said takes precedence over the difficulty of the
graphic, told me how much he loved Disney World. When I
found the Jorges, at what was apparently the civil ceremony
that routinely follows the religious ceremony in Brazil, Jorge
so erect and Jorgito so slumped it seemed as if there was
merely a six-inch difference in their heights, Jorge told me he
was glad to have found me, that we would be going as soon as
the Padre finished speaking to the father of the groom.
Finally, thirty minutes later, we left the wedding and found
ourselves once again in the perua, this time traveling to the
Fazenda do Senhor Jesus, the priest expressing his elation at
having received a donation of thirty thousand reais (about ten
thousand dollars) from the father of the groom. While he
spoke about the donation, the texture of earth below the car
changed from cement to rock and then to dirt, as the window
view reeled from city to suburb to farmland, the landscape
rewinding through the levels of urbanization. As soon as we
were far enough away, atop a hill with no apparent signs of
human existence upon it, we finally reached a gate, the gate
opened, and we had arrived.

Settled for the night in a dormitory all my own, where another priest regularly slept when on-site, I disrobed and put on sandals and shorts, which produced the same sensation as would adding a scarf and earmuffs a few days ago in New York, and was a clever addition to my suitcase at the last moment, courtesy of Camille. Despite consistencies in the temperature of São Paulo reported over the past week, it still proved impossible for me to avoid bringing several extra sweaters and different-colored dress pants, all of which were made redundant by the heat, which had thus far been bearable due the air conditioning in the perua and at the Biazi Grand Hotel.

My briefcase and suitcase locked into the armoire, I sat on the bed and picked up a copy of St. Augustine's *Confessions* from the dresser and tried to manage Portuguese, which was so similar to Spanish that it seemed as if both languages were being used interchangeably. My curiosity satiated after a page and still feeling not in the least bit tired, despite the number of things we had crammed into the day, I wandered from the room to the outer garden and up a large staircase that led to the upper level, where the car was parked. The entire encampment stood upon a large hill and was an auspicious place away from the civilized, addicted world. The tip, the pinnacle of the hill, seemed only a small climb higher and, as it looked to be only twenty yards from where I was standing, I decided to make an ascent to get a better view of the vast countryside and twinkling lights of Campinas in the distance, not to mention the stars, which, I reasoned, would in their light years away seem infinitely closer after I shortened the distance these twenty yards.

When I reached the summit, I saw a form in the distance sitting on the grass and, realizing it was Father Rahm standing with his hands on the ground and his feet in the air, I turned quickly away so as not to interrupt his prayers, but then heard his voice calling me. When I reached him, he said, "Hello! I

113

thought you might be coming," but he didn't tell me why, and I didn't ask.

"This is tremendous," I said, looking down below at the ranch. "I mean this is quite an accomplishment. I am really humbled to be in your presence." My words felt confessional and awkward—I was saying something that came from the heart. "Can I ask you...how did all of this come about?"

"I don't know." He blushed. "I guess I wanted to save the world, turn the slums around...but I didn't have the first clue how to. I just kept asking people for things. I listened to people when they told me about their problems. Things just kept happening. We worked hard. We had to really push. People get caught up in all the wrong things."

"What do you mean?"

"The rules. The literality. We need to choose our battles carefully."

I asked him questions about the issues, the very things he said we must not get caught up in, and he told me the laws of love are etched into our hearts and we don't need them written down in order to know how to live, that he reckoned a man can love a man just as much as he loves a woman, that if a person wants to be baptized they should be able to.

"But was it God?" I wanted to know. I felt like if *anyone* knew, it would be he. "Do you believe it was God who made all of these things happen?" I added.

He pondered the question for a moment. "Even with God, you have to put one foot in front of the other every day. You can't do anything unless you do it. You can't just pray for it and let God do the work. For me God's not a Coke machine. You don't put a nickel in and, click, he gives you a Coke."

I longed for my tape recorder. I knew this was the rub for a journalist, that tape recorders create unnatural environments that often preclude heartfelt statements but, without a tape recorder, I would have to rely on memory alone and could never reproduce them exactly. We continued to talk about religion, about his ecumenical Catholicism, all of the things about which I most wanted to interview him, and then he looked out among the stars and told me it was midnight and time to sleep. "But first, follow me," he said. We descended the small hill, and boarded the perua, which he carefully drove farther down the hill. We stopped at another encampment that we had passed earlier but that I hadn't noticed, due to its invisibility in the darkness, and got out of the car. We walked into what seemed to be, for its largeness, the main hall, and he flipped on the lights. "This," he said, "is Art's gallery."

I was surprised it was still here, still preserved, almost exactly as it had been, he said…like other intact pasts, other places that time, for whatever reason—or no reason at all—fails to refresh. The paintings covered the walls—there must have been two hundred of them—and though, naturally, they were easily distinguishable from Art's work, as they were painted by his students, they seemed to brim with his energy. What was most apparent were the colors—the sheer multitude of them, as if Art had pillaged a paint factory and returned with buckets; the number of them in each painting; the use of certain colors to do things they weren't expected to do (as in Art's own paintings): as in a tree painted orange, a green moustache or silver snow. This had a transforming effect on the room's personality that made every object in the room seem concomitant to the art in the same way that a desk in a room surrounded by books is a different desk than one in an empty warehouse, transfigured by the presence of new objects, the illusion of spatial alteration and colors. The paintings varied in size, and they were done on paper of a slightly thicker stock than computer paper. There was action in each of them—they weren't still lifes or portraits. In one, a barefoot young boy ran down the street with a radio in his hand, as a woman in front of her house held her hands to her face, which was emblazoned with varying primary hues of orange, red and purple. In another, several pieces of paper were taped together, and on the bottom it had been labeled Jardim Itatinga in a sort of graffiti script (obviously done by one of the more artistically gifted kids); it depicted women standing in front of their houses in skimpy clothing or nothing at all as cars slowly cruised by. Although the paintings were predictably amateurish, a complexity had been achieved in all of them. These paintings were alive.

At twenty one years old, Art hadn't been distracting these kids from the streets, he was sending them back down them, realizing their value as part of what had formed the kids and would give them an advantage rather than teach them how far behind they were. And he wasn't just teaching them to recreate these experiences, he was also teaching them the basic skills necessary to paint. The walls shook with energy; the room swerved and shuddered. As I looked back at Father Rahm, he shrugged his shoulders.

"Everyone was in love with Art," he said. "One of the young street kids, a young girl, was very taken by him. She even broke into his room in the middle of the night while he was sleeping. The painting she did is over there," he said and, as we edged up closer to take a better look, he continued. "The night before she came here, she nearly died of an overdose of heroin." Her painting was of a fire hydrant, in black on white—not a particularly life-like fire hydrant.

"It happened again a few years later when she was long gone from here," Father Rahm said. "And she died. He came back for the funeral."

"I didn't even know that," I said.

"Of course, there was nothing he, nor any of us, could have done," he continued. "Life is not easy, for anyone," Father Rahm said. "But there is still so much joy. We have to emphasize the joy!"

"That's right," I said.

We are obsessed with narrative. We find ourselves one day, strangely, walking the streets of a wildly complex world, having no idea how we arrived here. Yes, the womb. We arrive through the womb, activated upon enjoinment of sperm and egg nine months prior and, yes, we can follow our family trees back through names and names and names, and eventually, if our resources were not limited by the absence of written records from long ago or the flimsiness of the oral tradition, which requires no more than one person to get a story wrong or to provide an alternate perspective on the same event, we might then arrive at two names, the first father and mother—Adam and Eve, if you'd like—and though this offers the mind a cohesive, physical portrait of time, its defect is in its appearance of completeness, its overlapping equivalence in space. Narrative is a human creation dependent upon time and reliant in its presentation on beginnings, middles and ends; our concept of everything is completely enwrapped in its details—past, present, future, first, next, last, start, stop, seconds, hours, months, centuries, eons, when, then, now, before, between, after, yesterday, tomorrow, timeline, time frame, calendar, chronology. And how do we understand time, measure something that we cannot see, something that is not matter? Through distance and space—closeness, nearness, in front of, behind, here, there, forward, back, coming, almost, long, lengths. All is a question of power, of superiority through organization, order and accountability, sense, knowledge. How does memory account for lost time? It creates or listens to stories, religions, family trees, histories…and uses these to cement the gaps. The mind will create its tableau and, on the left side, it will place the beginning; on the right, the end. The brush stroke will not be interrupted, the painting will be smooth and polished, infallible. In the places where it does not have any information, no stories, no guesses, it fills in its own gaps, disappears unknown time, pretends it did not exist, creates a perfect image of a complete woman, her complete form as it exists before the eye. But if we were honest about our memories, it would be a different painting, a nose separated by a large fissure, body parts completely removed from others, hair follicles stranded, as if the tableau were a long piece of

117

paper attached to a moving conveyor belt whilst the artist stands immobile, continuing to paint his strokes upon the same coordinates.

I had seen a sudden flash, a sudden glimpse of this longer tableau but, unwilling to allow this disorder, I decided to turn the conveyor belt off, to unspool the paper and fill in the missing spaces. Since high school, Art's life had been communicated to me from various sources—friends in common, interviews on television and in magazines and newspapers and Art himself, through letters and our sporadic meetings. Our friendship superseded the gaps because I could interpolate data from the parts that were already known and create a whole painting. I saw him clearly for his quirks—the laundry list of things that were quintessentially and unalterably his, those things that I could predict from patterns that had emerged in his youth, those very things—facts—that in a newspaper article or magazine provides its readers with the sensation of knowing something, and I had extended these details to represent the parts of the tableau I couldn't see. But now Art's presence in Brazil, his galleries and his teaching and his donations—even his possible appearance as an activist in Rio under a false identity, which Father Rahm, by emphasizing the detail, perhaps suspected by instinct was Art himself—created in my mind a new Art, who, though inseparable from the actual Art, altered the tableau with such a pull that it could no longer be touched up in its spurious form, with a powdering of the nose or a freshening up of its lighter hues; the entire tableau needed to be repaired before we could again shrink back to what we are comfortable with, see him in miniature and then recover from what has jarred us, resume our positions as the masters of time, the controllers of a universe that has never been in our control.

And so it was, with this glimpse, that I began my official, conscious search for Art. I booked a seat aboard an overnight bus from Campinas to Rio in two days and filled my remaining hours in Campinas on assignment, finishing my interview with Father Rahm, driving around with the Jorges through towns of porcelain and oranges, learning more about Brazil and the world the priest had created, where, everywhere we went, we received a degree of respect from people that in the United States you would only get if you were rich or a celebrity. In a hotel room back in Serra Negra, I filed the story by email to *The Monthly* and filled the editors in on the change of itinerary and told them that I would email from Rio regarding revisions. At the rodoviaria, Jorge, who had become quite maternal with me, gave me a few sandwiches for my journey and a book on Portuguese idioms and told me to look out for his cousin Rosenilda, who he said was "very beautiful and capable." I thanked him, and then turned to Jorgito, who surprised me by pulling me to his chest, squeezing me tightly and patting me twice on the back of the head.

The bus departed from the rodoviaria and squeezed through a tight place between two other buses, slowing through the headway and the adjacent roads near the station and then finally loosing no holds barred onto the highway, the driver buckling his seatbelt, the passengers reclining their seats, and from my briefcase I pulled out Jorge's grammar book and settled on a section called "pleasantries." The bus joined others on the highway, traveling en masse toward Rio. Alongside the highway, the landscape turned green and coastal, the rivers bloated and the towns nearby glistened in the darker nightfall hues that beshined the landscape and gave it the personality of a silvering actor in repose.

The tableau flickered apart and came together again. Brazil waded in the ocean, still pulling away from Africa.

nosotras

Follow us por allí donde vamos, into the frosty Chihuahua night. But before you leave home, smell the paint as it settles into the walls a glossless white, a fuming colorlessness. Let the paint flare your nostrils and tickle your nose hairs, but don't linger, paisanos. Too many of our primos and hermanos are no longer coming down from highs induced by paint thinners and glue and spraypaint y todo eso. Come away from your doorstep, and follow us down to Anapra and Fronteriza Baja and to all the colonias, trash cans aglow in fiery refuse. Or down by the river. Smell it thick and pungent, the progeny of brick kilns and fábrica fumes and the exhaust of cars from decades before, the clouds pushing through the sleeves of a sweater sodden in sulfur dioxide, particulates, carbon monoxide, nitrogen oxide, hydrocarbons y todo eso. Vengan acá, carnales, away, and into our habitat, where we simmer onion peels tangling in the oil spattering with slices of mango and tomato, chile verde, garlic and sprinkles of salt and pepper. Everything is fresh. We got them all aquí a la vuelta, where we buy everything, and we know where these things come from. But we cannot stay for long; we must always egress. Onward to las maquiladoras, where our stories always end and begin. Perfumes bejewel those of us who cannot wear bracelets or necklaces or earrings because of the requirements of our employ. They clash with one another in their flower and fruit aromas. The night is cold and windy, but the freshness of the air must always surrender to the acrid winnows of the fábricas. And do you know who we are? Have you guessed? We are nosotras. We live here.

Padre Osvaldo, the monkish Jesuit priest, sitting afore the group of all-boy private-school grads, now on to university and high times, remembered adolescence and was struck again that the greatest myth of life is that you grow up. In the flesh, yes, he was older, his hair pushed away from the center as if by high-power winds, his eyes reflecting a less solid ember of light, his joints jerky and unpredictable, his hands a diagnosis short of rheumatoid arthritis. But growing up—when would it have happened, anyway? It couldn't be as sudden and tangible as baby teeth falling from gums and being replaced by adult molars and eventually the teeth of wisdom, condemned to the hidden part of the mouth and yanked upon first yammering. It wasn't so much growing up as watching the older people stay the same age. He remembered his eighteenth birthday—a rite months away, in either direction, for these lads, a grandiose moment akin to First Communion—his relatives from blocks away in Campestre, then other Juareños and finally the few from Chihuahua arriving, walking through the door, the overlarge red door from whose opening burst the redolence of pine, his uncles grabbing him and embracing him hard like reminiscence, his aunt kissing him on his lips and telling him how handsome he had become. And then they all went outside, populated the yard in small circles of conversation under the Summer Triangle and talked politics and education reform, celebrity and rumors, and then, for the first real time, for the first time without secrets and regrets and apologies, invited him to join them as they threw back bottled Coronas or Tecate and tequila and mezcal from shot glasses of myriad designs and decals—great serpents slithering, toros so ferocious they'd be wont to charge at any color, the marcas of all the major labels—gusano o no—a collection he'd never known his parents to possess. It occurred to him, for the first time, that instead of his classmates and him joining the ranks of his relatives and other adults, his relatives had instead been demoted to his class, where trading stories of drunken first times or wanting only those things outside of their material grasps or petty crimes—all the things he associated with the immaturity of youth—diluted the adult discourse he'd expected. In the summer before he was meant to go to college at the University of Juárez, he worked in his uncle's best friend's legal office in El Paso, organizing files, filing papers, answering the phone and escorting clients into the lawyer's office. There, he continued to observe the same things among his new office peers, all acting out the same rituals and expressing the same concerns his uncles and aunts did during his eighteenth birthday party. He thought maybe things might be different on the other side, but even there people seemed consumed by personal advancement, promotions, money, cars, status—he was surprised also at the number of second-generation Mexican-Americans who acted more Anglo than they did as heirs to a long line of rich history and familial ties. Although he was perfectly capable of taking on the gallantry and educación that was expected of him, he was deeply unsatisfied with life almost overnight, as if the magic carpet of adulthood had not only never started flying but had been ripped right out from underneath him.

He heard clapping and the overexaggerated pronunciation of his name—Padre Osvaldo Orozco—by the vice principal, who, Osvaldo thought, must have gone into education only after putting to rest designs on a career as a fútbol commentator. Osvaldo stood upon the podium, leaned forward onto the lectern and spoke the first words that came to him: "You may think today is the beginning of the rest of your lives, but for many of you it is the end. For many of you, today begins la carrera de locos, what in English is called the 'rat race,' the beginning of the amassing of things, a collection it will take you the rest of your lives to build; the only thing negotiable is the type of cheese molding away at the finish line. A proverb from our great country says, 'As you see yourself, I once saw myself. As you see me now, you will be seen.' The older you get, the faster time goes. What science will not tell you but age will is that the speed at which time passes is relative to the amount of time that has already passed. If I have lived nine-hundred-and-ninety-nine hours, then this next hour is one of a thousand hours lived and the hour following is one of a thousand and one—a slightly smaller fraction of a lifetime. When you grow older, time shrinks. They say that every hour is sixty minutes long; when I went to the seminary in the United States, there were days when they said the temperature was at zero, but the wind made it feel like it was more like twenty-below. Measurements can be deceiving. Similarly, you may arrive at the age of fifty with a car so sleek it looks as if it is polished every hour, so much money that you can afford to carry ten thousand pesos always in your wallet and a title and profession that wins over the respect of one hundred men and women, but you'll find that none of these things are as important as the things that are really important. So, then, what can we do to change the way we enter the world? The world is already unequal. Today, you and your classmates are on similar ground—the clothing you wear, the places you come from. But consider this: for every wrinkle on our faces are a hundred-thousand decisions and for every gray hair are millions of moments. By the time you reach my age, wrinkles will cover your faces like the

123

creases on your hands; such is inevitable. What will have differed will have been these decisions and moments. This is my proposal. Live the life you have planned on living up to this day, live it exactly as you have imagined, preparing for the same goals, the same successes expected of you—with one small alteration. When you get home tonight, before the music starts to play, before you finalize plans on where to meet your friends, before the alcohol intoxicates your system, before your adult life begins, make a decision to keep a secret from everyone else you know—write it down, sign your name, put it in an envelope and seal it—to do one thing for somebody or something for a group of people that will be great, that will send them soaring above the clouds. Dedicate the smallest portion of your life—one percent is enough—to this detail, but always be mindful of it, never let it out of your sight and always pay it its due. On your fiftieth birthday, count your money—go to your bank and ask for a printout—add it together with all of your assets, everything you own that can be counted. Then bring the envelope out—you will have saved it all these years—and though when you open it, it may have yellowed at the edges and the handwriting may look rushed as if you were on to a party and better things during an evening more than thirty years before, read the words and then compare everything you own to the feeling you have about what you did, in secret—all of those years—to ensure the world around you would be a better place, a part of your life that wasn't reached through the pursuit of glamour. Compare and decide which of the two is the one that makes you happier. I won't tell you the answer to this question. Even joining the priesthood does not entitle one to such privileges." As Padre Osvaldo said the word "privileges," the microphone sang a rankling note that pierced through the room like the sound of screeching chalk, and he stopped, looked up as if in thought, then, after several seconds passed, positioned himself in front of the microphone again, looked over at his colleagues and back at the microphone and said, "The reason

I'm up here is that I've been asked to lead a prayer. In the name of the father...' "

Later, as they drove away from the high school, Humberto patted Osvaldo on the shoulder and said, "Inspiring, Padre." Osvaldo, who often did not hear Humberto, was, as is said, elsewhere, pondering something else—*his* decisions—the many, glaring errors of his life that no editor could be called to redact.

Perhaps they traveled together. The two with the longer dark curly hair were best friends. They spent the most time together, drank together, told that same joke that ended with the punchline "chango descalabrado," and went further back with El Diablo than any other two and were therefore shown the trust afforded brothers, which is why, maybe, they were the ones chosen to meet the Egyptian in the prison as representatives of Los Rebeldes. And, now, they were coming back with information about how the murders were to be carried out, the precise and intricate directions so that the pattern, despite the time elapsed between murders, would repeat and each degree of evidence and speculation against the Egyptian would be reduced in strength with each new crime. They were a thick gang of miscreants, bearded in antagonism and fearlessness, unchallenged in their pursuits, equal to any delinquency and any malice. The brilliant caprice in their alignment with the Egyptian was that it was a huge sum of money per girl—one thousand pesos. Bodies were to be dumped in the Lote Bravo and other areas of uninhabited desert where no one would ever see anything, and, if anything went wrong—and why should it?—the hijo de puta was in jail and he couldn't really mess with them from there. Cops could always be paid off; the going rate for corruption betrayed its disparate resemblance to the value of things, and repercussions could be avoided as long as high-level government or mafia weren't involved. A good thing the

Egyptian knew so little of the Mexican judicial process and spoke only so-so Spanish.

And so they met El Diablo, perhaps, at the Pollo Mateo off Avenida Lopez Mateos, the maelstrom of chicken-smell pumping out of the store's vents such that El Diablo could do nothing to avoid calling his friends to him to share in his pleasure, and so, as soon as the two of them left the jail, they drove across town, found their leader in a corner booth, halfway through his third of three legs, and they ordered and sat down and got down to business, into a discussion of how the meeting with the Egyptian was a veritable call to arms and the troops would need to be assembled as soon as possible, as early as that evening perhaps. The Egyptian's style, the seduction and courtship, the bottles of wine and entertainment, could be skipped in favor of quicker and less risky methods, they agreed, as long as the same evidence remained. And yes, this would be a tricky endeavor, scavenging for particular articles of clothing rather than just taking loot. Perhaps unlike previous, unpremeditated ploys, El Diablo would have to ensure that everything was organized. Several of them could work at the same time in different parts of the city, but they risked multiplying the numbers too quickly, and therefore foiling the intent, which was to prove that the serial killer or killers were acting at their normal pace and range. Perhaps El Diablo decided that the money was in the details, making things look right—consistent—and it was for this reason that he'd asked the two to memorize the details the Egyptian had dictated to them. "Be sure, cuates," he might have said. "Something fails, and everything goes a la chingada."

Maybe they had someone on the inside, someone at police headquarters who would keep an eye out for them and let them know if for any reason the band was suspected. The same investigating officer would have ensured them that there would be no problems. This case was not high priority. Evidence in this investigation, as in others, had a history of being improperly handled—soiled by officers' hands, misclassified, lost, even burned when it took up too much space at headquarters. Maybe the officer assured them that people did get busted in Juárez but not the ones who were careful, and it was just as likely someone who wasn't even in Juárez during a weekend would be apprehended for a murder that happened while he was away. Maybe.

Perhaps they'd never dealt with anything like this. They weren't hit men, clinically insane, or myrmidons of the drug trade, who kill by profession or pathology. They had killed before, but only when it was unavoidable—when their lives were threatened by other street gangs fighting for the same turf, someone was on their tail or the victims fought back, for example. And maybe that's why El Diablo was careful, so careful that the two, as they gnawed down to the bones of the chicken, felt a different sensation when they swallowed. The day had taken on an eerie quality, as if they had awakened after bad dreams and realized what it was to feel powerless, the sky was fogged and rain poured in spurts like wind, a respected president had been assassinated, or Christian beliefs offered the threat of eternity when life on earth seemed too long as it was.

Plans were drawn, on paper, and El Diablo, who had seemed out of sorts while discussing the details, now seemed stronger, the way a great leader, after showing signs of vulnerability, suddenly and commandingly recovers his mask of impenetrability, and those who had observed its absence forgot their moment of doubt. The foundation was cementing. The money—their cut, anyway—was all but in their wallets. That was all. Nothing else to add. It was going to happen.

"¿Es todo, pues?" El Diablo asked, and the two nodded their heads.

It is painted on the mountain in white letters, and she reads it. These are two cities of graffiti and murals and letters painted on the mountain, where temporary messages become permanent, and the messages are everywhere. *La Biblia es la Verdad. Léela.* They say that if you get lost, look to the mountain. Once you become familiar with its bends and curves and angles—elephants and clouds and faces in the crowd carved and then disappearing into the rock—it becomes as familiar as the face of one's obsession or a bright image looked at directly and then viewed again behind closed eyes. *The Bible is the Truth. Read it.* Look for these words, follow them home, follow them to where they lead you. They have long since become a part of the landscape. They are the brothers and sisters of the cacti, the yucca, the foxes and goats and snakes, the secret living beings of the mountain biome. The girl walked from her apartment, walked in a city of cars, and she kept walking and walking, thinking again of Verónica and what might have happened to her that night at Amazonas, what arrested her from life, caused her to be erased, dissolved? Truth sounded like a good idea, truth in this world of uncertainty and theory—*that* could be a wonderful thing, a good place to begin.

Eventually, after walking several miles, she boarded a bus, taking it downtown to a bookstore to which she had always attached great prominence because of the elegant script of its name, which she hadn't remembered. There, she selected a tome, wrapped in plastic. She wanted a *new* Bible—not to preserve the book, but because with a new book she could chart her progress as the oils of her hands soaked into the pages and distinguished on the binding the pages read from those to come because, now, in her recently acquired twenties, she liked to see the lines of life and believed that behind them lay a new, palpable bloom. These days, when she looked in the mirror, she was beginning to see life happening to her; she realized that beauty wasn't entirely innate, that it arose from the various stations of life, arrived in spurts and disappeared. Before, she had wanted to be an actress because she thought that acting would stymie the aging process and keep the book binding clean and white forever against the dusting of time. Now, she almost couldn't wait to turn forty.

When she turned, her hair brushed her face, and she could feel the chill slipping into her body, and she shuddered, her keys jangling, her hair flocking back. Night began to fall, and things were much more quiet, and she could hear whispers behind her, so she whipped around to find nothing, then turned back the other way and bumped into someone—¡híjole!—apologized, inhaled the thick whiff of his cologne counteracting against the stink of a day's work and competing for control of his body, enough to elicit the smells of a hundred men: sweat-stained, beer-breathed men, and, though she had never before been nauseated by any smell, not even turpentine or burning trash or las maquilas, there was something in the air that frightened her, and she walked hurriedly down three blocks to Avenida de la Raza, the street where she worked, and entered the building hyperventilating, constipated with emotion, stupefied by her recourse, her easy surrender to the whispers of the night.

Inside, she sneezed. The smell of café brewing came from somewhere on the first floor. She knocked loudly at the door nearest her before wondering if knocking loudly would be mala educación. After about a minute, a woman said through the door, "¿Sí?"

"I'm sorry to bother you," the girl said, her voice shaky. "¿Can I come in?"

"Sure," the woman said, opening the door, allowing the exposed bulb above to spotlight her light-brown, smooth face and dyed blond hair.

"I'm embarrassed," the girl said. "I can't explain it. I was just suddenly overcome by fear. I work upstairs, but I needed to see someone, to…"

"It's okay," the woman said. She was at least thirty. She wore a sweater of multiple, horizontal stripes—red, pink and brown. Her eyes were large, her voice small. She transmuted her usual insouciance into maternal warmth. The woman, Leti, told Esmeralda about a time she had called la policía when her husband was working late and she had heard what she thought to be gunshots but what was actually an old car backfiring, and then Leti went on to divulge prideful details about her three children—Dulce, Octavio and Orlando, two years apart respectively and worlds of differences among them—and then how she had spent the day nearly sleeping through her work and that now she had to spend a few extra hours there, after everyone had gone, to finish what should have taken her the morning. Esmeralda told the woman about the various roles she played upstairs as a graphic designer and letter writer; she talked about how she'd dropped out of school at twelve, about her mother now many years dead; about her father, the exploitative drunk; her dreams of becoming an actress and marrying the first rich man who fell into her arms, and how these dreams had changed; she told her about Padre Osvaldo, the priest who confessed her every week, that after a month of speaking to him nearly every day, she discovered that he had also been her roommate's confessor—and then new tears for Verónica, always when she spoke about her and told the story: the phantom investigation, the donation of all the dead girl's clothing to a charity, the emptiness she felt every time she visited the grave or saw the pink signposts and the black crosses that were painted by women and men all over Juárez in remembrance of the murdered women and girls. How long ago was that? Just two years before, and it was that day, the entire twenty-four hours of it, that she remembered more than any other day in her life—the gringo vaquero and his fifty-dollar note; the delirium of having stayed up all night taking form in her distraída speech when Vero's Aunt Laura called and she answered groggily, stumbled in finding an excuse for where Vero was—"At church, I think"—which had actually been the truth, though unbeknownst to her, and it sounded like the furthest from it because of her hesitancy; her shaky hands, then writing the message in an illegible cursive script, tossing that in the

130

trash, rewriting the same words; going out to buy frijoles in a bag, flirting with the grocery store owner's son, his sexual advances, thinly veiled, which she had found flattering; then returning home to see Verónica curled into a ball on her bed, the message from her aunt in her hand, her innocence in her round cheeks and eyelids; then the rest of la historia: the night at Amazonas, the next morning, that hangover of a morning when for a moment one has to decide whether reality is fiction or vice versa, the shakiness again in her hand, her turgid limbs, this time not from lack of sleep but from anxiety, as she dialed Aunt Laura, the feeling of regret and utter loss when she realized that Aunt Laura had been calling to *see* her, that she was going to ask Vero to forget the ugly things she had said, that had Esme known this was going to be Vero's last night, she would have made certain she call her aunt, and then everything might have happened differently, and she sought solace in that hypothesis, because even when all hope is gone the body still clings to it, even retroactively.

"¿How old are you, Esmeralda?" Leti asked.

"Twenty," she said. "But I feel much older."

"You seem much older, not because of the way you look, but because of the way you carry yourself."

"I'm sorry. I always talk about Vero. I feel responsible for her."

"¿But how could you have been?"

"They say that surviving makes us stronger, but it has only aged me and made life more difficult than it was before." With that, she looked up at the clock, which insisted it was nine o'clock by forming a perfect right-hand angle between the minute and hour hands, and she said to Leti, "I better go." Leti implored her to stay; Esme could wait until she finished her work and they could walk out together...But Esme said she needed to get going; she thanked her for opening her doors and promised that they would meet for lunch sometime. She left the office and ascended the stairs to the third floor, unlocking the door with the key she'd been given just a few days before.

As she entered, the room was lifeless in its quietude, murky in its darkness. She flipped on the light switches and watched the coincident appearance of light in certain stratified sections of the vast room, which was divided by curtains; then, to duplicate the sounds of the room during the day, she flipped on the computers, the sound otherwise discernible only in its absence. She walked over to her desk and peered through the window at the street, the streetlamps, the carnival sound of a Friday, and, continuing to look down upon the street, she found there was something trancelike about the pace of people walking by and talking, something that was interesting about observing something public from a completely private place, safe from the world outside yet still belonging to its greater apparatus. She sat down at the desk and opened the Bible. Chapter One. *¿De veras?* It has chapters like a regular book? Esme leaned back in the chair and held the book above her head.

In the beginning God created the heaven and the earth. And the earth was without form, and void; and darkness was upon the face of the deep. And the Spirit of God moved upon the face of the waters. And God said, Let there be light, and there was light. And God saw the light, that it was good; and God divided the light from the darkness. And God called the light Day, and the darkness he called Night.

Esme continued to read, absorbed by the narrative voice; outside, the street quieted as if it had been submerged in water. The café smell from floors below had long since dissipated; if Leti still had work to do, it could wait until tomorrow. Esme felt her eyes blinking, her body tiring, but she kept reading. She stopped every few pages and glanced back over them to see if she had left something out, forgotten something or missed a word. She would not be taking in any partial truths. At three-thirty a.m., she gave up, pushed the chair back as far as she could and slept.

And the evening and the morning were the first day.

Maybe this is how it happened. The two sat in their car and talked. And selected. "¿Y ella? ¿What about her?" The one with the longer hair maybe asked, eyeing a girl as she crossed the street, emerging from la maquila across the street and choosing not to board one of the nieves, the buses that transported maquila workers to las colonias. "No importa, güey," the other replied, in a slightly contemptuous tone. "Son todas iguales." All equal. All the same. But neither of them moved when the girl, her hair a soft auburn dye, a slight hop in her walk, walked right in front of the car. "¿How old do you think she is?" the shorter-haired one asked, after she had passed. "¿Fourteen? ¿Fifteen? No sé." For minutes, they could not disturb the silence. What was it to them? Was younger better? Or worse? Hadn't this question already been decided for them? Wasn't it that the younger the girl, the stronger would be the reaction of revulsion from the community, the media, the police? Could they forgive themselves their act, if they deliberated upon such questions of ethics?

"Let's eat something."

"Good idea."

They drove through Anapra and settled on the first taco stand, ordering apple sodas and tacos, talking to the jovencita, a smile alighting her face when they joked with her about the tacos.

"These are the healthy ones, ¿verdad?" the shorter-haired one might have said.

"They're all healthy," she said, moving her hair away from her face.

"¿Hey, do you have a vegetarian taco?"

Perhaps she blushed. "¿Have you tried the beef tacos? They've got lettuce in them. I could take the beef out."

"No, just give us the beef ones."

The two of them sat at the outdoor bar while she served the other customers who had just arrived. When she came back, it was perhaps the shorter one who said, "Oy, these tacos are good."

"The best on the block," she might have said.

The two were quiet in the car, quieter than before, as they drove across the street to a gas station, filled up the car, then moved back to la maquila and parked nearby, between two other cars, farther away from where they had been parked earlier.

"She was the same, just works a different job," the longer-haired one maybe said.

Their dialogue ceased. Outside, no one walked by them, the wind stopped blowing, the occasional traffic had halted, and the two men sat motionlessly in their car. After a quarter hour, two girls in their late teens, older than the rest, walked right behind the car, and the shorter-haired one caught them both in the rearview mirror. "Vámonos, cabrón."

The other slid his foot onto the clutch, turned the key and eased into first gear, rocking through the unpaved lot and onto the asphalt road, following the girls by about forty feet. The girls moved at a slow pace, as if they were conversing, though they weren't, and the longer-haired one found it difficult to maintain an unobservable distance while still moving. Eventually, the girls turned a corner onto an empty gravel road that arched over a sickly stream of water and drew nearer the lights of the colonias, lights that in their lower wattage seemed to be in perpetual candlelight vigil.

Suddenly, a car lurched past the girls on their left side and the brake lights fluttered indecisively before staying lit, and two men with long curly hair emerged from both sides of the car. The girls thought to run, but, as in a dream, their bodies froze, as if wrapped in bedsheets pinned to a hulking mattress. Instead, they moved closer together, as they were sisters, and their parents had told them never to leave the other's sight. Soon, darkness covered them. All they could do was smell the freshness of gasoline, the odor of thought, a lingering scent of tacos…and neither cried for the other's sake.

The stink of their decomposing bodies, disfigured, naked and gnawed at by vultures, was the olfactory equivalent of washing one's hands in boiling water, staring directly at the sun, standing just below an aeroplane as it takes off or allowing a pill to linger too long in one's mouth so that the protective gel no longer serves as a shield from the pill's potent core. The night had turned up two more women, and the list was growing. A missing woman did not mean her body would be found immediately; sometimes, it would take several months before her body was discovered. Sometimes their bodies were never found. In a city of crime, numbers could go up disproportionately long before anyone would ever suspect something irregular at work, and it was months before anyone really noticed and, even then, even after arrests were made and suspects jailed and the end prophesied, even then, the only thing one could count on was more dead bodies lying facedown in the sand.

In the dark of his office with a desk lamp spotlighting one small area and then everything around it blending into darkness, as in the days when lucubration was not merely means by which to save electricity or practice one's vow of poverty, but the only way to work at night, Padre Osvaldo cut out the article about the two women—or girls, really, both sixteen—and wrapped it in the clear plastic slip inside his binder of clips from the Juárez press, and then he flipped through the book once again, looking for patterns, any clue that might lead him toward a solution. Here lay the photos of victims smiling, police officers in the desert investigating, family members grieving, human rights organizations hostile with disapproval. He would not think twice about trading his twelve years in the seminary for four years of forensics, four years of jurisprudence and four more of criminal justice. Then he would comb the desert in search of bodies and follow the trail to the killer. Certainly, with more than a hundred dead bodies, several must hold the key to the solution; no

135

perpetrator could be flawless in his or her work one hundred percent of the time. But there were no clues, just photos. No evidence, just examples. The articles provided facts, and the new developments were hard to find because so much was inconclusive, so much hearsay. The police, he thought, were like politicians, making promises, charting progress, and then every day you still woke up to the same mierda, the same shitty country.

Osvaldo found he was happy only when he reflected upon certain parishioners. Although he did not think of them favorably when pondering them collectively, he adored so many—the Chávez twins, his altar servers, one born with an extra finger and the other with one fewer, whose slapstick banter reminded him of radio shows during the fifties; the sixteen-year-old fútbol star who came for a blessing before every game and when in confession provided elaborate details of his sins because he seemed to think this would lead to proportionate exculpation; the obsequious elderly women, who dedicated their time, serving as volunteers, answering phones and attending to some of the bookkeeping and secretarial duties that would have otherwise been his; those like Verónica who came alone at hours when Mass was not being said and knelt onto pews and prayed fervently; and then, of course, the extravagantly poor, whose charity was often equally as extravagant.

But Padre Osvaldo felt priests weren't meant to be happy. On a daily basis they have to deal with the most wretched, squalid circumstances, the depths of human suffering—those smitten by disease, death and poverty; adultery, divorce and loss of love. And, even though over these taxing years he had gained knowledge about how to deal with these things—how to console a woman grieving for the loss of her husband, how to aid a man for whom death impends swiftly, how to fill the dirt-colored niños de la calle with ivory-colored dreams—the blow of seeing these calamities came from a knife whose blade somehow never dulled. Padre Osvaldo had heard the adage that undergoing tragedy and disaster makes one stronger, but he only felt weaker, only helpless. His bones felt more fragile and porous, his clothing looser, his inner disposition rankled and, when he stared at these women and their families and their helplessness, he wondered if ever there would be an end to any of it.

The madrugada caused the stars to disappear, and the earth was exposed; light existed all around. The sun rose slowly, melodramatically. Light rushed through the alleyways and colored the streets, turned on the lights of houses, flamed up the grills, ignited the anger of those sleeping on the streets, for there was no negotiating with the light. Whether from haciendas or shacks, people emerged from their homes smelling fresh, clean, perfumed. Breakfast steamed—huevos, chorizo, jalapeños and chiles tucked into tortillas and fried in oil; nothing burned yet, the day was inerrant. People whistled, and they could see their breath in front of them, leading the way, keeping them fresh. Others lit cigarettes, and the smell seemed to dissolve rather than stick to their clothing, as if this were the trial run. People were smiling, music filled the streets and cars, and everyone breathed in gulps of their long lives born afresh. This is beauty, their faces said. As the people walked their ways to work and the sun continued to rise, less-subdued—a beam rising like the shadow of an eagle spreading its wings—Padre Osvaldo looked out of the window of the cathedral and made his forecast: Yes, más mierda, another shitty day.

PART TWO

the crabs

When I arrived upon the River of January at about six in the morning on a humid March day, I quickly grabbed my bag and my briefcase from the luggage compartment, hailed a cab and was driven to Ipanema and dropped off on the beachfront where, sitting on a bench whose legs were buried in the sand, I saw a dark sky give birth to a fiery sun. At the hour of alvorada, Rio seemed unsure as to whether or not it wished to begin, as if the entire city might choose to malinger complicitly. As I walked along the street that conjoined Ipanema and Copacabana, activity burst forth like a sky aflame in snow. Trucks unloaded in front of restaurants and grocers, women with large, bulbous sunglasses walked their dogs, and hoary old men with their hands held behind their backs watched the changing angles of their shadows upon the sidewalk. I stepped into a hotel in Ipanema and arranged to

141

stay for the night. I ascended to the twelfth floor and, as I turned the corner looking down at the anachronistic key I had been given, the prototypical gaol-cell key that in cartoons a prisoner will call a dog to bring, I ran into a man of about thirty who was wearing a yellow cowboy hat over curly tufts of blond hair. He stuck his hand out. "Sorry. Excuse me. I am Robert."

Robert was a chocolatier from Luxembourg who was attempting to introduce his chocolates into candy stores all over Brazil and having very little luck. "They already have their bonbons and favorite imported chocolates, and they will not consider that Luxembourgers can produce chocolate just as well as the Swiss and Belgians," he lamented, later, after I had stopped by his room on his request to "have a chat," his hat concealing his eyes when he looked down dolefully. As it turned out, Robert spoke Spanish nearly as well as I did, in addition to six other languages—Flemish, German, English, French, Italian and Lëtzebuergesch. As I was leaving the room, after telling him briefly about my purpose in Rio, he called to me, "Wait! Have you seen Christ?"

His question was not evangelical. The Cristo Redentor statue on the top of the hunchbacked mountain, overhanging Rio like the prow of an enormous ship, had been obscured by clouds for the past week, and he was waiting for a moment of clarity in which to take the tram up to the top of the mountain and "see Christ." He explained to me that statues of Christ appear in almost every city in Brazil with a mountain. I told him I hadn't seen it and, though I hadn't planned on doing anything touristy, I agreed to go with him as soon as the clouds cleared. After leaving his room, I took the elevator down and found the concierge, telling him that I was looking for information about art in Rio, perhaps a newspaper or magazine that might lead me to where I could view exhibitions.

"Rio," he said, amiably. "We pronounce it 'Rio.' "

142

"Right," I said. "I forgot. My first language is Spanish, and we roll our 'r's."

"In English, it would be like the word 'hero' without the 'r,' " he said, and then he smiled. I'd eventually come to learn that the occasional lessons Brazilians were inclined to spontaneously give were less about condescension and more about seeking to impress, like children looking for opportunities to correct their parents.

"Have you heard of Arturo Serrano, the American painter?" I asked.

"Yes, of course," he said. "And of course, lately he disappeared. Where he's gone, nobody knows." He shrugged his shoulders.

"Right. I'm doing research on him for a magazine article in New York and am hoping to see some of his work while here in Hero."

"Are you a writer?"

"A journalist," I said.

"For what magazine do you write?"

I gave him the name of several of the publications. Instead of responding, he picked up the phone and after a moment said something into the receiver that I didn't understand, interspersed with the names of the magazines I worked for.

"...Ta. Ta. Ta bom. Otimo," he turned to me. "I have a friend who works at *Olha*, a magazine of marvelous repute in Brazil, and he has recommended you speak to a woman who is the magazine's art critic. If you want, you can meet with her for lunch. Do you eat meat?"

I thanked him for making the connection, slipped him a couple of ten-real notes, said goodbye and then walked out of the hotel front doors, up a block or so and onto Nossa Senhora de Copacabana, where I was hoping to find breakfast, an event Brazilians call café da manhã. Eventually I located a place on the street corner called Lanchonete Três, where many men were standing, crowded at a long lunch counter, and I ordered a shot of espresso, something called suco de

143

mamão (which turned out to be papaya) in a juice box, several pieces of cheese-filled bread called pão de queijo and a pastel, which I took to be a pastry because that's what "pastel" translated to in Spanish, but which I nearly spat out—not because it was especially unappetizing, but because it was filled with some kind of meat, and I'd been expecting something sweet. The men who crowded the counter were sipping juice through straws and talking to one another, finishing their drinks there before moving along. I left the place and its inveterate patrons, holding my pão de queijo and the suco de mamão in my hand and wondering if in fact Brazilians were on to something, that the secret to life was in standing immobile, listening to sports scores, eating fried food with fresh juice and laughing a whole lot at one's friends. I continued down Nossa Senhora de Copacabana, catching the glance of an attractive woman through the window of a clothing boutique and then deciding to enter the store; upon crossing the threshold into the perfumed environment, I realized the crowd inside mostly comprised employees, who seemed to outnumber both customers and merchandise. The woman I had seen through the window asked me something in Portuguese, then switched to English when she saw that I didn't understand, asking if I was looking for anything in particular and, when I said that I wasn't, bringing me six shirts, seven pairs of jeans and two pairs of shoes she insisted I try on.

Thirty minutes later, plastic bags in hand, I left the store, turning right on Hilário de Gouveia, passing a post office on my right and then looking ahead of me at the vast and luscious sands of Copacabana Beach. This time devoid of my suitcase and wearing my sandals, I walked onto the sand and felt its warmth between my toes. I ventured closer to the sea and finally sat down a few meters from its foamy, crashing waves that had been carried miles across the open waters, which now, in one last, magnificent burst of life, collapsed violently, dying onto the sand. I watched the cycle repeat itself: the endless waves lapping down upon the sand, which, wet and smooth, like the glossy varnish on a piece of furniture, seemed like the canvas of an increasingly difficult-to-please artist, whose compendium of ideas is discarded before he can even begin to paint them, or the newly installed memories of someone with a progressive case of short-term memory loss.

And then I realized another ceremony was in progress. Out of the corner of my eye, I suddenly saw a tiny crab scurrying across the sand and then disappearing into a hole. I waited for him to reemerge but instead a similarly dressed crab appeared, pausing, a bit surprised, disoriented perhaps, scooting, stopping, then scooting another several centimeters before also vanishing into the sand. I looked around me and found the beach almost completely empty of people. It almost seemed these crabs were playing this game of hide and seek for me alone, and I felt connected to them, as if these particular crabs belonged to me and were *my* crabs—and in some uncertain reality they were; these crabs really *were* mine.

I stood up and turned around, looking for the statue of Christ, wondering if he was normally visible from here. The blank wall of clouds circling above made it impossible to field this question. I looked down and saw the crabs dancing at my feet and, feeling frivolous, I ran into the water and the crashing waves and wandered farther out into the ocean. As I turned around to view the beach from which I had come, the zone of hotels behind rising up like some villain racing toward the sea, I was taken from behind by a massive wave, its undertow grabbing me by the ankles and causing me to contort underwater. When I reemerged suddenly, after what must have been ten seconds of being knocked around, I was panting, my lungs choking with air, and I moved quickly back to the sand, leaving the ocean, alive and carnivorous, behind. I checked for my wallet and documents and, finding them intact, looked around to see if anyone had noticed. No, I was alone. I looked below my feet, and the crabs stopped in their tracks, as they had before, but now they seemed different from *my* crabs, as if now years were wedged between these moments and the crabs I had viewed before were the ancestors of those that scuttled below me now.

When I returned to the hotel, I waved to the concierge, who seemed to be in the exact same pose of that of an hour and a half before, and now he proudly observed that I was wet and holding some bags, about which I agreed with him. He told me that I would be eating at O Rei de Cupim, literally "the King of Cockroach," a churrascaria in Arpoador, where at thirteen-hundred hours I would meet a woman called Marisa de Oliveira, who he said was looking forward to meeting me. I took the elevator back to my room and began to undress and shower. As I washed my hair, looking up at the showerhead, I saw that the electrical cords above were exposed and, even though I had never once died of electrical shock, it seemed a precarious place to drape them, as all they would have to do was come unattached from the showerhead and I would be dead.

I arrived at the city center two hours prior to my lunch with Marisa de Oliveira to look for clues that might lead me to the activist João Fabiano. All I needed to do was meet João Fabiano to disprove that he was not Art or, if he *was* Art, as I suspected he was, then finding him would bring an end to this quest. (*Why did I think they were one in the same?*—It had mostly to do with the look on Father Rahm's face as he told me the story about the other priest, his mentioning it at all when it would otherwise have been too banal to point out, the fact that it seemed somehow like something up Art's alley...). At the same time, I had to make sure before I met him that he not be clued in as to my presence because, quite obviously, his purpose in hiding here would be to keep from being identified, so I needed to choose a different identity. I chose Julio Vargas—Julio from our high school valedictorian, Julio Poitras; and Vargas, the last name of a prestigious family of doctors that lived in the house overhanging mine, when I lived on El Paso's Westside. Next, I created several different scenarios for which one might wish to meet the activist. In each of these, I felt it was essential I be Mexican, as it would likely create instant solidarity, Art having always preferred Mexican people to Americans, and it would be better not to be Mexican-American, I thought, because this might arouse his suspicions, if it were indeed Art. At first, I considered being a Mexican coming to join Art in his protests of the Brazilian government for their lenient or non-existent sentencings of police officers but, upon further deliberation, I decided it would make much more sense for someone to come from Mexico looking for João Fabiano if he was hoping to persuade him to assist him in his own, similar cause, thus meriting a trip all the way to Rio. It made sense—despite progress in communication that could all but teleport one person from one locale to another, it was only advances in transportation that had truly made the world a smaller place, and the best anyone hoping to convince anyone of anything from afar can do is hop on a plane and carry the miles with him or her in his or her résumé. Besides, this was Latin America, and nothing is ever accomplished in Latin America without dinner or a drink.

In front of the large Theatro Municipal, in the Praça Marechal Floriano, I found a kiosk that had listed upon it multiple apartment offerings, contact information for English schools and private tutors, advertisements such as "Férias Exóticas—Flórida!" and several notices of manifestações, protests or demonstrations. I took down the times and places and other information, tore down one flyer that was stapled upon the kiosk several times over, and then continued to walk, looking around the area for anything that might catch my eye, as my investigative skills were limited in this place in which I did not speak the language nor understand where anything was, in addition to being a rather poor investigative journalist to begin with, which is why I was instead often in charge of converting research already gathered into prose or writing human-interest stories that I could write without disturbing my heartbeat, which I always found to be an excellent niche in the profession because writing crime stories or politics had never interested me and seemed to require too many interviews, too many facts and figures.

I wandered through one of the neighborhoods that lingered near the theatro, through a row of shops selling juice, then into a more residential area where I walked by a group of college-age kids, many with afros and flowers in their hair, some shirtless and others wearing tie-dyed and multihued clothing who were beating on timba drums and dancing on the cobble-stoned street. The sun intermittently slipped through the gauze of clouds and flashed across their drums and naked backs. I approached one of the women from the back. "Hey, do you speak English?" I asked her.

"Yeah," she said, breathing forth the perfect slangy indifference of an American teenager.

I pulled out one of the notes I had about one of the manifestações. "Do you know how I can get to this?"

She looked down at the paper and then back up at me. "No," she said, less indifferent than before. "You want to protest globalization?"

"Yeah," I said, duplicating her indifferent tone from before.

She said something to another woman, one who had been dancing, the slope of her throat bedewed with sweat, a hardness in her look that curved into a faint smile on one side of her mouth and a beauty that seemed to be achieved through her total occupation of her body and not her physical traits alone, as if her body was a thousand-string marionette she operated one string at a time.

The woman whom I had initially addressed spoke quickly and exaggeratedly, and her hands moved in ways that did not seem to correspond to anything I could understand. And then, after several minutes, the other woman responded, her voice producing in its deep husk a short string of sounds that ended as quickly as they had begun. Finally, the first woman nodded in agreement and dismissed herself. The second woman turned and said something to me in Portuguese and, when I replied that I didn't understand, the two conferred for a moment, and then the first one spoke to me in English.

"Cool. But that event already passed," she said, looking me up and down. "There's something going on tonight in Lapa. It's contra-globalization also." She glanced over at the drums and then back at me. "Do you know Lapa?" I shook my head. "Look for the arches," she said. "And go there before ten."

I thanked her and, as she moved farther into the circle of drums, dancing to the ludicrously fast rhythm, I was left with the second woman, the guy seated behind her still watching me fixedly.

"Where are you from?" she asked, also speaking with an impressive, clear accent.

"Mexico City," I said.

"What are you doing here?"

"I'm on vacation."

"Cool," she said, leaning back onto one leg and eyeing me suspiciously. "What do you normally do?"

"Normally…" I repeated. I had not worked this part out. "Normally, I profess. I teach, in Mexico. And yourself?"

"I go to school here, in Rio, at Pontifícia," she said, moving her hair back to behind her eyes after the wind had caught it and dragged it into her face. "I'm a graduate student," she qualified. "What do you teach?"

"Journalism," I said, inventing; our lies are extensions of ourselves and our wants. We talked for several minutes more. Jucélia was twenty-five and studied politics. She was deeply involved in activism but never a leader for fear of public speaking. She had consigned herself to supporting roles, convinced that leaders were mobilizers and that the hard work is always carried out by someone behind the scenes. Her parents called her an abacaxi, or pineapple, because she was thick-skinned like a pineapple's husk. She liked to bronze on the beach, dance with her friends and talk about colonialism and political ideologies, especially Marxism. Jucélia was the type of person about whom you could assemble a biography in ten minutes but it would take you years to get to know, for she was full of contradictions and did not seem to know herself. Eventually, I asked her if she would be going to the manifestação that evening.

"Yes, I think so. Do you want me to meet you in Lapa?"

"Yeah," I said. "That sounds great."

We set it up so that I would meet her at nine-thirty that evening. I departed from her and her friends. The drum beat continued, fast and entrancing. I took a cab and arrived just in time at O Rei de Cupim, drenched in sweat from running the last several blocks to the restaurant because the cab driver had dropped me off a few blocks away misunderstanding the address I had given him, then hoping that Marisa de Oliveira would arrive late so that by then I would have cooled off, as the waiters were already giving me strange glances that seemed to communicate that this amount of sweat had far surpassed permitted levels. She did arrive late—half an hour late—and by then I had already drained two Brahma beers and declined no fewer than twenty pounds of meat from the waiters who circulated carrying skewers packed tight with chicken, beef and pork. Their importunity seemed unnecessary, as I had already chosen this as my restaurant, but after observing the other customers, I learned there was a dial on my table turned to green signaling that I wanted them to continue propositioning me. I wondered if such a device could have also been made available at the boutique, where I had earlier tried on as many as fifteen pairs of jeans.

When Marisa de Oliveira arrived in stiletto heels, large black sunglasses, an orange-and-yellow summer dress and matching purse, which was to be my signal, all the heads in the restaurant turned, not because of her beauty, but because she tripped and nearly fell into a fountain at the front of restaurant, which was full of some number of carnivorous fish collected from the Amazon. I rose and signaled her. We greeted one another, then sat down, and within minutes I learned of her charming familial ties—her second-cousin João Baptista de Oliveira Figueiredo had been president of Brazil during the early eighties and many of her family members were in upper-level government positions, her nephew was a professional *futebol* player, her aunt a famous movie actress.

"But my family connections are not the reason that I work at *Olha*," she continued. I nodded. "I went to school at USP, the University of São Paulo, the best university in Brazil, to study art and then made an internship here. I lived in New York, you know," she said, as if I had been versed on her biography and could confirm this fact, "for several years—in the LES."

"No wonder you speak English so well," I said.

"No. I don't think it's so good," she said, looking down at the table and suddenly appearing to be quite shy.

"No. You're excellent," I reassured.

"Do you know I actually met him once?" she said.

"Who?"

"Arturo Serrano. He was speaking at NYU. They had made large poster boards, replications of his paintings of the human form, the ones where the internal organs of people were visible, or blended with their skin so that both were shown in coexistence. I interviewed him afterwards and sent the piece to *Olha*, and it ran the next month. That article was really the bridge that connected my internship with my current employment because I hadn't contacted the magazine since I arrived in New York. But I remember what he said. I quoted it in the article. He said, 'We spend our entire lives living inside our bodies but don't know what goes on inside us. We live completely externally, know something about everything except for ourselves, our actual physical internal selves.' Isn't this tremendous?" she asked. (I wasn't sure whether she was referring to what Art had said or her ability to recite it so perfectly.)

"Was it difficult to get an interview with him?"

"No, not at all. I walked up to him after the speech and asked him if I could interview him. I even told him that I couldn't call it an official interview yet because I still needed clearance from *Olha*, but I don't think this mattered to him. But you know something else? You know—as a journalist—how easy it is, once you get someone talking, to lead them to almost any subject? When I went back to my apartment afterwards I had an hour of tape, but I couldn't find anything to quote him on. It was like *I* was talking more, or what he was saying was so personally directed at me that it wasn't anything I could include in an article." I wondered about my own interviewing adequacy at the moment and, for that reason, asked her if I could use my tape recorder for the rest of the conversation.

"Absolutely," she said, then continued before I could turn it on. "I'd never seen a photo of him before, so I was surprised to see what he looked like. He was very short—what would you say, I think, in American measurements, about five-feet tall. Is that right?" I said that he was a few inches taller but that she had estimated well not having been born into our alien system of measurements. "But," she continued, "It didn't surprise me when I read that he committed suicide. His paintings, even the most colorful, could be so *lúgubre*?" I nodded. "And he never smiled and always seemed to be thinking about something else. And his final painting—how depressing! To paint yourself out of the world just before taking yourself out of the world!"

Since Marisa de Oliveira had entered, I hadn't spoken much, aside from introducing myself and submitting my request to use a tape recorder, so it didn't surprise me that after interviewing Art she had returned to her apartment with an hour of tape but so little of her interviewee, though Art was clever in the way he could trick people into thinking they knew something important about him when in reality what he said was entirely a reflection of themselves. Still, the one thing she had captured *was* this quality, a quality I had not only forgotten but had later misappropriated to another person I later met, who, because of his similar Aztec features, I subconsciously imbued with the same personality traits as Art and thus enjoyed a brief period of undue solidarity until, after several months, I eventually realized how utterly repellent and antipodal to Art he was and why I had let him get away with saying and doing innumerable repellent things. "So…don't you have some questions for me?" She finally said, making me suddenly aware that I too had the power to break the silence.

"Yes," I said. "I understand Art staged an exhibit in Rio in the past year or two. I was wondering if you knew where, when, what it was called, etc."

She had begun shaking her head before I finished my sentence. "No," she said. "Arturo Serrano has not shown art in Brazil during the past five years."

"Are you sure?"

"Absolutely. I have been the chief art critic for *Olha* for the last three years. Before that I was an assistant. I would *never* miss an Arturo Serrano exhibit if it were in Rio. He was one of the best painters in the world, if not *the* best, and I'm not just saying that because of his enormous celebrity. He was light years ahead of the rest—I find it difficult to write about his work because I realize that the moment I start, I've already failed." Noting that I had been waving away waiters for the past several minutes, she flipped the dial on our table to red.

"That's strange," I said. "I have a source that says he showed his work here during the past two years, but my source didn't witness the exhibit personally. He only heard about it from someone else."

"Well," she said. "I'm sure he wasn't here. I would have known about it. Rio may be a city of sixteen-million people, but it is still actually quite small when you consider its smaller factions." She looked at me directly. "I was wondering what you were hoping to discover by talking to people in Rio about Arturo Serrano. You didn't come all the way to Rio based on this tip, did you?"

"Oh, no, I was actually doing an interview in Campinas with a Jesuit priest—Padre Haroldo," I said.

"Oh, yes, I've seen his television shows. You wrote a profile?"

"Yeah. The article is running in a magazine in the U.S. in about six months."

"I would love to read it," she said.

"I could take your email and send it to you if you'd like? Actually, do you think you could send me the article you wrote on Art from a few years ago?"

"Absolutely," she said, unconvincingly. "And I wrote one recently after his disappearance that I'll also send. One more thing. You keep calling him Art. We don't know him that way here. Is that a play on words?"

"Oh, no," I laughed. "As far as I know, he's always been known as Art in the United States, even when he was young. Actually, I am an old friend of Art's. He is, or was, one of my closest friends."

She asked me questions about what Art had been like when he was younger and even brought out her own tape recorder and began to record some of the details of Art's youth, details that had been enhanced by my reiteration of them over the past two months, and my mind kicked into autopilot as I relayed to her these now-dulled memories, clearing the way for an extra layer of thought that focused on pondering the locale, the churrascaria, its abundance of meat and waiters in circuitous routes, the eight televisions that offered eight different futebol games and then eventually the woman who sat across from me, and I wondered if in her face, an expert could find traces of a political lineage and a dynasty of greatness.

154

When I arrived that evening at the Arcos da Lapa, the arches of Lapa, Jucélia was waiting for me, standing in front of a carro de bombeiro, a fire-truck, its sirens reverberating against the rustic buildings, a crowd huddled around, some people with their hands over their ears. "Hello," she said, and leaned forward so that I could kiss her cheeks.

"What's the story with the sirens?" I asked.

"What? Oh, I don't know. Silvia—the black girl—she thinks the police have heard about our march and the fire truck is to keep people from congregating. Don't worry," she said. "We will congregate. But it's still very early. The manifestation won't start until later. Let's go drink something."

We waded through a crowd of people in streets nearby and found ourselves squeezed in closely together as the path between the buildings seemed to narrow. "*Ali*," she said, pointing to a bar directly in front of us, before the street parted into two; even if we hadn't chosen that bar, the centrifugal force, it seemed, would have led us there anyway.

"How do I ask for two…what do you like…mixed drinks?" I asked Jucélia.

"I'll have a batida de maracujá. You should order a caipirinha or something. It's the Brazilian drink they know abroad. Just say, 'Quero uma batida de maracujá e uma caipirinha.' Like that," she said.

I ordered at the bar, repeating myself twice as Jucélia looked around, trying to find a place for us to sit. When the drinks arrived, I joined her at a table in the corner of the room.

"Obrigada," she said, knowing that I wanted to hear her speak Portuguese. "You did really well at the bar. How do you find Portuguese?"

"It's a strange, strange language," I said. "Do you know the game where you stand in a line of ten people, and the first person in line is given a sentence, and he has to say the sentence to the next person and so on, until the end of the line has been reached?"

"Yeah. We do that in school, to simulate oral tradition."

"Exactly," I said. "To me, Portuguese seems like the entire Spanish dictionary having gone through that process, in an assembly line where one of the people can't roll his 'r's, another pronounces all the 'j's. A Frenchman and Russian are also present, which gives the language that nasal touch and the 'schtoe' sound, in addition to, of course, somebody who mishears a lots of words and just throws in his own."

"That's probably not too different from what actually happened," Jucélia said. "So…what are you doing in Brazil?" she asked.

"Oh, this is, in a sense, my vacation, but I am also looking for someone, a man by the name of João Fabiano, an activist and leader."

"Why are you looking for him?" She asked, showing no recognition of his name.

"I want him to join me in Mexico City. I am thinking about organizing, protesting the police in a recent scandal. He led a manifestation here against the police, and I want to ask his advice."

"Oh, that's great," she said. "Where do you expect to find him?"

"I don't know, really. I understand he's somewhat controversial. I was hoping he might be here."

She looked at me, puzzled, and her face seemed to change, as if she were suddenly frightened, but I wasn't sure if I was misreading her face or if she might have recalled who João Fabiano was and that was what had caused it to alter so suddenly.

"I don't know him. But Silvia might. We can ask her later. What's happening in Mexico City?"

I'd already worked this part out. During our high school years, in a stretch of only a handful of years, there had been several hundred unsolved murders of women just across the border—in Juárez. Art had been deeply affected by the crimes, constantly mystified that so many girls, mostly teenagers, could be killed without any arrests, or even leads. I doubted Jucélia or anyone else would have heard about the story and, yet, if they were to look it up, they were certain to find the story in the archives, as it had been covered in a number of publications. I also thought this was the perfect bait to reel Art in, especially as he would be curious about the unearthing of a story like this from the remote past.

She nodded. "I think I vaguely remember that. Usually when as many people die, there is a war."

As I took another sip on the caipirinha, Jucélia noticed Silvia, the girl I had met earlier in the day, and called out to her and the young man who was accompanying her. As they approached, Jucélia said something to the man with her, then turned to me and said the word "Julio," then what sounded like "meshicano." I had been so excited about becoming Julio Vargas, even if ephemerally—instead of answering the question as to where I was from with New York or El Paso, I had been forced to reply with "Mexico City," which was exciting because then I could judge others' perceptions of me based on this response rather than on what I was used to—but, like a child who, pretending to sleep, squeezes his eyes tightly together rather than closing them gently, I lacked the practice of deception, and if I had been a second slower in understanding why I was being called Julio, I might have responded by correcting her. Instead, I squeezed his hands too tightly, to the young man's discontent. The conversation went on in Portuguese, and I couldn't make out many of the words. Jucélia moved her hands passionately, and Silvia shook her head in disagreement. They started yelling at each other, as the young man and I watched on. He shrugged his shoulders at me, and I nodded in solidarity.

Eventually, both of them left. Jucélia turned to me. "The manifestation is about to happen," she said. "We should go." We finished our drinks and moved briskly back through the crowd to the arcos, where the fire truck no longer was. Now, a large crowd had assembled. Jucélia leaned into me and said,

157

"Silvia knows of João Fabiano. We can go meet him after the manifestation."

He's here? I wanted other details quickly. What did he look like? Did he have a beard? If you shaved the beard off, was he Art?...But it was better not to ask any more questions. She didn't know anyway.

By ten o'clock, a thick crowd had assembled. A large podium that either had not been there before or had been detracted from by the presence of the fireman or the absence of someone standing upon it provided the crowd with a direction to face and a person at whom to direct our attention. The multitudes comprised people both young and old: women holding signs, men in suits and ties, other people in swimsuits and flip-flops and masses in the retro threads of Jucélia's clan. Shouts and cheers rose up and died from various parts of the throng, usually fading before becoming the battle cry of the entire group. The man at the podium, a raised block of wood on wheels, tapped the microphone repeatedly—um, dois, três—then conferred with those behind him and inevitably returned to the microphone to repeat the same three numbers, as the audience continued to amass, reminding me of the inadvertent organization of the Martínez twins' fights at the park, where only when capacity had been surpassed and the seats at the top of the coliseum had been filled did the event actually begin. Jucélia looked at me every several seconds, watching my response to the movement in front of my eyes, the instant camaraderie of the people, the spectacle of a Brazilian crowd.

Eventually, another man stood up to the lectern and raised his left hand into the air like an American president, then changed his sign, shaking his thumb and pinkie in the air. The crowd cheered, and the chants and shouts that had taken over various parts of the crowd now became the momentary voice of the entire mass. After a few minutes, the man raised his left hand into the air again and repeated the thumb-and-pinkie sign, lifting his shirt slightly with the other hand, and then he began talking with a high voice that I had not expected but that distinguished him.

Jucélia leaned into my ear and translated, holding her arms on the small of my back. "People, friends. We have congregated. We are here. Congratulations. We are together, but we are being torn apart. And who, and what are culpable? Globalization, consumerism, imperialism, capitalism, neo-liberalism, the proliferation and monopolization of the media, colonialism, multinational corporations, the World Trade Organization, our governments. They are *all* culpable." He looked around him, as if to suggest all of these entities skulked the night air. The crowd cheered. The man was gaunt and wore wiry glasses. His hair was short and spiky, and he looked a lot like a Syrian broadcast journalist I knew through Joaquín Guzmán. He spoke very quietly, but his high voice struck a pitch that commanded the audience's attention, and they reacted positively to him and his authority. He continued to speak about the different threats of globalization. Most of the ideas he put forth in his speech were repetitive and did not offer any solutions; he just voiced his gripes and the gripes of his organization, which was called Global Não. He spoke of Marx's vision of the ultimate socialist paradigm and how that had failed in the Soviet Union but had been adapted improperly and had imploded when the leaders of the country began to seek power and capital. He talked about the disadvantages of free trade, which were often adopted by governments under the guise of benefaction but how it only caused the poor to multiply. He talked about how debts had piled up in countries that had once been in shambles and that corporatism proved the only way to salvage their countries, their only alternative to desiccation. He spoke of avaricious politicians and countries despoiled of their beauty and put the blame squarely on everyone and everything, including us, the audience, his supporters.

Jucélia and others seemed to be quite affected by the speaker. Jucélia had more trouble translating the further the speaker discussed the details because it seemed to cut into her impassioned response. She wanted to cry out with the others in contempt for all those who were to blame. When the speech ended, others ensued, and I wasn't sure whether they were from other organizations or members of the crowd; they mounted the podium and delivered truncated versions of the same speech, which I learned in sum from Jucélia after the speeches had concluded. After two or three speakers had come and gone, I asked Jucélia if the protest was over. "No," she said. "We still have to march."

We marched at midnight from Lapa all the way through Botafogo and to Copacabana, sweating together in muggy huddles, jimmying our bodies through tight spaces, trying to keep apace of our contemporaries who, like werewolves or alcoholics, intensified in their effrontery as night comfortably straddled the earth and deprived it of light, which only cast emphasis upon those things that were lit—apartment terraces that hung over the streets and made voyeurs of those living en route, neoclassical palaces, vigorous skyscrapers, streetlights and lamps and, eventually, when we arrived there, the beach, flourishing in the racetrack lights of the streets and the opalescent light protruding from bulbs on the wall.

At Copacabana Praia, the group disassembled, Jucélia called Silvia, and they agreed to meet somewhere in the favela called Macedo Sobrinho, in the neighborhood of Humaitá. My hands clasped in hers, as they had been ever since we had been so closely compressed while between city buildings, we hopped aboard a taxi that whisked us quickly in what seemed to be the direction whence we had come. After paying the driver, I realized we had come upon Rio's underbelly, or *one* of its underbellies, a reality far from the one under the lights by the beach—"Stay close," Jucélia said, probably sensing my apprehension as we walked through several alleyways and eventually made it into what seemed, on the outside, like a shanty, similar to those in the colonias of Juárez. The parallels were inescapable: having slipped through a side door from the luscious sand and bodies on the beach (or the first-world skyscrapers of El Paso), we had arrived into the middle of the slums, miniature makeshift cities identical the world over: with street kids and rogues wandering the unpoliced streets with concealed knives and weapons—men with the eyes of raccoons, accustomed to a different luminosity, lurking in the sidestreets for their prey. Suddenly inside, it was as if we'd tunneled into another, inconceivable unknown. The inside of the makeshift building, whose roof was made of tarp and surrounded on all sides by machinery, was elaborate and posh, replete with leather couches and televisions tuned to international news broadcasts. On its walls were papers tacked with graphs and charts and lists and other written things that I could only vaguely decipher. I had no idea what this place was, but my observations were stopped short as soon as three or four men turned from the computers they were facing and eyed us distrustfully as Jucélia spoke to them. Following us by no more than three or four minutes were Silvia and her friend. Eventually, from another room emerged the man who had been a speaker earlier in the day. He looked different up close. From a distance, his spiky hair and smart dress had given him the appearance of trimness but, close up, one could see alarming bags under his bloodshot eyes. Even so, his smile and affability immediately made him seem an ally.

"So, you are the Mexican professor," he said. "Here on holiday," he added, in the perfect accent of an Englishman.

"Yes," I said. "To whom do I owe the pleasure?" I asked, seemingly astounding him equally with my English fluency.

As it turned out, Ilnur was a Turkish man who had spent more than a decade in London and had been in Brazil for nearly twenty years and was a close friend of João Fabiano during the police manifestations a few years before. He described João Fabiano with such delight and in an almost biographical way that I almost felt as if he were merely an introducer and that João Fabiano would soon appear from another room, spotlights upon him, as a television audience clapped enthusiastically. But João Fabiano did not appear. In fact, when Ilnur got to the heart of the story, he revealed that João Fabiano had, just after that protest several years before, disappeared, leaving neither note nor forwarding address. He had emerged from nowhere, without a background or a trace of history, with a wealth of experience and charisma. He spoke Portuguese with the accent of a paulistano, someone from São Paulo. Although Ilnur was full of reverence for the disappeared activist, he said he had never felt more deceived. "It's not like João abandoned us with loot under his arms or traded away any secrets. It's just sort of peculiar that he would leave us like that, especially when most of our plans had to be discarded, many of which we'd worked for months to realize."

I had counted on João Fabiano's being Art so much that I was unprepared for the conversation that followed. Jucélia had told Silvia, who had in turn told Ilnur that the reason I had come to speak to João Fabiano was because I was hoping to assemble some sort of all-American group of activists and protestors for an important, underground manifestation in Mexico, and now he wanted to find out what our plans were. My spot ingenuity should have been somewhat embarrassing. I dwelled on the words "getting people together" and "marching" and described essentially the same situation as I had just observed in Rio, but I was unable to go into too much depth about disobliging police or government officials in Mexico in the situation of the murdered women. When he asked me what the death toll was at, I used vague vocabulary such as "a lot," "many," "for the most part," "officials," "several," "tons," "sometimes," "every now and then" and "some number" and hoped he would take me for a man of sentiment rather than detail, and I spoke passionately about a need for the world to take note of such tragedies, where there were as many deaths as in entire wars, while the wars get all the attention.

To my surprise, he said he was very interested in helping the cause, and he lamented the fact that João Fabiano would not be involved, for João had a great affection for the Mexican people and had even been to Mexico several times, a detail that in conjunction with the correspondence of Art's trip to visit Father Rahm and the other priest's spotting him aboard the bus, all seemed to me to be compelling evidence in support of Art's reinvention as João Fabiano. Still, I wondered why. Why, if João Fabiano had become a hero to the people of Rio de Janeiro during a short period of time, had he bothered to change his name and invent an entire persona? Certainly, it was Art's profession to convert blank pieces of paper into brilliant works of art, to routinely clean the slate and begin afresh, but why do this with his identity and body?

I told Ilnur that I would get in touch with him as soon as my preparations were finished. "When?" He asked. "It may take a few months, but I'll send for you," I heard myself say. When our conversation had ended, Ilnur escorted Jucélia and me from the lavish headquarters, then watched us leave without moving from the entrance, as the car turned the corner and moved through the favela and back onto the streets leading to Copacabana.

I awoke the next morning to the sound of knocking at my door. It was Robert. "The sky is clear, and I'm going to see Christ," he said. "Do you want to come?"

As I had not yet recovered my senses (nor yet re-learned how to speak), I asked Robert if he would mind checking back in fifteen minutes or so when I was more capable of issuing forth complete sentences.

"Great," he said, "Actually I was hoping to go at sundown or thereabouts." I told him I would drop by his room around four, as he requested, and closed the door.

Lying back down on my bed, I rubbed my temples for several moments before sitting back up and going through my notes.

What next? *Where to?* There was really only one place to go. All roads led east. *A thousand roads lead men forever to Rome.*

163

But *not* all the way to Rome, in Art's case?

Or maybe *so*?

I called New York and used some of my magazine connections to locate Ulick Martin, the fight promoter in Dublin who had bankrolled Art's Neoismo collection, and I eventually got ahold of a phone number. The deeper, double ring tone seemed out of time rather than out of place. He answered on the third ring with a frank, "Hallo. Ulick here," and in a short, perfunctory conversation I worked it out to visit him at his vacation home in Teddington, a borough of London, where he was on holiday with his family.

I called the airlines and, using some connections I had through the magazines, who are always privy to great discounts, I changed my flight so that I could fly to London and then back to New York in two weeks, which would give me the chance to travel through Europe and interview some of the people who had been associated with Art during his years there, where he had begun and spent the better part of his artistic career.

I had a late breakfast with Jucélia and later met with Robert at four. We took a bus that dropped us off on the backside of the mountain where we boarded a train that sat for half an hour as if immobile and then lurched forward just as Robert told me he was going to see if there were any complications. The train cut a path between the trees going up the mountain, a harsh contrast to the barren desert mountains of El Paso and, when we had finally reached the top, we detrained, ascended some number of stairs and were soon face to face with Christ, his hands outspread as if he were about to skydive from the top of the mountain, his feet immobilized in a square base, pockets of discoloration in the soapstone. After looking down below at Rio de Janeiro and then watching the experts explain to visitors what lay below, I turned back toward Christ, this time looking at his eyes, which were without lens or pupil, which made him seem spacey and vacant, blind. I wondered what Rio would be like—or the whole of

Brazil—without statues atop every mountain and hill. Would Catholicism still be the religion of choice? Would Father Rahm be the celebrity that he was? Robert returned from wherever he had been, approaching me with the excitement reserved for children and lunatics. "It's amazing, isn't it?" He said, referring to the statue. I nodded. When he again turned toward the statue, I watched his excitement deflate. "What happened to his eyes?" he asked, his blond curls shifting as one as he looked from the statue to me. "What have they done with them?"

baggage reclaim

During the several times I had traveled to Great Britain, I was always struck, as soon as I spotted the baggage reclaim signs, by how differently two groups of people who speak the same language can view things. In the United States, *new* things are what is valued—new houses, new movie theater complexes, new leases on life, the New Deal, New Age, even New England, New York, New Mexico, New Hampshire, New Orleans—the regions, states and cities of the *New* World. The English see no reason to bulldoze a perfectly nice, hundred-year-old house, cars stay with people for decades, people shine their shoes rather than constantly buying new pairs, York and Hampshire still look about the same as they did a century ago, and suitcases and bags are meant to be preserved over time rather than replaced, so, instead of claiming your bags, you are actually always *re*-claiming them. In the United States, people

166

use red ribbons and nametags not only as first lines of defense against theft but also because they are worried they might forget what their luggage looks like.

After settling into my hotel in South Ken, I found the Earl's Court District Line tube stop and, following Ulick Martin's directions, took it to the end of the line, Richmond, where I caught a bus that whipped me quickly across the Richmond Bridge, down through the anterior part of Twickenham's high street and into the borough of Teddington. I had only to disembark from the bus and walk several blocks in order to find Ulick Martin's house, implanted on the Thames River several blocks from Teddington Lock.

The cars parked along the street were strange and miniature, and their license plates looked different. What is jarring to me about other countries is most often not the things that I have never seen before at home but those things that are familiar to me but slightly different elsewhere, such as street signs, airports, spellings with slight deviations from American English, dial tones, license plates—all of which we expect to find a certain way, as when we look at a person's picture in the newspaper or see them on television and later meet them in person and are surprised by the mutual resemblance and lack of resemblance at once.

I knocked upon the bus-red door, just below the archaic script numbers that denoted the address, and within fifteen seconds Ulick Martin himself cheerfully answered the door and gave me a hug with two pats on the back, in the Mexican style. His moustache and sideburns were composed of the same curly hairs. He had long hair and no neck and a slight squint to his eyes. He looked like a pirate without the costume. Even his "Hallo, mate" seemed less like a British salute as it did a slightly benumbed version of "Hallo, matey." He welcomed me into his house, took my coat, offered me a cup of tea or glass of beer. I accepted the tea.

"Shame, isn't it," he said, as soon as we formally sat down in the living room, a Victorian fireplace churning out heat

from the center of the room, which, with its burgundy
Victorian parlor sofas and Queen Anne side chairs, would
have looked like a showroom of the nineteenth century were
it not for the infinite DVD titles stacked haphazardly on top
of a bookcase, several game cartridges and a video game unit
in the corner on a smallish period end table and an unpacked
flatscreen television lying inside its box on the floor in the
corner. It looked as if the twenty-first century had suddenly
moved into the nineteenth overnight, with little regard for the
century between or the year-by-year process of obsolescence.
I was glad also to see the bookcase was overflowing with
books, and I wanted to get a closer look because the presence
of a bookcase often momentarily trumped all purposes I had
for existing in the space of a room, but I was deterred from
doing so when he continued his thought.

"Mind you, I have my suspicions that he hasn't exactly left
us, that inconsiderate twat."

"You think he might still be alive?"

"So do you. Otherwise, you wouldn't be here, right?"

"Right," I said, "I agree."

"So where shall I begin?"

"Can we talk about how you met him?—Do you mind if I
record this?" He shook his head. "So…when did you meet
Art?"

"Ah…it was not intentional, you know. Arturo was the
guest of Lord Brandenburg at a dinner party my wife and I
had gone to, begrudgingly, in London, in Holborn, an affair
with a number of artists—musicians, actors, painters—the
actor Stanley Sheen was there, as was Peter Rae and Jenny
Neville. My wife, who is an actress, and I were showing our
faces, hoping to sort of go in and slip out the exit while no
one was looking. I was bored, mentally sorting through some
of the cheese and cracker hors d'œuvres to decide which I
wanted when Arturo trotted over to where I was and, sans
deliberation, took some of the grapes and fruit on a toothpick
and inhaled them. He looked out of sorts to be at the

party—he was well-dressed, of course, but he didn't look like he was happy to be there. When I asked him what he did, he said he was a painter. 'What kind of painter?' I asked—he said he was probably the worst person to ask about that. 'What do they look like?' I asked, and he said, 'They look an awful lot like paintings.' I quickly learned that he was also there begrudgingly. He told me frankly that he was hoping to get some money for an exhibit out of Lord Brandenburg, who I knew to be, despite his reputation for his exquisite taste—don't quote me on this—as stingy as a packet of crisps. We got on well from the start, especially as soon as I learned that he was as two-faced as I am for, though I promote fights and other sports, I'm also devoted to charities, particularly Comic Relief and Sport Relief, both with the BBC. Although Arturo was a prodigious painter, his passion was centred elsewhere, in his social campaigns. I guess the best example of those is 'Know Your Baker.' "

"Excuse me?" I said, stunned, for more than in the art gallery in Brazil that bore the trademark of Arturo in its colors, there was something in hearing these three words in an atmosphere so foreign and produced by a man so different and seemingly removed from Art—an effect similar to that of street signs or the British license plates—that brought me instantly nearer to Art, nearer to the way I knew him then, as a young man, full of dreams but not having accomplished any of them yet. The outdoor cafeteria tables, the food fights, the swindlers who said they would give ten dollars to anyone who could eat two pieces of bread in thirty seconds without water, the gangs of kids sitting together by sport or club, Coach Escobedo's lack of success in discovering who was throwing tortillas (we all were), the bearded lunchladies, the pedantic administrators, the theories Art would spout out when others were talking about sports or lunch, the feeling of displacement those three words had wreaked upon me—all of this reclaimed me like a hand reaching back through the tunnels of the past, eager to identify me as baggage.

"Know Your Baker," he repeated. "That was his credo, his existence, his solution."

"What does it mean?" I asked, exasperated, fearing that he too might point out that I was from the Westside.

"Do you know your baker?"

"*My* baker?" I said, frustrated.

"Literally. The person who supplies you with bread."

"No, I don't know him…or her."

"Know your baker," he said, and laughed. "Arturo used to take the piss out of people who didn't know what it meant from the start by saying that it was misspelled, that it should have been 'know your maker.' But it *could* have been 'know your maker.' It could have just as easily been so," he paused, reflectively, then noticed my presence, my irritation that this was a joke I was on the butt side of and continued, "Know your baker, know your cobbler, know your barber. Know your butcher, your carpenter and farmer. Know your mother, sister, brother, father. Form relationships with the people around you. Keep things small and simple. Cast your pound—or dollar—votes on things created by the people you know. We've begun, here in London as well, to create large distances between people and the things that they buy. The superstores have replaced bakeries. The so-called global village has replaced the village. Quality. Responsibility. Connections. Everything else is sacrificed. Things are made as cheaply as possible and made to go out of style as soon as its warranty has expired. If it's food, there's a good chance it has been made heavier with animal waste, grown by the use of pesticides, the natural taste spoiled by artificial flavours. They can make a dirty sock taste good, but why do that when they can make something that looks like a cake taste like a cake. If it's a car, they'll make it run like a car, speed down the motorway like a car, but when it crashes, you'll find out what it's made of. Customer service is a phone number rather than a conversation. Your phone call will be forwarded to India, Sri Lanka or the Philippines, where underpaid 'personnel' who talk just like computers coach you on a product created in another part of the world by different people, and you will be at their mercy because it's loads easier to hang up on people than it is to push them out your front door and lie to their faces. The new world order supports our lifestyles. It's meant to be good for our wallets. And it is. At first it is. But you know what happens when large companies gain monopolistic status? They control the government, the politicians, the power. Theirs is the earth and everything in it, and which is more—which is more!—our children will grow up powerless and without recourse. They won't have any choices. They will struggle—as do so many people all over the world—to put anything more than milk, potatoes and loaves of bread on their tables. They won't be able to go anywhere without ID cards—not something that will be required by the government but by the shops, the newsagents, the superstores. These days, we're quite willing to do that sort of thing if we can get a discount, aren't we? We'll sign our name and allow it to exist in some computer network, we'll hand over all our numbers and middle names and our mum's maiden name to seventeen-year-olds in their A-levels or high school who won't give a shite where the beets are or where they came from, and they'll do price checks on computer scanners that resemble what the police use to catch you for speeding—all to save you two quid and a walk around the block. It's the society of torpor, the day of the hack. Keep profits in the black and give fuck all about everything else. You live in Brooklyn? [I nodded.] You can still know your baker in Brooklyn."

I thought about justifying not knowing my baker by the lack of a proper bakery in my area, but he continued before I could interrupt.

"By the time Arturo had arrived in London, he was already known as a sort of prodigy in the art world," he said. Ulick Martin seemed to have settled down by now and was soon speaking with less fervor. "You've seen his earlier work, so you know that it was his unabashed use of colours and his representation of personalities and events of his youth, the depictions of your hybrid culture on the river, and the number of paintings he produced in such a short time—what was it, maybe five hundred at Grenoble alone?—that validated his genius, and with the number of awards that he won there and abroad in such a short amount of time, he earned his right to be identified as the art world's so-called 'next Picasso.' Nevertheless, when we look at the work of Matisse, Renoir, Klimt, Vermeer or any of the greats, we can see their genius in their early work, but this work is almost never what we come to know as the quintessential Matisse or Vermeer. If you consider Arturo's career as having lasted fifteen years, because he was painting quality pieces at twenty, it was around the time he was 26, I think, that he really began to flourish, and that was when he was here in London, when he struck upon this new objective, and all of the precursory work representing the border and his portraits made it possible for him to give the Know Your Baker paintings their ardour. Do you know what I mean?"

I nodded, then asked him which of his paintings began the Know Your Baker series.

"The first one…to think back…must have been a collection of a dozen or so paintings he'd done in the first couple months while in London. You'd get the idea, if you were to see them, and I don't know where they are—I think most of them have been sold to individuals—you'd get the idea very quickly that these paintings had a different agenda than those he painted in France, and in Mao, Ireland, where a friend of mine has a cottage, where he sodded off from the rest of the world and painted for six months without interruption. The technical skill was still the same, so very much his style because his signature—his voice—has always been present in his work, but what he began painting in Know Your Baker withdrew from portraiture and landscape to more concept-driven work. One of the paintings, for instance, which is called "Objectividad—El Presente" shows several individuals sitting in a coffeeshop in Soho—where they proliferate—eating cakes, sipping coffee and reading newspapers. It is a large canvas, and in it about four or five people hold newspapers in different languages so that you can see the title of the paper, but in place of the actual name of the paper, he put the name of the owner of the paper along with *Times* or *Daily Mail* instead of the name of the city. In an almost identical painting, called "Objectividad—El Pasado" the same people drinking coffee and holding newspapers are in the same places, except they are all wearing the vibrant colours consistent with the sixties and seventies and only one of the titles bear the name of the news empire that owns the paper. In the third of the three paintings, called "Objectividad—El Futuro," the people are in the same places and wearing the toneless and drab clothing of the future, and all of the newspapers are named after the same man while still bearing the same titles—*Daily Mail*, *Times*, *El País*, *El Diario*. This was one of the paintings he showed me later, the week after I had met him at Lord Brandenburg's flat. From his flat, which was on Baker Street—you know London a bit, I suppose [I nodded]—we proceeded directly to lunch and he told me about Know Your Baker, and then I told him I would pay all of the costs of his materials and his room and board in Central London, as I have a large, three-room flat in the city proper that I let from time to time, for the next year so long as he continued to paint in this vein and if twenty per cent of the takings of his work could be held for charities such as Comic Relief."

Ulick Martin continued to talk about his first experiences with Art, the logistics of their arrangement, the disarray of the flat in Central London he had let him, and then the work that Art produced there, including the Neoismo painting, the McDonalds storefronts, both of which now seemed like prime examples of the Know Your Baker collection. During the year, Art's profits from selling his paintings and staging exhibitions had generated him more than enough to hand

Ulick Martin a sizeable contribution that he found ways to disperse among the charities with which he was involved. What he found most interesting, however, was not this generation of profits or the success of Art's work, but the new cult following Art had won with this new "thematic" collection, and how Art embraced these people, who often befriended him at galleries or sent letters by post, people who had reacted to the statements Art was making through his paintings. According to Ulick Martin, Art had not drawn boundaries around his person and was very accessible, perhaps too accessible if you considered the types of people who would clamor for his attention. "Women, especially," Ulick said, looking up toward the ceiling and causing me to follow suit, quickly realizing it needed paint. "Arturo was often surrounded by women, some of the most beautiful and charming women in London and then some who seemed quite unspectacular. I don't know where they met, but they followed him around like dogs on leashes, and they only ever seemed to show up when he was leaving a party or an event. And when I asked him about them, he was always so smug. He always found a way to divert my questions or ride out the silence past the statute of limitations in which the question was answerable with a deep stare or cocky smile, so I never learned their surnames or who they were. It almost seemed as if it were the one thing he was proud of or maybe he thought the whole game frivolous. I don't know."

Art would meet with his fans in coffeeshops and bars and discuss his visions, which Ulick said seemed ridiculous—the messages were all in the work, and there was something inherent in the beauty of art that precluded and forbade explanation, which was something that would limit the free range of interpretation. I understood his point. I could never explain what I had written and often felt that when I had spoken about my writing I was actually deterring people from having a look, and I was happy that I did not have to promote my collection of essays because I was sure sales would have been much lower than already they had been.

"Another thing about Arturo," he said, pausing, granting the approaching detail an attention, a squint of the eyes, that made it seem as if he could literally see what he was about to describe. "When I would meet him to go to the West End or encounter him on his walks through the city, I could always determine the emotional nature of the painting by intuiting his emotional nature when I saw him. He was very difficult to talk to when he was in the middle of painting something but, when he was between paintings, he always seemed to be the carefree person I had met at Lord Brandenburg's. It was a very curious thing, this metamorphosis, but fair play to him. No one can create a uniform list of quirks that all artists share—penchants, proclivities, pet peeves, favourite foods, favourite positions, times of day in which they best work and that sort of thing—it is much more apt to say that art wrests from each artist's life something different, and the terms the art itself draws for them is what they should accept as their lot rather than seeking out taboos and superstitions to replicate an effect. That's just feeble."

I continued to ask him questions that would lead him to the same answers—because I was excited that he *had* the answers—and quite delightfully, sparing me these same responses, Ulick Martin was always able to invent ways to introduce new material while still answering my questions. The more he spoke about the Know Your Baker philosophy, the more he kept coming back to the importance of relationships, and I realized that Know Your Baker extended far beyond anti-consumerism and globalization and was more a philosophy of human kinship and social proximity. According to Ulick Martin, Art had always had a great disdain for war, an aversion that far exceeded that of those who are opposed to war and violence but see how it can be necessary—and the more Ulick Martin spoke about this aversion, the more I began to remember Art's outspoken anti-war stance during our high school days. I suddenly remembered him having once come up with the idea that if two soldiers, one from one country and one from another were put into a room for an hour and, if language were no barrier, were told that for the next hour they must talk openly about their families, their lovers and friends, the things they most feared and the things about which they most cared, when they left the room they—many who just five years before were just thirteen-year-olds—would be far less apt to murder one another. He'd likened it to Christmas Day in 1914, when British and German soldiers, after spending hours in the field collecting their dead, exchanged words and decided to play football instead of resuming the battle. According to Ulick, Art had said that there should be a law decreeing that, as a prerequisite to declaring war, leaders of country should have to risk death to themselves—either by having to fight a duel with the leader of the other country or to pass a kidney stone specially inserted in them at the United Nations.

"I never understood that one. You can't assassinate the leader of a foreign country, when usually they're the only bastard worth assassinating," Ulick Martin commented, his eyes bulging out of his head, his mouth splitting in laughter. "But it's true that when people know one another, they're less likely to steal from the other, more likely to benefit from knowing each other and, if we build strong relationships into all the things we do, we'll live much more fulfilling lives and feel less alone. Art never had a problem with globalization itself…but rather the problems *caused by* globalization."

We spoke for another thirty or forty minutes about Art and, as darkness began to slowly enshroud the house, I turned off the tape recorder and thanked him for his time.

"For my time?" he said.

"For the trouble."

"You're going to leave?" he asked. "Stay for dinner. Why would you want to leave now? You just got here."

He offered me a beer from a keg of Guinness on tap in his cellar, and I accepted, and we clinked glasses, toasting Arturo. His wife—a hybrid of Northern Irish and Spanish, which made possible such phrases as "ven acá, lad," arrived about an hour later, their two teenage sons in tow, and Ulick Martin left me in his wife's company as he went off to grill steaks and bake potatoes. The boys joined us and, as soon as I finished a beer, one of the boys or Ulick brought me another. The food was excellent, and Ulick Martin and his wife shared stories about the many times they had dined with Arturo—the approbation shared by the boys, who looked forward to evenings with him; Art's affinity for English rock music, which he would occasionally listen to while painting; his "frightfully British table manners" that—according to Ulick—Art had inherited from his mother. I took another drink, and we discussed such things as the Six Nations rugby championship, played in nearby Twickenham; Teddington Studios, at the corner of the road, where many major situation comedies are filmed. I looked at my watch to figure out what time it was, but both hands were frozen together, facing nine o'clock. My body wobbled against the floor, but I was no longer concerned about others noticing how often I went to the bathroom. When I returned from the toilet one time, I found them all in the living room, and I sat between Ulick Martin and his wife, my arms around them and told them how wonderful they were, that this was the beginning of a lifelong friendship and I would never forget this evening.

"Know Your Fight Promoter," Ulick Martin said, his moustache twittering at the corners like a pinwheel, his laughter squeezing from the sides of his mouth like a kazoo. The boys positioned themselves dreadfully close to the fireplace and, as the night continued on, Ulick Martin's wife ornamented her sentences with more and more Spanish vulgarities in an Irish accent. At one point in the night, I began telling jokes and, when I ended one, the boys always supplicated me for another. "Oh come on," "Carry on;" "Go on," they would say. The beers were cool, and I did not see Ulick return to the cellar each time to refill them, nor did I know how long it took me to drink one before the next arrived. The room swirled, and I felt as if all of these characters gyrating on the proscenium of my mind were the product of imagination rather than human reproduction. One of the boys, who were both also drinking, turned to me and asked if I was all right. "Pst," I said. "Do you want to tell me a secret, or are you trying to say 'pissed'?" he asked. "No, I'm just slurring," I said. "Yes, pissed. That's what I meant." Drunk and without the faculty of mind to refuse another drink or decide to leave or to stay, I eventually watched the gesture emerge from my lips and saw myself move from the table, thank the Martins for their hospitality, emerge into the quiet and stumble home.

la detective

Listen to the saturnine moan of the mountain. Escucha, and let it soothe you. She leads a life of omniscience but cannot react, for she, like us, feels immobile and powerless, enthralled, and so she grows agave, cacti and yucca to ward off people and other surface nuisances. Listen to the desert and its secrets, whirring like the chants of some Eastern religion in one ceaseless monotone, drowning out the sounds of the cars that pass every day, the synergic beat of the city nearby, los gritos sin ecos. I have often wandered from the city to the mountain and desert to find a kindred soul in the symphonic bliss of the world beyond my realm. But I cannot stay. The city and its blaring trumpets, its delicately pinched guitars strings, its honking cars, its famous itinerant musicians who play the same old songs of star-crossed lovers under the sidereal skies bid me return, for I am a Juareña, frustrada and full of dreams, strong and indefatigable, and I must die someday but not before I have witnessed a change in tide, a calmer, softer lapping of waves upon this shore of gold. I am a listener—that is my job—and it takes me to where girls and women are, so I spend my hours in the maquilas, listening to the machines and their clangorous palpitations, the commotion of scooting and movement, rusty chains and scuttling shackles. But the bell that symbolizes the hour—that is a song they long for. It is not a song, but it is as sweet as one. Listen to me. Listen to me. We are dying in the night. We are dying in the night. What does it take to listen, to stop talking and truly open your ears? All you have to do is turn your head slightly, and I will hold the seashell of my voice to your ear, and in it you will hear the sounds of the collected voices of so many girls, and their voices are beautiful. What is more sacred than the voices of children? Close your eyes. Listen closely. Listen for clues. Listen to me. Listen. Listen…

The brush whisked briskly against the signpost, the sound of sweeping the street or brushing one's teeth, leaving upon it a pink color that rose from the base upward and furthered their campaign into Jardines Campestre, Del Valle and Campestre San Marcos, neighborhoods looming near the centro. Laura Delgado went on to the next signpost, allowing the paint to dry before she and Pablo, her taciturn eighteen-year-old son, would return to paint black crosses into the pink, the new, but now-universal symbol of las desaparecidas, that made black and pink as symbolic as the two-tone colors of the national fútbol team. Sand flecked into the paint, the wind whistled, the dust drew up into small clouds that swept across the atmosphere like swarms of bees. "When we finish these…" she said, not finishing her sentence, but communicating enough. Pablo nodded, swabbed several vertical strokes upon the signpost, then stared impassively into the bucket for a moment before dipping his brush into it again, thickening the glob and bearing down afresh onto the signpost.

180

A bus returned them to their own neighborhood, Felipe Ángeles, where Laura's husband, Armando, awaited them, fresh from the repair shop, clothed in dirt and grease he did not remember, drinking Tecate and combing his moustache with his index finger and thumb. "¿Cómo te fue? He asked, when she entered.

"Good," Laura said. "All painted. It was a nice day to be outside, too."

Armando slumped in a fold-up chair looking at cartoons in a copy of *El Diario* that he had taken from the bus. Laura, boiling black beans in a pot, listened to his unmitigated laughter, which softened as he read further, eventually fading as he fell asleep and became replaced by snoring, which began softly and then turned into loud snorts that sounded like he was dying. The sand blew against the walls of their abode, and night began to settle, but the sand continued to assail against their walls, always regrouping and trying again moments later. As the darker hues crept up on las colonias, Laura Delgado, inside, lit the cylindrical church candles, each bearing the figure of a different saint or religious figure on their sides, then secured the black cloth that draped from the top of the shrine in the corner of the room to the table on which it rest and on which were affixed pictures of Verónica and her parents—her mother resplendent in her eternal smile, her father's stern expression, the only photo of him in existence, which captured an aspect of him that no one had ever seen in life, causing him to look even more foreign immured in the deep matte of the black-and-white photo. An entire family disappearing nearly overnight. Y la pobrecita Verónica. She'd called a day too late. A day earlier and she would have been alive. She hadn't meant to let the lesson go on for so long—she'd wanted to deter her, so she'd pronounced loudly her judgment: "Prostitution is worse than death." She remembered it. She had said it. She had chosen to abide by it. But, no, it wasn't. Death was much worse.

The wicks of the candles floated in puddles of wax, and they swayed from side to side, all in the same direction, as Laura knelt in front of them. Yes, an entire family disappearing almost overnight, and Verónica and her mother both killed by villains who lurked in the shadows. Verónica's murderer was faceless, nameless, came from out of nowhere, did his or her work in the darkness, and left behind a body that no longer drew breath, an indurate vessel it seemed no life had ever been fit to occupy. As Laura peered into the photograph of Verónica, a photograph she had looked at hundreds of times in the months after Vero had left the house, she still tried to find something in her face, any clue that would reveal to her that Vero indeed had been capable of selling her body to men. It was unnecessary, really, she knew, because Verónica had long since departed, but she still felt there must be something of one's moral character visible in the face, but she still couldn't find it—something in her face that suggested a malevolence of spirit, that would allow Laura to forgive herself her guilt at having sent the girl away. All she saw was innocence, an absence of lines in her face, stained diapers, first steps, childish giggles, First Communion in Coatzacoalcos, then the trip—the girl leaning her head onto the window of the train, her head shaking with the rumble, completely asleep.

And then it came to her, finally, after more than six years. There would never be anything there in the photograph, nothing in the face, nothing that served as an augury or hint of what it was in a person's capacity to do. The reason she couldn't find it was that it didn't exist. *Anyone* could sell herself. It is life, one's environment and means and not a preexisting moral condition that causes people to do things that compromise themselves and their bodies. And now Laura felt even more terrible, incapable at the time of recognizing the most basic of things—that the earth was cruel, and—many times—the best one can do is to cut his or her losses, to become *part* of the evil of the world in order to rise from it—to turn into the perpetual skid that cut into one's path. If Verónica had not begun to sleep with men for money, she would have later lived the life of Laura Delgado, a life that existed in exiguity, a tarpaper and aluminum-foiled life in a city of trash and a lifetime penance of poverty.

The sirens seemed to take on a different tone in the night, as if they, too, knew the night was more serious, when traffic accidents were more common, diseases could kill, drugs were sold not only in the alleyways but in the major thoroughfares, bodies were rented and, even though the girls were the ones who were dying, Laura wanted Pablo home, in the safe bosom of an abode in shambles.

The candlewicks swayed, casting oblique moving shadows of the photographs upon the black construction paper, as Laura moved from her knees to her feet and then returned to the beans. She added onion, queso fresco and jalapeños in rajas to a frying pan and turned on the gas. The heat browned the cheese and softened the chile. The onions crackled.

Eventually, Pablo returned home, and Armando woke up, but neither knew about the time Laura spent in the darkness with her knees on the ground and her head buried in her private hell. Dinner was served; in the corner of the room, the candles burned.

The priest's hair had whitened completely in the four quick years she had known him, she told Leti, as soon as she noticed him down below on the first floor of the mercado that they overhung from their perch on the third floor. "I guess this is how we notice that time passes," Esme said, as they looked. "¿If things didn't grow old—if the trees didn't grow and the children didn't become men and women—do you think we would have a concept of time?" she asked.

Leti smiled. "I'm anxious to meet him, even though I can't stay. You know, I don't think I've ever met a priest outside of a church or a cemetery."

Eventually the priest—his now-whitened hair accentuating his gray eyes, his purposeful stride, the glow of his silver years transfiguring his middle-aged grump into an evening charm—arrived at the top of the stairs near where the women were eating and gallantly strode across the floor with the poise of a handsome suitor come to collect his dowry.

After an impulsive speech the priest had made at the graduation of one of the city's Catholic high schools in place of a prayer, Padre Osvaldo had almost never been requested for funerals and weddings and other ceremonies, which had always been his forte and one of his greatest pleasures, but now, in the past year or so, there was hardly a day that he wasn't booked for an event in Juárez, and having this afternoon free with which to visit Esmeralda and finally meet Leti was a rare pleasure and he envisioned spending the entire day with them.

"You are my two best friends," Esme said, introducing them, considering how strange life was that a twenty-four-year-old could have as her best friends a sixty-four-year-old priest and a thirty-seven-year-old accountant. "Have a seat, Padre," she said, and he pulled out a chair and joined them. "Gracias, Detective," he said.

For the few minutes that Leti could stay before returning home to her children and the new baby—whom he was scheduled to baptize—Padre Osvaldo entertained them with stories about baptisms: parents more squeamish than their children, a six-year-old who pretended to be the priest by walking up to the altar, putting his hand on the newborn and saying "I baptize you in the name of the Father, Son and Holy Spirit," tardy padrinos (godfathers and godmothers) some who were replaced before fulfilling the first duty of their new post, babies peeing, mothers fainting, fathers belching… "Pardon me," Osvaldo said. "I didn't meant to be so crass." Esmeralda laughed, and Leti made mental notes about what to prevent from happening. Padre Osvaldo asked himself, Was it true? Was he really a happier person around Esme? Was it true for her, too?

It began when Esmeralda came to him one day with a Bible she had read twice. After the first time she read it, she decided to read it through again, and this time to make marks, ask questions, underline the things she didn't understand and make a list of things from one section that seemed to contradict another. The first thing Osvaldo told her was that she had accomplished something that even some priests couldn't say they have done. With a book as lengthy as the Bible, one could claim to be expert after a single read-through, but Esme had read it twice. *¡Jesús!* But Esmeralda wasn't impressed with herself. "¿Órale, padre, but can you explain to me what I got wrong?" she asked. "What I don't understand." And so they began to meet—every Saturday in the beginning, and, when Osvaldo's calendar began to fill again, they met on Thursday evenings at the cathedral. Osvaldo felt like he was back in the novitiate, defending and challenging semantic doubts, erecting and then bulldozing theological arguments, using epikeia to justify deviations, mystical theology to interpret. "¿Pero por qué?" seemed to be Esmeralda's favorite question, as soon as she grew comfortable with him and knew he was likely to say, "No sé. Let's look it up" or "We don't really have answers, Detective. Just questions." She asked more questions than a detective investigating a homicide, he said. When she showed up at the cathedral, he would say, "Let's see what questions La Detective has for us today" or "It wasn't me. I am only the confessor."

In the meantime, Esmeralda had been attending the University of Juárez, taking night and weekend courses in politics and law. She would spend the day working—she now commanded the (still-paltry) salary of a full-time employee and lived with a roommate—then go immediately to class three nights a week and fall into bed around two in the morning. After a while, however, and somewhat contingent on what she had learned with the padre, the classes grew

185

easier, more bearable, though still challenging. She discovered the strange phenomenon wherein all her courses, including her study of the Bible, affected one another. Everything seemed relevant—her study of psychology and irrationality would lend itself to her understanding of a character in a Carlos Fuentes novel, which would, in turn, in Fuentes' character's obsession with Rousseau, lead to the study of philosophy and the principle that all people are inherently good, which seemed to hark back to Judeo-Christian beliefs and la Biblia. While on the bus, several times she missed her stop, when previously her body had always mechanically risen at the appropriate moment; once, she had even caught herself walking past the street she turned onto to go to work, so otherworldly were her thoughts. In time, her Thursday evenings with Padre Osvaldo transformed, and instead of strictly talking about the Bible and Catholicism, they eventually began to talk about all of life. Padre Osvaldo encouraged her to reconsider her contempt for men and instead to create adjectives by which to classify them in order to leave room for the possibility that there was good in men, too. "We're not all villains and rapists. Rousseau would probably say that our environments have corrupted many of us savages." "I'm not ready, Padre," she said. "I don't know if I ever will be." And she began to teach him about law, about politics—subjects he had been interested in since even before the murders began. When she received her acceptance letter for law school, she said, "Padre, we're going to law school," and he appreciated this, even though she would have less time, because he understood this to be a gesture of love. Standing up from her chair and dropping several ten-peso coins onto the table, Leti protested both Padre Osvaldo and Esme's implorations that she stay. "No, the kids. We must always be there for our children, so they can teach us about life." After she left, Padre Osvaldo turned to the waiter who had been bringing them agua de papaya, asked for refills and then turned to Esme and said, "She's a lovely woman. I approve."

Esme laughed. "You should see the things she's entrusted with at work. She handled a multi-million-peso transaction this past week."

Esme talked for a while about Leti the way friends sometimes do—predicting her success, her future promotions with the company, what was to come for her three children, all adolescents and teenagers: "Dulce—she's seventeen—she wants to be a lawyer, too," Esme said. "Sometimes she quizzes me on the cases I have to learn for that pre-law class."

And then he asked her, "¿What new cases did you learn about this week?"

There were many, so Esmeralda always had to pick the ones she thought would interest Osvaldo the most. So she told him about how several years before the Supreme Court of Justice in Mexico City had upheld the Robles Law, which permitted abortion in cases where women have been raped, risked danger to their lives, had a fetal defect or an unwanted artificial insemination.

"The significance of the case is that this was practiced for a short time in Mexico City, but now it is precedent all over the Republic. Women were dying when they could have lived. They were having unwanted babies. One girl I knew when I was fourteen killed herself because she didn't want a baby. She was only fifteen, her only source of income was men, and she couldn't get an abortion without paying five thousand pesos to some back-alley bruja. ¿Qué podría hacer? The law is waking up and slowly realizing what life is like out here."

"And, sadly, the church is even slower," Osvaldo said. "In Rome, they're still trying to decide whether women should be allowed to be priests. Of all the professions of the world, which are women not more qualified to do? I haven't heard a good argument against it yet, but it will certainly take some time before the curmudgeons allow it...if they ever do. They're so insistent on a division. Men over here. Women over there. If men got pregnant, abortions would be as acceptable as appendectomies."

"¿So...no weddings today?" she asked, when their conversation had veered away from the law.

"No, nor baptisms or masses, but I'm on-call, if I'm needed."

They paid the bill and then left the mercado through a side door and were immediately engulfed by the outdoor maze of booths and food stands, the festival sounds and mêlée prevailing, in places where the supply always seemed to outnumber the demand several times over. Esme grabbed the priest's arm by his sleeve and led him through the market, past the vendors and their children, apprentices in their trade, past the women searching for more coins in their purses to make change..."I need canela," she said. "For my avena." She laughed at her comfort with the priest, the public display as she moved briskly through the orgy of goods with a Catholic priest, with whom she was so profoundly connected, all the way back to Vero.

They continued to walk, farther from the mercado and the accidental bazaar nearby and into the clogged city streets, where a completely different, non-historic district dwelled. Padre Osvaldo was reminded of his days in the seminary, those long aimless hikes into the countryside, where sometimes he walked through a small town, or the remnants of a small town he'd never known existed and sometimes found some old country route that no one took anymore because it had been replaced by a highway, central to only its rundown convenience store that supplied candy and sodas and chips to country school kids and beer for the locals. It was strange, he thought, to superimpose this ambulatory lifestyle upon a landscape so intent on being driven upon. As the haze of evening descended upon the earth, concealing some objects and magnifying others, they found they had moved so far from the center of the city that they had reached the fringes of another colonia, Esme feeling unthreatened because she was with a priest and therefore under the protection of God, Osvaldo in a spell of contentment due to the strange inconsequentiality of all events when he was with Esmeralda. Finally, he suggested they turn back around.

"Claro. We need to find a bus or a taxi. ¿Do you ever take buses, Padre?"

As she said this, they saw a girl running toward them from behind a row of lower-middle-class houses. The girl was barefoot, about fourteen years old, and she ran with a limp and nearly came crashing into them; she was out of breath and hugged Esme as hard as she could. Her knee was covered in blood, and it didn't seem she was looking at either of them.

"¡Jesús, mija! ¿Qué pasó?" Esme said. "¿What happened?" she repeated.

Tears rushed down the girl's face, some catching at her mouth, from which there emerged a wailing sound, and she did not answer Esme's and Osvaldo's repeated questions of identity, the cause of her problems, the whereabouts of her family or whether she was in pain or not. It was unclear as to whether the girl was registering anything that they were saying—as soon as she had fallen into Esme's arms, she was unresponsive, as if her body had carried out the actions that would lead to her safety and then shut off as soon as she had come upon someone safe. Padre Osvaldo went to look for a phone to dial an ambulance and, within a quarter of an hour, one came roaring down the gravel, and the street, which had seemed otherwise vacant, was soon speckled with a number of concerned individuals, some who rushed over to the three of them, others who stood at their doors and waited for the ambulance to take them away.

Everyone dies of natural causes. Isn't death as natural as birth? Isn't it guaranteed everyone? Isn't it the real reason that doctors' methods can't be foolproof and medicine is an art, not a science? If someone were to die of synthetic causes, then wouldn't it be a synthetic death, the kind of death where the next day you show up at your job and everybody runs for their lives because you were supposed to be dead—a death for cinema audiences or the kind arisen from after some number of days. In Mexico, nobody dies completely; here, deaths are partial. Spirits live on, and they linger because they are allowed to, and it is in this unknown zone, this porous barrier, from which things emerge dead and others survive. The body clamors for more air, or it runs, or at the last second, a deft maneuver cheats death, cheats murder, and that's what they were up against, maybe, if you believe what the girl said before she took everything back.

Maybe it happened like this. On a dusty gravel road distanced from the city by a great length that stretched out beyond several divisions of shanties, the girl boarded the bus, preparing for the early morning shift at the maquila. Her maquila identification card showed that she was eighteen, but she was really fourteen, though she probably could have passed for sixteen. As she moved to the back of the empty bus—it was almost always empty, as this was the beginning of the route—she pulled her knees up and rested them against the seat in front of her, and she tried to sleep because the night before she'd had anything but rest. A strange thing had happened the night before—her uncle and her uncle's new wife had come up to Juárez from Durango, a city due south and half the way to Mexico City. Her uncle had arrived by surprise, had decided to drive up on a moment's whim, he said, though she would later find out that financial troubles had gotten the best of him, too, and so the night before had been one of great festivity, marked by the men drinking cervezas and the women cooking tamales and all the children, including the girl, learning from the new aunt how to make maracas out of soda cans, paint and garbanzo beans. Maybe this is what she thought about, entranced by the thrills of the evening before that she wished she could live again or commit to memory, when she fell asleep, as the bus barreled through the empty desert. Eventually, lines the shape of the seat in front of her cut into her skin and her circulation, causing everything below her knees to feel weightless but still existent, like a predicament assuaged by a distraction but still hanging on the outskirts of the diversion. Perhaps she awoke to find that the bus had stopped and that another bus had pulled up alongside hers. She looked out of the window; darkness still abounded, and she couldn't make out where they were, as it seemed by now the lights of the city would have proliferated, and, for a moment, she wondered whether the city might be in a state of blackout. Maybe before she could even become frightened through contemplation, two bus drivers came toward her—one obese and slobbery and the other gaunt and scarred—and everything else happened quickly. She was underneath one of them and then the other, pushing against them, trying to claw at them, but then, after a while, she realized her resistance was futile, so she decided to put everything into one last effort, one sink-or-swim maneuver. She bit one of them in the ear and the other in the groin and, as soon as they slumped down in agony, she darted for the exit of the bus, her body moving more quickly than her legs, such that she fell to the ground and landed one knee crashing against the cement. As she battered against a sweep of sandy daybreak wind, the blood surged from her knees, forming a trail back to where the bus had been parked, as she made her way toward the lights of the city.

"I wish we could have heard it from her," Esme said to Padre Osvaldo the next Thursday in his office in the cathedral, a room of dark wooden bookcases filled with volumes by Anthony de Mellow, John W. O'Malley, Karl Rahner and Harold Rahm, the Jesuit priest who had inspired Osvaldo to join the seminary. "Now," Esme said, "more mysteries, more one person's word against the other's. All I would have needed to do was to look in the girl's eyes, and I would have known the truth. Pero la policía—they come out of nowhere."

"They always have," Osvaldo said, and then he thought back to when that had been historically true. He remembered the many times that they *had* come out of nowhere, and he remembered hearing stories about how his friends and classmates had to pay mordidas to the police even if they hadn't done anything. He remembered his father telling him that if he had any trouble with la policía, all he had to do was call him—his father knew some of the officers and could guarantee that he would never spend a night in jail at the whim of some maleducated marrano. But while his father's relationship with the police made him feel his own safety was less tenuous, the contradiction bothered him—the purpose of la policía was so that you could go to them for safety. You shouldn't be worried about *them*. It was a contradiction in terms on the same level as a stomach medication that *causes* stomach pain or a car mechanic who, while trying to fix one thing, breaks another. He hated when things did not perform their function. "They really always have," Padre Osvaldo said again.

"It's all so difficult," Esme said, and she turned to Osvaldo and said: "Listen," not because he hadn't been listening, though his attention did sometimes stray, but because she wanted his complete notice. "A girl who has not spoken runs into our arms. We escort her into the hospital, we stay by her bed, we wait for her to speak but, as soon as she does, we are ushered out into the waiting room, among the media, the photographers, her relatives and the masses, and only the police and doctors can stay with her. Within hours, a very specific group of men called Los Choferes are rounded up and within a few more hours they have confessed to raping, choking and nearly killing the girl. Y, más loco, they confess on television. They know and give the complete names of the girls—their victims. They give first names, middle names, last names and mother's names. And the same story of what happened to Los Rebeldes is repeated, that the Egyptian is the murderer, paying these men from his cell, asking for women's underwear and upping his offering to twelve hundred American dollars for each girl. And then, days later, one of Los Choferes dies in jail. And then along the highway, one of their lawyers dies. People keep dying everywhere. ¿Where is the justice? This has been going on for six years and since the beginning of time. ¿How, Padre, can we stop this? ¿Where is God at a time like this?"

Padre Osvaldo, who often did have the answers to questions, said, "I don't know. This is the hardest part about religion, about Catholicism. There is so much pain and suffering in this world. We look forward to heaven and its eternal bliss, and we hope that this is the trade-off. ¿But why do bad things happen to good people? I don't know. I don't have the answers. I can only try to help. I can only open my doors and say, 'My children, come to me. It is safe here.'"

He took Esme in his arms as her face quivered in anger, and then he said, "But you—you are La Detective…"

"¿And what does that mean?" She said, angrily—even angry, perhaps, at *him*.

"It means that you are a doer, not some passive priest."

"You're not some passive priest."

"No," he said. "You're right. I'm out here with you, but what I wouldn't give sometimes to be something else, to have just a little bit more power."

Esme looked into the face of the priest and thought for a moment: *No, better that Padre Osvaldo was a priest.* "If you weren't a priest, I'd never have met you. If you were just a man, I'd never trust you."

"You clearly don't know that much about priests," Padre Osvaldo said. "Don't be fooled by this uniform. A lot of priests, just like all types of people, are villains, too."

"But not you," she said.

"I certainly hope not," Padre Osvaldo said, shaking his head.

numbers

Did those children really outdrink me, I wondered, as I slid the card into the appropriate slot aside the doorknob and stumbled through the door of my hotel room in central London. The room did not look the same as the one I had checked into earlier, but then I wasn't sure I had devoted enough time earlier to remembering it. There was nothing inherently wrong with the room. It was not booby-trapped. There was only one bed, and it looked comfortable; a copy of *Where* magazine rested lasciviously on the nightstand. And then, suddenly it hit me—smack!—I had forgotten to check my email in Rio. And then a series of regrets connected to this warning signal: what was I doing in London looking for Art when he was more than likely dead, what had I really gotten out of interviewing Ulick Martin, shouldn't I call Camille, how many siblings did Joaquín Guzmán have, when was the last time I had gone to the Tequila Derby in Juárez, how had I gotten so deliriously drunk...and, as I thought this, my pants, which were wrapped around my ankles (as I had been trying to undress), twisted me into an impossible position, causing me to topple onto the floor and producing a noise loud enough to—through some sort of chain reaction of which I was not privy to the specifics—encourage one of the hotel's staff to come check on me.

"Yes, everything's all right here."

"Are you sure?"

"Absolutely. I heard the sound myself, but I think it came from the room next door."

"So you know there was a noise?"

Where had all of these thoughts come from? How do our thoughts work that certain ideas pop into our heads seemingly from nowhere? Had they been dislodged from my brain during my drunken affair? Why do we think things *when* we think them? I understand the relationship between our senses and their interaction with our memories. We smell a light wisp of honey and are reminded of our mother, who used to make banana and peanut butter sandwiches with honey, or we hear a song on the radio and it brings us back to the year when that song was popular, and in our memory suddenly appears a film trailer for that time in our lives. But where do the *other* thoughts come from, the ones not drawn from the sequential development of thought? Perhaps, as soon as we have stopped thinking new things, like a radio show on a weekend that recycles banter from the weekday midnight hours, tidings of a repeat historical gaffe only remembered in books in other languages disturbs a stretch of peace or an ecosystem that looks to old prototypes of weather in order to create the day, thoughts and memories from the past are dredged out and assigned a value and then put into something resembling a lottery wheel, the wheel is spun, and then a thought or memory is plucked from the schizophrenic shuffle of non sequiturs. Or do things in the natural world trigger this revolving belt; in other words, does our memory work the way lenses do, refracting and reflecting off things in our environment, signals and satellites of which we are not even aware but that control us?

At certain points of my life, I have asked my memory to guard these moments of my life and then return them to me when I ask for them, and the only thing that I have learned from these experiments is that it is impossible to record their success. If I document them in a notebook or journal, I am affecting my memory because encountering them in my notebook on another day strengthens its value. If I memorize them by connecting them with a sensory detail, such as, for example, the next time I hear a bird chirping, I must remember a night I spent walking through the rain, drunk in London, from the house of a friend of Art Serrano, then I am more likely to remember it. But what if I attach no other insurance to the thought at all and ask my mind to remember something on its own? What does my mind owe me? What relationship do we have?

Our concept of who we are—our histories, our goals, our existences—is completely based on our memories and the memories of others and, because we have very little control over these memories, we create birth certificates and documents and statistical data to furnish proof of our identity, we write journals or books to record our ideas, we make video and audio tapes to record our voices and our bodies, and we use planners and calendars to remember what we have in store for us in the future. And, after four or five years, just as our skin replenishes itself almost completely, shedding old layers as quickly as the new ones are produced, not memories but these things independent of time, these items—planners, tapes, books—are most of what we have left, and we allow these things to rekindle memories or provide us with new memories for the things that have come before. Few of our thoughts and designs of the quotidian survive an interval of time as short as a presidential term. We forget what we had for dinner on the night of our fifteenth birthday. We don't remember what we did for light on the night of the great storm that severed all ties between houses and their electricity.

And yet some things do come back, and we wonder why they are there, why these memories are the ones that we saved, what process of spring cleaning our mind went through to be limited now to these choice moments, and then we put them side by side with the things we wish we would have known, especially about the people who were in our lives but have since gone, the events we feel define our lives but of which we no longer remember the specifics, the person we once were all those reincarnations ago in the same body, in the same lifetime, and they do not compare—our priorities are not where our memories are—and we think that maybe our memories are the cruelest mechanisms in the world, so deceptive and selfish, so spotty and inconsiderate—that I would remember a mathematical equation but not what my mother's voice sounded like.

After closing the door on the night watchman, I was feeling nauseated and, eager to prevent this feeling, I drank a glass of water, which seemed not to assuage but to enhance my nausea, so I instead clambered onto the bed, pulled back the sheets and felt the seismic tumult of my brain, which reminded me of my experience in the ocean in Rio, and when I fell asleep in what could have been as few as five seconds later, I am sure that sleep came as suddenly and unexpectedly as that undertow.

Morning in all its finery arrived just in time to wake me up. I spent an hour or so attempting to defuse my headache by diluting the alcohol settling in my stomach with water. I then took my briefcase and went to search for an Internet café, which I found in The Strand and, as soon as I signed in to my account, I discovered a stream of emails from *The Monthly*, commensurate with the number of days in which I had failed to check my messages. I sent a long letter of apology, complete with fallacious details ("...ill for many hours, suffering from some sort of strange—let's just say environmental—circumstance that affected my mobility. Upon arrival in London, I was deterred from properly entering the country as they were concerned I might be the carrier of a certain strain of bug, which I thankfully do not have..."), in addition to the information they had requested regarding my story—extraneous details they were hoping to pull together for a bio blurb on Father Rahm. That accomplished, I discovered an email from Marisa de Oliveira, which included, in fact, her article on Art from several years before and, already, a draft of an article based on her interview with me, which she had translated into English, asking me for confirmation of some of the details, some of which she had either made up through extrapolation or misinterpreted despite her excellent English. The only other email sitting in my box was one from Camille from a few days before asking me where I was and whether or not I had been swallowed by a piranha. The letter was fifteen lines long and dealt exclusively with piranhas and their prevalence in Brazil. Her final words were "Whether you may like it or not, Omar, piranhas are carnivores and are much more likely to eat people than, say, herbivores. I hope you are keeping about with yourself, whatever that means. Love, Camille."

I decided I would call her as soon as I arrived back at my hotel room. From here, I followed The Strand back whence I had come, through St. James Park, where I found a crowd of about fifteen or twenty people assembled around an American man who was asking several audience members where they were from—and they were unanimously American as well: one from Pittsburgh, another from Boise, others from San Francisco. Then, as soon as five or six city names were taken, he started shaking his head, as if to say, "No. This won't do."

"See?" he finally said after a few more moments of disapproving head-shaking. "Everybody wants to tell where they're from, whereas I want to know where you *are*." He said this with such conviction, and with such resonance, that I found myself in admiration of his rare powers of oration because, as with a church congregation whose members are invited to consider the possibility of their going to hell, he had captivated an audience he had insulted on the strength of a philosophical conceit that was incisive but spooled into the wrong analogy. And though his message did make sense as a legitimate philosophical argument, it seemed the effect of his words would only deign to create in the audience members an unnecessary indisposition to questions of origin, which are harmless and in my experience only endow people with a sense of pride for belonging somewhere and carrying that place with them.

I eventually returned to my hotel, where I had a breakfast of bread, jam and coffee, and then I called Camille.

Why is it that the first two minutes of nearly every transatlantic call are, despite our knowledge of the sciences and the universal understanding of the significance of fifteen degrees of longitude, spent painstakingly comparing—and then marveling at—the time difference?

"I can hardly believe it myself," I said, then asked her about the weather.

"Oh, it's fine. About the same as when you left," she groaned.

"Really?" I asked. "In April?"

"Hey, I don't have control over these things. You know who does?"

"Who?"

"I don't know. I was wondering if you might."

She asked me what my agenda for the next several days was, and I looked over the notes I had loosely scribbled on the airplane from Rio to London. I knew I needed to meet with Professor Keating at some point and, since he taught in Grenoble, I imagined he would be the next person I'd try to reach. In my preparations in Rio, I had taken down the number of his university and would call him as soon as I hung

199

up with Camille. I had also sent emails to several others, including Kristof von Behren, the famous German artist who had been shown shaking hands with Art on the cover of *Die Zeit*. I'd left messages with a museum curator in Madrid and an art historian in Prague. I'd emailed Marta Herrera, the librarian at the Universitat de Barcelona, and contacted a few of our high school friends, including Julio Poitras, by email.

"What about Art's sister, the one who works for CNN. Isn't she often in Europe?" Camille asked.

"Yes. I didn't consider it, but she might be a good person to talk to."

"How did you plan this trip? Where did you get the idea about who to interview?" she asked.

"I don't know," I said. "I've never been that good a journalist. I don't really know what I'm doing. I lack the necessary organization skills to effectively plan a trip. I don't know what questions to ask when I'm interviewing, and I have the tape recorder and notepads to prove it."

"Do you have *any* sort of strategy?" she asked.

Camille went on to inform me of a recent discovery she had made by cleaning out one of our closets, a feat that in the several years I had leased the apartment I'd never thought to undertake. Inside, she had found empty beer bottles from before the prohibition era, an antique dish set of entirely broken dishes, New Year's 1981 noisemakers and tiaras, a tee ball tee, a box of Jewish hamsas, one of the first IBM personal computers, six pillows, a collection of figurines from the television show *Alf*, a stowaway sleeper and a five-by-seven-foot chalkboard with basic math equations still written upon it. As it turns out, what we had always thought was a closet was actually the back exit, an emergency staircase that led to a door to the apartment on the first floor.

When we hung up, I immediately called Professor Keating's university in Grenoble and recorded a message with the department secretary, who informed me that Keating would be in touch with me "in some time." (He sounded like *me...*) When Keating eventually returned my call that afternoon, he told me he was in Paris on a conference and that he would be there for the next several days if I wanted to have lunch with him, so I made arrangements to depart Waterloo the following day for Paris and then, despite my wishes to walk around London for the next several hours, following an ambulatory course prescribed by a newspaper article detailing a "Posh Spice Walk," the return of my headache required immediate attention, and so I repaired to my hotel room and rejoined the sleeping world.

Standing in front of Davioud's fountain across from the Saint-Michel metro station in Paris, I scanned the crowds and tried to remember what Professor Keating looked like. I had seen him on television during the first month of heavy press and remembered him to be in his sixties or seventies, of medium build and cherubic disposition, a man capable of shamelessly using the word "preambulary" in an interview, an ex-pat of more than a decade, for whom France, and the Alpine city of Grenoble specifically, was likely to have taken residence in his body, his gestures, his movements and his tongue—especially whilst on this soil. When he finally did arrive, he walked right into the center of the open area in front of the fountain and looked directly at me and where I was seated and, as soon as I raised my hands to signal him, he very quickly and spasmodically jerked his head into another direction, and for a moment I wondered whether I should approach him.

"Professor?" I said, coming up from behind him.

"Yes," he said, cheerfully, turning his body awkwardly to face me, as if his movements all had to equate to exactly forty-five degrees.

We headed south down the Place Saint-Michel and turned right on Boulevard Saint-Germain and walked for several blocks before we arrived at a restaurant called Le Jean George. He asked how my flight had been. I told him it went well. I asked him how he was. He told me he was well. And the conference? Normal, no fusses. How was my room? Oh, it has a nice balcony overlooking one of those busy city streets near the Place de la Bastille. Great. Great.

"This is the first restaurant Art dined at in Paris," he said, triumphantly, as soon as we were seated, and I wondered if this is where Professor Keating took people when he wanted to show them the city. By the attention he received from the staff, one could presume he was either a regular, a celebrity, the owner, a restaurant inspector or just extraordinarily charming in French.

"Art had the tourte d'artichauts et aubergines farcies, an artichoke pie and stuffed eggplant," he said. "It's a popular dish."

As it turns out, Professor Keating and Art's first dinner at Le Jean George had been one of recruitment, and much of Professor Keating's reflection upon that time regarded his own sell strategy—boasting the school's preeminence in the art field, the prestige of the Montparnasse fellowship, the school's skyline (which included the Alps). Now, he talked at length about the school's record, the number of artists who had distinguished themselves in Europe, but, of course, he said, none were as celebrated as Art Serrano.

"And, Professor, what was it about Art then that led him to be your choice for the fellowship?"

"Call me Patrick," he said, looking away from me, toward some bookstores to my left. "But to answer your question, we were excited about the landscapes and the exotic characters in his paintings. Here, most of the students seemed to be replicating styles. Art already had his own style, and I think the influence of Mexico and the border were so unique to him and your portion of the world that the same would be unique to the program. The program was founded on fostering diversity and creating a dialogue among artists. In the first year of the Montparnasse fellowship, we brought in a guy from Morocco, and you should have seen his ability to create brilliant surrealist art that depicted life in that part of Africa.

But, as you know, Art far surpassed this fellow. The number of awards he won during his two years there, in addition to the number of awards he won afterwards, you know, all the major ones—the Hugo Boss Prize, a Guggenheim, a MacArthur Fellowship, grants from everyone—the Louis Comfort Tiffany Foundation, etc. He would have won the Vincent and a Turner Prize had he been British. And then of course, if you consider all the magazines and newspapers that did stories on him…"

The more Professor Keating spoke, the more it seemed strange to me that *he* was the one who had wooed Art all the way to France. Although his knowledge of art was compendious, his sell strategy—the very thing he seemed to pride himself on most—seemed to be more about promising preeminence and laurels than it was about artistic development. His was a world of statistics and retention rates and class ranks and ostentation, the kind of world where a brilliant Saint Germain des Prés restaurant was used to impress in the same way a jersey with a high school basketball phenom's name already on the back of it (or a BMW) might be used to court the player into committing to a "program." Of course, there was nothing wrong with this, but it did seem curious that this was an environment in which Art had participated, as Art seemed so immune to affectation. As I had met both Keating and Ulick Martin within a period of three days, I couldn't help but compare them. Like the speaker in St. James Park in London, both were charismatic characters with deep voices, and they both showed inestimable knowledge of the art world but, whereas Ulick Martin seemed to be more focused on Art's evolution as a painter, his messages, his *art*, Keating seemed to regard Art as an image, with a name value and an identity, inseparable from his "product." It seemed even more interesting now that in Art's absence, it was Professor Keating who had emerged as Art's great representative, finding his way in front of the cameras, interpreting the painting as an "artist's suicide note in visual form," which was a phrase repeated so many times in the media that it had already entered into rhetoric, had already been grouped together as a set of words that sounded appropriate together, that produced the effect of one word rather than a composition of six, in the same way that certain letters jumbled together immediately signify their aggregate value as words rather than being the sum of their parts, as they are for children. Conversing with Keating now, I wondered how significant he had *actually* been in Art's career or if he was, like the numerous magazines and publishing houses that publish bound commemorative picture books paying homage to deceased celebrities such as John F. Kennedy, Jr. or Princess Diana, merely profiting from a position of adoration and feeling ennobled for doing so. For Keating, success, especially the kind that was pecuniary, was often brought about through numbers and statistics, bests and worsts, public relations, networking, fine dining and payola.

I asked Keating whether, based on his intimate knowledge of Art, he thought Art might still be alive.

"I really don't think so," he said. "And I think the painting is evidence enough. Let me tell you something. Something about Art that you may or may not know is how much of himself he put into his paintings. He essentially *was* his paintings, and his paintings were him. To put it another way: Do you know how they say that if one dies in his dreams, his body processes the sensation of death and follows suit? I think that's analogous to what happens when Art paints himself out of a painting." This was something that Ulick Martin had commented on too—Art's seriousness and his inability to disconnect from his work when at the heart of it, but I wondered if Ulick Martin would go so far as so say Art's work was his equal in form rather than something completely independent of him that sprang from him but was not him in the same way that for Christians people are made in God's image and are given power through His creation but have minds of their own. I felt Keating was right in recognizing

Art's intensity, but I wondered whether he might have been taking this a bit too far, cutting into mystical, Dorian Gray territory. Keating was a deeply intelligent man, but I didn't like him. By reputation, he was a distinguished professor, an eminent name but, upon meeting the man, you realize he is taking everyone to the same restaurants, delivering the same lines, moving like a brownnosing student into the spotlight, keeping others from excelling.

The food was excellent—I had just devoured the sole meunière, my main course, and was now awaiting the soufflé glacé aux cerises, which I had ordered at the beginning of the meal. Keating took his own advice and, à la Art, ordered the tourte d'artichauts et aubergines farcies, which, probably because I had declined his recommendation, he chewed with such ecstasy that I searched his eyes for accompanying tears of joy. As he ate, he continued to point out numerous occasions in which people who had died were thought to be alive by their cult followings, and it occurred to me that Art's disappearance provided an opportunity for him, whether intentional or not, to expand the renown of his program, enjoy some moments in the limelight and, ex post facto, favor some details to the exclusion of others.

In order to change the subject from a sentence that included both Amelia Earhart and Tupac Shakur, I asked Keating what he thought of Art's Know Your Baker campaign. For a moment he seemed ready to answer the question but was merely struggling to find the appropriate words, but then he shrugged his shoulders and said, "I guess I don't exactly know to what you're referring, but, trust me, it wasn't his best era."

"Do you know your baker?" I asked. I was hardly the person to pass on the Know Your Baker philosophy, as I had just learned about it in London two days prior, but I found myself duplicating Ulick Martin's interrogation almost completely. However, in my adaptation of Art's original question outside the cafeteria, I had accomplished something that neither Art nor Ulick Martin had—I was talking with complete condescension, as if Know Your Baker were as common an expression as Know Thyself.

When we departed from one another outside the restaurant, Professor Keating seemed to, at first, save the night its awkward ending through sheer social agility. He said, "Well, Omar, our night has come to an end. I really have enjoyed talking with you about Art. Let me give you my mobile number in case you have any more questions, I can answer them as best I can. And thanks for the discourse on Know Your Baker. Good luck finding whatever it is you're looking for." But, by the time I had walked away from him, I realized it was he who had had the last laugh, because even though he'd seemed quite amiable in the way that he said "whatever it is you're looking for," the disdain was in the words themselves and, by the time he and I were so far apart from one another that I could have screamed it without him hearing me, I could not help but detest everything about Professor Keating.

I turned right on the Boulevard Saint-Michel nearly oblivious of my surroundings, the city that flashed into my vision but could not penetrate the thick cloud of thoughts that cloaked me from the world. I couldn't understand why I was so angry, why someone such as Professor Keating had compelled me to react as I did. I'd met plenty of people in my life who were ten times as deplorable, rude, even sinister, and here Professor Keating had taken time from his busy conference schedule to meet with me, spend two hours having lunch with me and talking about Art and his relationship with him, and all I could feel was repugnance. Soon I reached the Jardin du Luxembourg, a name that delighted me, as it brought up kind remembrances of Robert, my companion in Christ, and I entered the park still slightly agitated by Professor Keating and wondering why I had such revulsion for him, when the environment, and specifically the thrilling La Fontaine de Médicis, did effectively pierce the cloud of thoughts that hung about me and caused me to set them aside. As I moved farther into the park, a park I had visited before, but formerly in the dead heat of summer when Paris was one molten, uninhabitable beast, I was moved by the lilting spring breeze, the park's serenity and quiet. As I walked past the pond with its racing fountains and chairs circumscribing the pond and the manicured grass, I eventually found three strips of lawn, two of which were completely empty, the other upon which people were nearly sitting on each other's laps. It was like seeing three bookshelves, two of which were empty, the other with books double and triple-stacked so tight it would take a sizeable degree of alacrity to remove one while keeping the others from falling from the shelves; or, it was like our world, with its clusters of populations magnetized by the centrifugal force of cities, while most of the earth was left fallow, unpopulated. Obviously, the operators of the garden, as in many places in France with "pelouse interdit" signs, were trying to preserve the grass by delineating which of the lawns people could sit on each day and then rotating them, but it still seemed silly and—in a small and probably unjustified way—arrogant to tell people which grass they could sit on and which they couldn't. I felt incredibly angry, pissed off about everything, especially as the conversation with Keating continued to replay itself in my head, each time dwelling on the part where I had plagiarized Ulick Martin's line, "Do you know your baker?", at which point each time I felt a pang of guilt for acting so inappropriately, for treating him so condescendingly.

And then, finally, I discovered exactly why I was so upset. Keating and I had a lot in common. All of my criticism of Professor Keating, I realized, could be accurate criticism of me. After all, when had I myself become most involved in Art's life but after he was no longer here? When had I begun talking about him to the media but after he had gone missing? What did I know of his paintings, his campaigns? Since high school, our conversations had been brief, our letters no more than three hundred words long. In the past nearly twenty years, we had really been little more than acquaintances.

The clincher was, of course, that *neither* of us had been included in Art's great inside joke; neither of us had appreciated what Art had meant by "Know Your Baker", and the embarrassment that I could read in Keating's face communicated that he, too, had been excluded and was only pretending, nodding, masquerading, as I had done during the longer lunch days when I had said, *Yes*, when Art had asked me if I knew why these words were so important to him. My acknowledgement that the friendship between Art and me had passed into acquaintanceship whilst I still seemed to regard it as the great friendship it had perhaps never been was a disconcerting realization. Searching to console myself this thought, my mind found its way to the will, to the letters left me—and, I reasoned, this evidence of his opinion of me far surpassed the manifestation of acquaintanceship that masked our relationship's chronology. As I further clung to a rationale that would mitigate some of the damage of my discovery, I reasoned that Art's friendships were, like these lawns, very strictly divided, and the information one friend might have, another wouldn't. Like many people, Art had a split personality, but he had taken his further, such that his lectures on art in front of Brazilian street kids differed greatly from his conversations with me and then further in his conversations with Ulick Martin. That is why the only time I noticed a trace of Art's mother's voice in his own was during the few occasions that I had seen him speaking before crowds, instances in which he was required to communicate with perfect precision and intelligence, and for this he chose his mother's manner, as she was a university professor and the comportment that characterized her was more likely to be successful in front of an audience, as it had been so often for her.

Further, the will that Art had left, which had in it twenty-seven names, represented twenty-seven different modes of conversation, inside jokes, histories, and personalities that the different essences or personalities of Art stretched to capacitate, not because he was conforming to them and their personality but because he was reverting to the personality he had previously set up as his when in their presence. And then, of course, there existed the Art that only Art himself knew, perhaps the Art most separate from the other twenty-seven, for this Art viewed himself completely from the interior, like a person inside a limousine who exposes to the external world his or her personality through the shine of the hood, the length of the cab, the dimness of the windows but is otherwise completely invisible. In order to better know Art, understanding him from the point of view of all these other people would allow me to fathom why he had decided to take his life or convince everyone in the world, including those most dear to him, that he had.

As I pondered this, I had already made my way out of the park and toward the Sorbonne, which during my many visits to Paris, despite my desire to see new places and experience the less-touristy parts of Paris, I was drawn to innately. When I reached the university, which was compressed into one or two buildings with a sentry at each door so that the masses could not penetrate its walls, I found myself in an outdoor mall and made my way into a bookstore that housed books on philosophy, political science, journalism and literature. Finding the literature section, I could not help but, without anyone watching me, trace my fingers along the bindings of great books. Eventually, I found an English-language section and, curious to see which books composed the English-language canon in this store, I came upon a book called *Paris Reflections: Walks Through African-American Paris*, which caused me to leave the store immediately, as it reminded me of the strict divisions among men that Americans impose on one another, and it bothered me considerably that such a quintessential American concept would be so presumptuous and ethnocentric as to extend the landscape of its divisions to foreign territory. When

I left the bookstore, I saw a number of men my age and older walking together through the mall and quickly spotted Professor Keating among them but, not wanting to bother him, and embarrassed at my earlier gaffe, I moved more quickly around the corner where he wouldn't be able to see me. I continued to walk away, north toward St-Michel. But, again, as this sudden flash of anger from the book in the store persisted within me, I realized it was the result not of the book but, in fact, of my discovery of my relationship to Professor Keating that caused this sting to persist, camouflaging itself among all sorts of other, minor annoyances. I turned and headed through one of the alleyways of the Latin Quarter, onto the Rue des Écoles and away, navigating northeast through the parts of Paris where people lived.

The following day I called Ella Serrano, asking for Beatriz's email address and received both her email address and cell phone number. Art's mother was surprised to hear from me in France and asked if everything was all right. I didn't tell her I was looking for Art and merely said I was seeking to catch up with Beatriz while in Spain on assignment. During the day, I walked north from the Bastille up Boulevard Richard Lenoir, following alongside the Canal Saint-Martin. After going quite far north on the canal, I reached a point where people were sitting alongside it, and I followed one group of people who were carrying a table and chairs, wine and baguettes to set up for lunch aside the canal. When I eventually turned, looking for the métro at La Place de la République, I found the site in the throes of a large anti-war protest. Discouraged from taking the métro at La Place de la République because of the large traffic and signs pronouncing hostile anti-American sentiment, I decided to walk down the Boulevard du Temple where I was witness to one of those rare, incandescent marvels of life—on the sidewalk, a woman was burying her head deep into the arms of a man. As I noticed this, it struck me that in a world that was so adroit in crossing sexual boundaries quickly, the embrace was dying out as an expression of love.

Later that afternoon, I went to view the Arturo Serrano paintings that were housed inside the Centre Pompidou, the colossal, glassy building holding the Musée National d'Art Moderne. Because the room was so full, it was difficult to get an intimate and lingering look at any of the paintings. According to the exhibit's information card, this special showing included some of Art's paintings that "blend Surrealism and Expressionism with Mexican mural style" and were dated the year he was twenty-five, the year he spent in Paris before taking up his flat in London.

I was impressed with how Art had, when he moved from one style of painting to another, whether it be impressionism, expressionism, neoclassicism, etc., always found some way to suffuse whatever he was painting in the most vibrant hues of dissimilar colors. And this had been a part of his œuvre since the very beginning, as I remember from the sketchbooks and paintings he had shown me in high school; colors had always been used boldly to highlight strange aspects of the work. One of the paintings turns El Paso's skyscrapers into the faces of ominous men overlooking the city that rests below (in homage, the description below said, to the German expressionist style). Another is of a man working as a mechanic at an auto shop; this one is predominately in black and white, but the man's sweat drips in yellow, orange, green and blue. A third is called *Autoportrait—Self-portrait*—and shows a man whose face is a skull, the jaw agape in a skeletal smile, painting upon a canvas the viewer cannot see. I tried to linger here longer than most of the people who had come into this room, as I wasn't here for the other galleries. Still, the whirlpool traffic of the room fumbled me along the wall and I arrived prematurely at the last of the paintings, which was a simple painting entitled "El Padre Bicicleta," which reveals a white priest on a bicycle pedaling through the streets of South

211

El Paso, as a crowd of drug dealers, prostitutes, aristocrats and children look on.

These paintings, which in technical skill alone far exceeded those he had painted in high school, still bore the stamp of the child who had come before him, especially in their extraordinary contradistinction of colors, but also in his particular way of viewing human figures, that it was as if his art held immured beneath it the very strokes of youth in the way that a closer inspection of an older man's face reveals the child. It is this transcendence from youth to adulthood that is more fragile a period than any other. The weaknesses of any fledgling artist are likely to become the secret ingredient of the expert artist who will someday pick up the paintbrush and hold the easel and paint upon the canvas the same "error" he made at twelve with the hands of a man of fifty. At some point I am sure that an art instructor or colleague must have expressed disapproval of one or more aspects of Art's work—perhaps of these extravagant colors themselves (his critics saw them as gratuitous)—and I wondered what stretch of logic Art had to follow in order to convince himself to brazenly continue, to realize that if those thick globs of color and other things that were intrinsic to his work were to disappear, then so would every other original aspect of his painting.

Later that evening, I called Beatriz in Spain and, though she was covering a story in Budapest, she said she would be back in Barcelona in two days, and I could meet her there. As I still hadn't heard from Kristof von Behren in Munich, I decided to go to Barcelona the next day. I had dinner at a place on Rue Charlot and then bought a bottle of wine that I uncorked in the wine store and carried with me as I walked alongside the Seine, as boats drifted by, apace with the speed at which the fading light was turning into night.

On the morning after I arrived in Barcelona, after breakfast I found my way to the Universitat de Barcelona where, passing through the foyer in the main building, I came across a photography exhibit: *exposició fotogràfica*—which instinct told me was misspelled, lacking the "n" at the end of "exposició," the direction of the accent mark over the "a" in "fotogràfica" reversed; words that in English and French end in "-tion," in Portuguese in "ção" and Spanish in "-ción," in Catalan end in "-ció," cutting short that last sound and for Spanish readers creating the appearance of something missing, like seeing the words "garag sale" in English or your father without his nose. I looked at the exhibit, called "Platja," a number of pictures from the beach that seemed to be striving for some sort of statement by cropping parts of heads and essential parts of the photos off, leaving the rest to the imagination. When I finally arrived at the library, I stood at the door for a moment and looked in, trying to decide on a course of action but, when several people came up behind me, I realized I was blocking the door and *had* to enter, and I arrived at the counter prematurely—and when the woman asked me if I needed any help, I realized that I didn't know the name of the librarian. "Disculpeme, un momento," I implored. I opened my briefcase and found the name, Marta Herrera. "¿Is Señora Herrera here?" I asked, in Spanish. "No, she just left for lunch about five minutes ago." She answered me in English, perhaps because she had mistaken my Mexican accent for an English speaker trying to speak Spanish. It was all the same to me. "Would you like to leave a message?" she asked. "Yes," I said. "Let me leave a card. Can you tell her I'll come back some time this afternoon?" "Sure," she said.

I left the building the same way I had come and, after thirty minutes of walking desultorily, my thoughts following the logic of dreams—the magnetism of Barcelona's esoteric balconies set against the hypnotizing grid of its streets (several times, I found myself running from the middle of the street to the sidewalk as the oncoming blaze of honking cars and motorcycles rushed me)—I came upon some smaller streets not as visibly articulated by signs or numbers. In this area away from the city despoiled of its grid by the disorganization that lies beyond every city center, I began to walk haphazardly without destination, killing time but also surrendering myself to the part of my mind operating independently of consciousness, perhaps the same part of the brain that randomly spits forth memories, and to which the peripatetic appeals. At just after one, the store owners peeked out of their boutiques, giving the street one last glance before pulling down the security grilles and heading off for siesta. The restaurants filled at this hour, and I kept walking into quarters that led me farther from the historic-touristic center, walking only the way one walks in a foreign city. I grabbed a bocadillo with jamón serrano, and I walked out past another avenue and among some alleyways where I chewed on the sandwich as crumbs fell to the ground from both sides of my face.

It was just a quarter past one that I looked into a vitrine and saw it, inside a vintage clothing shop tightly hugging the figure of the mannequin: *the* shirt, the same one I had seen in Seville a few years before, a black shirt with the white words Conozca a su Panadero written upon it in a graffiti font and slightly faded—the translation of Art's philosophy, a shirt I had all but forgotten about as a result of the story about the sevillano war vessel I had been writing.

I looked over at the door, but the store was closed and not due to open for another two hours, so, after standing there for another five or six minutes staring at the letters and the message, which, unlike the 14-year-old who had first heard the phrase, I now understood, I made mental note of the location and headed farther away into a city dense with buildings and bereft of people.

I wandered for another hour and, by then, my sense of direction had been completely disrupted. Where was I? I started looking for landmarks or the seafront. I had money and could have hailed a cab or asked for directions at any point, but I wouldn't allow myself to, whether for pride or for obstinacy or fear that someone would say "¿You're looking for *what*? You're nowhere close." Instead, I continued walking. Eventually, I came upon a discount supermarket that was open and in which there were only a few customers. I had been hoping to see something different, perhaps something local, or bizarre, the kind of thing one finds in a book several centuries old where the language, even if it is your own, is formed of letters whose curlicues and elegance has long since been stripped and now, for this reason, could only be seen and processed through the disfamiliar demarcation of its century. Instead, inside were the same products one finds the world over: cereals, coffee, cookies, pasta, rice, canned goods, some produce, some frozen things and a small deli that sold different meats and cheeses.

Where was Art? I thought about going to another gallery, but the answers to where he was wasn't going to be found inside the paintings. And besides, Art wasn't here in Barcelona. This city belonged to *other* artists—and most particularly the living memory of Antoni Gaudí, whose balconies, churches and parks were of the few examples in the world where fantasy had triumphed, where the dream had leaked into the superstructures and living spaces of men. I thought about the shirt. How could I have possibly found my way directly to it? The scattered remnants of everything could be found somewhere if you went looking for it (almost as much as when you weren't looking for it). Life could be lived backwards, or out of order, and lost one sometimes finds himself. And where was I? Would the shirt fit if I found it again?

I wandered back out; now I was totally lost and, as the streets began to come back to life, I began to trace my steps in reverse. I turned back toward streets and avenues I'd only ever seen in reverse but that still bore some trace of familiarity. I made a few wrong turns, gave up several more times before changing my mind and committing again to the search before finally coming across the name of the street of the clothing shop. I had to follow this street for twenty minutes, walking in each direction to the end, before I found it again. I opened the door and walked inside.

I told the merchant, exhausted, in a tone of voice prohibitive of small-talk or dissembling. "¿How much for that shirt in the window?"

"We have several more," the man said. "I suggest you look around first. But if you don't like what you see, I'll undress this mannequin."

Despite the yellow marks around the collar and under the arm, I was intoxicated by my discovery of the shirt because it was tangible—this was about as tangible a piece of evidence of Art's alternate reality as one could find. Also, it symbolized his past in activism as opposed to his past in art. What was more, this was a line Art had uttered during the longer lunch days, and this shirt seemed to me to be tangible proof of *that* conversation's existence as well. As soon as this shirt multiplied all over the thrift shop, in alternate colors—always colors—I finally found one that looked less worn than the others, and I paid for it and left.

The hour had strayed to three p.m. and, needing to return to the university to meet Marta Herrera, I hailed a cab, and the driver quickly reduced the hours of distance I'd walked into minutes, and we arrived at the university shortly thereafter. When I returned to the front desk and found myself in front of the same woman, who once again insisted on speaking English, I learned that Marta Herrera had taken ill and would be back at work in an "indefinite period of time." I asked if there was any other way of reaching her, and the woman looked at me with a scorn that seemed to be more the anger quotient of years rather than minutes, and thinking that this scorn had for some reason come as a result of our speaking English, I asked her in Spanish why she was speaking to me in English.

She said, "Because you are American."

As much as I would have liked to respond that I wasn't, I *was*, and, because people not from the United States tended to consider our notions of heritage and descent and ancestry to be less meaningful than questions of citizenship, I did not respond. I left the library, perplexed as to why I had been treated as such and wondering deeply what Marta Herrera's stringent reasons were for avoiding me.

Morning the next day came like rain from a clear sky. Even with the blinds turned open, the sun preceded me in awakening, had already danced upon my face in horizontal lines and when I awoke seemed to be sitting there on my bed with me like a hallucination. It took several moments to adjust to this other world because, unlike the world of sleep, in this one my whims needed acting upon in order to produce movement, which required use of my limbs. It eventually registered that in just several hours I would be seeing Art's sister Beatriz and, as I looked across the room and caught sight of the Conozca a su Panadero T-shirt lying across the back of a chair, I was suddenly seized with the desire to wear it.

The shirt came on tighter than I had realized it would and, affected by the Spanish sense of size, it wore in such a way that it accented muscles I had managed to forget about but that in the mirror of my hotel room's bathroom, in light proportional to that of daylight, did not make me look ridiculous. Excited about my meeting with Beatriz, who, unlike my other interviewees, I had met and knew and liked, I sped through all the activities I had relegated to the morning and was ready for lunch at about ten, even though we were to meet at one thirty. One of my morning's accomplishments had been to check my email and, upon discovering an email from Kristof von Behren ("…So journey on, man. Give me a call when you get to Munich. I can give you directions, a place to stay, whatever you need…") I booked a bed on the overnight train for that evening so that I could arrive early the next day, the day I had mentioned in my original email to him.

I packed my bag, and the hotel agreed to keep it in a downstairs office reserved for luggage.

Annoyed that it was only ten in the morning, I needed to fill the time and I debated as to whether to give the library another go. Feeling put off the past two times by the way I was treated by the woman at the front desk, I decided I would go anyway, if anything just to annoy her. When I arrived this time, she was nowhere to be seen and, waiting my turn, as several students were held up at the front desk, I was able to see what a work of art the library was, the shelves full of books bordering the entire room on several levels, the sleek computers dispersed throughout, students in smart dress studying and researching in the stacks. By the time the students had been directed out, back through the door we had just entered, I caught sight of the woman who had turned me away both times. She sped up to the front desk and gestured to the other workers that she would take care of me and, as soon as she began speaking to me in English, the others turned away.

"Hello. I told you she is sick," she said, her eyebrows creasing into a frown on her forehead. "Where did you get that shirt?" she said, pointing.

"A friend of mine made it."

"Who?"

"The painter Arturo Serrano," I said, then repeated "Art."

"Art," she said. "Did you really know him?"

I didn't reply; instinct told me not to. I waited for her to say something.

After several seconds of staring at me, she continued. "I haven't seen that shirt in years, but seeing it now takes me back…to before, when it had just been the idea of this man whom I had met through a friend at a party—a dinner party—and then that idea transformed and became a movement. There wasn't a person in Barcelona who didn't know what Conozca a su Panadero means."

"And in London," I said, attempting to show her that what she said did not betray her, that I really did know Art. "They know it as Know Your Baker. And I remember Art asking me if I knew my baker when we were both thirteen, eating lunch outside the cafeteria instead of inside because we were rebels."

"¿Verdad?" she said, switching to Spanish. "I thought you were a gringo." And here this woman, whose shoulders had been tense, forehead wrinkled and speech impolite suddenly surrendered to another ego. She led me through the library and into a back room with a large circular table, a white screen pulled down and a film projector on the other end of the room and invited me to sit down, asking me if I wanted water or something to drink.

"I'm fine."

"I'm sorry about yesterday," she said, now speaking exclusively in Spanish. "I was growing tired of the press. The European press wasn't half bad, but the American press blew all the wrong things out of proportion. They focused too much on the painting in his studio, disregarding an entire life of stewardship, passion, diverse paintings and rallies that drew the support of all of Barcelona and other cities. I was upset yesterday. I apologize. It wasn't you. In the morning I woke to the sound of the phone ringing and, when I answered it, I heard the voice of a man and, when I waited about ten seconds for him to finish, I tried to interrupt him, but he wouldn't stop talking. I realized it was a recording, and I was incensed because the phone call had awakened me, but there was no human being on the other line that I could lash into. I felt it in the morning when I went to the supermarket on the corner of the street. The employees were wearing new uniforms, they were using scanners to price the food, and the friendly owner I always greeted upon coming in was no longer there. It had been consolidated into a huge chain, and the effects of the transformation were just beginning. How terrified I felt, when everything around me was being converted into machines and I was powerless to control the change. Of course, the worst aspect of this is that it must work. People must be stupid enough to stay on the line and then buy whatever it is being offered for something like this to persist. And our grocery stores are gradually being converted into corporate chains. So when I saw you and knew you had been the one who sent the email, I reacted harshly. I didn't know you were Art's friend. ¿You grew up with him?"

I briefly explained to her the extent of my relationship with Art, trying to speak honestly about how close we had been at our closest point and how close we were up until the time of his disappearance. But *my* story did not interest me. "¿What does Conozca a su Panadero mean to you?" I asked.

"As I mentioned before, probably most anyone in Barcelona would be able to tell you. Arturo had just come from Oaxaca, Mexico, and before that he had lived in London, and during that time, he had been painting the Conozca a su Panadero series. He came to Barcelona because the curator of the Picasso museum called him to stage an exhibition in a space several blocks from the museum, calling it 'Arturo Serrano—Picasso of the Americas.' As I said, I met him at a dinner several weeks after he had arrived and, eager to ask him questions about his art, I found a way for Garza—the curator—to introduce me. He seemed very disenchanted. When I asked him about his art, he told me, 'It's useless.' I asked him what he meant. Knowing him now as I do, I doubt he really wanted to talk to me about it, but he was affable and he explained to me what he meant—that it provides no solutions to any of the grand-scale problems of our world—and I would say that in twenty minutes he gave me a deeper glimpse into his soul than had anyone else I've met since adolescence. He told me that he was abandoning his career as an artist, that he no longer received the same satisfaction with his paintings he once had. It was heartbreaking because I think he was wrong—because art does a *lot* for people. We don't know its effects because, like the paintings themselves, the effects are abstract—incalculable.

But once you got into his head and understood how ugly the world looked to him…"

I interrupted her to mention that Art had once made a statement nearly identical to what she'd just said. That it was only through art that men would understand one another.

"¿Really?" She said, "That's hard to believe. I would have liked to have met Arturo the boy—Arturo the idealist. It might explain some of his earlier work. It might explain *all* of it. Or maybe it is just that the birth of the artist includes, to some extent, a death—perhaps the death of idealism. Anyway, by the time Arturo was thirty, art had become to him something weightless and empty. I said to him when we were having dinner one night, '¿Why don't you just take a break? Don't paint anything for right now, and in the meantime, find something else to do.' I didn't think he would really appreciate what I said, especially so quickly, but the next day he came to my apartment with sketches for several T-shirts, one of which you are wearing, and all three said the same thing. We got a small T-shirt company to produce them, and they caught on—people were wearing them all over Barcelona. The fact that they had been created by Arturo—and you realize Barcelona has always been a city of art that supports its famous artists—only made their value that much higher. By the time we organized the very first Conozca a su Panadero conference, thousands of people from Spain and Europe-at-large found their way to Barcelona to hear our speeches."

She went on to explain the details of the Conozca a su Panadero campaign. Art's idea, she said, was to make it impossible for anyone in Barcelona not to know those three words. He canvassed sidewalks in chalk, rented billboards, organized rallies at the Universitat de Barcelona, in the Plaça de Catalunya, on the streets and at his exhibitions.

"But now that Arturo is gone," she continued, moving her hands through her hair and for a moment avoiding eye contact with me, "you don't hear about any of these things. You instead hear about his final painting, the one where he painted himself out of the world. ¿Do you know why he painted himself out of the world? It's because he felt like he didn't exist in it anymore. Whether he killed himself or not—that's a different story. But, that painting is not a suicide note—it's the final expression of Conozca a su Panadero. If we stopped knowing our bakers—if we allowed everything in our environments to become branded, order our food from home and have it delivered and left at the door, allow computers to make phone calls for us and images and name brands and categories to define us, then we don't exist. ¿Because to whom would we exist? Arturo did not paint *himself* out of the world. He painted anyone who looked at the mirror out of the world. He painted people out of a world that has been taken over by images and machines."

As I registered what Marta Herrera was saying, I was also pondering the number of transformations she had made over the span of the last two days. First, she had appeared to me as a library desk clerk, taking my business card in order to pass it along; then she had become the irate woman who had sent me away, informing me that Marta Herrera was ill; next, at the sight of my shirt, a comrade; then an activist; an enlightener; and soon the person in the world whom, for a moment, I felt I understood the best. And each time it was she in front of me, and yet it was our interaction that changed the way she looked to me, that made her seem suddenly more familiar, more physically alluring, more intelligent, as if the conversation dressed her more than her clothing did.

It occurred to me, of course, that she had been in love with Art, that she had been one of his "lovers," though I couldn't decide how or why I knew this. The thought arrived like a word we haven't heard in ages arrives on the page when we are writing. We spend hours talking and never use the word, but as soon as we sit down in front of the keyboard or the typewriter, here it comes, wearing the vestments of another century, the obscurity of a secondary or even tertiary meaning, and we turn to our dictionary and realize, yes, this is the appropriate word that fits exactly what we are attempting to describe, though we are completely unaware as to how it came to be on this screen in Garamond.

I went with her to her apartment for dinner—she lived in Sant Gervasi Sarria, near the Parc Güell (another Gaudian design), on the top floor of a three-story building. I lingered beyond the meal—and beyond the arrival of several neighbors from upstairs, who descended upon her apartment in the hopes of dragging us off to sing karaoke—in order to ask her more questions about Art, hoping to be led to something that might further deepen my understanding of who he was, something that might provide me with information heretofore in shadow. Finally, when we were alone, she once again transformed, her features suddenly darker than they already were: her hair, eyelashes and deep, black eyes.

"I can't believe he's dead," she said. "And yet he *is*. He never belonged to this world."

"¿Was he in danger?" I asked, suddenly considering something I hadn't before.

"He had an ugly side to him that only few people saw. On the surface, in a crowd, he put on a face. He could endear himself to anyone, not through any display of specific charm or wit but just by being in the room. The darkness wasn't to do with, I don't think, any regrets about his own performance: and he wasn't affected by people's reaction to his art, or at least he never mentioned it if he did. He painted because it made sense for him to do so—it was like cooking dinner or having sex. But there was a part of him that really hated the large majority of people, how we constantly lie about ourselves and our intentions, how willing we are to hurt someone else for our own gain. Yes, I'm worried he's killed himself."

"¿But what would he have done with his body?" I asked, taking in the shock of a statement that should not have been specifically shocking in light of the events of the past several months. "That's the part that most makes me feel he's still alive."

"No," she said. "You don't understand. Arturo would *never* have left behind his body—that would have had too much of an environmental impact…¿Gas yourself or jump off a building? Think of all the carbon, the cost of a church-funeral, the embalming fluids sinking into the soil. No, Arturo would have disappeared first, and *then* he would have done it."

"¿He was an environmentalist, too?

She didn't respond. What did my question mean, anyway?

"¿Were you *together*?" I finally asked.

"¿You didn't know that? ¿Isn't that why you came looking for me?…We shared that bed"—she pointed at the partially made lump of sheets in the corner of the room—"for 131 days, from the moment I met him until he left Barcelona."

"¿Why did he leave?"

"¿Why would he have stayed?" She said, her eyes wet with tears. "¿For *me*?"

"¿Why not for you?" I said.

"He left me a note when he went. It said, 'I can't stay. You and I both know that. And I can't tolerate goodbyes…' "

"¿He couldn't tolerate goodbyes?…*I'm* the same way," I said.

"That's what he always said. His dreams were always dreams of disappearance. He said to me more than once that he wanted to learn to play the tuba and paint under a pseudonym and just completely withdraw from all the world—from everyone; only his parents would know where he'd gone. He said he wouldn't say where it was that he wanted to go, but *he* knew where. I think he meant Rio—that was the place he most romanticized."

"¿Do you think he might be in Brazil now?"

"I wouldn't be surprised if he were."

"¿Do you think he's dead?"

"I've already answered that question."

"It's time I go," I said, thinking that maybe I'd already taken up too much of her time.

"Don't," she said, staring intensely at me, her eyes becoming dilated. I returned her gaze. After a moment, she leaned into me and kissed me. Her tongue felt strange in my mouth, but the tenderness of the kiss helped me to confuse it with affection.

Did I dare go? Let's face it—it didn't happen too often that a woman just suddenly kissed me.

I stayed the night with her there in her apartment—in her bed—sleeping very little and, when she fell asleep, staring at a ceiling Art had looked up at for at least several of those 131 nights.

What followed, after I left Marta, proved disappointing since, instead of seeing Art's charismatic twenty-three-year-old sister the next evening, I was given a note from the owner of the restaurant that she had phoned in a cancellation, as she had suddenly been summoned to Madrid, where a train bombing had killed twenty-two people and injured countless others. She was sorry not to be able to see me, unsure as to when she would return and hopeful that she could see me at some point in New York; she had tentative plans to attend an event there in July. And so it was that I met one woman whom I had not expected to see and did not see another whom I thought I was sure to.

I collected my things from the front desk of the hotel so that I could make my move on toward Munich. I was growing tired of lugging the same things around and even more tired of my lifestyle over the past two weeks. I thought about coming back to Barcelona to do more interviews and see Beatriz. Perhaps I would. But nothing seemed more enticing than returning to Brooklyn, spring electrifying the street and preparing the way for summer—the bandstand at Prospect Park, eating brown rice on the stoop, the promise of all those artifacts unearthed from our stairwell and wondering what Camille had chosen to do with them.

the activist

On the overnight train from Barcelona to Munich, I shared a cabin with four others—a man from Berlin, an American woman from Detroit and a young couple from Barcelona, who throughout the night whispered pledges of love back and forth in nearly inaudible voices as the train whooshed across the continent. Europe brings strangers closer together in shared sleeping cabins, hostels, hotels and tables at restaurants, where the maître d's do not think twice about seating people less than half an arm's length away. I loved sleeper cars for their novelty, especially as we do not have such comfortable terrestrial travel alternatives in the United States, and because I relished the idea of moving while sleeping away the night since, so often, we find our ways to sleep, dream thousands of stories during the night that have changed us, but wake to find ourselves in the same place and state we were in eight hours before. In a sleeper car, we awake to different languages, new countries, fresh lives.

In the email reply I received from Kristof von Behren, he said, "…Glad to receive your travel plans. Call me if there is any change. Otherwise, I will see you outside the S-Bahn at Hauptbahnhof holding a sign with a nickname I have created for you. Then, I will take you to a party under a bridge…" When I woke up, the Detroit woman was gone, the couple had fallen asleep in the same small bed, and the man from Berlin was standing just outside the cabin staring out the window. I walked past him in my sandals to the bathroom, where I found two women in their twenties wearing nightgowns and slippers—one had a toothbrush in her mouth—waiting for the water closet. The expressions on their faces foretold annoyance were I to make the mistake of conversing with them or attempting to bribe them to let me go first. When my turn finally came, I noticed something I had also observed on board the train from Paris to Barcelona. Water closets on trains have signs above the toilets indicating what sorts of objects you aren't to throw in them. This train from Barcelona to Munich suggested not throwing a newspaper or soda can into it. I wondered who got to decide which objects are represented in the diagram, and if these objects changed from country to country based on the culture (I did not remember which objects were represented from Paris to Barcelona) and, if it could be taken a step further, perhaps by picturing objects associated with the countries the train traveled through. In Belgium, there would be Brussels sprouts, waffles and beer, in Mexico—pozole, sombreros and mariachis.

When I finished, I returned to outside the cabin and, not wanting to enter again for fear of causing the young lovers to awake in the presence of someone they did not know, I spoke to the Berliner. He told me that he was returning to Berlin on a later train from Munich that evening and that he had just been to Porto, Portugal, where his son was living with a woman who had just left the convent she had belonged to for the past decade. The man was now retired and he spent his time traveling from place to place using a discount pass for the elderly, but he said he did not really enjoy this privilege—his wife had died a year before and, as he rode through endless town after town, in every place he went he always felt he was turning around to say something to her, but she was never there.

Reaching the Hauptbahnhof, the train finally slowed, with little warning, except I'm sure to the Germans, who understood the announcement (Spanish had been abandoned hours ago) and, in a rush, I quickly grabbed my bag and left the train, wondering if the Spanish couple had intended to stay on and, if they hadn't, whether this would enhance or diminish their eternal love. By the time I reached the main hall, I looked around for anyone holding a sign and, finally, without any doubt, began to approach a man in his late forties with a shaved head who was holding a sketch that I recognized as a recreation of the poster for the American film, *The Mexican*, with a question mark over the shadow of a figure, where Brad Pitt would have been shown almost kissing Julia Roberts with his hands clasped in hers.

"What do you think?" he said, as I approached him, "Well, it only took me five minutes," he said, handing it to me. Within seconds, he was leading me out of the train station and toward the street, where he had illegally parked his car. As I sat down in the passenger seat, I thanked him for the offer to stay with him but tried to beg off as, I told him, I could easily stay in a hotel.

"A hotel? No, no, no. Some of the hotels, you know, are converted Nazi barracks. There are probably swastikas still on the walls and moustache hairs clogging the sinks. You can stay with us—with me, my wife and my daughter. Besides, we live over by the Englischer Garten—the English Garden—well, so does half of Munich, and you can go out there and sun with the naked men in the afternoon."

I thanked him for the kind gesture and the poster.

"Lots of thank-yous from Americans. It is a thanking culture. You know, Arturo is much more Mexican than you, but he is still an American. I tried to convince him of that, but he would not listen. So, I guess it fits that I made you Brad Pitt, but it's an old movie now and a not-so-good one, though he's still a really great actor. Could have been the voiceover. The voiceover artist in *12 Monkeys* was great. He's the same guy who does Gary Sinise."

"Gary Sinise—they've got two completely different ways of talking."

"Not in Germany," Kristof said. "I think he also does the voice for Kiefer Sutherland. Anyway, it's time for us to go eat lunch—we have to make it to the bridge by five o'clock."

During lunch, we did not talk about Art; instead, he asked me questions about writing, listening with such attention that I thought he was either considering going into the field or wanted to know everything he could about it so that he would never have to hear about it again.

After about an hour in which almost all of my questions to him were deferred until later, as he wanted to continue asking me about writing, he said, "I read the B-35. Art gave it to me when he left Munich three years ago. It's a fabulous collection of essays, but the name—did you really expect to sell any copies?"

"I don't know why I named it that. I just thought the picture of the bus on the cover could be amazing. When they replaced it with a picture of a man with a German Shepherd, I think maybe people confused B-35 with K-9 and thought the book was about dogs. I don't know."

"But the essay is much better. A lot of truths. And very funny. You're not as funny in person as you are in your book."

I explained to him my theory about how senses of humor were like blood types, how everyone's not funny to everybody else but some people are and how some people think everything's funny but others only enjoy certain senses of humor.

I asked him about his own work. "Well, let me put it this way," he said, "Arturo's and my styles are as similar as American actors and their German voiceover counterparts. I paint concepts, and he is a true genius of the brush. Arturo is a rarity these days, in this world, because he is strictly a painter, whereas I do sculptures, graphic design, printmaking, fonts, mobiles—you know, things to hang over the baby's crib—and now movie posters. You should feel honored to appear in one."

I had finished the food, even polished off the garnish that had appeared as an optional side, but Kristof hardly touched his food. I insisted on paying the bill, but he refused.

"Don't worry. I have an account here. Do you see that sculpture?" He pointed to a large sculpture of a tongue with a nose hovering above it in the middle of a fountain; the tongue licked the water, and the water sprayed upwards. "The owner and I are friends. Ever since I made this sculpture for him, the food has been on the house. I guess you know what the sculpture is supposed to signify."

I shook my head.

"No one can *ever* figure out what it means. But it's simple—the two organs of taste are the tongue and the nose, even though we most often rely on the other senses—what a restaurant looks like, the texture of the food and what we hear about a place—to decide whether or not to go there. Of course, sculptures are all about pleasing the eyes. They're also the only art that can be experienced by the blind, though, sadly, museums don't like it when you touch their sculptures. Some even keep signs up that say, 'Do not touch.' Fortunately, these are signs the blind cannot read, so I always think they should touch them anyway."

After what ended up to be an early dinner, because we stayed at the restaurant until nearly five, Kristof drove through the city, pointing out major sites, including

Marienplatz, with the gorgeous Neues Rathaus, which, like the Sagrada Família in Barcelona, depicts miniature scenes upon the façade; the Olympiastadion, where he said he had seen some of the most exciting football matches of his life; and BMW headquarters, a building in the shape of a six-cylinder engine. He turned onto a road flanked by trees and several miles down the path turned onto a smaller dirt road and parked halfway into a ditch. We opened our doors and walked through the glaze with which spring, in conjunction with the sun streaking through the trees, had coated everything in our view.

"Can you hold this?" he said, and loaded me up with multiple bags, which held, among other things, a grill, bottles of wine, beer and ice. "Is that enough?" he asked.

We cut a path through the trees until we reached the ledge aside the Isar. "Hello," he called to a few people—one man and two women, who were already below. We handed our bags down to one of the men, and then climbed down the ledge with the help of the others.

The man was a political science professor, one of the women was a television journalist, the other a photographer. They had already managed to bring down fold-up chairs and some beer that they had buried in the shallow part of the water. The bridge and the trees were our skyline; the frosty water flowed gently past. I helped Kristof set up the grill, as the professor brought over the coal, and the three of us attempted to ignite the fire and begin cooking the Weißwürst. "Wah!" Kristof, said, as the grill flamed up. "How many academics does it take?"

We sat in the chairs and, as Kristof monitored the sausages, he told me about the history of the Friday evenings—with added lore from the others, the faithful—an evening that had been a monthly tradition for the past eight years, sometimes with friends or family joining, but usually limited to the original four. When spring and summer came, this was the patch of shore next to the river that—higher tides

232

notwithstanding—they would always find their ways to because, as Kristof said, proudly, "Tradition is either the sign of true friendship or the first indication of decadence."

It didn't take long before the sausages were cooked and, though I was not hungry (I now understood why Kristof had eaten so little at the restaurant before), I managed to eat two of the sausages, which were improved by the taste of stout lingering in my mouth. By the time everyone was eating, Kristof introduced me, though they seemed to already know who I was and seemed, ridiculously, to regard my knowing Art as secondary to my feats as a writer, which substantiated Kristof's claims that he was one of the people who had actually read my book.

When we did eventually turn to a discussion of Art, the conversation seemed to change tone, similar to the hush that descends upon a room when a powerful figure unexpectedly enters. The atmosphere of jubilance quelled, the candles pulsating in the sunset dim, the photographer turned to me after a brief pause in conversation in which they were discussing an exhibit they'd seen at the Zentralinstitut für Kunstgeschichte, the Central Institute for Art History, and said, "What do you think happened to Art?" For a split second, though I am not sure why, whether it was the inflection in her voice or the utter impossibility that she could mean anything else, I actually thought she was referring to *art* rather than *Art* and only after allowing the question to echo in my head for the remainder of the second was I able to consider an answer.

"I don't know," I said, taken aback because it was the question *I* was normally the one to ask. "That's why I'm here. That's why I'm trying to discover his past. Do you know Art, too?"

"Yes," the photographer said. "I was the one who introduced him to our little circle. I introduced him to Kristof. I thought that the two of them would get along instantly. I actually met Art when I was doing a photo story on him—for

Heftig—" she said, looking at the others, who nodded, as she named the magazine—"when he first moved from Barcelona to Munich. It was quite a feat to convince him to be photographed, as photos of him are rare, and he made me promise that I wouldn't make him look taller, less indigenous and that I would not use imaging software to smooth out his face. After the shoot, I brought him here so that he could meet Kristof, hoping that perhaps Kristof could convince him to start painting again. In effect, the reverse happened."

"What do you mean?" I asked.

Kristof continued the story. "I didn't produce a work of art for six months—not even a sock puppet," he said. "Instead, I became a minion of lost causes…" He raised an eyebrow. "An activist." As Kristof spoke, and the others contributed, he lit perhaps twenty tea candles that he passed on to the professor, who placed them onto the table and, when it was amply lit, he used them to form a square around us while we sat listening to Kristof as he elucidated the details of their collaboration. The first thing they did was translate Conozca a su Panadero into German—*Dein Bäcker Kennen*. Kristof remarked that it had already been translated into French (*Connaître son Boulanger*) and Italian (*Cognoscere il suo Fornaio*) and, of course, English, and that it would later, during Art's visit to Brazil, which occurred at about the midpoint of his time in Munich, be harvested in Portuguese (*Conheça o seu Padeiro*).

I interrupted Kristof to ask him when and why exactly Art had gone to Brazil, and he explained that Art had maintained contact "with a priest called Padre Haroldo" with whom he had spent some time volunteering in his early twenties. He didn't mention much of what Art had been doing there, merely that it was connected to the priest's social work. As I expected, the time corresponded exactly with the time João Fabiano had led protests against the police officers who murdered street kids in death squads, though this was more of a confirmation than it was new information. According to

Father Rahm—or Padre Haroldo—he had been selling art in Rio. When I asked Kristof about this, he said, "Not to my knowledge. As far as I know, Arturo did not resume painting until he had left Munich and gone back to El Paso."

"But he did translate Know Your Baker into Portuguese? What did you say it was?"

"Conheça o seu Padeiro," Kristof repeated.

"Did he do anything with it in Brazil?"

He assured me that the translation was the extent of what he knew. He then launched into the details of Art's campaign in Munich. As it turned out, since the Second World War, NATO had held an annual conference called the "Summit for Safety Policy" but, in recent years, according to Kristof, this conference had seemed to be little more than a coordination of capitalist countries in preparation for war. Kristof, who was surprised that I had not heard of the protest, said Art was intent on making a huge statement opposing preemptive wars and 'seeking peace through war.' As officials and media increasingly became aware of the exact nature of the protests, they briefed several hundred police officers, in addition to other armored personnel, special commandos and snipers, on the protest that was to take place in front of the Hotel Bayerischer Hof, the conference venue. Art and Kristof, with other key protestors from all over Europe, discovered that not only had the city been alerted to their extensive preparations, but it had also banned all demonstrations over the week, thereby permitting officers to make as many arrests as they wanted. Even though Art and Kristof relished in the idea of having thousands of people assembled in front of the hotel, they decided to split into smaller groups of several thousand and protest at various points across the city and then march into one large congregation during the peak of the conference.

When the day of the event finally came, Art and Kristof learned that the Germans who had organized protests in the years past—whom the two had joined as leaders this year—had been arrested in their homes the morning of the protest. The many activists convened in their designated places but, because the leaders were neither in Marienplatz nor downtown, the protest was disorganized and chaotic.

"By the time we arrived downtown, the scene was hectic," Kristof said. "Cops were arresting protestors everywhere. There was an armed officer for every three protesters. It all ended up this huge mess."

"How did you and Art manage not to be arrested?" I asked.

"Well, it was somewhat important to us—to Arturo especially—that our names not be disclosed. Since a lot of our allies were the ones who made the connections with the people who publicized the protest, the police and the press never really knew we had been involved," he said.

"But wouldn't it have made sense to use your names in order to better publicize the event?"

"Not mine, of course. But Arturo could have. However, I think in Barcelona he found that almost all of the attention was put on him and felt that the cause was much more important than his involvement. He wanted it to be the people's crusade rather than *his* crusade because if you saw the way the media responded to his anti-globalization protests there, they did paint it to be his mission rather than the people's, which he felt trivialized it. Our supporters in Munich knew that he was involved, and we were thankful. He took it very personally, of course, when all of these people were arrested because he felt it was *his* plan that had failed, when, of course, it was the fault of whomever had leaked such detailed information to the authorities."

"Or the fault of the city officials who interfered on our right to assemble," the photographer added, knocking against the table as she leaned forward upon it, causing the tea candles to shudder. Her voice slurred a bit when she talked, at times making her all the more forthright, at times invalidating what she was saying. "It was the conference itself that was protested, not capitalism in general. If it had been capitalism

236

alone, some of the placards would have been much more on the mark."

I didn't know what she meant by the placards being "more on the mark" but Kristof seemed embarrassed by this comment. Somewhat petulantly, perhaps a bit drunk, the photographer said to Kristof, "You should at least tell him what happened."

"What do you mean?" he asked her.

"About how Arturo was almost arrested," she said. "Or I can tell it."

He seemed almost not to have heard her request and went down to the water and took several other beers out from under the rocks. "One of these days we're going to forget to take the beer out of the water," he said, not detailing what the repercussions of such an oversight would be.

"Go ahead," he said, as soon as he had returned. "What can it hurt to tell him? I think we can trust that you won't abuse this information," he said, looking at me.

The photographer continued: "Arturo was angry when he found out that the other people leading the protests had been arrested. As a result, during the arrests of the other protesters at Marienplatz, he went there and protested side by side with them. Kristof was with him there. It was a non-violent march, and even those who were arrested were asked not to resist. Kristof came across Arturo a few blocks from the main area of the protest with one of the delegates, who we later learned was at the conference promoting the use of unmanned aerial combat vehicles in war. We don't know if Art knew this or not. We do know that Art was holding a knife to his throat."

"I don't understand," I said. "He was threatening the delegate with a knife?"

"He was," Kristof joined in. "I asked him what he was doing. Arturo had *always* said that we were never, under *any* circumstances, to protest violently. This was, in fact, the whole point of our protest. After I convinced him to let the delegate go, he told me that violence could be used

237

strategically and, as a threat, it was a particularly strong one. I wouldn't have been surprised had these words come from almost anyone else, but from Arturo, for whom non-violence was the sacred seed of his entire philosophy, this was more than shocking. He talked about the power brandished by many men in suits who never yield weapons but who send the children of others to die on battlefields...how can the value of life be understood, he said, when no one was threatening *their* lives? But we'd had an entirely different discussion just two or three weeks before, in which he explained to me why he believed no one should ever carry a weapon. In that conversation, he had said that if you carry a weapon, whether you know it consciously or not, your fate is *always* to use it."

According to the group, several weeks after the protest, Art left Munich to go back to El Paso, saying that he wanted to compose himself and return to painting. The group had been sad to see him go, but they knew it was for the best that he went away from Europe and away from the epicenter of protest and hostility and back into the much-safer environment of the art world in which he was so prominent a figure.

I was taken aback at what the photographer had led me to discover, just as it had surprised and embarrassed them. Art had never been hostile, and the knife that he carried showed that the action was not simply a reaction, but also on some level premeditated.

We all continued to talk by the bridge for another hour or so, as the slow current breezed across the bed of rocks and sand and beer, until eventually Kristof took me back up the path through the forest to his car, then back to his house, where I met his exceptionally tall wife who had waited up for him, the kids already tucked in and asleep, a bed in their guest room made up for me and what would be my last night in Europe, as the next morning I would wake to an urgent email from a magazine offering me several thousand dollars to do an exclusive cover interview with a prominent celebrity known best for his incredible sensitivity and on-stage temper tantrums. (But wasn't I secretly hoping for a reason for my trip to be cut short, having only been led to the revelation that *I* was the Patrick Keating of the Americas?—Or was I being too hard on myself…?)

As I lay down in the unfamiliar room, a different, equally as unsettling, feeling remained as I looked up at the ceiling, and it was connected to the night I had spent with Marta, just after she told me not to go and then kissed me.

I had let what followed happen despite the fact that I knew full and well why I had been invited into her bed: Art had been there before, too, in her apartment, among her plants and a cat and a dining room table that folded out into the living room to make room for as many as eight. I was taking advantage of my relationship to him again, as perhaps I always had, riding on his coattails, following his footsteps down the sandy beach. This wasn't the first time I was sleeping with a woman because of him. Hadn't there also been a journalist at a conference in Philadelphia to whom I'd mentioned in all earnestness that I could make an introduction?

If I had achieved a degree of intimacy with the legendary Art Serrano, then certainly *I* couldn't be all that bad. Certainly *I* had it all together.

Wasn't that right?

salsa de manzana

Taste the sap that abseils down trees. Chew it slowly and savor the movement of every muscle in your jaw that allows you the degustatory pleasure of licking a tree's soul. That's what Padre says, and he heard that from his Padre, who is now somewhere in América del Sur—Brazil—telling people that the soul is what animates the body, encendiendo todo—the lungs breathing, the heart beating, the stomach bleating. Relish it all. Life is beautiful, and anything that reminds us of that is saccharine. We live fast lives, busy to the hilt. When we started dying, we still hadn't started living yet. They tasted us, put their tongues into our bodies and created terror in a place designed for love. Somehow I got away, but I am still running, with sweat rushing down my face and into my mouth. I am much older now, and I know all the best places to hide, but I am still a woman, and the only place safe

240

enough is age, briny skin, wrinkled eyelids—to no longer be wanted. We are always living on this line, trying to repulse and attract at the same time. But men are impossible, and there are only two types of them—good and bad—and, really, I'd rather be old so I don't have to figure out which is which because oftentimes they look the same. I have chosen to taste other pleasures, the kind I return to every day after work—the tortillas I make with my hands, the masa I roll and bake, enchiladas verdes, tamales dulces, heart of palm and sun-dried tomatoes in pasta—the sabor of this world. Miren acá, mis hermanas, it is time we take this life into our hands, rub our bellies and fill our souls with language, la Biblia, art. Let's taste from a world that was so intent on tasting us.

The taste of salsa de manzana always reminded her of the first day of law school because, just before the class began, she'd felt nauseated and so had gone to one of the university stores and bought applesauce in a small pudding container. The anxiety feeling had leaked into the sauce, or vice versa, and for months afterward every time she ate it, she felt anxious and nervous and was instantly back at a desk amid a hundred, with her notepad and her pen, her heels and her black skirt, her hose and her lipstick, her hair put up, her white button-down shirt reminding her of the fresa Catholic schoolgirls. She was twenty five years old, but she felt ten years younger—when the function of her dress had been to make her look older, more mature.

The professor, a stern, burly man—El Ano, The Anus, as he was known to the students, a nickname that, when he caught wind of it himself, he used himself self-aggrandizingly, allowing it to encapsulate his reputation among students and faculty—was the school's name brand draw for his incomparable case record in Mexico City and coincident number of times his name was implicated in cases of precedence, and several years before he had asked that he be the one in charge of the incoming law students' first class. The classroom was completely full, and no one was talking, but an even greater hush that reminded Esme of the way a judge enters a courtroom, from a side-door that no one else comes through, something connected to a whole other world, a lavish apartment with legal books strapped onto built-in bookshelves, an immense oblong desk that is completely empty but for a pen and, of course, secrets—secrets in the walls, in the dusty binding of the books and the closets and in the pencil shavings on the floor—descended on the room when the professor entered.

"You," the professor said, pointing at no one in specific, but in her direction. "¿What are you doing here?"

"We're here to uphold the law," one man, obviously quite young, yelled from the front row, after a few moments had passed, and many of the students in the class laughed, more out of relief that they hadn't been called on than of admiration for the young man's nerve.

"Of course," the professor said, nodding his head in agreement. "¿What is your name?" He asked, walking toward the student and smiling that of a benevolent grandfather.

"Emilio Sánchez."

"Emilio Sánchez," the professor repeated, walking away from him and then addressing the rest of the class. "Class, it is in your best interest to make sure el señor Sánchez never becomes a lawyer. The law is not for us to uphold, but to mold into our own shapes. The law is written in words, and words are flexible, we give them the meaning we wish. We can turn any good word into a slur, any bit of profanity into an apostolic incantation."

He paced from the left side of the room to the right without saying anything, then asked, louder than he had the first time: "¿*Why* are you here?"

Esmeralda, from the middle of the room, yelled out, "¡Justice for the women of Juárez!" and the several other women in the room and some of the men clapped at her response.

242

"¡How great!" the professor said. "¡What a thrilling moment for my career! Someone willing to combat the ills of the world with the very idealism that allows it to happen, that is the reason why women walk into the darkness of night, that is the reason so many lawyers fall flat on their faces. Great, when I need an emotional lawyer, I'll call you, señorita. ¿What is your name?"

"Esmeralda," she said, almost proudly.

"Fantastic," he said, loudly. "She has a fairy tale name and no surname. ¿From what fairy tale do you come, here to sprinkle on the world your fairy dust to save us all? Emotions have no place in a lawyer's repertory. We must hide our emotions rather than screaming them out like wailing babies. I assume, everyone, that we will always remember Esmeralda and her wonderful ideas, and perhaps she will make a great lawyer some day in Wonderland."

Esmeralda resisted the urge to leave the room. She looked straight ahead and watched the professor's mouth move, his Adam's apple bouncing with every word.

Here he was, maybe, standing on the corner of the block, fully uniformed and on-duty, when he saw her leave the pharmacy across the street and walk in the opposite direction. He was an officer of five years, sworn by the code to protect and serve, a history of salient arrests, camaraderie with several of his superior officers, a chance for promotion, married for four years, two kids, a house in a decent zone, a VCR player and connections with a satellite dish provider, who offered him free cable in exchange for occasional help knocking off occasional misdemeanors—a small price to pay for the immediate gratification of so much television. He radioed another officer parked several blocks down, taking lunch in his car. "¿Mira, güey, do you see that vieja?" There was no response for several seconds, the airwaves crackling. He was supposed to be checking out the cars along the road, always waiting for that Cadillac with the windows tinted, the

243

compartments stuffed with white powder and somewhere therein a wad of cash, something he might be able to get a piece of before one of the other officers did. Of course, it was all a dream anyway. He didn't work border patrol—it was unlikely he'd get away with the big loot, so he just had to keep satisfied with the occasional bite. Maybe he thought back upon that time he *was* on a drug bust. A few years before, on a country road outside of Juárez, they'd pulled over this car for a routine check. And with his gun slung around his shoulders, he had asked the guy for his information—¿De dónde son? ¿Qué hacen?—But there had been just too many people in the car, all cooperative and practically amiable, and not the religious types, practicing Christian educación, but clever types, sarcastic types, held mute by their complicity in something. How he and the other officers had combed through the car, asking the man and his associates to stand with their hands upon this massive tree on the side of the road—a convenience of landscape—and stuck their hands in all the gaps and all the places drugs were ever found and, eventually, after a quarter of an hour, found underneath the car the mother lode, enough cocaine to keep Mexico City running for an entire month. The payoff, that was worth it, that warranted being a cop. But now, perhaps, resigned to watching a neighborhood away from the centro, a repeat event would take a miracle. "¿Pues, did you see that girl, güey? *No mames…*" He maybe called again into the radio, this time frustrated. The guy eating lunch was a pendejo, probably didn't hear the radio and didn't see the girl. Pinche pendejo.

But then, perhaps someone *did* respond into the radio. "I'm just around the corner. I'm going to drop by and pick you up," the voice maybe said. He recognized the voice. It was someone in his precinct. Jesús, I hope he isn't angry at what I said over the intercom, he thought. But he didn't have enough time to turn this uncertainty into anxiety. As the car pulled up aside him, the driver stretched his arm across the seat and unlocked the door so that he could get in. "So," the guy said, his face expressionless "¿Y la vieja?

"Just saw her walk around the corner, pero ya se fue. She's gone now."

"Too bad," the officer driving the car maybe said. "¿She was pretty?"

"Unbelievable. Should have seen her ass."

"Should have," the driver said, and then he looked into the officer's face, as if threatened with the possibility that he had forgotten something. "I want to show you something. Radio to the maricón that you're going with me for the next hour."

Perhaps they drove away from the centro toward the desert, zipping from lane to lane, their sirens spanning volumes, until they reached a residential area and then slowed the car, disabled the sound system and drove on for another ten or twenty minutes, crusted in silence, the officer on the passenger side wondering to what death he was going.

"Aquí estamos," the officer who was driving said. The other officer closed his door and followed him into what looked like a police station but seemed deserted for its bedraggled appearance and its location nowhere. Another police car and a civilian truck were parked in front. The two officers walked into the building, knocking first on the outer door and identifying themselves, then entering through the doorway, the exposed trusses on both sides making this place look as if it had never been finished in the first place. The officer who had been driving introduced his friend to the others, and each of the officers, whom he had seen before but did not know, welcomed him, asking him if he wanted a cigarette or a drink. He accepted a cigarette, but it was too early for him to be drinking, he said, though when they insisted, he downed a shot of tequila from a paper cup.

Maybe the tequila threw him for a jolt. He could feel it slip down his esophagus toward his stomach. And then he saw the difference, the translucence that extended to the world around him, a heightening or dulling—he wasn't sure—it only lasted a few seconds. He followed the officer who had been driving and a third officer into a room at the far end of the station and, on the inside of the door, he saw what must have been a hundred or more photos of women and girls pasted to the wood. "¿Are those…?"

"Yes," the third officer said. "Nearly two hundred of them."

Later that night, as he pushed his wife, who had been snoring, onto her side, he tried to stay calm against the current of thought that kept him awake, and he thought to himself that he would rather not have known, that this was too large a secret for a man to have to keep, and he wished he would never have radioed about the girl crossing the street because then he may not have been brought to that place in the desert, as knowledge of it seemed to insist a responsibility to the secret and this responsibility, and the others' doubt about his maintenance of this responsibility would likely, at some point, threaten his life. An hour passed, and his wife began to snore again and, though he lay still and breathed deeply, sleep, something that with practice one can fake, skipped entirely over him, and he didn't begin to fade until the water truck came roaring down the street, blasting its tune, ringing his doorbell: twenty pesos the garrafón, and you can always sleep later, my friend.

In the time since Esmeralda had begun law school, Padre Osvaldo saw less and less of her, but he took this as a sign of their relationship developing rather than slackening—like a new hobby that has been practiced with feverish frenzy during the initial stages that later either attenuates to nonexistence or blossoms into habit, the two of them, the law student and the gray-eyed priest, always found a way to meet weekly, though only once weekly and, despite the fact that in the past she had stayed longer in his office or at the cathedral or wherever they had met, she now excused herself after precisely one hour, without apology, so that she could recommence her study for the night. Perhaps Osvaldo, in his occasional rumination over this extraordinary relationship with Esmeralda, which far surpassed all his relationships with other priests and other parishioners because it was of the few relationships in his life where the full gamut of subject matter was thrown open to discussion—religion, philosophy, literature, culture, fine arts, comedy, the underworld—would have lamented the partition law school had created in divvying up time into hours rather than evenings had his ministerial duties not been so overwhelmingly required all over the metropolis of Juárez. On the Thursday in question, he woke at five a.m., scanned the newspaper, adding no new clips to the binder but still leafing through it briefly. These days, he did not eat between midnight and noon, calling breakfast "desayuyo" instead of "desayuno," because he felt those twelve hours would serve to de-weed his stomach of everything in it, cleansing him of food and causing him to apperceive the suffering of the hungry, as throughout his life breakfast had always been his favorite meal. In the seminary, he had found a similar coincidence of language convenient to English as well, always decompounding the word to "break" and "fast" and, by this time in his life, by the time the last follicle of his hair had turned white, he had refused breakfast for more than forty years. Six-thirty was the time preordained for the celebration of the day's first mass and, in a white vestment, which he selected for la Fiesta de los Ángeles, the Feast of the Angels—Gabriel, Rafael and Miguel—he stood in front of the small congregation of regulars. Padre Osvaldo could not regulate the length of his homily. Sometimes, he would end dreadfully early and, other times, go on for twice as long as he should have. Additionally, as this was the feast that marked the beginning of the academic year in which Esme participated, he felt emotionally connected to this day in a way he never had before. In the homily, which he would repeat later in the second mass with even further digression, he spoke of the prayer that was often given to San Miguel, the

247

most hallowed of the seraphim and the angel most referenced in the Bible; he had decided not to use the famous prayer of Pope León XIII that began "San Miguel, the Archangel, defend us in battle…" because he did not like prayers that seemed to endorse violence or that, as later in the prayer is incanted "thrust into hell Satan and all other evil spirits," asked God to declare unfavorable judgments upon spirits or villains. Padre Osvaldo incorporated the specifics of his editorial decisions into his homily, something that in his earlier years he was less prone to do but now saw as crucial—and he no longer felt the censorious heat of the Catholic church's feared doctrines upon his back when he preached. He explained to those who were willing to listen that he did not believe in hell anyway because to him God was a good God, He created us, and like any artist who loves that which he has created, he would not destroy his creation or condemn it to eternal flames. "After all," he said, with a sidelong glance to one of the female volunteers who helped to write up the weekly bulletin and whom his uncensored remarks had caused several years before to consult the bishop regarding whether what he said was consistent with church doctrine, "eternity is a really long time, and no one has done anything evil enough to merit spending it in a place like that." After mass, he listened to the confessions of the men and women in their seventies and eighties whose sins were often those the younger generation wouldn't even consider to be immoral, which reflected not just the difference among the generations but also the change in the Catholic church over the past century. In the morning, he spent a rare interlude going over some of the financial matters with Padre Humberto, who, since his empowering revelation about Leviticus, had rarely left the cathedral during the day, attending merely to the economics of religion, and only on occasion was it remembered by those who spent time at the cathedral that Humberto lived there, too. But, Osvaldo often thought, Humberto's hermitage had, most unexpectedly, been one of the greatest blessings bestowed upon him, for Humberto was a skilled writer and had managed to secure millions of pesos from foundations and aristocrats and other organizations that benefited the church and Juárez; what Humberto lacked in savoir faire, he made up for in his ability to write begging letters with the precise blend of desperation, confidence, respect and humor that inspired donations and grants. Additionally, the money was almost always spent exclusively by Osvaldo—except for the catalogue items such as cassocks, votives, paraments, bulletins, incense, etc. that Humberto ordered—because he was the one involved with the community, orchestrating the diocese's social programs and interacting with the parishioners. On this day, Humberto had been soliciting Osvaldo's advice regarding the clothing he wished to wear when not celebrating mass or attending to clerical duties that required his cassock. Catalogues were compared, and eventually Osvaldo decided on a few button-down shirts from a company called Friar Tuck. At nine-thirty, he visited a parishioner at the Hospital General in Partido Escobedo. The woman had been battling with chronic kidney failure, and he performed the last rites, humbled by her stoic disposition, which he had seen in the faces of many dying men and women over the years, something that intimated a faith far beyond religion, a tolerance of pain that was exclusive to certain types of people that he recognized in them immediately by instinct. At ten-thirty, he returned to the office and Humberto, where he put his signature on some of the letters Humberto had written (because Humberto operated behind the scenes, having Padre Osvaldo's signature next to his improved their odds). Twenty minutes later, he left for one of the nearby primary schools, where he taught a religion class. At noon, he ate, and at twelve-thirty and one-thirty said two more masses. At two, he presided over the funeral of a man he did not know but was able to deliver a speech that left even the man's widow thinking he had. At five, he celebrated another mass and at seven-thirty he ate dinner with Humberto in the offices of the cathedral, before going to the house of a member of the city government, and he blessed all of the rooms and gave the children prayer cards of Nuestra Señora de Guadalupe. At eight-fifteen, he implored the aristocrat to drive him to the cathedral so that he could be there by eight-thirty, but the man was delayed, caught in the bathroom with a bout of diarrhea, and his wife could not drive because of a broken foot. Padre Osvaldo did not make it back to the cathedral until eight-fifty, and by then Esme had left. Although she left a message with Humberto, he would not know how her first class went. He had waited a week for this moment and, now that it hadn't arrived, he was, quite simply, disappointed. He crossed the threshold into his bedroom and took a book randomly from the shelf. His eyes glossed over the words, but his mind did not register their meaning. In a little over eight hours, he would soon find himself locked into routine again, and the week would pass quickly that way. Funny, he thought, considering this particular moment in light of all the others that had come before and those that would soon be. The present, he reasoned, is just one moment sandwiched in between the endless past and the eternal future. And only the past grows.

The words leapt from the page onto the wheel that turned in his subconscious, finding their rhythm, and, within minutes of lying down, Padre Osvaldo was asleep.

When the evening had ended and Esmeralda walked home to her apartment, a dingy studio that she had recently moved into, one of the apartment complexes on Adolfo de la Huerta, the first thing she did was catch sight of her face in a mirror, and there she located all too quickly the naïveté that had settled over her face—how she had spent the past decade swaddled in an infant's cloth, under the protection of a priest and a rosary. She lay in her bed, regretting her decision to go to law school, wondering if it was not enough to be one of the women in charge of an important organization that publicized the murders of the Juárez women and gave relief to the women and lobbied for response from la policía. She wished Padre Osvaldo had been there at the cathedral when she arrived. She needed him to tell her she should continue or whether what she was already doing now was enough. And eventually she calmed down, drank a glass of water and sat on her bed, and she looked at her white walls and saw colors dancing upon them—startling, vibrant colors athrob with emotion. She wished she had paints, but the owner of the building did not allow painting anyway, so instead she found a blank piece of paper and a pen—no crayons or colors, just a blue pen and, on the page set down, one by one, her words. She wrote:

Let me roll paint on your walls and then I will tell you a story full of the colors of life. Or better yet—come with me to las colonias, where the colors already exist in the brightest shades.

As soon as she had written this, she pushed away from her desk and let out a breath of air. She felt as if she had broken something, as if she had destroyed something that could never again be whole. *What have I just done?* She asked herself. She read the words again, changing a few and then looking at it again—the words were malleable. The Anus was right.

She took the pen and once again bore into the page as if she were afraid it might otherwise fade, pouring her anger into the paragraph, which, when she stepped back from it, looked to her like it was still simmering like a smoldering fire. *Fuck him*, she said, *and all men like him, for that matter.* She wrote this, and, even though she was struck by the weight of her profanity, she let the words hang on the page in its astonishing reality. I can always erase it later, she thought. Until then...

Later, after the second class, she met the professor's eyes with a cold stare of her own and, as long as she did not taste or smell salsa de manzana—which would always magically inflame the area around her belly button, making it feel as if squeezed—she never again felt the anxiety she'd felt on that first day of classes and, forevermore, when trying to find a face for the hidden perpetrator of women, she always allowed her professor's face to embody that of the greatest villain of Juárez, simply because his was a face she despised and to her there were no other faces more malefic. She knew it wasn't fair. She knew that the only person or persons to blame were the killer or the killers, and that everyone else—la policía, the government, the maquila owners, the media, the drug underworld, God—were only secondary culprits, worthy of derision but undeserving of condemnation.

But, as she lay on her bed on nights when she felt rage, when the newspapers pronounced another dead, when alleged culprits were arrested by the police and then found to be completely innocent, when the government delineated hours for curfew that made the nights the more tenebrous, when the maquila factories promised to offer more safety to their workers but then carried on with their old unmindful ways, when the professor said something else in class that made her despise in him all men—she wrote new passages about the women of Juárez, telling their stories, their sagas, and then going over and over them, trying to make the words curl the page because, she had realized that, though the professor's pedagogy might have been flawed, there was something about which she felt he was right, and that was the way pure emotion unleashed would come across in a courtroom, whose chambers would stand or be demolished by words and the logic that they wrote. Yes, the law was a place for facts, but real injustices can only be settled by the law when someone *felt* the injustice, the anguish, the suffering.

How on earth did I get to this point? She wondered. I'm in law school, she thought. *Me.* And then she looked down at her paper, and she saw that the word was good.

And the evening and the morning were the first day.

Perhaps when he next returned to the station in the desert, two weeks had passed, and the first of those two weeks had been wrought with torment. For several days, it had been as that first night had gone: tossing and turning, moving his wife over into different positions so that she would cease snoring but, then, as the nights progressed, different forms of unrest manifested themselves, and he returned to the station morning after morning with little more than two hours slept, his mind a torpid, sludgy winter ground during the day—at night, a pitfall of free-floating aimlessness that never seemed to end.

On the seventh night, he rested. The world that he had created in his sleep was full of despair, and he had never before been such a wreck. But the world in which he still seemed to dwell called out to him from the other end of the long tunnel, asking him to resume his roles within it, and finally he slept, drifting away on the couch in front of the television, surrendering finally to his body's call for equilibrium.

When he awoke ten hours later, the dawn glimmering, it was as if the week before had not even existed, as if he had proceeded from the afternoon when he had been led to the station in the desert to that evening and this morning, the week before fodder for déjà vus some years in the future. Instead of spending his morning in the area to which his superior officer had assigned him, he set off for the same street on which he had been that afternoon the week prior and radioed again: "¿Mira, güey, do you see that vieja?" He gave them his coordinates, and several minutes later the same officer picked him up.

"¿Where is she?" The officer maybe asked.

"She's everywhere," he maybe said, as they drove off.

They headed back down the same roads at the speed their sirens allowed them, as they didn't have to stop at traffic signals or school crossings or, of course, random checks provided courtesy of la policía. When at last they reached the

253

station in the desert, he was the one who knocked; the other officer followed, dumbfounded, unable to explain what had spawned such a complete transfiguration.

"I want to be involved," he said, brazenly, and he was not surprised to hear himself speak thusly because he had removed all level of doubt. Perhaps he had decided that the only way to keep silent was to be just as up to his ears in blood as the rest of them. Maybe this is why he had been so emboldened as to propose, as soon as he arrived at the office he'd only been to once before, that anyone who saw these offices from this point on had to prove their hands were stained in blood in order to avoid being murdered themselves. And he was willing to be the first person to abide by that new rule. In the next three days, he would be responsible for the rape and murder of three girls in Juárez—all done in the thick of night, in the desert of darkness. He would return to his wife and his two children, one a boy of nine months who was still suckling on his mother's breasts and crawling around even though he could walk, and a girl of seven whom he worshipped above all of creation, a girl who was excelling in her primary school, who wore dresses on Sundays at the downtown cathedral, who loved her father—her first word was papá—and rushed to the door with her arms wide open as soon as he arrived home from work.

As he fell asleep that night, in the clutches of sleep that bore down tighter every minute, it came to him that all men are motivated by the same things—power, riches, love—but the difference among them were how far they were willing to go to get these things, and, he felt, now, that he could pride himself on being one of the ones who would go just as far as it took.

254

the chalkboard

I was jet-lagged: slapped across time zones, the alcohol consumed out of miniature liquor bottles, the physical wear and tear rasping against my bones after enduring question after meaningless question regarding my bag, which was subjected to a sophisticated sifting-through that made me wonder how accurate those metal detectors are if they still need to ask so many questions beforehand, I felt like I had just spent the night in the overhead compartment tossing and turning, my stubble had upgraded to a beard, and I reeked of Europe. Suddenly, public transportation in New York seemed the greatest inconvenience in the world as I stepped back onto the platform and, for the moment, looked around at the faces waiting for the train, trying to figure out which of us would refer to Sixth Avenue as "Avenue of the Americas," how many of us would say "subway" as opposed to "train" or "on" line as opposed to "in" one.

When I arrived back at the apartment, after walking from the train in my jacket through the humid May shock, I rang the bell to warn Camille that I had arrived, then walked up the steps to my second-floor apartment.

Camille was not home regardless of how many times I shouted her name in various parts of the apartment. In the kitchen I found the beer bottles from the prohibition era that Camille had cleaned and then used to decorate a windowsill in the dining room above printed signs that said, "Bottles from the Prohibition Era." Apart from the bottles, the only other obvious change to the apartment was the existence of the large chalkboard that had been wheeled up against one of the walls in the living room, which, because of its indentation, made it appear as if the chalkboard had been part of the building's architectural plan. Camille had written the word "¡Bienvenidos, Omar!" on the board in large letters. After dropping my bags in my bedroom, I returned to the living room, turned on the stereo to an evening jazz number and lay down on the couch, falling asleep as soon as my breathing slowed to the music.

A window open, some cans that had been set upon another windowsill in the kitchen leapt from the ledge and rattled onto the floor, and my body started, my eyes flicked open. Camille was frozen en route from her bedroom to the bathroom. She had probably figured that if the sound had not awakened me, the combination of the sound and her movement across the floor might in conjunction cause me to stir. She didn't look at me, probably also deciding that looking at me directly would spook me if I were to wake. I extrapolated her motives from my own psychology.

"Camille," I whispered.

"I am not Camille," she said. She was wearing the clothing of someone who had recently been to a bar. The only thing that did not match this outfit was her bare feet, which had surrendered her shoes at the front doorway. "I am no one. Go back to sleep. I'm not here."

She hesitated for a second longer, then moved the rest of the way down the hallway.

When she returned, I was still awake. "Hi, Camille," I said.

She acknowledged herself this time—"Yes, you've figured it out. I really am Camille." Then she pointed to the welcome words on the chalkboard, tracing them with her finger.

"Thanks," I said, smiling. "What time is it?" I asked.

"One o'clock. How long have you been here?"

"Since about eleven-thirty. I fell asleep in this position."

"In *that* position?" she asked.

"Probably something close to it," I said.

"Oh," she said, then she turned back to the chalkboard. "What do you think of it?" She said, wincing at my potential response.

"I like it. Fits right into the groove," I said.

"Do you plan on being awake for a while?"

I told her I hadn't planned on anything.

"I've got to tell you. I saw Joe...do you remember Joe?" I nodded. He was the guy she had broken up with—the one she had talked about to a tape recorder in order to get over. "Right?" She continued. "I feel like I haven't seen him in *years*. I hear of sightings occasionally...My colleagues at work see him, you know? But I was walking near Chelsea—or *in* Chelsea—I don't know where these neighborhoods begin and end—and I saw a beardless man crossing the street in front of the Flatiron building. At first, I thought, this guy looks just like Joe without a beard. I thought, 'This is what Joe might look like if he shaved off his beard.' I wished I had a camera because I'd always wondered what it would be like if Joe shaved off his beard, and now I could take a photo and show him. Of course, then I noticed the other things. He had Joe's exact walk. The same clothing style of polo shirts and khaki pants. I caught up to him, and I still couldn't get over his face.

257

It changed who he was, his personality—completely. His face looked bloodless, naked."

"It *was* naked," I said. "In what ways had he changed?" This excited me, for I loved the idea of external changes affecting internal character. I was afraid to undergo any changes to my physical appearance for fear that my persona would be altered irreversibly.

"You might think that it would have made him look younger, but it didn't. It made him look *older*. He was timid, shy. Remember when I told you how boisterous and full of pranks he was? This Joe was nervous, jittery, as if he thought people were following him, but I looked around. Nobody was. It probably didn't help that he was drinking coffee."

Camille continued the story, revealing that this was the moment she was officially "over" Joe, especially because Joe had pleaded with her to take him back and settle back into the lavish Upper West Side lifestyle that had been theirs for the past several years. "It's as if the only way to get over someone is to finally be given a choice," she said. "Anyway, here I am blathering. What about Art Serrano?"

It would have taken me only about fifteen minutes to describe the entire trip to her were it not for her extensive interruptions with questions and commentary. Instead, it lasted about an hour and a half, and I told her more things than I seemed to have taken in myself. When I told her about a new character, she insisted on knowing his or her name, while I was quite satisfied referring to Robert, for example, as the Luxembourger or Jucélia as the Brazilian activist. In recounting all the individuals that I had met over the past two weeks, it surprised me how many characters there had been—Father Rahm, the Jorges, Robert, Jucélia, Sylvia, their jealous friend, Marisa de Oliveira, Ilnur, Ulick Martin and his family, Professor Keating, Marta Herrera, Kristof von Behren and his colleagues. I never heard back from the museum curator in Oaxaca or from an art history doctoral student in Prague with whom I'd spoken on the phone, who was mostly keen on discussing the final painting, which she interpreted as part of a *presence-absence* motif that she said Art had been developing since the beginning of his career. I also explained that I had heard back from several friends from high school, none of whom had any information to offer other than what I already knew. One of my former classmates, Quique Delgado, who had inherited the painting "La Senectud y La Decadencia," spoke to me at length about the offers he was getting for the painting well into the tens of thousands. He said he was upset that Art was not around to explain to him what the damn thing meant.

"So what about Jucélia—did you sleep with her?" Camille asked.

"How did you know?" I said, flabbergasted by her explicit accusation.

"You do sleep with women from time to time, don't you, Omar?"

"Occasionally," I said. "But they have to more or less lay it out on the table for me before I'll make a move."

"You mean," she said. "*They* have to seduce *you*?"

"I know it sounds stupid," I said. "But I'm just not a hunter. I'm not wired that way."

"That's not good, Omar," she said. "*Women* aren't wired that way. If you were after me, you'd *have* to make the first move. It's not that hard."

"I know," I said. For a moment it was almost as if she were waiting for me to make a move right then.

"So how's the book coming?" She eventually asked. "The story—it's died out in the media. They don't talk about him nearly as much. What did you find out?"

"I don't know," I said. "I didn't figure *anything* out. And I haven't learned anything about him that would change what has been since the very beginning the fundamental mystery—whether he's dead or alive. All I know is that he was once *very* alive."

"Are you sure you didn't pick up any clues?" she said. "Maybe the thing to do would be to write everything down and then try to guess where he went based on all the information." She took a box of chalk from the coffee table and pulled out a full long piece of white chalk that she broke into two and began writing on the chalkboard.

"Right now?" I said.

"We all have a blind spot," she said. "Why not?"

She wrote: "Art in High School." That's when you first met him, right?"

"Yeah."

Before I knew it, the ground beneath the chalkboard was drizzled in a thin layer of chalky residue. The street visible through the three large windows in the living room seemed to be sparser, though those automobiles on the road now streaked across in quicker and louder fashion, and ambulances and police sirens embroiled the night soundtrack. On the chalkboard, lines were drawn connecting facts to other related details. While I filled in details from my journey, Camille brought in her laptop from her room and looked up biographical information on the Internet about when Art had won certain awards and the dates of some of his gallery openings, which gave us a general idea, in conjunction with my interviews, where he had been during specific years. My interviews filled in some gaps between countries and provided his philosophical mindset and interests during each time period.

When things were put in order, the chronology was essentially this: As a young man, Art had already been frustrated with the problems of the world, and so he had turned to painting as a way to vent his frustrations and distance himself from the world. He received a full scholarship to a prestigious college in the Northeast, where he studied art and immediately established himself as a genius. Despite this genius, which had brought him laurels and awards and invitations for residencies all over the world, he felt that he wanted to do something that would satisfy his need to improve the world, so he went to Brazil and worked with Father Rahm for a year. His finances running out, he accepted Professor Keating's invitation to study in Grenoble for two years, at which time he produced most of his paintings that reflected on El Paso and the borderlands. With enough money to venture out alone, he left the cities and spent six months in the sparsely populated Irish province of Mao, with its lush countryside and purple majestic mountains. Feeling that he needed to return to the vivacious city life he had been fond of since his upbringing in El Paso, he next went to Paris, where he painted some of his most renowned works. By the time he had taken up an apartment in London, his paintings had changed subject from the El Paso landscape to what he and others would refer to as the Know Your Baker series. By the time he had gained a cult following, he returned to Mexico—to Oaxaca, where he adapted Know Your Baker to the country of his father's ancestors. Next, he went to Barcelona, where, disenchanted by how slow in effect art itself was and how much more immediate organizing and protesting was, he extended Know Your Baker from the landscape of his paintings to the actual world, making T-shirts and organizing marches, on which he capitalized a few years later in Munich, when he led a demonstration against the greatest symbols of capitalism—the governments of the most powerful capitalist countries. When the demonstration did not go as he expected, he lashed out with threats of the very violence he had always disapproved of, claiming that it was in some cases necessary. By then, he had almost completely abandoned painting. When he returned to El Paso, he painted only sparingly and, eventually, in deep frustration, he grew depressed, painted his final œuvre and left notes in his apartment that communicated to most people that he was dead. He had gone from being an unequivocal pacifist to someone who carried a knife. He had gone from being an artist with an interest in activism to an activist with an interest in art. He had left El Paso sixteen

261

years before and had returned to it, but what for?…To end his life where it had begun?

It was four o'clock in the morning, and Camille and I were drinking coffee, charged with energy from some combination of the caffeine, the rush of the mystery, the feeling of proximity to the truth. "I hate to say it," she said. "But I think I've figured out what the next step is, that is, if what we're doing is at all logical. It may not be. Life is only as logical as we pretend it to be."

"What do you think the next step is?" I asked.

"This chalkboard is about as good an endorsement for suicide as you can get. While his artistic life was nothing but a success, he cared more, in the end, for what he believed in—which was Know Your Baker, something that he felt was completely unsuccessful. So he killed himself. Or," she said, now seemingly excited about what she was about to say. "He only killed himself metaphorically, meaning he killed off his identity, all of his interpersonal connections, etc., to devote himself to being someone else. Have you ever read any biographies on Hitler?"

I said that I hadn't.

"When Adolph Hitler was young, he wanted nothing more than to be an artist, and in his later teens—or his early twenties—he actually lived the life of a starving artist. He lived out of homeless shelters and hostels and supported himself by making a couple of bucks here and there scribbling drawings, watercolors, advertising posters and selling them to people on the streets. This time on the streets and in coffeehouses and hostels taught him something about life, and he became a German nationalist. After serving in the First World War, he joined the Nazi party and quickly became known, rather, for his skills in elocution. The older he got, the more he believed in his cause. The more demonstrations he led, and then eventually he turned into the psychopath we're familiar with today. We all know what eventually happened to him, but few people know that he was always interested in art. After the

German army took France in the Second World War, Hitler
went on a tour of all his favorite buildings of Paris, admiring
each of the major pieces of architecture, saying that it was a
dream come true. It's the same for people such as Bin Laden,
who, despite his billionaire family wealth, found his principles
to be worth sacrificing his way of life for—or Ted Kaczynski,
the Unabomber, who mailed bombs to people because he
wanted to put out a message that technology would kill us all,
so he used technology—bombs—and mailed it to people,
killing them."

"So…you think Art has gone the way of Hitler?" I asked.

"No, of course not. I'm not saying *anything*."

What Camille was saying made sense. It did complete the
portrait and, for some reason, like the hypochondriac who
leafs through a medical book for his symptoms and identifies
instantly with the one that poses the most imminent and grave
danger, I immediately feared that she was correct, and the
evidence of her claim lined up before me on the chalkboard.
But, if I really had just borne witness to the evolution of an
artist into a terrorist, then where did Art intend to commit his
great terrorist act, and if he had already or would soon do it,
would it bear the stamp of its creator? Would I be able to
identify it as he who had revoked his identity and devolved
everything that was his to others?

There was also the equally plausible idea that he was in
Brazil, playing the tuba…

Or *dead*…

I was back to square one.

Dawn was beginning to assemble itself on the residential
blocks and avenues of Brooklyn and, instead of bowing down
to the lag in time due to my travel across the ocean, I stared
directly at the sun instead of avoiding it by closing my blinds
and covering my face with sheets. I was delirious with
exhaustion and would probably have acceded to claims that I
had stolen a car earlier in the evening were someone to claim I
had. Camille looked as if she were equally beleaguered, having

had to bear witness to her ex-boyfriend's exsanguinous face and then propose a theory that her roommate's famous artist friend, who had been the focus of the media for more than three months, had faked his own death in order to stage large-scale terrorist acts. When I woke the next day, the possibility of this hypothesis as truth afforded me a glimpse of an Art that was one-hundred-and-eighty degrees different from the person I'd understood him to be at the time of his disappearance. Now, when I thought of Art, the examples from the past that I recalled were always those that supported Camille's hypothesis. Like the same sick man who by the time he arrives at the doctor's office no longer admits the symptoms he is experiencing but instead describes those he has read about—the symptoms for acute kidney failure or cancer of the lymph nodes—I no longer considered that if he were alive, he would be unarmed and harmless. Why else would he vanish from the world without even telling his parents?

Several nights later, Art visited me as I slept. He was sitting on the edge of my bed; his smile drawn exceptionally wide as in a caricature, his eyes wide and intense, as if charged by a high-volt battery. "Don't do it, Art!" I yelled at him, but no sounds emerged from my lips. He sat there, smiling. "What?" he said. "It's already been done. Your time is about to expire." He had dumped chemicals into the atmosphere, making it impossible to breathe, and it was only a matter of time before the chemicals reached us, causing us to suffocate and die—the entire human race. He came back two nights later. "Stop me," he said. "I dare you." We were in Leicester Square. People were falling everywhere and, as I turned and looked into the crowd, I saw Robert, the Luxembourger, as he reached forward to escape the fire but then was thrown backward into it. I cried out for him, but he was no longer visible. The fire had consumed him.

For several weeks, Art came and went as he pleased, and I awoke exhausted, finding myself napping more often in the afternoon, sleeping when I should have been working and then staying up later working when I should have been sleeping. I sought counsel in Camille, who was now willing to take back everything she had said about Art's terrorism so that I could sleep better, but this only served to make me more convinced by her theory. As I ruminated further about Art, his disappearance, the trails he left behind him, some of which had already been rained upon and grown thick with grass and shrubbery, but others that were left exactly as was, as if he had never left, I continued to ponder my role in his disappearance. The letter and will had been left to me, a journalist, a person who, at least in theory, had the power to investigate, to find him, to chase the sound of his footsteps stamping through the pouring rain and, eventually, to stop him—to call him off whatever it was he was planning to do (though it was the chemicals and fires, I was sure—my dreams wouldn't lie). Maybe, in his heart of hearts, he knew he wanted someone to find him and talk him out of whatever it is he had chosen to do. Art had selected me to be his savior, so now it was my mission to stop him from whatever it was he would attempt to bring off.

But regardless of what I had been filling my mind with, I had no idea where he had gone, and my continued theorizing that kept me awake for weeks led me not a step closer to him. I was exhausted with Art and my theories, which had taken over my life for several months, even caused me to travel from New York to El Paso, Brazil, England, France, Spain and Germany. Finally, in early June, the dreams stopped, and for the sake of my sanity, I tried as much as possible to keep thought of Art from entering my head.

The remainder of spring gave way to summer; then summer turned the earth a golden hue before disappearing into the hearts of leaves turned brown. In the three months that passed after Camille and I had spent the night pondering what might have become of him, Art was no longer mentioned in the media. As far as they were concerned, the story of Art Serrano was a story for the archives and, even though if the story had ended there it would have taken years for people to forget who he was, his name was not mentioned as often and soon slipped back into the place from which it had emerged, in the way a city flooded by rain eventually restores its water to its rivers and lakes.

I continued to think less and less about Art and more and more about other things—the stories I was writing for magazines, one of which was on a famous director whose work I had always admired; a new computer I was thinking about purchasing; a yoga class I was thinking about taking (or was it French cooking?; I don't remember); and the lease on my apartment, which I was, through bribing my Polish landlord with an annual five-hundred-dollar Christmas gift, hoping to renew without an increase in price. Camille had recently in some strange rationale of bureaucracy been "promoted," even though she had lost some of her benefits and her salary had increased only a pittance.

Life went on. It moved on like a New York City taxicab cutting through Central Park to avoid traffic. Inside that cab, I told the driver not to stop—to just keep moving on.

PART THREE

el pasado

I once ordered an iced tea on Long Island, hoping that I would be brought a Long Island Iced Tea, but instead the waiter brought me something in a can, then proceeded to pour it into a glass with ice in it, even though it was already cold. From then on, I specified. Even when in Manhattan, I enunciated when ordering it, which was not appropriate barroom behavior. Better to mutter something incomprehensible under your breath, stumble about when heading for the bathroom and repeat yourself several thousand times when talking to someone at a bar. Enunciation betrays a deficiency in sobriety, and bars are in the business of intoxication. If you ever doubt that, order a glass of water and watch the bartender's reaction. Even though according to New York lore a good percentage of them are out-of-work actors, it is hard for them to hold back the grimace that results from your ordering something that is free, whether you have a five-dollar bill rolled up in your hand or not.

At a neighborhood bar just off the Hoyt-Schermerhorn A-train stop, I sipped on a Long Island Iced Tea at the bar, waiting for my longtime friend and closest New York buddy, Joaquín Guzmán, to creep in. Logs were stacked up high over the fireplace, and a late-September cold front had breezed into the city, threatening the recurrence of winter, which would have seemed unwelcome were it not for the humid torridity of the city at present. Joaquín arrived in trademark fashion, slipping his hands around my waist, under my arms and squeezing my nipples, as he was apt to do, and so pleasured was he by the experience of catching someone off-guard that I was often prone to face the wall so as not to deny him this delight, which could put him in an upbeat mood for the rest of the night.

"¿Qué pedo, huevón?" He said, as soon as he removed his arms from me and sat down at the bar, now patting me on the back, as if we hadn't already had enough physical contact with one another.

"Great. ¿And yourself?" I said, then, as I listened for his response, leaned forward onto the bar and asked for two shots of tequila and a bourbon for Joaquín.

"I'm doing well. Working on my tan," he said. "Just kidding, güey. But that's all these gringas were concerned about all summer long—their tans. You even see men going to tanning beds. ¿Who are they trying to be?"

"Back in the day," I said, as we clinked shot glasses, "Back in the day, everyone wanted to be white—whiteness was godliness."

"They go to these tanning beds, and they turn out red. You know, I'm almost glad the winter is here because at least now all the white people can go back to being marshmallows." We licked the salt and threw down the shot, that powerful, benumbing sensation of having swallowed poison gripping our throats in an ephemeral clasp of death that loosens as the alcohol slithers down into our stomachs. "Now brownness is godliness, huevón. ¡A toast to the godliness of La Raza!"

I started to say something about tanning, but he immediately talked across me, saying, "But speaking of La Raza, I'm tired of all these Americans calling me a Chicano. Chicanos are this-side-of-America-born Mexicans, like you, güey. Some studies show the word came from Chihuahua, and there's no way I'm going to let myself be identified as a Chihuahense."

"Chicano—it's too close in sound to 'Chicago,' " I said. "It's difficult for me not to think of Chicago when I hear Chicano, even though they're completely unrelated."

"If I were born in America, I'd still want to be called Mexicano. If you're Jewish and born anywhere in the world, you're still Jewish. ¿What do the Jews have over us? Mexico gets under your skin in the same way. I'd even call *you* Mexicano."

"I actually don't mind what I'm called," I said. "Latino. Chicano. Mexicano. Just as long as you put something in front of the 'ano.' "

We spent the next thirty minutes talking about the labels groups are given—all the delineations, and in this city of New York, there were many. People of Latin American descent were called Latino, Latinoamericano, Chicano, Mexicano (or Dominicano, Boricua, etc.) Mexican-American, Hispanic, and so on. And every other race/ethnic group dealt with the same labeling characteristics. People from China and their descendants, for example, could be classified as Chinese, Chinese-American, ABC (American-Born Chinese), Asian, Asian-American, Oriental, etc., and each of these classifications seemed to say something different about the people who called themselves each name, seeking individuality by classifying themselves as part of a group, which has always been the American way. Joaquín had recently got his master's degree at Columbia in humane studies, which I had always found interesting because he was a Marxist and had only enrolled in the school to, as he put it, "study the enemy." But he felt the past year had been a waste and was now studying for a second master's in linguistics, which suited him much more because now he could spend all of his time studying nomenclature and sociolinguistics.

When our conversation on the names of groups concluded, a silence prevailed as we finished our first round of drinks and ordered another. Then, Joaquín turned to me and said something strange. "Omar, I'm really surprised you called me yesterday."

"¿Why is that?" I asked, noticing that Joaquín had changed tones completely and seemed to be speaking seriously, with a degree of sentimentality that I was completely unaware he possessed.

"¿Because when was the last time we saw each other? ¿When was the last time you called me?"

"¿You're angry because I don't call you every day?" I said.

"¿Every *day*? Forget about it. ¿When was the last time I saw you? January this year. ¡The last time I talked to you before yesterday was on the phone during the time when your friend had gone missing, and that was almost nine months ago!"

He went on, "You know that I call you. I even emailed you a couple of times. But you don't respond, and then you tell me that I'm your closest friend in New York. It's a complete contradiction."

"You *are* my closest friend in New York," I said, and I meant it.

"¿You see the closest friend you have in New York twice, maybe three times a year?"

What Joaquín said made complete sense, so I argued with him. And the more I argued with him, the more convinced I was of his claim. Joaquín proceeded to describe how he always spent weekend nights with his friends, just as he had in Monterrey. His friends and he would go to restaurants in the evenings, and then sometimes bars or clubs, sometimes places where they would dance the salsas and cumbias and corridas of the world half a hemisphere away. During the summer, he would habitually go with friends to Summer Stage in Central Park, where he saw major bands from all over the world—Skank, Café Tacvba, Ladysmith Black Mambazo, Antibalas—plays of Broadway caliber and orchestras led by the likes of Wynton Marsalis. Apartments were smaller in New York, but, he said, you could still fit a lot of people in the rooms, onto the fire escape, in hallways and on stoops. Had I ever been to Washington Heights or farther north to Inwood? He asked. There, summer packed the sidewalks full with people playing chess in the streets on turned-over box crates, listening to music in their cars or hanging out against the chain-link fences where pick-up basketball games spawned street legends.

When I later walked away from the bar toward my apartment, which was several stops away but worth the walk under the darkened sky, I thought about what Joaquín had told me, how even he, whom I'd known so well, had shown a compassion and sensitivity that had never before been realized in my presence that proved how little I actually knew him, though within the space of five or six hours, I probably could have written a feature story on him of several thousand words that would convince any reader that there were few I knew as well as him, so wonderful was the paradox of knowledge. As I rounded Grand Army Plaza, which lit up the sky in such a way that I wondered whether the light above the statue was the light of the moon or that of the men galloping on braying, hurtling horses, I saw the vast superstructure of the Brooklyn Public Library, and as I drew closer I read the words engraved on the façade—*Here are enshrined the longings of great hearts, and noble things that rise above the tide; the magic word that wingéd wonder starts; the garnered wisdom that has never died.*

Inside this library lay thousands of books, each grouped categorically by genre—books of literature lined the stacks on the inside, with those in languages such as Polish and

Portuguese and Italian and Spanish on separate shelves, and if you crossed from one end of the library to the other, you would find a book as unrelated to the other as two human beings who have never met or conversed and live in different parts of the world with different moral philosophies, the greatest divider: the inability to connect itself. What was most fascinating about the library—though I could not at the moment enter, and instead found myself at a great distance from these books, the thick-glass wall and chains and locked revolving doors equivalent to the physical distance of antipodal countries—was the process by which new books would be added, as every new book would find an appropriate place next to another book that determined its relationship to the other books, and it was this building of relationships, this closeness, that created the particularity and brilliance of the layout that far surpassed the value of a mass of books in a room not sorted by any characteristic other than that they were books, as in a world where people, if we were incapable of growing closer to others, would be like stranded books on empty shelves, merely furniture in a world without common denominators and languages—human things wandering deserted plains without cities.

I moved away from the door, which I had drawn closer to the more I had thought about this notion. For the first time I noticed that there were people sitting or standing outside of the library, as if they had arrived considerably earlier than others to form a ticket line for an imminently sold-out concert. One of the men appeared to be homeless but did not have in front of him any signs nor did he ask me for money as I walked past him. Another sat in pensive repose on the steps, his hands resting on the top of his head, where, if he were feline, his ears would be. On the streets, people were walking near where the landscape swept up and became the structure of the Brooklyn Public Library, toward Prospect Park and Park Slope and in the opposite direction, toward Prospect and Crown Heights. I joined the latter group and, as I walked on

Eastern Parkway toward my apartment, heading the direction the name suggested, I wanted to travel back against the tide and to the bar and through the alcohol and ask Joaquín how to make a friendship.

When I arrived home, I checked my email and found a lone message in my inbox from a name I had nearly forgotten. It was Jucélia, and the message subject was "Juárez." I clicked on her name and saw her message carefully reconstruct itself onto the page. "Julio, Ilnur should have arrived by now in Juárez. I know this 'event' is classified and that I'm not supposed to mention it to anyone, but I just wanted to offer my full support. I think it is wonderful that you are finally doing something about this "femicide," and to put yourself in such a vulnerable position shows an even greater self-sacrifice. I am curious—does your signature in the letter to Ilnur imply that you have finally found João Fabiano? Abraço, Jucélia"

The first feeling that overcame me was one of guilt—I had misled Ilnur despite liking him and promised that I would get in touch when I'd never had any intentions of doing so. But someone had contacted Ilnur with similar purpose, providing details that made Jucélia confuse its sender with me. I had sent no such letter. Further, something about the signature in the letter implied its author might possibly have found João Fabiano. Finally, the proposed plan made by whoever had contacted Ilnur would require "self-sacrifice," perhaps putting one's life at risk (in Juárez), and now every piece of the puzzle had been put in place with the exception of the very last one.

"Camille," I shouted, standing quickly up from my chair and rushing down the hallway toward the light of her room. "Yes," she said, "Hold on a minute," she said into her cell phone. "Are you ok? You smell like my father. I love bourbon."

"Yes, yes, yes. Finish your phone call, then we'll talk."

I went into the living room and took a new piece of chalk from the box, broke it into two, then filled the newest detail into the chart, which had remained on the board for the past several months—since that night Camille and I had spent dissecting Art's life. It had been under my nose the whole time. How could I have overlooked the most powerful clue, that of his return to our home front, his easy escape across the border, which would have cost him a quarter and no proof of identification had he crossed over the downtown bridge no more than eight blocks from his apartment? I had always thought he would have fled to Munich, Paris or elsewhere in Europe, perhaps because that's where I might have gone and where he had been, but instead he had gone no more than a mile. In his letter, he had written: "When are you going to write a book about la frontera? You know it's your duty to keep things alive when everything else is dying." In the will he had bequeathed me a book about the story of drugs in El Paso and Juárez and a painting with the squalid colonias underneath the buildings of downtown El Paso (a painting I had not yet received). He had been alerting me to his presence in Juárez from the very first moment.

"What is it, Omar?" she said, her excitement feeding off mine.

"Art is alive, and he's in Juárez," I said. "He's organizing something of which I do not know the specifics. From the email that I received from the Brazilian grad student, from Jucélia, it seems that whatever he's doing down there is going to be violent, or at least illegal. I'm going to Juárez in the morning."

"That's amazing," Camille said.

"Do you want to go?" I asked.

"I'd love to," she said, without a second of hesitation, "I'll have to call in sick, but a certain number of sick days are on the house. Since I'll be calling from my cell phone, they'll have no idea that I've skipped town. I'll cite stomach and bowel problems, so they won't ask further questions. Let's go."

Later that night, as sirens echoed, the voices of teens emerging from the backyard connected to ours growing clear—"You going to smoke all that yourself, son?"—and then fading away as the wind blew and the snow began to fall, I sat in my bedroom with the lights on, a desk lamp creating an extra pool of light over my computer, and pulled together probably a hundred or so pages of articles, websites and other literature about the murders of the women in Juárez which, contrary to what I'd thought before, did not belong to the past and had *never* stalled, nor diminished in number. As I mentioned before, the first I ever heard of these murders was from Art himself, during our freshman year in college, the year these murders had begun. Despite the fact that, according to these documents, over four hundred girls had gone missing since—some even suspected that there were as many as three or four thousand missing, as so many of these cases went unreported—this phenomenon had never engaged the full attention of the media. Full-length articles had appeared in various national and international magazines and newspapers, but they were scattered. In other words, Art's disappearance had captured the interest of the public over several weeks, so that all of the cameras were shining on him at once, whereas the same number of cameras—maybe even more—had focused their lens on the girls of Juárez, but over such an extended period of time that the phenomenon never stirred a media frenzy. I had learned superficial details about the murders over the years from various echoes, but I'd never been able to appreciate the full scope of the situation.

As I pored through the articles, each seeming to be a cry for help, a plea for intervention, I came upon details that further seemed to confirm Art's involvement. The bodies of the girls in Juárez that were found in the desert were often difficult to identify, as clothing was sometimes switched and bodies would appear months after the person had gone missing, such that there was always a lag between disappearance and identification. Wasn't this the same thing that had happened to Art's paint-stained clothing, which had been found next to the bones of a dead mountain goat? Had this been an intentional effect on Art's part?

What did he plan to do? As far as I could gather, the police and government in Juárez were still merely offering suspects and theories—a band of bus drivers, an Egyptian psychopath—but every time someone had been arrested, the murders continued. Perhaps Art's trip to Rio de Janeiro had been some sort of a trial run for what he was going to do in Juárez that would require his complete change of identity. Due to the escalation of his activism, it was clear to me, through Camille's reasoning—and my adoption of her reasoning—that the only reason one would go so far as to remove themselves from the world would be because they wanted to do something violent, some sort of kamikaze mission that would have, had they decided to do it without disappearing first, sullied their family name. Art knew that his family's pride for him was insatiable and could only be reversed were he to do something drastic. Even though I was at times quite certain this was the case, I couldn't figure out what specifically Art aimed to do, especially since the enemy had not been identified and seemed to be a number of people, all disparate, none convicted and perhaps on some level protected by corrupt members of the police or government.

Something violent. Perhaps something illegal. You don't fake your own death just to organize a march. Art was dangerous, and it was up to me to stop him. I continued to theorize, but individual and strange as those paths of reasoning or lack of reasoning my mind would lead me to, as colorful and fleshed-out as these theories became, the fact of the matter was that I did not know the truth and would not know the truth unless I found him and, as I thought about our eventual arrival in Juárez, my eyes heavy in their sockets, the noise of the neighborhood dying out as snow fell thick and angrily, I cringed at the thought of the search that lay ahead, as I had no idea where to begin.

The car service was to pick us up at four forty-five the next morning. Despite the fact that the operator took down all the information when I called him the night prior, he had decided to call at three forty-five and four the next morning, on both occasions asking if I was sure. Each time, I offered details that I hoped would assuage his fear that at the last minute I would stand him up—"Yes, my bags are packed and by the door." "I'm showered and am nearly completely shaven."

Eventually, the car pulled up to the curb at four thirty-five honking. At four-forty, he left in a rush. Camille watched through the window as she waited for me to finish using the bathroom. I called the car service. "You weren't ready," he said. "It's not even four forty-five yet," I rebutted. "You lack respect," he said and hung up. I called another car service, and we were picked up at a quarter past five and despite the tardiness made it without any trouble to La Guardia Airport, where we sat for an hour watching early-morning television that had been put at such a high volume that everyone within earshot had to condescend to listen to it.

The first flight took us to Houston, the next to El Paso. Had El Paso become more accessible since the last time—nine months before? Camille and I sat next to each other, both of us reading, Camille elated that she had found a way to rescue some of her time away from her advertising firm.

Camille was buoyant in the morning and excited about this trip to the Southwest and Juárez that, as she had grown up mostly in Denver, Colorado, awakened her childhood fascination with the Old West, the barren desert, Mexico, etc. Her experience of Mexicans was mostly based on those in Brooklyn and New York, who had gone north in search of better lives, most of whom were from the region of Puebla and occupied the lower tier of New York's work force—the waiters and busboys in Little Italy, those who worked in the stockrooms at grocery stores all over the boroughs, the entire community of Sunset Park, many of whom slaved arduous hours undocumented and therefore below minimum wage and stretched their dollars so that they could send money home to be converted into many more pesos. Despite Camille's obvious acceptance of all races and economic groups—she had even spent several years volunteering at a homeless shelter in Crown Heights on the weekends and lived in a fairly "diverse" neighborhood in Brooklyn—she had never encountered a culture where Mexicans composed the lower, middle and upper classes, and she was excited to suddenly become a minority to some greater majority within her own country.

"I can't wait to see the cacti that are like the shape of the palm of your hand. What are those called?

"Nopales. In English, it's 'prickly pears,' I think. The fruit is called 'tuna.' "

"Any relation to tuna—the fish?"

"No."

"What's tuna in Spanish?"

"Atún. And did you know you can cook tuna?" I asked.

"Atún?"

"The fruit from prickly pears."

"What does it taste like?"

"Like everything. I don't know…chicken."

Camille started nodding her head. "I like it. This goes on my language list, after French foods that sound like terrible ways to die."

In Houston we changed planes and were among the first to board the flight to El Paso. I watched the different faces as they emerged onto the plane, the curtain dividing first and second class having been pulled apart to allow the passage of others of the lower stock, myself included, to the lower order. The people who boarded wore El Paso in their clothing, in their hairstyles, their brand of Spanglish—even the "Anglos" who came on board the plane seemed to belong to something distinctly El Pasoan. Just as spouses are said to look alike over time—they vacation together at the same time, undergo the same tragedies and deal with the same children—people begin to look similar to other people in their same environments, who are living at the same pace, under the same sun, moving their mouths in similar ways to produce similarly accented words. El Paso, for its isolation—an eight-hour drive to San Antonio, twelve to Houston, four hours to Tucson and five to Albuquerque—has very little outside influence and is like a culture apart, with its own vernacular, accent and civilization, and it is always a shock to recognize this distinctiveness after having spent so much time away.

After returning to my reading, I looked up once more and saw a woman who wore sunglasses, a white blouse and a long red shirt that looked Indian in make and hugged her figure perfectly. She sashayed down the aisle toward us and finally stopped at a seat several yards in front of us. She was carrying a suitcase that a young man in his early twenties volunteered to put in the overhead bin for her. She thanked him with the nod of her head and a smile, something that seemed so regal and familiar that I searched laboriously through my brain wondering when I had last seen such a gesture, as it endeared me to this person more than the display of generosity by the young man could ever have. As much as I reflected, the only thing that increased was the familiarity of the gesture, and as soon as I had given up attempting to discover from where this had been duplicated, thinking about movies and counting painstakingly backward through the women in my life, the scene when I had last observed this gesture played back to me in full. It was the moment when I had been in Art's studio in El Paso and had finished reading the will and letter and Ella Serrano had returned from her walk. I had given her a quick synopsis of the letter and the will, and she had, just before crying uncontrollably, gushingly, nodded to me graciously, the nod of a demure, sophisticated woman.

And this is how I had recognized Beatriz Serrano.

For a moment, I stood from my seat to move over to where she was sitting but, as the flux of people moving

283

toward the back of the plane continued without slowing, I sat back down in my seat. Camille, who had fallen asleep moments before, had asked me, with her eyes closed but her hand pushing against my arm, if I could bring her a magazine, and then immediately fell asleep, and I wanted to fulfill her last conscious request. Eventually the traffic subsided, and I moved over to where Beatriz was seated and startled her when I called across to her.

"¡Por Dios!" she said, putting her hand to her chest immediately. "Omar! You're everywhere these days."

I told her I had gotten the latest strain of a travel bug that had been infecting people in their mid-thirties. Maybe Kristof von Behren was right—maybe I *wasn't* funny in person.

"But what are you doing going to El Paso?"

"What are *you* doing going to El Paso," I asked.

"I'm visiting my parents."

"Oh," I said. "Well," then I pointed back at Camille, who was licking her lips with her eyes closed. "I'm bringing my girlfriend to El Paso to show her where I'm from."

"That's great. How long have you been together?"

"About a year," I said.

The seat next to Beatriz was empty and, as there weren't any other passengers boarding the plane, I asked if I could sit next to her and, for several moments we both relished in the coincidence that had brought us both onto the same flight. Beatriz talked about how she had needed to come home because she had been homesick and had taken flights from Barcelona to Paris, Paris to London, London to Houston and now, after nearly twenty hours of travel, was on her way, "finally to the pass."

"The *past*?" I asked.

"No, The *Pass*. The Pass to the North. You know, El *Paso*?

As soon as she said this, someone who had boarded the plane late nudged me on the arm and showed me his ticket. Beatriz said she would find me when we were in the air.

I returned to Camille, who was now awake, and told her that Art's sister was aboard.

"Do you think it has anything to do with what's going on?"

"It must," I said. "Her flight from Barcelona stopped too many times for this to be a trip for leisure. Something's going on."

When finally we slipped through the last of the clouds, the pilot turned off the seatbelt sign and, a few minutes afterward, Beatriz got up from her seat and made her way toward us. In the brief conversation that ensued, I introduced Camille, and Beatriz told us that she would meet us after the flight. Her parents were picking her up at the airport, so all of us would be reunited. "My parents think the best of you. Your coming before Art's funeral was great consolation for them. And then Art left the will to you," she said. "How bizarre."

After the flight had landed, I watched the same young man bring down Beatriz's bag. She nodded graciously in the same manner. As we walked up the ramp, the heat immediately filled my nose and caused me to breathe more fully in the absence of the artificial air conditioning. Beatriz had waited for us, and now I was able to properly greet her. She kissed me on both cheeks, in the style of the Spanish. Although her accent was still quite Mexican, she seemed to have developed a preference for Spanish terms and kept repeating the word "guay", even when she was responding to something in English. She had spent her undergraduate years at the University of Missouri-Columbia's School of Journalism and when spending her junior year in Barcelona had landed an internship with CNN, where she'd been working since graduation. I was impressed with how natural and articulate she was for twenty four.

We reached the escalators—I looked below, where I saw Hector and Ella Serrano looking up in our direction for their daughter, and Ella's eyes locked with mine. While I'd thought they might be perplexed to see me here again so soon, they instead waved to us with excitement.

After the initial hugs and kisses that Beatriz gave her parents, she said to them, "And look who I found." I greeted them the same way I had months before and introduced Camille, who kissed them on the cheeks herself. "What are you doing here?" Ella Serrano said.

I told them that I'd wanted to show Camille where I came from, adding the new detail that we were engaged because it seemed to lend credibility to our story. When I noticed that Hector Serrano had looked at Camille's ring finger for the evidence, I added that we would have loved to have shown them the ring but that we were having it resized. We agreed to have dinner with them at their insistence, told them where we were staying, thanked them for the offer to give us a lift and parted ways.

Our rental car sorted out, Camille and I drove downtown, checked into the hotel and went for a walk around downtown El Paso. We walked mainly down South El Paso Street and I pointed out Art's studio, which we were to visit the next day; Father Rahm St., several blocks from the border; then the border itself, which in the early evening on a weekend, was almost completely devoid of traffic.

When we returned to the hotel before venturing out for dinner, I noticed the light was blinking on the phone in our room. I dialed up the answering service and listened to a message from Beatriz, who said to give her a call at my earliest convenience. I dialed the number I had known since high school. Now I noticed how short the number was; bereft of the area code that is obligatory in New York, it seemed as if I were dialing into another century. The phone rang several times and, just as the answering machine was picking up, Ella Serrano answered, "Hello?"

"This is Omar. I was returning Beatriz's call."

"I know," she said. "Omar, you're a terrible liar. Why are you really here?"

Instead of supplying her with yet another fiction or an abridged version of the truth, I told her about everything that

I had done over the past eight months—my trip to Brazil, Ulick Martin, Professor Keating, Jucélia's email. She listened intently, merely acknowledging each new detail of my story with a series of stock, terse conversation sounds.

When I finally finished, she said to me, quickly and frankly, in the voice I had always associated with intelligence and kindness, "Omar. We've been lying to you from the start."

el padre

Touch my face. Feel my skin. Hold me close, mi querido, my lover. What a two-faced villain life is—always mixing pleasure and pain like tequila in a shot glass with sal y limón. I was not ready for this, but here you are—mi paisano from centuries past, when we walked the same barren earth searching decades for the eagle perched on a cactus with a snake in her mouth—tenochtitlán, mi vida. Feel my skin—smooth your hand across my thighs and up my belly and along my side and to my mouth. You are the first I have ever allowed here who didn't have to pay my fee. Can you believe that? This worn surface has never known love; it has only been a runway for men—and boys, too—with enough money in their wallets. They fell in love, too, but this was no place for love—jamás ha sido así. No, Juárez is no place for love. Love is an exception, a compromise. It cannot be wrested from us in the same

288

opprobrious way with which they take our bodies. Love is love, and that's it. And now, these days, can you feel the rumbling below your boots? We are beginning to rise. The signposts are painted thick in pink on black. We women and those who love us are watching the street, looking out. We're going in numbers everywhere. We're carrying stuff that will make you go blind, ¿sabes? And the world is starting to pay attention to us, too. We've been shooting flares up in the sky from the border for years now, and they're finally starting to notice. They're sending their planes down to our little town of three million, this collector of dreams washed up from the south like broken bottles on the beach, this last stop before we all go swimming to the other side. I would be standing at the gate like everyone else, but I'm not going to wait another second. Besides, nobody knows this city like I do, and it's going to take an inside job to get everyone out. So grab ahold, take my hand, come with me. Let's shake them off our planet.

Esmeralda picked up the phone and spoke into it—Bueno—in a voice rife with confidence and a sort of jurisdiction over the airwaves. When she used to answer the phone at the women's rights group, her voice had been small and hushed, and sometimes people asked her to repeat herself—¿Mande?—even if she had merely helloed. But now, a lawyer in one of the largest cities in the country, a diploma that indicated she was of the top graduates from a school of law, and all of the other things—her skin tighter in her face, forcing her cheeks to conform to her jawline; her hair grown long and thick and parted straight down the middle; only slight daubs of makeup that blended into her natural tones; her body healthy from her daily sprints on the university's track—Esmeralda operated her body like a woman of sixty in a body less than half that age.

"Hello," she repeated, and then she heard the voice of Leti on the other end identifying herself, asking her how she was.

"Good. Busy. ¿And you?"

"Good, thanks. I was wondering if you wanted to eat lunch together today."

"¿Lunch? Yes, of course. I'll be busy until one. ¿Can we eat after then?

"No problem."

Esmeralda returned to her books and her notes regarding past lawsuits against the Mexican government. Even though it was not necessary in the courts of Mexico to establish legal precedence, she wanted to find out how it had been done in the past and with what sort of success, so she had photocopied several hundred pages pertaining to cases, some of which she had studied in law school, that dealt with individuals or groups suing the government, la policía, former government officials, companies, etc. As she pored over the photocopies, she underlined, highlighted and set apart anything that she considered might be useful—similar to what she had once done with the Bible after following the signs on the mountain—even considering that she might need to use international influence to sharpen the blade because nowadays there wasn't a country in the world you could go to where they did not know about the Juárez women, dying in numbers comparable to the statistics of war.

She moved on to her next case, that of a woman from a rich family who was suddenly forced out of her house by her husband. The woman had had to walk across the city to her mother's house—she didn't have a peso in her pocket—her feet bleeding first from the discomfort of her heels, later from walking across the pavement in bare feet. Esmeralda's niche in Juárez was what allowed her to have a practice at all and, even though at the moment she was just starting out, she'd set herself apart as a lawyer who worked exclusively in cases dealing with women who were raped, abused or mistreated. The women's rights group that she had worked at for the past eight years had found the necessary funds to help Esme open an office, and she would act as their representative in all legal proceedings from then on. New law students, young women

290

and men at her alma mater, volunteered to help research and file and answer phones and make coffee, so that her office was always occupied by herself and at least one other. Apart from them, Leti's daughter, Dulce, also spent several hours a week volunteering—answering the phone, running errands and organizing things in the office; she was twenty-one now and would soon be applying for law school. This woman's case would not require too much work. She was only seeking divorce and, according to the couple's marriage documents, their property was communal, thereby entitling her to her part of their estate.

Esme was printing some forms for the woman to sign when one of the law students knocked on her door, entered and announced that Laura Delgado and her son Pablo had arrived.

She arose and walked toward the door, where she saw Laura, escorted by her handsome son around the front desk and into her office. Laura balanced herself on Pablo's arm, moving slowly and laboriously, and Esme moved the chair, which spun on wheels, toward her, to cut the distance.

Esmeralda had seen Laura only twice since the "investigation" of Verónica and, during those times, Laura had never seemed robust, but she had never seemed this physically debilitated. If these pains were indeed in her knees, anxiety and inactivity had extended the dominion of the disease over the rest of her body; her eyes appeared slightly tinged with a pinkish color on the sclera, her face had broken out in smallish red blotches, and her hair was thin and damaged. Still, Laura wore a skirt, and her short hair was kept in place with hairspray, and she spoke to Esme as if the knee injury had been just a scrape from adolescence long since forgotten into a scar.

"I'm so glad you came," Esmeralda said. "It's been ten years since that night. Ten years."

"You've done well, mija," Laura said. "Mi hija," she repeated, referring to her with the sense of affection by older

291

women who refer to younger women as their collective daughters.

What Esme hoped to accomplish by calling Laura here was to depose her regarding the investigation of Verónica's death. Laura was the first of the many victims' family members she planned to call for cooperation over the next several months. She had heard the stories of all of these families, often the working poor, but to her knowledge no one had ever interviewed all of them, and certainly no one had sought to represent them in a class action suit against la policía and the government-at-large. What Laura told her at first seemed to be the details Esme had always known about Verónica, as she had been there that night and the following day during the investigation. But then—as Laura began to talk about the years that followed—new details were divulged, such as the fact that la policía no longer kept a record of her particular case because it had been so long ago now. Still, as Laura had continued to make demands that they reopen the case several years after Verónica's disappearance, they eventually called her in to identify Verónica's body only to discover that the body was not hers though the clothing *had* belonged to her...Laura recognized a patch that she had sown on the skirt that Vero had worn that night.

"How strange it has all been," Laura said. "They have all of the evidence, but *none* of the evidence. Our daughters and nieces are found dead, dressed in the clothing of other murdered girls. And ten years pass in ten minutes. And we're all still here. And the problems remain the same. Entire wars last less time, and countries are rebuilt, but here the girls still die, and they still can't hold on to evidence. They still don't know. They haven't solved *one* of the murders, not one in over four hundred."

Esmeralda excused herself for a moment to call Leti and ask her if she could meet for lunch the next day instead—she hadn't finished the bulk of the work she'd intended to make it through. "It's just like that day when you were still at work—the day we met," Esme said.

Esme continued to depose Laura for another hour, going over the same old facts and, as she pressed for more specific details, new facts continued to emerge. When they had finished, as Pablo sat in a chair in the corner next to his mother, Laura stood from her chair, moved toward Esme, put her arms around her and said, "I was so unfair to Vero. It was all my fault. I didn't understand her. And I will never forgive myself."

Esme returned the embrace and, as much as she wanted to say something to console the aging, frail woman, she knew there was nothing she could say nor do that would keep Laura from blaming herself. She knew a wound ten years old continued to bleed no matter what pressure or bandage you applied to it.

As he left the office of the century-old archdiocese of Chihuahua, Osvaldo could not believe what had just happened. During the past several weeks, he had become increasingly aware that the inevitable, which had for years been approaching with slow, meticulous steps, had drawn intimately closer—close enough to whisper in his ear—but it still hadn't completely sunk in that today would arrive, that today *could* arrive. He had always put faith in the Divine Magistrate, and problems had always seemed to be solved before they arose—that is, his own problems: his health, his job, everything that concerned his own particular standard of living. He understood his covenant with God to be that, if he was taken care of, then he could expend his energy on the people who he had been called on to serve. But this was a huge blow. And now what could he be expected to do?

It all began in the homily during a Mass several months before, when, standing in front of the congregation, Padre Osvaldo had been talking about the murders and said, "The Mexican government is right to have made allowances so that women who have been raped can have legal abortions." He knew when he said it that he shouldn't have, that, though he was sure that what he said was at least as fair a statement as any of the Bible's verses, his practice of speaking from the heart was at odds with his representation of a two-thousand-year-old institution. It was Catholicism that gave him a pulpit on which to speak and a congregation to address, and even though during these days he often felt as if the institution had too much power over the will of the people—the will his faith told him it was God's alone to decide—he had to listen to the church's demands in order to retain his position. This is how life works, he thought. We are constantly allowing ourselves to be governed by authorities we outgrow and no longer recognize. Two days after the Mass, he received a call from the Archbishop of Chihuahua, from whom he'd expected to hear as soon as the words slipped out of his mouth—from whom a scolding could have been written into the calendar. And though he had been reproached for "controversial practices" on numerous occasions before, this time the archbishop said it was "the last straw" or, as he clarified, though without a hint of humor, "the final of several last straws." Padre Osvaldo was now on his way to Chihuahua to receive his penance, a full year of suspension from celebrating mass and interacting with parishioners, something that would easily disturb the balance at Nuestra Señora de Guadalupe, where Humberto had long relied on Osvaldo for these things.

But this was ridiculous, Osvaldo thought. How could Humberto be expected to say mass when he has slowly but irreversibly gone eremitic? And how could he—Osvaldo—be kept away from his parishioners who depended on him for confession, funerals, last rites, etc.? When he posed this question to the archbishop, the archbishop replied, "We play the roles God asks of us. You know what a Jesuit's life is like. Look at it as God's will."

As he drove through the Chihuahua desert to Juárez, Osvaldo felt the anger pushing upward from his stomach to his chest, causing him to feel inflamed deep within. They'd been waiting to blackball him from the very first moment he arrived in Juárez, he thought. He had been full of ideas and ready to bring about grand-scale changes, so they had put him in the most visible of the churches, the cathedral, so they could keep a sharp eye on him and wait for him to make mistakes. And for years he had held his tongue, put on his best performance for clerical visitors but never made pretenses about being fond of any of the rest of them. They were all interested in fine dining, vestments, ceremony. They were estranged from the world they hoped to guide and enlighten.

An afternoon sandstorm blasted the car, causing Osvaldo to slow for safety's sake. As he pushed down on the brakes, he felt as if this storm was an extension of all the other storms that were responsible for the intractability of this world, so under the illusion of being classifiable and governable, yet so terribly plagued and imbalanced. The storm intensified in its resolve, and the priest pulled the car to the side of the road. He looked into the rearview mirror and saw that his Roman collar was not properly affixed to his shirt, but instead of setting it straight, he took it off. He unbuttoned his shirt, revealing his chest hair clustered in thick, white whorls.

Your life can flash before your eyes in a second, but sometimes, Osvaldo thought, every trivial detail haunts you. But the part that he remembered most, always, was the process of decision—the decision to work in his uncle's best friend's legal office in El Paso over the summer; the decision not to go to college at the University of Juárez but instead to become a priest; the decision (several weeks after ordination) to return to his hometown of Juárez instead of staying in the United States; the many times, such as now, that he had chosen to remain a priest despite all of the things that were so terrible in the world, that made this gift of life so dubious: the way people lied to and hurt one another, adultery and murder, dire economic situations forcing young women to sell their

295

bodies, governments sinking in corruption, and then those things that people did not have control over (hurricanes and earthquakes, diseases and injuries, our bodies disintegrating from within, human suffering...), and yet, even so, he believed in God, believed in the beauty of creation, the intricacy of not just the human form but of all of nature and its evolution—he believed that science was proof, that something had to create all of this, that all of this suffering, it must be for something...it *had better* be for something. He came down hard with his wrists and hands onto the steering wheel. "¿What the hell am I going to do?" he yelled, and his voice did not echo.

Outside, the wind hissed; the sand swung up like blankets whipped in the air. The world was dry, damp, cold and hot. It rotated on an axis. It managed around the sun in a slow, calculating motion. And centuries above, in the brilliance of conception—as many light years away as the beginning of time, the answer to the mystery of life gleamed.

Maybe the Egyptian never committed a crime in this country of Mexico to which he had escaped. Turning over a new leaf, as they say, or, synonymously, rotating a mattress, tossing a tortilla or flipping over the cutting board, he decided his life of iniquity was a life that had culminated in his last crime, and he retired to his duties as a chemist, in Juárez a life of generous remuneration, sometimes translating into houses with maids and servants, VIP status at clubs, restaurants and sporting events, marriage to an attractive woman—but most certainly a life where one need not brood over the daily concerns of the populace: food, shelter...safety.

And then, of course, Los Rebeldes and Los Choferes would have never met the Egyptian because he wouldn't have hired them to continue crimes he never committed, and unless they committed these crimes on their own, which was not how la policía had presented it, they were equally as innocent.

And, as the years rolled by and the murders still continued, these theories had only been replaced by newer, equally implausible lies, seemingly all fed from the mouths of the very people who were meant to be the protectors of the land.

But Mexico, this is a different country. And here la policía is just another group of men from whom we have to protect ourselves. And maybe there are no villains out there—just officers of the law. So then maybe we don't need a government and, though maybe anarchy would be no better—nor worse—then at least we'd be killing one another rather than paying someone else to do the job.

That's what some people say, anyway.

Maybe that's taking things too far because it can always get worse, and we don't know what changing the variables would do. We don't know what life would be like if one small detail were altered, and we don't want to do anything that will cause more women to die in this country of colors and perfumes and tastes, the moans of the mountain, the textures of love.

Or maybe it wasn't so. Maybe la policía was just as stupefied by the immensity of contradiction as the rest of us. Perhaps there weren't any photos on the back of the door nor, for that matter, a derelict police station in the middle of the desert.

Maybe it was, as they have said, an American man. The border is easy to cross for those who have the right color passport. This deranged psychopath slipped into the city during the day, committed murder in cold blood and joined the clusters of teenagers on the bridge traveling back to El Paso at night, his hands washed, his shoes shined.

Or if not El Americano, then Los Juniors, the children of aristocrats, sons with rolls of bills and bodyguards, devoted sybarites and collectors of beautiful girls, who, under the protection of their family names, their money and connections, make evidence disappear as quickly as cocaine.

Or could it be the drug cartels, with their numerous tributaries that stream into every place imaginable—the homes of reputable people, the churches, the schools, their mansions, clubs and prostitution rings? They control everything down here, so why wouldn't they have their hands in this, too?

Or perhaps the local media, backroom club owners, the brokers of an illegal human organ trade? Could it be a scheme harvested in government offices, sports clubs, the backrooms of maquiladoras? Maybe men are killing women, or maybe women are killing women.

But most likely men.

These are our daughters, our sisters, our mothers and our cousins. Hundreds have died—maybe even thousands. Decades have passed, and we continue to die—

Didn't they ever tell you that in Mexico, alive or dead, it's the same?

That's because here the dead crawl out of their graves to eat, and the living eat fruit fresh from trees planted in unmarked cemeteries

When the sea dies, all living creatures will end. The roots of trees will die, every last animal will become extinct, one by one. The august rose will be reduced to its thorns, the winter will come and go unnoticed and without snowfall

The salt will lie face-down in the sand, the crabs will bury themselves in their own holes

It has gotten to be very, very late

After rescheduling again the next day ("¿You don't ever want to see me again, do you, Esme?" Leti said), Esmeralda and Leti were finally able to meet for lunch. They selected a torero-themed restaurant boasting comida corrida with sopa de frijol con chicharrones—bean soup with pork rinds—alongside chicken with rice and beans, unlimited flour tortillas and agua de jamaica but, at the last moment, Esme ordered enchiladas verdes, which, when served, bristled with spice and steamed with heat, and Leti followed.

After they ordered, Leti promptly moved on to the latest from Esme's old building: "There's this strange guy who took the large office on the second floor a few months ago, and I think he's *living* there. I've only seen him twice, but he has a thick beard and long, curly hair. The only time we see him is when deliveries are being made. They are always boxes, never anything such as a desk or refrigerator—just boxes."

"¿Have you asked the super?"

"My boss asked him, and he said he didn't really know. So long as he pays his rent on time, you know. But I was working late the other night and, as I left the office at eight o'clock—it was dark—I heard his footsteps behind me, but then they stopped, and when I turned around I didn't hear anyone. ¿Can you call upstairs and ask them if they've seen or heard anything strange?"

"Sure. Of course. I talk to them every day."

"¿About the case?"

"And other things."

"¿How is that going?" Leti asked and, by now, Leti had already become involved in the case as well. Even though she still spent most of her evenings at home with her children, she volunteered her bookkeeping and tax accounting abilities so that Esmeralda could dedicate herself exclusively to her work.

At this, Esme apologized again for not having seen her for the past several days. She told Leti that she'd been interviewing the victims' families, the first of whom had been Verónica's tía Laura, who informed her that in the years since they'd last spoken, Verónica's case had been closed, the evidence lost, the body misidentified. Esme then went on to tell about a girl called María de Los Ángeles, whose parents revealed similar details—that the police had found a body they thought to be hers but, when they arrived to identify it, they realized the clothing was hers but the body was not.

"It's as if the clothing has been kept in one vault and the bodies in another, and when it comes time to try to make sense of things, they mix and match the two," Esme said.

"¿Do you think it's la policía that is guilty?"

"I don't know. Maybe. Anyway, they're not helping. I'm developing a fairly powerful case against them for their negligence. There's no excuse for the way they've handled these cases. Regardless, they seem to be operating under the full support of the government, and I think the government needs to be held responsible for their role in this collective obliviousness."

"¿You're going to sue la policía and the government?"

"¿Why not?"

"It's dangerous. They'll kill you."

"I know," she said, and then she paused, changing tone and subject. "Dulce's been a great help." The girl was doing remarkably well in college, achieving all the top marks and honors. Phone calls from young men in their twenties filled up the answering machine and made Leti feel old with their señoras and ustedes and kept her busy—despite the fact that she was interested in none of them (or so she told her mother), she was too polite and seemed to have, in her admiration of Esme, inherited her disgust for the opposite sex. The girl seemed to be so in awe of Esmeralda that she copied her hairstyle, borrowed clothing and even tried to talk with the same authority in her voice, which she couldn't pull off, as her voice was much sweeter and higher.

Later that day, Esmeralda called the office of the women's rights organization, hoping to check their files for alternate contact numbers for one of the families, when she remembered that Leti had wanted her to ask about the mysterious man who rented the colossal office in between their floor and Leti's. Her old boss told her, "Yes, we've seen him, too. We probably wouldn't have noticed him, but he has such a thick beard and long hair. He looks like he must be in his forties, though he's always wearing T-shirts. But, really, we don't know anything about him."

Curious about the unsettled identity of the man and already angry at him for being the cause of Leti's apprehension, which must have already caused her unnecessary anxiety, Esme told her old boss that she would go over to the office later in the day to look through and photocopy some of the files. If anyone was going to confront this man, she reasoned, it was going to be her and, in order to avoid embroiling her old boss or Leti in conflict with their new neighbor, she decided she would go there by herself and find out what this guy was all about, so she walked the ten or so blocks west, past the bookstore where she had purchased the Bible to Avenida de la Raza, where she entered the building, walked up the flight of stairs and knocked on the door.

For a minute, no one answered, so she knocked again, and as she did this, she looked up at the peephole and wondered if the bearded man's eyes had already met hers. She thought about knocking again, but instead resolved to cross her arms and wait, whether he was there staring at her or not.

Eventually, she heard footsteps coming from a distance maybe three meters away, and a man with a thick, coarse beard wearing a white button-down shirt with tight-fitting trousers and matching European loafers emerged at the threshold. Esmeralda looked up into his deep-set brown eyes and felt as if in them lay a wisdom and refinement far beyond anything she'd ever borne witness to before. Now, she finally understood why age was beautiful. It is not a reblooming, as she had often thought. Now she considered that the lines and wrinkles of people's faces stretch and curve to represent the decisions and events of their lives, as a tree wears its age in rings. She had seen the way anger furrows and malice wrinkles, and she had often related the kindness in a face to the kindness that dwelled deep within, as in the face of Padre Osvaldo. When she encountered someone young, someone without the understanding of his actions, his face remained unchanged because in youth people do not yet wear their faults on their foreheads, their morals in their eyelids. But age bears all. As Esmeralda looked at the man, she already felt comfortable, as if they had known each other for years, as if he was her paisano from centuries past, from that other lifetime, that other reincarnation, back when they walked the same barren earth searching decades for the eagle perched on a cactus with a snake in her mouth—tenochtitlán, México.

The man stared at her expressionlessly for a second; then, his face twisted into another expression equally as resilient. "Buenas tardes," he said.

Esmeralda didn't say anything.

"¿Can I help you?" he asked.

bridge stories

Back in the day—that is, as soon as I turned fifteen—we used to cross the Free Bridge leading to Juárez almost every weekend night. Our parents thought we were sleeping at each other's houses. Instead, we had decided to leave the country. The Juárez club scene was extraordinary—disco balls, jungle themes, the seven-dollar drink-and-drown at Tequila Derby, dance beats straight from the capital and all over Latinoamérica (before the American Música Latina craze), the Vegas-like lights of the Strip, the gorgeous Juárez girls.

And then when the night had ended, we piled back into our cars and headed bumper-to-bumper toward the bridge to join the exodus back to the other side. "¡Chingao!" Someone would say. "Look at this line. How long y'all think it's going to take?" And then we'd take bets. An hour and a half? Two hours tops. And then it ended up being three. The street kids scrambled between cars trying to sell chicle and flowers and sodas and damn near everything you could want, and there was honking and jerky movements by cars trying to find quicker lanes. Sometimes, there were accidents. Sixteen and seventeen-year-olds driving drunk at three a.m. would fall asleep or lose control or drift into neutral and hit the car behind them, and a couple of times there were fights on the bridge—really bloody things with switchblades and bottles and fists full of misplaced anger. Cars were packed so tight that people wanted to get out of them, to join in the commotion and have bridge stories to later tell their friends.

And what would happen was that, instead of parting ways with our friends at the end of a long night dancing and trying to scam with girls and getting bien pedo, we would find ourselves packed tightly together with our closest friends, and that's when we would talk about life and who we wanted to be and how we would arrive on life's great stage—the future. There was Julio Poitras, our future valedictorian, who wanted to convert the Plaza Theatre into a dance club that rivaled those in Juárez; Patrick Finnegan, the red-headed gringo, who wanted to become a disc jockey for an alternative music radio station; Felipe Quiñones, who wanted to invent something ("Like what?" "I don't know. Me vale verga. Just as long as I turn famous." "Hey, maybe they can shave that hairy stuff off your neck and make sweaters."); me, who wanted to live up to my nickname as El Periodista by editing a major New York magazine; and Art, who simply wanted to revolutionize the world.

On some nights, we'd find ourselves alongside a car-full of girls. Strangely, we often heard stories about how Felipe had kissed one girl in the corner for forty minutes or how Julio had acquired three girls' phone numbers, but none of us had seen these things happen. In fact, it seemed as if no one ever had any success while in the clubs. On the bridge, however, safely enclosed behind metal and chrome, the right amount of distance separated us from the girls. We summoned the boys selling chicle. "Hey, bring this note to that girl in the car over there, and I'll give you fifty cents when you come back." And notes were passed back and forth and, before you knew it, Julio Poitras had been replaced by a girl called Gabriela, who was now holding hands with Felipe Quiñones, while Julio sat in another car with a girl named Amanda. Cars would cross the border bringing back not drugs or duty-free, but a completely different set of people than had gone over in the first place. I'd heard of occasions when people ended up driving other people's cars and, as these were the days before cell phones, some of my classmates and friends had very interesting stories to tell their parents about the whereabouts of their vehicle, especially when they were supposed to be sleeping over at their friends' houses.

The bridge could take as few as five minutes to cross or as many as four hours. As we grew older and were finally willing to tell our parents that we were spending time in Juárez at night and, if they approved but gave us a curfew, the bridge became the greatest excuse in the world ("It's 'cause we left the club really early—about one-fifteen, but the wait on the bridge was like four hours, so that's why I'm coming home at five-thirty"—when really we left the club at four and waited on the bridge for thirty minutes, and that's the reason we arrived home just as the sun was yawning and beginning to stretch its rays above the horizon…).

I later discovered in emails from friends that when they returned to El Paso during the summer after their freshman year in college, the clubs no longer stayed open until four. The government had put the city on curfew. And then the word from friends was that the Strip had been like a ghost town some nights, especially when there had been shootings by drug barons or scares of people going around injecting people with diseases. As my contact with friends from high school and the world of the border became less frequent, I stopped hearing about El Paso and Juárez, though my research in the past several days showed that the curfew had been applied in response by the government to the uproar in the community by human rights and women's groups about the murders of girls and women. It seemed terrible, now, as Camille and I drove across the free bridge into Juárez, that we had spent those nights basking in the frivolity of youth and had no idea what was happening to the girls our age, who at the end of the night did not return to cars and the other side, but instead to the constant uncertainty about whether they would live to see the end of the days, the weeks, the beginnings of their twenties, the rest of their lives.

We were not stopped at the immigration checkpoint entering Mexico and, as we moved from the bridge and onto a jagged city street of Juárez, I turned to Camille and asked her to look at the map that had been provided courtesy of the rental car agency—which I had interpreted as their blessing that we enter Mexico—and tell me where and when I needed to turn.

"Avenida de la Raza," she said. "Should be coming up on your right. We're getting close. I can feel it. It reminds me of being a little girl and going to my grandparents'. The closer we got to their house, the more familiar everything on our way became. The supermarkets, the shops—everything suddenly had names and memories devoted to the times we went to each place. Of course, by the time we got there, we wanted to leave because of that large ticking clock."

I listened inattentively to Camille, on some level registering what she was saying and, instead of responding to her, I continued to lament my error in perceiving the hidden intentions of people. "I can't believe I got it all wrong," I said. "Beatriz had no idea why she was in El Paso until she arrived, and Ella and Hector Serrano knew all along. They convinced the world he was dead." I had been repeating to myself similar utterances for the past half hour.

"Maybe they *did* phone it in to the media," Camille added.

Still, Ella Serrano had been vague. After I'd spouted the extent of my trips to Brazil and Europe, she told me they had lied to me. I remained quiet on the phone, listening for the details of her lie and, finally, she said, "Arturo is alive. What is more, we've known he was alive from the beginning." It was then that she had given me the address that we were heading to now, advising us to go there immediately. As we still had not eaten since arriving in El Paso, I took Camille to Chicos Tacos on Montana St., an El Paso institution—which I remembered only when we were passing the Raynolds exit on the freeway on the way from the airport to downtown—for a quick bite of juicy rolled tacos in a paper trough of sauce, which in addition to fries and a soda had always been the perfect gluttonous snack. From there we crossed the border, eventually found Avenida de la Raza and parked on the street near the three-story building indicated by the address Ella Serrano had provided me. It was four-thirty in the afternoon.

We ascended the stairs to the second floor, knocked on the door and, no more than five seconds later it was opened by a man with grayish eyes, bald but for the white hair that formed into a u-shape on the back of his crown, a white shirt with a collar and brown pants. He extended his hand with a smile. "¿You are Omar, verdad?" I nodded, then, in the strange custom that united us, where one introduces a person he has just met to the person accompanying him, I introduced him to Camille. This gem of educación had been my favorite during the Manners Games.

"I spoke to you on the phone about Padre Rahm just before you went to Brazil to visit him," he said, looking at me for recognition I gave him immediately, though it would take the next sentence of this declaration before his identity registered with me. "You called me in Juárez—I'm Osvaldo. Never mind what I'm wearing. I'm a Jesuit priest." Then, I was reminded of the phone call I had made to him months before. His voice seemed softer now, and the body that complemented it seemed less dispirited than the man he had

307

seemed on the phone, when he had before told me such things as "We always said that Padre Rahm had a direct line to God; that was years before saying that was a cliché. Now they say that for any priest." Padre Osvaldo quickly closed the door behind us, and we turned our attention to the vast office, a room swarming with people of all sizes, shapes and ethnicities. Some were answering phones; others seemed to be inventorying several hundred or thousand boxes that were set up in the corner and then moving some of them out once they had been counted. I noticed a woman of about thirty in all black, her hair parted in the middle, who went from person to person checking in on them or advising them.

"¿And Art—where's he?" I asked.

"¿Art? Sorry—his mother should have told you. He's going by a different name. He's finishing the project, but he should be back soon. Until he tells you otherwise, call him Julio Vega."

"¿Julio Vega?"

"After all of your research, you can't be surprised that he has chosen not to be known as himself."

"¿So that credit for his missions goes to those who labored for the cause?" I said, relying on what Kristof had told me.

"No," he said. "Anyone can know in the end, but it can't leak now. He wants people to know in the end. His celebrity is very important."

I was surprised that Padre Osvaldo knew so much about me to say "after all of your research." Had Art been watching me from the shadows since the moment I opened the letters? If mine had been a long, arduous quest designed by him, then what role was I meant to play now that the day of reckoning had arrived? As I pondered this, now in a haze of contemplation as Padre Osvaldo spoke English with Camille, I continued to watch the woman in black, who moved agilely like a bee from flower to flower, and it impressed me how without cinematic effect of spotlight or costume this room could so completely revolve around her. My gaze followed her as she moved across the room to the other side and, enraptured by her calm authority, I didn't notice the door open from behind me. Camille and Padre Osvaldo had already turned around, and it took Camille's calling my name several times before I noticed they were trying to get my attention.

When I turned around, I saw before me not my friend Art but instead a man older than he who had borrowed his body and used the process of age to change it. His chin and jaw were covered in an immense thicket of hair, and his head of black hair had been slicked back like his father's and then pulled into a ponytail, a look I never would have prophesied his adopting. Still, he looked the part of a disheveled artist—his white shirt bore traces of paint and his jeans were faded and the hems had been worn thin and stringy.

"I didn't know Aztecas could grow beards," I said.

"I'm half English, remember," he said. From his straight-faced demeanor emerged not even the most generic of smiles, though there was something in the voice that communicated the lightheartedness of this comment—this voice that for so long I had tried to reconfigure when writing articles that dealt with his disappearance. Journalism was besotted with the type of details I could not usually provide and, in the interest of publication, it had been necessary for me to work around these things by supplying details of another sort that would create the illusion of these details and, in turn, supply a similar reader gratification. In effect, I had learned to write by avoiding convention and the result had been my style, which seemed to advertise a flouting of convention, but which had actually been avoidance. Now, it was clear to me that his voice, regardless of whatever it had been like during those freshman days of half-baked dreams, plastic-wrapped lunches and drinking our sodas as fast as we could so that no one else could have any, had now matured into a voice similar to the gentle voices of authority of the Mexican Christian Brothers who had run our high school. And though, like myself, Art had been away from El Paso for the past twenty years, unlike myself, the past lived on in his voice, grew old with the body that had wandered from place to place, from cause to cause and from one continent to another. And while I had endured conversation after conversation in New York where people asked me what had happened to my Texas accent (I had always replied that we have a different accent in El Paso, and they had said, "Ok, then what happened to that?"), it now made sense that the past lives on in ways individual to people and their memories, which become enfolded into the skin of their arms, the inner ridge of the ears, the mucosa of the vocal cords.

"How could I forget?" I said. Before I could think to initiate the gesture, Art came forward and hugged me, a strong, almost penitent embrace, from which emerged a sensation of unity, and I felt as if his energy had been transferred from the tips of his fingers onto my back and shoulder blades. Was there not also a charge of malevolence that I had also felt intermixed among the blast of energy and emotion?

Camille and Art were introduced, and we all stood in a half-circle somewhere close to the door.

"I'm glad you came, Omar, but I must say that I'm surprised you're here. Why did you come?"

"You left me clues. The letters. The will. The painting of El Paso. I was destined to be here. You led me here."

"Omar, you're incorrect," he said, seemingly disappointed in me. "These 'clues' were so that you would write stories about the border, so you could revisit *your* past. The one thing that I noticed when reading your book was that you never mentioned the border. This is where you're from. This is the place that formed you."

"But why did you leave the will to me?"

He laughed. "I put your letter and the will together, with the same paper clip—they weren't supposed to *both* go to you."

I was embarrassed. Everything had been just a series of misinterpretations. Camille and my arrival here was in no way part of his plan at all. I had gotten everything wrong, nothing right. And yet I had still arrived in Juárez on the night of Art's great act.

I asked Art if I could speak to him privately for a moment, and Camille said she would stay behind with Padre Osvaldo, who seemed to be happy to practice his English. I followed Art into a small office to the side of the large room. This room appeared to be the only other room aside from the colossal one from which we had just come. I listened carefully to everything he said, waiting for the moment when he would tell me what was happening in Juárez, wondering whether I would, if necessary, have the courage to confront him.

"So everyone was in on it—all of these people I met while abroad? They all knew you were alive, just condescended to entertain me," I said, somewhat rankled by having been left out.

"No, Omar. The only people who knew were my parents. My sisters didn't know. Professor Keating didn't know. It was only when my mother called me moments ago that I learned about your trip."

"There's so much I want to ask you," I said.

"You're going to have to save it for later. The sun sets at seven-thirty, and that's when we begin."

"What is this all about?" I asked, as I looked back toward the door and the faint sounds that emerged from it—printers running, boxes moving, phones buzzing.

"It's about retribution. It's about *finally*. Do you remember, Omar, those years ago, when I used to talk to you about what was happening in Juárez? I learned it from a girl that I had met in Juárez during our freshman year. A friend of hers had died. And then another girl died a week later. And soon, bodies were falling everywhere in Juárez. It was like a solitary drop of rain had fallen from the sky, and above are dark patches of clouds in the sky, and then another drop comes and you think, it's going to pour, and it does. Every time it rains, it always stops, but what if it didn't? What if it just kept raining? It's been too long. I've been haunted by this for nearly two decades. I want this all to end." As he said, "end" his eyes gleamed like the brake lights of a car that had been speeding down the freeway but had suddenly become aware of a speed trap.

"The boxes," I said, pointing. "They're explosives, aren't they?" I said. What else could they be? Nearly nine months had passed since he had disappeared, long enough to give birth to a child. But what would Art's child look like? What form would it take? And how would I talk him out of whatever it was he was about to give birth to? My memories of my dreams were so vivid that it was as if the future had already happened in a past relative only to me. The only difference between the reality of my dreams and so-called reality was that my dreams were mine alone; in other words, no one shared my experience of these dreams, in the same way that no one had shared my relationship with Art. The question was again before me: what *was* my relationship to Art? What did I remember of him? Locked within it, my memory mostly held instead small pieces of our youth, my search for him around the world, the details Camille and I assembled upon the chalkboard, my nightmares about the crimes he would commit. But what was real and what wasn't? Who was this person in front of me and who wasn't he? What happened and what hadn't happened? Was the part I had tape recorded, my interviews in Brazil and Europe, and what they suggested real? Why was it that my memory—my internal tape recorder—had been running in my dreams but not in my past? I couldn't trust myself. All that was real was my fear, bisected into two equal parts, the part that was afraid because of all that had been lost and the part that was afraid because, based on all the evidence of what was real, it meant I had to act, that I had to stop Art Serrano because the evidence foretold the presence of a great villain.

Art studied my eyes, as if he were searching for answers from me rather than fielding questions himself. "And if they are, is it that you've come to stop me, my friend?" He glared at me for several moments. I watched his beard, which had sat still for a moment, no longer conforming to the movements of the muscles in his face. Finally, he laughed, exposing his gleaming white teeth. "Omar, now you know what I have done with my life," he said, after a few moments. "You know that I have chosen to dedicate my life to what I believe in. In your position of complete neutrality, what you fail to understand is the conditions I have lived in over the past twenty years—the things that I have had to see. The shanties in las colonias here in Juárez—a wake-up call every time I drove to the Westside—sitting there like ant farms on the hottest hill on earth. Then I went to Brazil to stay with Padre Haroldo, and I met ten-year-olds who had HIV and were addicted to crack. I realized that life is in ruins everywhere. I recognized that people were always responsible for the problems of other people. I realized the people with money were perpetuating their existences by branding their products, creating mega-chains and very rarely looking out for the people who had nothing. And then wherever I went, the border went with me, stamped behind me like a child in muddy shoes, following me everywhere I went, making it impossible to enjoy this life. I never felt success; did you know that? Every step of success has always been to me a step in the wrong direction, further from the people, the earth I came from. So—as you've discovered—I gave up painting and spent my time trying to make a difference through organization, protesting businesses and governments who are only looking out for themselves. And people followed. We walked through city blocks and screamed, and we were unified and there was a proud sense of camaraderie and ebullience, but when the next day came, the governments still went to war, the corporations continued to multiply, the poor were still poor and the women of Juárez kept dying. Morality is flimsy. It is situational, and some morals are in conflict with others. Do you remember freshman year when—what was our religion teacher's name?—Brother Ramiro! Do you remember when Brother Ramiro taught us about white lies—lies that save feelings, lies to avoid tragedies, lies for the sake of utilitarianism? I think it was then that I first understood the in-between, that the world was not a duality, that there existed planes and dimensions of appropriateness. What is a law? What is a moral? What is a rule? If I stand idle and three hundred people die, is it better than shooting one gun once at one person so that everyone else will live? It is a question of perspective, Omar. The rules are imperfect because humanity is imperfect and our laws are based on demarcating and separating. When we stare hard, we realize that we just created order in the disarray that is life because of power and prestige, but if we look much more closely, we realize that the other side is this side, perspective is counter-perspective, the past is the present, immorality is morality, and there are a thousand shades in between that make moralizing a condescension to the scope of life."

I asked whether what he was saying was meant to be support for terrorism. He gave me a look of repugnance that seemed to indicate the ridiculousness of the question. He moved his bottom lip underneath his teeth, drew in air as if to speak, then paused, the measured silence producing an effect usually reserved for seasoned actors, professors or expert storytellers. "You should know better than I that 'terrorism' is a dysphemism, a word meant to cast unfavorable light on what, in this case, is rectifying iniquity," he said. "Terrorism in its various forms and labels can also be referred to as military operation, massacre, assassination, war, crusade, freedom fighting or *any* resistance to oppression or act of oppression itself. It is all a question of perspective. Yes, I decided to kill whoever was responsible for the murders. Yes, I realized that this would mean doing something illegal. Yes, I am willing to sacrifice my life for it. Yes, I decided to end my life as an artist and begin a different life, and I couldn't remain Art Serrano; I couldn't continue to own things because these objects and materials had too much power over me. I needed to leave this identity in order to finally live my philosophy rather than just protesting other philosophies, to be someone else in order to finally put into action my crusades, my peace-seeking, my terrorism." He paused here for a moment, looking at his watch; as he did this, there was a knock at the door from Osvaldo, who briefly conferred with Art about something; then Art returned to me and proceeded to give me a brief outline of what happened next. Before I could begin to present my case, he went on to tell me about the time period directly following his disappearance from the United States and subsequent appearance in Mexico. In order to compile the following, I have supplemented it with details I would learn from him when I visited him in jail a few days later.

By the time Art left El Paso, his beard had already grown thick, and his hair was longer than he usually wore it—he'd spent the past several months almost entirely in his apartment, leaving only to go to his parents' house. When he first arrived in Juárez, he immediately set up an office on Avenida de la Raza in between a burgeoning women's rights office and a well-established accounting firm. His face and head grown thick with hair, his cheeks drooped and turned sallow from his lack of attention to his physical nourishment and his inability to find gastronomy that would satisfy his vegetarian demands. In the meantime, the wave of hysteria regarding his death and final artistic product having been considerably less ubiquitous in Juárez, he was able to conceal himself and therefore prevent any identification or sightings. He lay low and then emerged from his cache only to watch in the darkness, clamber to bars, establish nascent friendships with members of the underworld who would be able to provide him with the artillery necessary to erase landscapes and men, but chiefly he began an investigation that he hoped would eventually bear fruit in his discovery of who was responsible for the murders of the women. But this search led him down many roads—from an Egyptian, to a street gang, a group of bus drivers, an American terrorist, la policía, the sons of aristocrats, the government itself.

And though evidence existed to indict each of these groups and individuals, the entire bed of information was a cesspool of contradiction, each with a different series of incomprehensible variables and dead ends. Despairing and desperate, he stood in the vast, empty confines of his office one night and cried out, the sound of his voice echoing for a length so excessive he wondered if he was going crazy. As he had allowed the canvas of his body to grow mangy and unkempt, he decided the next day to shower, to spend an hour in the afternoon in ablution—clipping toenails, scrubbing his face, trimming his beard and hair, hoping exterior order would seep inward and allow him a fresh perspective. As he was finishing up in the bathroom, he heard a knock at the door. He clipped a final hair from between his eyebrows, then strode across the enameled floor, his footsteps like the sound of an ax against a colossal oak; before him appeared a woman a few years younger than he. Her fixed stare into his face seemed the most deep and penetrating glare he had ever received, as if from it she were downloading all of his hidden thoughts and emotions. He couldn't resist her. She had discarded her exterior and stood before him like one of his paintings of the body.

"Buenas tardes," he said. "¿Can I help you?"

But what he really wanted to say was "¿How did you take off your mask?"

Her name was Esmeralda, and from her poured the most exquisite story, full of transformations of names and identities—María Magdalena the prostitute, Esme the mentor, Esmeralda the law student with a fairy tale name, then finally Señorita Santiago the lawyer—spanning the past ten years.

She introduced Art to Padre Osvaldo, the monkish priest with the gray eyes and white hair, who was obsessed with the death of the women as much as Esme and Art—perhaps even more palpably, as his face was overtaken by a constant rage that bulged with the veins in his forehead. What was more, Osvaldo and Art were united by ties even greater than the pursuit of a common goal; incredibly, they shared a common mentor in the Brazilian priest Padre Haroldo, and this mentorship was rooted in the most important transitional stage of their lives—the passage from adolescence into adulthood.

One night, Art confessed his plan, and Osvaldo supported him at first tentatively—later completely. A partnership formed. But their complicit act, which neither involved nor was communicated to Esme, was delayed. Although now Art and Osvaldo had access to Esmeralda's inordinate files and occasionally worked as associates-in-disguise, meeting the families of the disappeared women in order to pursue their own investigation, they met time and again with the inconsistencies of mishandled evidence, cracks in memory and fissures in time, contradictions and a lack of authority by which to carry out a proper exploration. Art grew frustrated and angry for a second time, and this time he was joined in anguish by Padre Osvaldo, and in their lassitude the two resolved to purchase explosives and hoard them in the rented office, willing to let them detonate not on the murderers themselves but on those who had shown neglect in solving the murders—the media, police headquarters, specific government buildings and the special office for the investigation of the women.

I coughed, which was unrelated to what he was saying but did succeed in creating a reverberation in the small office. Art now seemed eager to move on to the next step, though his hostility toward me for my oversimplification had cooled.

"But Art," I said, finally. I had let him speak, and now was the time for me to intercede. However, as I hesitated, trying to think of what to say, he interrupted me. "You're too late. Everything is done," he said. Art moved toward the door, gestured to me to wait for him, leaving me in the small, cold office furnished with several chairs, an empty desk and a file cabinet. After a few minutes, I checked the door and, finding it unlocked, sat down on one of the chairs. Like a patient in a doctor's office who has already been weighed and had his blood pressure checked and is now being sent to his own personal waiting room, I began to wonder after a few minutes, given the absence of other things to amuse myself with, whether Art had chosen to leave me here indefinitely. I stood up to have a look outside but, as soon as I did so, Art entered wheeling in one of the boxes on a dolly. He opened the box, exposing six buckets, then, using a knife, opened one of the buckets, exposing a thick, white liquid, which he dipped his finger into, then came toward me and painted a dot on my forehead.

"Paint," I said.

"Paint," Art repeated.

"Art, what's going on?"

"Omar," he said, looking me directly in the eyes. "Tonight begins the revolution, and Camille and you can play an important role in it. I told you I was going to revolutionize the world. Since everything is about relationships, I had to figure out which relationship had been ruptured in the unsolved murder of the women and restore that relationship. The reason these murders persist is because we allow them to. We stopped protecting our women a long time ago. El Paso has denied the existence of Juárez for decades, and the Mexican government has never taken care of its people. Tonight I'm going to make it impossible for anyone to avoid the subject of the women forever. Do you know what I'm going to do?"

"What?" I said, prepared for anything.

"I'm painting the mountain."

I looked into Art's face as he mouthed those words and, in a flash, saw only the fourteen-year-old, as if this image had, through some black hole of time, slipped out of its spot from the past, from the longer lunch days, and into Art's body, here, now.

But what was it that changed his mind? Art loved to play games. It seemed to run in the family and perhaps that's why he waited until the end of our conversation to tell me that the boxes contained paint rather than explosives. But it wasn't simply a game. Art's story was true. He had spent more than a year in intensive study of weapons and explosives, even before he had left El Paso. He had made the right connections with the appropriate people. And when I had confronted him about this, instead of immediately denying my allegation, he wanted to show me how close he had been. Instead of looking with derision back upon that moment when he and Padre Osvaldo agreed on their violent solution, he embraced this former self, this obsolesced decision. He understood how he had come to this resolution, understood its validity and the validity of any decision come to that challenges the ideologies of a former self. And that's what he was responding to when he challenged me after I asked him if the boxes contained explosives: "…if we look much more closely, we realize that the other side is this side, perspective is counterperspective, the past is the present, immorality is morality, and there are a thousand shades in between that make moralizing a condescension to the scope of life."

One afternoon, Art and Padre Osvaldo were at Art's apartment, finalizing their plans. They had all but hired the team that was going to take these plans to the final step. All that remained was for them to allocate carefully the bombs to the places they were meant to go—which was no small matter. At about four o'clock, Esmeralda entered the apartment—he had given her a key by then—and caught them at Art's desk, a pencil in his hand, a map of Juárez rolled out in front of them.

"I needed to catch you in the act," she said, as soon as she entered. Art and Padre Osvaldo were stunned. They hadn't expected her at the apartment for several hours. "…Before I said something," she concluded. She had known for some time. She could see the presage of their act in subtle changes in gestures, their rage, their use of language and mannerisms.

319

Art and Padre Osvaldo stayed where they were sitting and listened to Esmeralda, as she spoke, the two men embarrassed, having known she would oppose them and having commended themselves for their ability to keep the secret below her radar.

"¿What are you men doing?" she said.

Esmeralda quoted Bible passages and philosophy, appealed to their intelligence as much as she did to their emotions. She spoke as if from a list of reasons that she threw out at them one by one without letting them pause to reflect on each. She told them not to commit a violent act on an already disheveled battleground, saying that more bloodshed would only serve to expand the content of violence in Juárez, would only make the city become irreparable on yet another level. She argued on their shared background, hoping to uproot their present plan through their camaraderie that lay somewhere in the past, through the personage of Padre Haroldo, whose philosophy, she said, in her extensive, vicarious knowledge of the man, was that one must always concentrate one's efforts on building up things that were good rather than tearing down the bad, much in the same way a doctor who practices alternative medicine insists on reinforcing the immune system rather than destroying the perpetrators meddling within it. Did Art and Padre Osvaldo think that the families of the victims would endorse such a reprisal? If they did, then they should think again. That wasn't the Mexican way. We've been turning our cheeks for centuries, she said. And we find it much easier to love than to hate.

But perhaps her greatest argument was her appeal to Art based on the philosophy called Know Your Baker. She told him the one thing he was losing when committing this great crime was his life philosophy itself. For didn't he once tell her that the secret to life was in relationships? He said that the key to painting is in forming relationships among lines—not, for example, drawing faces—but assembling lines that will together represent those faces and seeing the relationship in lines and spheres between the ears and the nose and the mouth, the chemistry of the human form, the formula that is the physiognomy. And subsequently practicing law is about forming relationships between laws and behavior, a lawyer and her client, a jury and their recognition of the perspective of a lawyer's client. And writing, as he told her when he looked at her poems about colors and sounds, etc., is all about building closer relationships between sentences with the intention for the sentence that begins the piece to be related to the one at the end because of everything between. Relationships close the gaps between things—they allow for connection and sense, they obviate wars, they allow for progress and solidarity, they tolerate variation and strengthen similarity. But what relationship would one establish were they to commit an act of violence that would kill many people? The bombing of these places would only serve to widen the gaps that already existed. It would create inconsistencies and holes. It would not be an improvement.

When she finished her speech, Esmeralda, still holding her purse, not having even removed her jacket, didn't wait for a response from the two of them. She said, "Now, I've got work to do. You two do whatever it is you think is right." As she turned to leave, under her breath, but audible enough, she uttered, "A priest and a world-famous artist," leaving the apartment without making a sound.

As Art and Osvaldo looked at each other, humiliated, Esmeralda walked into the apartment again, her shoulders and joints no longer tense but, like a candle that had just been blown out, all that was left of her rage smoked and whittled away from her, leaving her center calm and unspoiled by the fire that had ignited it. According to Art, she was smarter and better than all of us, and she had returned because she preferred not to leave two grown men alone in a room with their shame.

"Listen," she said. "This is your philosophy, but you've made a wrong turn. I learned this from you—my great loves. This is your crusade. Your philosophy has a built-in safety net. Whenever anyone who believes in it decides to go against it, there are other people around to remind them who they once were, what they believed in and why it was important. That's why so many successful terrorists work alone. They don't have anyone to remind them. They don't have a network of people they are close to. They've never met their bakers."

cómo pintar una montaña

We were the thousands moving rocks, following the intricate gridlines drawn by Art and his team over the months—the uniform graffiti font he had designed as appropriate to the mountain landscape, letters of varying sizes and shapes—and snugly laying them next to one another, painting them white with thick globs of paint, lime, salt and cement and pulling the weeds in between them so that there would never be a moment of doubt as to what the names of these women were. We moved swiftly, spoke to one another only when there was question of detail, but such questions were rare; we had only to stay between the lines illumined by the glow of the full moon. Ilnur descended for a moment and tapped me on the shoulder, surprising me, asking how we were coming along, ending his sentence with "Julio, Omar or whoever you are," one single thread of his hair blowing in the wind whilst the rest remained spiky and intact as they had been in Rio, and I answered him that our group would be ready to move within the hour, that we could join him in finishing the main words on the El Paso side, the words that said "We are nosotras, las muertas. Nosotras somos we, the dead. No nos olviden. Do not let us fade." Camille and I joined about twenty-five others, including Laura, a frail woman with a cane, whose son and husband had escorted her up the mountain hours before—they were the family of Verónica, the girl whose name we now washed into the stone. In the midnight darkness, we painted the names of the hundreds of girls and women into the mountain landscape, covering both mountains—the lower Rockies, the northern Sierra Madres, divided in name and by country but now inextricably linked by words.

When we finished Verónica's name, we radioed to Esmeralda, whom Camille and I had met earlier that night, as soon as my conversation with Art had ended—when she had asked us, with both of her hands in mine, to paint the name "Verónica" into the mountain, as she would spend the night in Juárez in the office coordinating the various groups on the mountain. She had explained to us who Verónica was and how with the end of her life had begun the movement inside Esmeralda that would eventually culminate in this project and the next stage, a class action suit against la policía and the Mexican government. Now she told us to move up and help Ilnur's group finish the words at the top, the words she had written, which began with "We are nosotras, las muertas…"

Camille and I worked side by side, renewing our brushes from the same buckets, which had for months been stored all over warehouses and offices in El Paso and Juárez. Flickers of light emerged from various spots all over the mountains, but the sun had set hours before, the mountain was unguarded, always left alone to the foxes and plants and snakes and people without houses who slept among arroyos. These dancing lights went unnoticed.

I did not see Art until the next day, when the cities awoke; by then the last of us had left the mountain, and now, in both cities, everyone was standing on the streets, in their front lawns, on sidewalks, looking up at the mountains, now completely covered in letters and, on the El Paso side, in the middle of the mountain, surrounded by names, the silhouette of a lone girl with a flower in her hair and a trumpet in her ear.

Not even the skyscrapers of Manhattan would have been a canvas as broad or as visible from everywhere as the immense mountains of El Paso and Juárez that ran through and around the two cities. There was very little space left over at all, and these specifications were yet another testament to the genius of Art.

The journalists who had been to El Paso for the unveiling of the painting and the funeral rushed back to the border to take pictures and explain the most elaborate instance of graffiti in the history of the world. Unlike media that had focused on the missing and murdered women, having been spread over the years like the birth of a city in the desert, now the whole world found itself staring into the great barrel of the past, into the faces and names of the girls and women of Juárez.

At about six p.m., the citizens of Juárez gathered in La Plaza de Armas in front of Padre Osvaldo's cathedral, chanting, "¡Viva Art!" and, minutes later, he arrived there to great fanfare, made a speech about the stupor that this country and government and the neighbors to the north had been in over all these years and then took a car across the bridge to a similar congregation that was amassing on the streets of El Paso, near San Jacinto Plaza, where, despite the chants and cheers, when he emerged from the car, he was immediately arrested.

And several days later, when he was advised to post bail, he decided instead to stay in jail, and this decision was greeted as sacrifice, the cause of the murdered women amplified.

Within days, coalitions and groups formed, and already-existing groups received increased support. Activists, celebrities and other members of the community made demands of the Mexican and U.S. governments to find the killer or killers and implement more measures to prevent these crimes from happening. The maquiladora factories, worried that they would bear the brunt of public repugnance and contempt, immediately hired buses to transport workers safely and implemented security measures meant to be interpreted as proactive, rather than reactive. Leaders of the Mexican government, including the president of the republic and the governor of Chihuahua, made speeches in Juárez promising to immediately set aside more money for solving the murders and to enhance the special task force that had been created years before.

In the next several days, I interviewed Ilnur, Esmeralda, Padre Osvaldo and many others and pieced together a story for *The Monthly* on the inner workings of the organization that painted the mountain white with names. As I still had to finish the story, with which Camille helped me—her attention to detail and language always far surpassing mine—I took her to the airport for her flight back to New York. When we arrived, leaving the rental car in short-term parking and then walking in, it seemed strange to me that I was merely dropping her off, rather than leaving with her. As soon as we arrived at the point where the only people who would be allowed to pass were ticket holders with identification who could resist making jokes about security, Camille and I hugged, an embrace that rivaled the one I had seen on the Boulevard du Temple in Paris. "I guess you have to get back to work," I said, as soon as we had let go of one another. There could not have been a more useless thing to say to someone with whom one had shared such an experience.

"Yes," she said. "If not to get back to work, then to pick up my engagement ring from the jeweler. See if it fits my finger." We hugged each other tightly again and, when we let go, she pulled her ticket from her back pocket and moved along, the slow-moving escalator delaying her ascent. Then, before I knew it, she was gone.

I got back into the rental car, heading immediately for the panadería on Alameda, where, as soon as I opened the door, I found Julia, Jimmy's wife, walking into the main room of the bakery with a fresh batch of pan de huevo. She remembered me immediately and told me that she had been closely following the events as they unfolded in Juárez. "I should have put it together when you came that you were talking about Turi," she said.

"Turi?" I asked, and then it registered. Turi was another nickname for Arturo. This was El Paso, after all, where people were known by something different to everyone. It was for a similar reason that in high school I had introduced to my friend her own cousin, who had been excited about meeting the person I referred to as Carlos, whom she had always known as Popo; as a child, he had been known for his temper, as explosive, they said, as Popocatépetl.

When I asked her where Jimmy was, she told me that he had been diagnosed with Alzheimer's disease a few months after I had last visited and that now, most days, he spent putting together model cars, which had apparently been his hobby as a young boy growing up in South El Paso. When I visited Art in jail later that day, after learning from him the complete details of his alliance with Padre Osvaldo and Esmeralda and all the others, I asked him if this was indeed the Jimmy who had been his baker.

"Yes, he was," Art said. "My youth would not have been the same were it not for Jim's endless stories and lessons about life."

I asked him if he knew the story of how Jimmy and his wife, Julia, met.

"Of course," he said. And when he had recounted most of it, which I listened to as if it were the first time I was hearing the story, I asked him if he knew what the story had to do with tres leches.

"Of course," Art said, again, in his slightly pedantic, know-it-all manner. "At the end of that first date, when Jim and Julia were reunited after a decade, they both ordered tres leches for dessert after their meal. It was at this moment that Jim expressed to Julia his dream of opening a bakery, and it was then that Julia fell in love with him—that had always been her dream too."

When I left the visiting room, Art called back to me. "Hey, Omar, thanks for helping me paint the mountain."

"Anytime," I said, and I left wondering when the next chance I'd have to do something like that again.

And now that the past had been etched permanently onto the landscape, visible from anywhere in either city, or the collective metropolis, as I now saw it, it was up to people, as it has always been, whether to choose to further ignore it. A similar question now stood before me as well. I was still blinded by so much else—the mystery that is life, the fallibility of the universal conception of moral order, that illusion of progress, when it is merely time that passes. But I now saw myself more clearly than ever I had before. And what I would choose to do with this information, now that I had it, was another matter altogether, for one could never be sure what future versions of himself will do or remember.

When I emerged from the El Paso County Jail, a place too provincial to be the short-term residence of someone as universal as Arturo Serrano, reminding me that rarely ever has a cloth or world truly suited a revolutionary, I thought to look up again at the mountain, as I had been doing for the past several days, imagining that once again it would shock me, render me nonplussed and time lagged due to the irrevocable changes that had been made to the backdrop of my childhood. But when I looked up, the names lying one after another did not startle me; instead, they seemed familiar, as if they had always been there, but had all those years been standing in front of a mirror that did not detect their presence nor reflect them back.

Brooklyn, New York
June 2004

acknowledgments and notes

This book was completed nearly ten years ago, in 2004, and the bulk of it remains unchanged from its original shape. At the time, I was convinced this book might do something to help bring to light the incredible atrocity that was—and *is*—the murder of the women and girls of Juárez. What I had not anticipated was the difficulty in bringing into existence a *book*, and so it sat for nearly a decade until one night this past year when I took it out of my closet and dusted it off—and saw that everything inside it was still, sadly, relevant.

I could not have been surrounded by more outstanding human beings. This book would not have been possible without my grandparents, Don and Mary Hogan, who taught me the power of literature and words. A thousand thanks to Ernesto Mestre; it seems quite insufficient a gesture of gratitude to provide only several lines here of adulation for the inordinate things you have done for me, for this book and through your friendship. Padre Haroldo J. Rahm, S.J., you are a dear and wonderful man of insuperable charity and compassion. These pages are for you.

I could not be more indebted to the dozens of writers, journalists and photographers who've been crusading for and, in so many cases, risked (and lost) their lives so that the story of the murdered girls would be brought to the attention of a larger audience.

Thanks also to my friends at Brooklyn College, and to many others still, scattered about: at Kingsborough, in Xalapa and Puebla and on the El Paso/Juárez border, in Brooklyn and London...; for Kathryn Venzor (a beautiful soul, who gave me the real-life, tangible "Conozca a su Panadero" T-shirt that I still wear to this day...) For Christina Johnson, with whom in conversation the phrase "Know Your Baker" found its way into limited, but meaningful, circulation.

And, as always, a thanks to all the rest, including most especially my family: Glenn, Margaret, David—my cousins, uncles, aunts, and all the rest...!

Brooklyn, 2013

Alessandro Clemenza

about the author

John M. Keller is the author of *A Bald Man With No Hair and Other Stories* (2012). He has taught writing at the City University of New York; the Universidad de las Américas in Puebla, Mexico; the Universidad de Montevideo, in Uruguay; and St. Xavier's College, in Mumbai, India. His fiction and journalism have been printed in the United States and abroad.

To the memory of my beloved mentor, the distinguished Brazilian educator, Dr. Emanuel Cicero, born in 1907 in Ubatuba, São Paulo. Rector of the College of Rio Grande do Sul from 1943 to 1978, he died in 1988 in Lisbon.

–Maximiliano Reyes, publisher

-FIM-

DR. CICERO BOOKS

31125423R00208

Made in the USA
Lexington, KY
01 April 2014